Above His
Proper Station

Tor Books by Lawrence Watt-Evans

THE OBSIDIAN CHRONICLES
Dragon Weather
The Dragon Society
Dragon Venom

LEGENDS OF ETHSHAR
Night of Madness
Ithanalin's Restoration

Touched by the Gods
Split Heirs (with Esther Friesner)

THE ANNALS OF THE CHOSEN
The Wizard Lord
The Ninth Talisman
The Summer Palace

THE FALL OF THE SORCERERS
A Young Man Without Magic
Above His Proper Station

LAWRENCE WATT-EVANS

Above His Proper Station

VOLUME TWO
of
THE FALL OF THE SORCERERS

A TOM DOHERTY ASSOCIATES BOOK
NEW YORK

This is a work of fiction. All of the characters, organizations, and events portrayed in this novel are either products of the author's imagination or are used fictitiously.

ABOVE HIS PROPER STATION

Map by Rhys Davies

A Tor Book
Published by Tom Doherty Associates, LLC
175 Fifth Avenue
New York, NY 10010

www.tor-forge.com

Tor® is a registered trademark of Tom Doherty Associates, LLC.

ISBN 978-0-7653-2280-7

First Edition: November 2010

Printed in the United States of America

0 9 8 7 6 5 4 3 2 1

Dedicated to the memory of
Brian M. Thomsen,
whose input was invaluable

Above His
Proper Station

1

In Which Anrel Murau Returns to Lume
and Faces a Dismaying Reception

The sun was directly overhead, but a cold winter wind blew fiercely from the northwest, sucking away the sun's warmth and chilling Anrel Murau to the bone as he came stumbling up to the gates of Lume.

Two guards watched his approach with mild interest, but made no move to assist him. They wore the red and gold colors of the burgrave of Lume, rather than the green and gold of the Emperor's Watch. There had been a time when Anrel found the division of duties, where the emperor's men were responsible for keeping order within the capital while the burgrave's men merely guarded the walls, to be perversely amusing, but right now he was far too concerned with other matters, such as not freezing to death, to care about such details.

The cold was not even what most troubled him; rather, it was his recent memories. He had, just that morning, seen a woman hanged for witchcraft—and not just any woman, but the sister of Tazia Lir, the woman whom Anrel had hoped to marry. He had tried to prevent the hanging by rousing the townspeople of Beynos to free poor Reva, but without success; she had been enchanted by the abominable Lord Allutar Hezir, landgrave of Aulix, and had quite literally put her own head in the noose.

It seemed to Anrel that Lord Allutar was responsible for all the great disasters in his life, of which Reva's death was the latest—but not the least. Anrel had not merely seen her hang; he had heard her neck snap.

He would have shuddered at the memory had he not already been shivering with cold.

Seeing his own hopes thus dashed by Reva Lir's death, Anrel had fled the scene by diving off a bridge into the icy Galdin River, and had then made his way on foot to Lume.

He had not tried to reach Tazia, to speak to her, and his heart ached with the realization that he would probably never see her again, but he had not dared to make the attempt. He could not believe that Tazia could ever forgive him for allowing Reva to die, and he could not bring himself to face her after so ghastly a failure—better to know he was no longer welcome in her presence than to actually see the grief and anger on that beautiful face. He had spoken to no one in Beynos; he had simply swum away, leaving behind his history and his hopes.

This was not the first time he had abandoned his old life and set out to start anew. When he had seen his friend Lord Valin li-Tarbek murdered by the same landgrave of Aulix who would later hang Reva Lir, Anrel had given a fiery speech in Naith, the capital of the province of Aulix, denouncing the landgrave. That had gotten Anrel branded a traitor, and had turned him into a fugitive.

He had found a new place with the Lir family, but now that was gone. He had nothing left to him but the clothes on his back, the dagger that had once belonged to his father and was now concealed in his boot, and a few dozen guilders hidden in his pockets and the lining of his once-elegant but much-abused brown velvet coat.

He did not even know how much money he had; a seam had torn open while he was in the river, and several coins were lost forever in the dark, icy water.

Swimming while fully dressed in midwinter was a foolish thing to do, and Anrel had been suffering for it ever since. His hat had been carried away by the current and was lost, so he had been walking bareheaded in the cold, his coat, blouse, and breeches soaked through. The wind had dried his clothes, yes, but only at the cost of all his body's stored heat, and he had not been very warmly dressed to begin with. His hands and feet and ears were numb, and he was shivering uncontrollably. He wished there were a watch fire at the gate where he could warm his hands, but the guards had none; they were dressed in several layers of wool and leather and apparently felt no need for additional heat.

"You look miserable," one of the guards said, sounding not at all concerned, as Anrel neared the gate.

"I am," Anrel said, clapping his gloveless hands against his sides and trying to keep his teeth from chattering. "My hat blew into the river, and the weather was considerably warmer when I left the inn in Beynos."

"And what brings you to Lume?" the other guard demanded.

"I'm coming home after visiting my uncle in Aulix," Anrel said, feigning surprise at the question.

"Where is home, then?"

"The Court of the Red Serpent, number four, third floor, at the rear," Anrel said. That had been his home during the four years he had lived in Lume as a student at the court schools, and still came readily to his tongue. He did not want to admit being homeless, or give some fictional address he might stumble over or later forget.

"Student or clerk?" the guard asked, demonstrating that he knew who lived in Red Serpent Court.

"Clerk now," Anrel replied.

The soldier nodded, and raised his pike so that Anrel could pass. "If you've been gone for a while, you should know—there's a curfew in effect now. No one is to be on the streets between midnight and dawn."

That was bad news. Anrel had known there was considerable unrest in the capital, as there was many places in the empire, but he had not realized it had reached that point. "Thank you for the warning," he said. He hesitated, then asked, "Is there anything else I should know? Did I hear something about a prince?"

The guards in Beynos had told him the empress had borne a son, and the news had been confirmed, but Anrel wanted to judge what these guards thought of this birth.

"Prince Lurias," the guard said. He smiled as he spoke, obviously pleased by the news. "Born three nights ago. Mother and child reported to be doing well, thank the Father and the Mother!"

Whatever discontent might be abroad, it had not reached the level of stifling this man's delight at the birth of an heir to the throne. Anrel managed to stop shivering enough to smile in return. "Wonderful! And . . . there were rumors at the last inn that demons had been seen in the streets. Is that why the curfew was set?"

The smile vanished. "No," the guard said. "There are no demons. Just rumors."

"There are foreign magicians at the palace," the other guard said. "Who knows what they might be doing?"

Anrel looked from one man to the other, trying to judge what he should believe. Did the first guard know what he was talking about, or was his denial mere instinct?

"It's just rumors," the first guard insisted, annoyed. He waved for Anrel to pass. "Go on, then, get on to the Court of the Red Serpent!"

"Thank you," Anrel repeated, ducking his head and hurrying forward, past the two guards and into the shadowy passage through the ancient city walls.

The "gate" was far more than a simple gate, of course. The guards were posted at the outer end of a sixty-foot stone tunnel, where massive wooden doors stood ready to be slammed shut, and iron gratings could be dropped into place on a moment's notice. The floor of the tunnel was hard-packed dirt for the first fifteen feet, but then Anrel's boots thumped onto thick oak planks, blackened by centuries of shoe leather—planks that Anrel knew could be retracted into the walls, revealing pits and other traps beneath.

The corridor smelled of stone and damp. Dark shafts led up into the walls and ceiling here and there, where other defenses lurked, their exact nature a military secret.

Anrel could also feel less tangible defenses—the magical wards that generations of sorcerers had woven around the city. The burgrave of Lume was responsible for maintaining and extending those spells, and for that reason the title was generally given to the most powerful sorcerer in the empire. Normally burgraves, who ruled towns and cities, were outranked by the landgraves who administered the sixteen provinces, and were assumed to need less powerful magic than the margraves who guarded the empire's borders; accordingly, they were usually chosen from the second or third tier of sorcerers. The position of burgrave of

Lume was an exception, and the present incumbent, Lord Koril Mevidier, was said, despite his relative youth, to be the most formidable magician in the world.

Certainly the wards Anrel felt as he made his way through the passage were strong ones. He supposed that most people would be completely unaware of them, but he was the son of two sorcerers, and although he had deliberately failed the trials himself, rather than ever risk facing whatever doom had befallen his parents, Anrel had inherited some magical talent. He honestly did not know how strong his gift might be, since it had never been evaluated accurately by a sorcerer, but it was definitely real. He could feel the wards as a faint crawling on his skin, a slight tingle, a vague pressure on all his senses, and he knew they were powerful indeed.

Those wards, and the various more mundane traps and devices, had helped Lume hold out against attackers many times, though it had been almost a century since a foe had gotten close enough that the gates had been closed and the defenses readied. Not since the Barley King's War had an enemy besieged the capital, but the emperor still saw to it that the walls and gates were properly maintained and manned, and Lord Koril had obviously tended and elaborated the protective spells.

Of course, that maintenance had contributed both to the empire's security and the emperor's financial difficulties.

Right now, though, despite all these intriguing features, what interested Anrel the most about the gate was that it sheltered him from the bitter wind, and was leading him into the city.

Lume was the capital of the Walasian Empire, but it was also the only place left in all the Bound Lands where Anrel thought he might still have connections he could draw upon in establishing a new home, and a new life, for himself. Everywhere else he had ever lived was now closed to him.

He had been born in a village called Verien, in the province of Aulix, but his life there had been swept away when his sorcerer parents died horribly, apparently from a spell gone wrong. He had been a child, only four years old, and remembered almost nothing of Verien. He had no family there, no friends, no debts owed or owing.

After he was orphaned he had gone to live with his uncle, Lord Dorias Adirane, the burgrave of Alzur, and had sometimes visited the provincial capital at Naith, but in Alzur and Naith he was now a fugitive, condemned to death for sedition and inciting a riot. Some faint hope lingered that perhaps someday he could once again make contact with his uncle, and with his cousin, Lady Saria, but for now he dared not attempt it. To return to Alzur or Naith would be to put his head in a noose as surely as Reva Lir had.

When he had escaped from Naith he had fallen in with the Lir family—Garras Lir, his wife Nivain, and their three daughters. They were travelers, with no permanent home, because the four women were all witches—practitioners of magic who did not have the blessing of the empire, who had not passed the trials to become recognized sorcerers, who had not placed their true names on the Great List that the imperial court maintained. Witchcraft carried the death penalty, but it was rarely enforced; it was too useful to have magicians who would take the time to dowse for wells, treat fevers, tell fortunes, and perform a hundred other little magics for the common people, magics that the acknowledged sorcerer-lords could not be troubled to provide.

The death penalty had been enforced for poor Reva because she had dared to try to perform a binding on Lord Allutar himself. The landgrave's sorcery had proved far more effective than Reva's witchcraft, and she had been sent to the gallows not so much for the crime of witchcraft, but for her effrontery in using it on Allutar.

Technically, Anrel himself was a witch, but he had never used his abilities to earn a living. The Lir women had given him some rudimentary training in witchcraft, but he had as yet done nothing of any significance with it. If he were to be hanged it would be for his speeches, not for witchcraft.

Anrel had traveled with the Lirs for a season, but now that he had allowed Reva to die he believed himself to be as outcast from their company as he was from Alzur or Naith or Verien. That life, as the Lir family's friend and Tazia's would-be husband, was behind him.

But before he had made his treasonous speech in Naith, before he had antagonized anyone, Anrel had spent four years at the court schools in Lume. He had made friends there—not as many as some of his class-mates, but he had not by any means been a hermit. He knew a few students who still remained in the capital, and was on friendly terms with some of his old professors, and had acquaintances among the clerks and shopkeepers and taverners. He had come to Lume in hopes of using these contacts to start fresh.

He had no idea what he would do once he had established himself, but there would be time to work that out later. For now he wanted a warm fire and a warm meal and walls that kept out the wind.

And then he emerged from the tunnel, past the two immense doors into the sunlit plaza beyond, and he was once again in Lume, the greatest city in all the known world, capital of the Walasian Empire, home to the Emperor Lurias XII. The plaza before him was paved with fine stone laid in elegant patterns, and the buildings surrounding it rose to as many as six stories in height, their hundreds of glass windows gleaming in the midday sun. Every street leading out of the plaza passed under a grand stone arch, and raised walkways, twenty feet up, connected these arches into a network, almost a second level of streets, though this upper level was reserved for watchmen, soldiers, and couriers.

People of all ages, of all shapes and sizes, wearing every sort of attire, were going about their business. A nobleman's carriage rattled across the pavement, the coachman holding his whip ready should anyone be slow to clear the way.

Anrel had never before entered this gate on foot; in the past he had arrived by coach. Still, he had done that often enough that he had no trouble in finding his route; he crossed the plaza, dodging the other pedestrians, and hurried under the arch that led into Cutler Street. That eventually took him through another arch into Blacksmith Square, where he followed Saddler Street down to the Promenade along the bank of the Galdin.

Some of the people he passed paused to stare at his shabby attire; his velvet coat was almost in ruins now. An ugly brownish stain tarnished the lace at his throat, and although it was not visible under the coat, he could feel that a shoulder seam on his shirt had ripped open.

There had been people of all classes in the streets he had followed, and he had not particularly stood out, but on the Promenade the dandies and their ladies were on display, with furs and fine woolens to keep out the cold. Not just one carriage, but half a dozen, rolled along the red brick pavement, brass fittings and gilt trim glittering. Here, his battered clothing drew sniffs, snubs, or disapproving stares from almost everyone.

Anrel ignored them. Ahead he could now see the ramparts of the emperor's palace looming above the streets and the river, the red painted mouths of cannon protruding from the battlements. Behind those defenses several towers rose, their bronze-wrapped spires gleaming in the sun.

He was not going that far along the Promenade, though; half a mile short of the palace he turned right under the Magistrates' Arcade, and began making his way through the maze of squares and alleys that surrounded the court schools and the Lesser Courts. He passed the ruined entrance of the Court of the White Dove, where a sorcerer's hurried defense against an attempted assassination two centuries ago had rendered several buildings uninhabitable—no one could sleep there and remain sane—and turned down Chalkcutter's Alley.

Dozens of students and clerks were going about their business, despite the cold; most were wrapped in good woolen cloaks, though, not dressed in near rags. Anrel thought he glimpsed a few familiar faces hurrying by, head down, but no one gave any sign of recognizing him. The only people who paid him any attention at all were those who stared at his inappropriate clothing.

Then he spotted faded red curves on a pillar ahead, a sinuous figure that was now little more than a blur, but which had once presumably been a painting of a red serpent.

He knew his own familiar little room was undoubtedly occupied by some eager newcomer by now, but he hoped to take shelter, at least initially, with one of his former neighbors. He turned in at the pillar, under the arch carved with a fanged, inhuman face, and hurried through the passage to the octagonal courtyard, where seven tenements faced each other across the cobbles.

The door to number four was closed, locked and barred, and his knock went unanswered. When at last he was convinced there would be no response, he turned away, shivering, to look at the other doors.

Little Orusir tel-Panien had had the ground-floor front at number three; Anrel decided to try there next. The door was closed, but opened when he tried the latch; he ducked into the hallway, glad to be inside.

No one had ever accused the landlords here of overheating the tenements in winter, but the corridor was still warmer than the outside air, with the familiar smell of cheap wine and boiled cabbage that seemed to permeate most of the student tenements in the city. Anrel stretched a little, unhunching his shoulders for the first time in hours, then turned his attention to Master tel-Panien's door. He knocked.

"Just a moment," came the reply.

Anrel waited, and a few seconds later the latch rattled, and the door swung open a few inches. Orusir tel-Panien's timid, beardless face peered through the crack. "Yes?"

"Ori? It's me. Listen, I need a place to stay."

"Do I know . . . oh, by the Father, is that you? Anrel Murau?" Tel-Panien stared.

"Yes, it's me," Anrel said.

"What did you do to your hair?"

Anrel sighed. "Bleached it, for the sake of a woman."

"And where's your cloak? You must be freezing!"

"Yes, I am," Anrel agreed.

"What are you *doing* here? I thought you went home to your uncle in Aulix!"

"I did," Anrel said. "It didn't go well. Could I come in?"

Tel-Panien glanced over his shoulder, then turned back to Anrel. "I . . . I'm sorry, Anrel, but I don't think that would be wise."

Startled, Anrel said, "Why not?"

"Things have changed since you left, especially since the solstice. The court was not pleased with how the Grand Council turned out."

Anrel blinked, trying to guess what the Grand Council had to do with anything. "I don't understand," he said.

Ori peered out into the passage warily; seeing no one else, he continued, "There are rumors everywhere, and I don't know what to believe, whether it's the empress or the Lords Magistrate or the burgrave of Lume or someone else who ordered it, if *anyone* actually ordered it, but the watch has been keeping a very close eye on us all. We don't dare do anything to draw their attention."

"Why *not?*" Anrel demanded. "What are they going to do?"

"You tried the door at number four?"

"Yes, I did," Anrel acknowledged. "It's locked."

"By order of the watch. They hauled everyone out of there. Some of them were released, but ordered to find other lodging. Some never came back, and we don't know what became of them. Deola Arimar never came back; neither did Sabirin li-Karopiel. Old Vardissier—the landlord, you remember?"

"I paid him rent three times a season," Anrel said dryly. "Of course I remember him."

"When he came home he was limping and something was wrong with his left hand. He wouldn't talk about it. He packed everything up, locked up the place, and went to stay with his sister in Kerdery."

"But *why?*"

Ori glanced up and down the hallway again. "You know about the Grand Council?" he asked.

Anrel knew more about the Grand Council than he had ever wanted to, but he did not immediately see what the connection was. "I know something about it," he replied warily.

"You know they meet in the ruins of the Aldian Baths because the emperor doesn't trust them in the palace?"

"I heard something about that," Anrel admitted.

Ori sighed. "All the wrong people were elected—at least, the emperor thought so. The empress was furious. And she and the emperor and the others all say it was clerks and students who were responsible. This Alvos, who started a riot in Naith and got Derhin li-Parsil elected—they say he was a student at the local College of Sorcerers, and of course Master li-Parsil was a clerk. Students passed the word to other cities, they say, and many of the troublemakers on the council were clerks and students— after all, we're the ones who have studied rhetoric and oratory, and argued about every mad theory of government ever devised, so when the call went out for candidates for the Grand Council, students and clerks spoke up. The emperor apparently expected a bunch of merchants and farmers, but that wasn't what he got, so now they blame *all* of us, they're watching us . . ." He shuddered.

"I see," Anrel said, dismayed. He made no mention of the fact that he, himself, was the infamous Alvos; he had invented the name in a vain hope his true identity would remain unknown when he gave his speech in Aulix Square, and while the magistrates had quickly learned who he was, apparently that news had not reached the general population. Nor were other aspects of the tale accurate; he had not been a student at the Provincial College of Sorcerers. In an attempt to shift the subject away from his own folly, he asked, "I had heard there was a curfew; is that part of the same effort?"

Ori nodded.

"But surely you can let a friend stay for a night?" Anrel pleaded. "Just until I find a place of my own? I don't want to defy the curfew."

"I don't think so," Ori said, shaking his head. "They'll want to know who you are, why you're here—you said you had a falling-out with your uncle?"

"Well, with others in Alzur, really."

"You have no cloak, you have no post, you are no longer a student—I'm sorry, Anrel, but it's too dangerous. You don't belong here anymore."

"Oh, but Ori—"

"*No,* Anrel. I'm sorry. Others may be more generous, but I cannot risk it. Go away, please. Now." He pushed the door.

Anrel resisted for a moment, then stepped back and let it close.

He had no choice, really; what was he going to do, *force* Ori to take him in? No, he would need to find somewhere else. Perhaps Dariel vo-Basig, over in the Court of the Blue Dragon? Dariel had always been fond of defying authority.

In small ways, at any rate.

Anrel tugged his ragged coat more tightly about him, then stepped out into the courtyard. He turned toward the passage out of Red Serpent Court.

A watchman was standing atop the arch, watching him. The afternoon sun gleamed from his brass helmet, and he had his gray woolen cloak flung back to reveal the green and gold tunic of the Emperor's Watch.

Anrel grimaced, then waved cheerfully and trudged onward, trying not to remember Tazia's face or the sound of Reva's neck snapping.

2

In Which Anrel Finds Shelter

Dariel vo-Basig had vanished; none of his neighbors admitted to knowing anything about him. Giel Darai refused to speak to Anrel. Beyir Astemin had fled back to his grandmother's farm in Vaun.

When Anrel tried to speak to his old history professor he found a notice on the study door saying that Master Telsis was available by appointment only, and only to enrolled students. A quick look around found similar notices on several other doors. The proctor at the school entry was watching him warily, so he did not stay to investigate further.

By the time Anrel had learned this much the sun was sinking low in the west, and he saw that the watchmen on the arches, like the proctor, were taking far too much interest in him—his increasingly desperate search had been observed. He realized he was not going to find a haven anywhere in the courts district.

He waved jauntily to the nearest watchman, then ducked under one of the arches, out of sight of the patrolling guards, to count his remaining money and make new plans.

He had been hoarding his funds as best he could since leaving his uncle's house, but he had paid his share of expenses during his season with the Lirs, and a goodly sum was now lying on the bottom of the Galdin River where his coat had torn when he dove off the Beynos bridge. His pockets held four guilders and a few pence, and the lining of his coat concealed another thirty-five guilders.

Almost forty guilders—at the prices typical of Lume he would be able to live comfortably at a decent inn on that for at least half a season, but that time would pass, and what would he do then? He had left most of his possessions behind—first at Uncle Dorias's home in Alzur, and then again at the Boar's Head in Beynos. He owned the clothes he wore, these stacks of coins, the dagger in his boot, and nothing more. Even his hat was gone, last seen floating down the Galdin. Spending his limited funds on lodging indefinitely at an inn did not seem wise.

Besides, if Lord Allutar or Lord Diosin were sufficiently aggravated to send men after him, the city's inns would be the first place they would look.

He had already restored most of the money to its hiding places in the coat's lining when he heard boots on stone, and quickly stuffed the remaining coins into his pockets. He looked up as a watchman marched around the corner of the arch.

"Is everything all right, sir?" the watchman asked, in that tone Anrel had so often heard as a student, the tone that meant everything had *better* be all right if Anrel didn't want to be hauled off to see a magistrate.

"Fine, thank you," Anrel replied cheerily.

"Might I ask where you are bound?" Again, the tone made it plain that only certain answers were acceptable.

Anrel smiled crookedly. "Well, I didn't want to do this, but I do believe I must resort to visiting my aunt in Old Altar Street."

That was not the answer the watchman had expected. "Old Altar Street?"

"Yes, behind the temple of the Cult of the Ancients." Anrel waved in the right general direction. "Over that way."

"Ah." The watchman nodded. The answer, though unexpected, would do. "Very good. Undoubtedly a better idea than staying here." He gestured at the nearest tenement, at the entrance to the Court of Ancient Snow.

"Yes, well, if my friend had bothered to write and let me know he was leaving the city . . ." Anrel shrugged. "Aunt Alisette it is, then."

"Have a good evening, sir," the watchman said with a slight bow.

"And may your own be as pleasant," Anrel replied with a gesture that would have been tipping his hat if he still *had* a hat. Then he ambled off in the direction of Old Altar Street, hoping the watchman would not follow.

He did not.

Anrel had no Aunt Alisette; so far as he knew the Murau family was extinct save for himself and a few distant cousins he had never met, and neither of his aunts on the Adirane side was still alive. His actual intention was to take a bed at an inn tonight—as unlikely an inn as he could find, just in case someone was pursuing him—and then to see about renting an inexpensive furnished room in the morning.

Anrel did not want an officer of the Emperor's Watch making suggestions for lodging, though, and perhaps accompanying him to make sure the advice was followed. He had created a fictitious aunt as the best way to avoid further discussion.

Where he would rent a room on the morrow he had not yet decided—Catseye, perhaps? Or overlooking the Galdin Steps, where the smell from the fish markets kept rents low? Or in one of the ancient alleys of Old Heart? Almost anywhere in the city that he could find inexpensive lodging would serve—anywhere but the courts, where he might be recognized.

Then, once he had a home, he would need to find employment. He could not risk the sort of clerical career he had once assumed he would pursue, but he was young and healthy, he could read and write in more than one language, he had some modest facility with numbers—surely there was some way to earn an honest living in Lume. Perhaps one of the banks, or the mercantile firms, could find a use for him. He was not particularly big or strong, but if all else failed he could probably manage to work at the docks, loading and unloading the barges that plied the Galdin.

First, though, he needed to find an inn before the curfew.

There were any number of establishments scattered through the capital, of course, though they tended to cluster around the gates, the coach stations, the docks, and the magistrates' offices. Those clusters were the first places that anyone looking for him would inquire, and were therefore eliminated from consideration.

He glanced back, and saw the watchman climbing the stairs that led back up to the top of the nearest arch. Anrel picked up his pace; he wanted to be around a corner and out of sight by the time the guardian of the imperial peace regained his elevated vantage point. Anrel hurried toward the Ancients Temple and under the Green Arcade, which took him safely out of the watchman's sight.

He promptly turned sharp right and cut through the Scholars' Market, ignoring the crowd there, then doubled back along Dazarin Avenue. At the ancient and mysterious statue the students called the White Pig he veered onto the sparsely populated Guev Way, and a hundred yards farther brought him to Executioner's Court, which was blessedly deserted. He hurried through the arcade there, on the far side from watch headquarters, and out of the courts.

From there he made his way quickly past a few streets of expensive homes, across Jeweler Street, up and over Zudil Hill, and into the Catseye district, where he began looking for a signboard indicating an inn.

Catseye was a district of shopkeepers and workmen, and not one students or travelers were likely to visit. That meant any pursuers seeking him were unlikely to look there—but it also meant there were few inns. The sun was well down and the twilight fading by the time the glow of a torch finally guided him to an establishment with the unlikely name of the Emperor's Elbow. Anrel was sure there must be a story behind such a name, but he was in no mood to hear it; he was exhausted and ravenously hungry, and once he was certain that the Elbow was indeed an inn he wanted nothing more than a chair and a meal. He pushed the door open and stepped inside.

He stopped just inside the door as the sight, sound, and smell of the inn's interior registered.

This was not the sort of welcoming traveler's rest he was familiar with from previous journeys to and from Lume, nor was it the sort of cheerfully shabby tavern frequented by the students in the courts. The Emperor's Elbow did not bother with beeswax candles or oil lamps; what dim illumination there was came from a few scattered rushlights, and the place reeked of burning fat. The casual chatter and friendly laughter Anrel associated with inns was not to be heard here; instead what little conversation there was seemed to be conducted entirely in angry whispers. The few tables were crude and heavy, slabs of rough wood atop crossed-beam trestles, and the seating was an assortment of mismatched stools, with no proper chairs to be found. Dirty straw covered much of the floor, but those portions where the straw had been kicked aside revealed hard-packed black earth, rather than flags or planking. The low-beamed ceiling was so black with soot that Anrel was not sure whether it was wood or something else entirely.

He had some difficulty in believing what he was seeing; how could so crude a place as this exist in Lume? In the outlying provinces people made do with what they had, and Anrel would not have been terribly surprised, but the capital had always had higher standards than the farther reaches of the empire. An inn like this could only have been established during the chaotic years that immediately followed the Old Empire's fall, and for it to have survived the subsequent centuries unimproved was astonishing.

But then, it was in Catseye, where no one had had a reason to build or improve an inn for hundreds of years.

Under other circumstances Anrel would want nothing to do with such a place, but he was here, it was warm, and at least it was unlikely to be expensive. He shuddered one last time, then trudged to the nearest empty stool and sat down, glad to be off his feet—all the more so because he had thought he could feel something moving in the earthen floor.

That might, he told himself, just be the natural flow of magic through the ground. Most magic drew power from either earth or sky, and here there was nothing separating him from the earth but the soles of his boots. Still, he was glad to be able to tuck his feet under the stool, off that strangely lively floor.

He had been sitting for a minute or two when a man in a wine-stained leather apron appeared out of the shadows to stand beside him. "What do you want?" he asked, glaring down at Anrel.

"A meal and a bed," Anrel replied.

"Sixpence."

Anrel grimaced. "Fine," he said. He could easily have paid twice that in a decent inn, but he suspected it was more than the Elbow's offerings were worth. If the accommodations were too unpleasant, perhaps he could dicker it down in the morning.

"In advance."

So much for dickering. He had agreed to the price; he could hardly balk at the timing. He fished a coin from his pocket and handed it over.

The innkeeper, if that's what he was, held the coin up to the nearest light and studied it before nodding and tucking it out of sight. "Wine's another penny," he said, still standing over Anrel.

Anrel stared up at him, openmouthed with astonishment. "And if I don't pay it?" he said.

"You get water."

Whatever passed for water here would probably give him the flux, and a decent glass of wine would cost a penny or two anywhere. "What sort of wine do you have?"

"Red."

Anrel suppressed a shudder that had nothing to do with the winter's chill. The possibility that this wine was decent looked very slim. "Fine," he said. He produced a penny, which was inspected as the sixpence had been, and accepted. The man in the apron then turned and marched away.

Anrel watched as he vanished through a door at the back that presumably led to the kitchens, then looked around at the other customers.

There weren't very many. Three men were arguing quietly in the back corner; two other men were facing each other across a table, discussing something intently. A man sat by the hearth with a girl on his lap, and even in the half-lit gloom Anrel could see enough of her painted face and low-cut bodice to guess her occupation.

Then he realized that her skirts were tucked up behind her, and she was moving rhythmically on the man's lap, practicing her trade right there. Anrel blushed and looked away. None of the whores around the courts had been quite so blatant.

He let his gaze wander back to the two men facing each other, and then to the three in the corner. They all had a certain similarity to their appearance, he thought. They were all lean, for one thing—very lean, the sort of thin appearance that came from not having enough to eat. There was a faint air of desperation about them.

A thought struck him. He glanced over toward the door, and saw no pegs or hooks, yet none of the customers here wore winter cloaks.

These people were poor, Anrel realized—not the sort of genteel poverty common to many of the students at the court schools, but *really* poor. He wondered how they could afford to patronize even so low an establishment as the Emperor's Elbow.

Then he noticed that none of them had plates before them, or any other sign of food. In each party a single wine cup stood on the table— just enough to convince the landlord to let them stay and talk.

He risked a quick look at the couple by the hearth, where the girl was now adjusting her skirts. She and her customer were both smiling; presumably the transaction had been completed to the satisfaction of all concerned.

She was as thin and hungry in appearance as the men at the tables; her patron, on the other hand, was somewhat better fed and better dressed. He patted her hip, and pushed her off his lap.

Anrel was beginning to develop a theory about the nature of the Emperor's Elbow. This place did not stay in business by providing food and lodging, he supposed, but by providing a relatively safe meeting place for illicit transactions. That was why everyone whispered; those other customers were probably involved in criminal enterprises of one sort or another. It was a place where no one would intrude—certainly, no one but the innkeeper had shown any interest in Anrel. A penny's worth of wine bought light, warmth, and a semblance of privacy.

Such a business would never be profitable enough to pay for improvements, but apparently it managed to survive.

He frowned. Were the authorities more likely, or less, to look for an escaped traitor in such a place? Would they seek it out as a known haunt of criminals, or would they assume Anrel had better sense than to come here?

Did his pursuers even know it existed? It was well inside the city, nowhere near any of the gates.

It was, he realized as he thought over his route, not far from the Pensioners' Quarter, and rumor had it that even the Emperor's Watch did not venture into the streets of the Pensioners' Quarter except in parties of three or more.

If he really wanted to avoid pursuit perhaps he should seek shelter in the Pensioners' Quarter itself, rather than here on its periphery—but then, he was not eager to venture into those streets alone any more than the watchmen were.

He was not particularly eager to stay in the Elbow, either, but he was here, and he had paid for a meal and a bed, and he did not think anyone would find him here.

That assumed that he was being pursued at all; he did not really know that he was. He had been condemned originally by the Lords Magistrate of Naith, but Lume was not Naith, and his accusers had no direct authority here. He had incited a riot in Beynos, which was at least close by, but again, the burgrave of Beynos did not hold sway in Lume.

Despite all that had happened between them, every cause they had to hate each other, Lord Allutar, landgrave of Aulix, had not particularly wanted Anrel to be apprehended. He intended to marry Anrel's cousin, Lady Saria Adirane, and had not cared to complicate their betrothal with Anrel's capture—but that had been before the incident in Beynos. The landgrave might have changed his mind.

Or he might not.

The more he thought about it, the more Anrel suspected that he was not, in fact, the target of serious pursuit. Probably Lord Diosin, the burgrave of Beynos, had sent word to the Emperor's Watch, and Anrel's name would be added to the long list of people they should apprehend should the opportunity arise, but a concerted manhunt was not very likely at all.

There was almost certainly no need to resort to the Pensioners' Quarter, or even to a cesspit like the Emperor's Elbow. He regretted paying that sixpence; he could have stayed somewhere respectable.

But he was here, he hadn't found anywhere more respectable, he *had* paid, and the innkeeper was approaching with a plate of stew and a mug of wine. He would stay one night here, and in the morning he would go looking for better and more permanent lodging, and seek employment that would allow him to pay for it.

The stew was bland, and he was not entirely certain whether the grayish meat was mutton or a poor cut of pork, but it was warm and filling and really not bad at all; when he had cleared his plate he stared at the remaining smear of broth and wished there were more.

The wine, on the other hand, was just as bad as he had feared. For the first time in his life Anrel wished the innkeeper *had* watered the wine. The best he could say for it was that its foul odor did seem to partly obscure the stink from the rushlights.

When he had eaten, Anrel rose, tugged at the innkeeper's sleeve, and asked to be shown to his bed.

The man grunted, and led the way up a steep, narrow stair to the second floor, which was presumably his own residence, and across a narrow landing to a stair so steep and narrow it was effectively a ladder. This led to an attic where half a dozen straw-stuffed mattresses were tucked close under the rafters. The smell in this upper chamber hinted that the chamber pots hadn't been rinsed in some time, and although there was single small window high in the far end, at this hour the only illumination came from a rushlight the innkeeper carried. Still, it was reasonably warm, with no obvious drafts, and the beds were far enough apart that Anrel need not worry about being bumped should one of his neighbors turn over in his sleep.

Not that he had many neighbors; only one bed was occupied, by a boy of ten or twelve who lay curled into a ball, apparently already asleep. Anrel took the mattress farthest from the boy, and settled onto it with a sigh of relief, ignoring the suspicion that the rustle he heard was made up of fleeing vermin as well as the crunch of straw.

There was no sensation of something flowing beneath the floor up here, of course, which was a relief—but curiously, there *was* a very faint hint of some arcane activity, like the lingering traces of an old spell. Anrel could not say whether it had once been a warding, or a binding, or something else entirely, only that it was very old and weak.

Well, the inn was centuries old; probably a witch or sorcerer had stayed here once and set a few wards, and these traces still remained. Or perhaps the place was haunted.

Whatever the cause, Anrel was not interested. He wanted nothing more to do with magic of any sort.

"Breakfast is a penny," the innkeeper said. "Twopence with egg."

"Of course," Anrel replied.

"A rush is a penny."

"I will manage without one, thank you."

The innkeeper shrugged. "As you will, then." He turned and clambered back down the ladder.

Anrel watched him go, and watched the light fade away to nothing. Then he rolled over, arranged his velvet coat into an improvised pillow, and fell quickly asleep, without even bothering to remove his boots.

3

In Which Anrel Makes New Acquaintances

Anrel was a restless sleeper, given to tossing and turning in his bed; nonetheless, it came as an unpleasant surprise when he felt his head thump onto bare wood. He came fully awake in an instant, blinking up through the near-total darkness at the shadowy rafters, and without thinking about it groped for his coat, meaning to tuck it back under his head.

It wasn't there.

He sat up and flung his arm about, first on one side, then the other, and then simultaneously heard a creak and a rustle, and saw movement. He stared into the darkness.

A faint glimmer of light came from the lone window, and by that Anrel could see someone swinging around to climb down the ladder, someone small who was clutching a shapeless something in one hand, something that Anrel guessed was the missing coat—his coat that had his entire fortune, thirty-nine guilders, in the pockets and lining.

He almost cried out, raising an alarm, but then he caught himself. Calling for help in catching a thief might mean talking to a watchman, and that prospect did not appeal to him. Furthermore, he did not know whether there was anyone other than the thief who would hear, and even if the other mattresses had been filled while he slept, calling out in this darkness might only create confusion that would aid in the thief's escape.

Instead he lunged out of bed toward the ladder.

He tried to move quietly, but the figure on the ladder looked up at his approach and hastened his own descent, half sliding, half falling down the steep slope, still clutching the velvet coat.

Anrel reached the ladder and swung around, hurrying down the steps, but could not match the thief's speed. He had a vague fear that the thief would stop on the second floor and take refuge in the innkeeper's quarters—it did not seem impossible that some member of the landlord's family was dissatisfied with honest income—but that concern proved groundless; the figure did not pause on the landing, but sped down the steep stairs to the ground floor.

The rushlights had long since burned out; the entire inn was dark. Anrel found his way as much by sound and feel as by sight. When he reached the bottom of the stair he stumbled, disoriented for a moment, then heard his quarry's fleeing footsteps and followed them, through the inn's main room, where a faint orange glow still emanated from the banked fire on the hearth, to the front door.

For the first time Anrel gained ground, as the thief had to pause to draw the bolt and lift the latch, and Anrel thought he was almost close enough to grab a shoulder when the door swung open and the thief dashed out into the street.

Anrel followed close on the thief's heels, and was startled to find himself in a new world, completely unlike the warm, still darkness of the inn. The two had run out into a snowstorm, where the low gray clouds overhead and the smooth white powder that blanketed the city suffused their surroundings with a faint colorless glow, a glow compounded of diffuse and reflected light from those portions of the capital where lamps still shone. The air was cold and fierce, wind tearing at Anrel's ears and cheeks, but he could see again, albeit only dimly. He had not expected that.

The streets were deserted, silent save for his own breath and the thief's snow-muffled footsteps; Anrel did not know what time it was, but it was plainly well after midnight, yet still hours before dawn. White flakes drifted everywhere, but the only other movement was the two of them.

The thief, Anrel could now see, was no more than a dozen feet ahead. Though it was difficult to make out any details in the dimness, Anrel thought he was very young, wearing a ragged dark tunic and breeches, with feet wrapped in rags. The light was insufficient to see colors, and of course Anrel could not see the thief's face while the youth was running away, but he was fairly certain this was the boy who had been asleep at the far end of the attic earlier.

Anrel's velvet coat, its brown color faded to dark gray in the snowy gloom, was tucked under the boy's right arm. The thief was running as fast as he could down the street to the southeast—toward the Pensioners' Quarter—with Anrel close on his heels.

They ran under a watchman's arch, and the sudden transition from snow to dry cobbles caused the boy to stumble, but he barely slowed. Still, Anrel was gaining, by virtue of his longer legs.

"Drop the coat and we're quit," Anrel called, his voice ringing out unnaturally loud in the nocturnal silence and echoing from the stone arch.

The boy did not bother to reply, and did not drop the coat. Instead he suddenly dodged to the right, through a ruined gate into a yard. Anrel followed, hand outstretched ready to grab, but was startled to see a light, a spot of bright color in the pale world of the snowy night. A small, smoky fire was burning somewhere ahead, and the boy was running directly toward it.

Anrel felt a sudden chill that had nothing to do with running coatless through the snow. Where were they, and what was that fire? He tried to remember how far they had come from the Emperor's Elbow, and what lay down this street.

He thought he knew.

"Give me my coat!" he shouted, hoping to frighten the lad into dropping it; Anrel wanted to get his coat and get out of this place. He lunged for the thief, but the boy shook off his hand and kept running.

As Anrel had feared, shapes stirred in the shadows at the sound of his voice. The two of them were not alone in this court.

"Come *here*!" Anrel said, making another grab.

This time he got a good, firm grip on the lad's upper arm, and the two of them went tumbling forward onto a patch of dead, snow-covered weeds. Anrel snatched at the coat, but the boy held on to it with grim determination.

He heard shuffling and murmuring in the darkness around them, and a glance toward that fire thirty yards away showed half a dozen shadowy figures surrounding the little blaze. Most of them were moving.

"I don't want any trouble," Anrel said. "Just give me my coat and I'll go." He took a good hold on the garment in question and pried it loose.

The boy, who still had not said a word, released his prize at last and fell back on the snow, looking silently up at Anrel.

This sudden surrender was not reassuring; in fact, it frightened Anrel. He knew where he was.

He was in the yard of the old, long-abandoned Pensioners' Hospital, the entrance to the Pensioners' Quarter.

The name was a relic. The Pensioners' Quarter and the Pensioners' Hospital had not held pensioners for half a century. The quarter's original inhabitants had gradually died out, and rogues and outlaws of every description had replaced them. The hospital had been abandoned and fallen into ruin, and the tangle of streets and alleys beyond had become forbidden territory to the city's ordinary citizens. Watchmen never ventured down from their arches and walkways here except in well-armed groups with a specific goal in mind. The emperor ruled these streets only in name, and it was generally thought that no sorcerer had set foot in the quarter in Anrel's lifetime.

And Anrel was here alone, in the middle of the night, chasing a young thief who had run into the quarter seeking sanctuary. The dagger in Anrel's boot was not likely to be any use in defending himself; in fact, drawing it at this point might well be suicidal.

Anrel got quickly to his feet and pulled on his coat, aware that several pairs of eyes were watching him from the surrounding gloom. Then he turned back toward the gate. "I'm going now," he said quietly.

"I think not," a man's voice said, and although he had not seen or heard anyone that close, Anrel felt a faint pressure on his back, just to one side of his spine. He froze. He was fairly certain that it was the point of a knife. An arm swung around and across his throat, and Anrel could feel warm breath in his ear. "Not without a little explanation for your presence at this hour. What brings you to our neighborhood?"

The man's tone was calm and conversational, as if the two were seated at a table together, rather than standing in the snow in the middle of the night, one holding a knife to the other's back. Still, the threat was obvious and real, and Anrel did not think an accusation of theft was wise.

"It would seem I dropped my coat," Anrel said, trying to speak just as calmly.

"Oh?" The voice seemed friendly enough, but the point of the knife did not move. A faint scent of onions reached Anrel's nose, seeming oddly incongruous in the cold, snowy gloom.

"Yes," Anrel said. "And this young man found it. I would be happy to reward him with a penny or two."

"One or two?"

Anrel tried to remember exactly what coins he had in his pockets. "Perhaps fourpence?"

"Do you suppose that to be fair compensation for the lad's efforts, on a night such as this?"

The man was willing to bargain; Anrel suppressed a sigh of relief. If this person had intended to kill him anyway, there would be no reason to discuss prices. "Why, then, what would you think fair, sir?"

"I scarcely know. I do not know how far he ran through the streets, trying to return your fine garment."

"From the Emperor's Elbow, sir, no farther."

"And he has surely left the innkeeper unpaid, sir, which cannot be per-mitted! What's more, it may well be that along the way some of his own plentiful funds might have found their way into your pockets. Shall we say, then, that the boy might take a look, to see whether such a mishap has occurred?"

Anrel knew what that meant; they intended to take every penny he had in his pockets. Presumably they would then allow him to go, with the coat and his life, and though they didn't know it, with thirty-five guilders still in the coat's lining. It would mean a loss of a little more than four guilders—hardly a negligible sum, but far less than Anrel felt his life was worth. Best to cooperate and be released.

"Certainly; I should hardly wish to deprive him of that which he has earned."

"Very good, sir! If you would be so kind as to remain as you are, for just a moment?"

"I would be happy to oblige you," Anrel said, holding very still.

A moment later he felt a small hand plunge into his right-hand coat pocket. Fingers rummaged through the contents, then pulled out the little wad of cloth that held the larger coins and kept them from jingling. The hand plunged back again a second later, then once more withdrew, this time taking the smaller coins that had been lying loose.

At that Anrel thought the transaction was complete, and he was about to say something to the man holding the knife when the same little hand dove into his left-hand pocket.

There was no money there, Anrel knew—a tinderbox and a handkerchief, nothing more. The thief removed the tinderbox, though.

There was a faint rustle, and a clink.

"Four guilders and tenpence," a child's voice said.

For a moment there was silence; then the man said, "Four *guilders*?" Anrel no longer felt breath in his ear; presumably his captor had turned to stare at the boy.

"Yes," the boy said.

"He was staying at the Elbow?"

"Yes."

"You will pardon me, sir," the knife wielder said, his breath once again filling Anrel's ear. "I am puzzled by my companion's discovery."

"It does seem peculiar that a lad his age would be carrying so much money," Anrel said.

"Let us drop this pretense, sir. Although that money is ours now, it *was* yours, and you surely knew it was there, yet you took lodging at the Emperor's Elbow?"

"I did."

"While I regret the necessity of speaking ill of a local institution, and particularly one that has been the pride of the Guirion family for a dozen generations and of great use to many of my friends, it cannot have escaped your notice that the Emperor's Elbow is in all likelihood the worst inn in all of Lume. You had the money in your pocket to pay for a far better one. Why, then, your choice of lodging?"

"I had other uses for that money," Anrel said.

"Would you care to be more specific?"

"No."

For a moment there was a baffled silence as the man considered that response; then the boy spoke up.

"It was heavier than this," he said.

"What?" The man's breath was gone again.

"The coat. It was heavier. Four guilders and a tinderbox—it was heavier than that. There's something else in it. That's why I held on to it as long as I could."

"Four guilders is a good night's work in any case," the man said.

"There's more," the boy insisted. "I know there is."

"The coat's velvet," the man said, not convinced. "That's a heavy fabric."

"Not as heavy as wool, and that coat weighs more than it should."

"Well, friend," the man said, addressing Anrel anew, "is there anything you would care to tell us? My compatriot is young, but he knows his trade well."

Anrel hesitated, and the man added, "We would regret the necessity of cutting the coat apart to discover your secrets. We would likewise regret the necessity of cutting *you* apart, should you fail to cooperate."

"And if I do cooperate, you'll release me?"

"That is indeed the bargain I propose, yes."

Anrel hesitated again, thinking over his situation. He held no weapon, but his father's dagger was still in his boot, and he had one other weapon that these people could not know about. He had denied it for most of his life, and he was unskilled in its use, but he did have his magic.

If he gave up all his money, what would he do with himself? He had no friends or family, no home, no income; he was an outlaw, a fugitive who had violated the empire's laws and who could therefore expect no protection from them.

It might be simpler if he did die here, alone in the snow, fighting these thieves. He had failed Valin and Tazia and Reva; he scarcely deserved to live. He scarcely *wanted* to live, knowing he would never see them again—Valin and Reva because they were dead, and Tazia because he was not worthy of her.

He would resist. He would fight. The Mother and the Father would decide whether he lived or died.

He began to draw power from the earth beneath his feet up into his heart. He did not yet know what he intended to do with it, whether he would attempt a binding or a ward or some other spell, but he meant to try *something.*

4

In Which Anrel Agrees to Terms

The knife pressed a little harder into Anrel's back. "You seem reluctant to speak," the thief said. "What secret can you have that's worth your life?"

That question, combined with the growing awareness of forbidden magical energy in his breast, the memory of Reva's death less than twenty-four hours before, and his despair at Tazia's loss suddenly struck Anrel funny, and to everyone's shock, not excepting his own, he burst out laughing.

The arm around his throat loosened, then withdrew, and the knife-point's pressure lessened.

"He's mad," someone said—a new voice, one that Anrel thought was probably a woman's.

"Or perhaps he truly *does* have a secret worth more than his life," the knife man said.

"Not *more*," Anrel said, struggling to catch his breath. "But a secret worth my life? Oh, yes. More than one."

That was no more than the truth. The knowledge that he was the infamous Alvos who had incited the riots in Naith and inspired the commoners to vote dozens of populist radicals onto the Grand Council was worth his life. The fact that he was a witch, a magician whose name was not on the Great List, would also be sufficient to hang him. Compared to those the thirty-five guilders hidden in the coat's lining were trivial, yet the money was the secret he had chosen to keep.

"You intrigue me, sir. You will not say why you were at the Emperor's Elbow, nor what weighs down your coat?"

Anrel was suddenly tired of this confrontation. It was the middle of the night, and he was out in a snowstorm, in perhaps the most dangerous part of Lume, arguing with thieves who had threatened to kill him, one of whom was still holding a knife to his back. He was cold and angry and exhausted, it was less than a full day since he had lost any hope of marrying the woman he loved, and he could feel the Mother's energy in his heart, ready to be used.

He would indeed use it, he decided. He would attempt a ward, a protective spell—wards were simple, and the only magic he had any real experience in using. It would be as general as he could make it, designed to turn aside blades or fists. In his present sorry state he did not have the subtlety to ward off anger or other emotions, but physical attacks were straightforward.

He doubted he had the skill to cast a truly *effective* ward, but it might help. He turned the power in his breast outward, but did not release it.

That might be enough to save him from the attack he expected, or it might not, but in his present slough of anger and despair he did not really care. He wanted this over, one way or another.

"I will say nothing to you, sir," he said. "You have your four guilders, and I am going back to my bed." He started walking toward the gate—not running, but walking slowly and deliberately. He waited for the feel of the knife plunging toward his back, and wondered whether the ward would turn it aside, or whether it would stab into him. Perhaps it would be deflected enough to turn the stab into a slash. He debated stooping to pull his own dagger from his boot, to be ready for the fight that now seemed inevitable.

Shadows appeared, blocking his path. Anrel stopped, frowning. He could not see any features in the darkness, but the size and general outline indicated that he was facing at least two large men.

"Did you think there were just the two of us?" the man with the knife asked, his voice as casual as ever.

"I had thought that at this time of night even most denizens of this unfortunate neighborhood would have the sense to stay indoors, out of the snow," Anrel replied angrily. His hand fell toward his boot.

"Sense hasn't a thing to do with it," said the voice that had called him mad, from somewhere on his right. "Now, what's in that coat?"

"*I* am," Anrel said, "and I intend to stay in it."

"I admire your nerve, sir," said the man with the knife. "But be reasonable—if you leave here, where will you go? Back to the Elbow? Surely by now you've realized why Master Guirion requires payment in advance."

In fact, Anrel had not thought of that, but now it was obvious. The innkeeper clearly *knew* his guests were likely to be robbed, and did nothing to prevent it, or even to warn them. He probably received a share of the proceeds. Anrel could expect no safety there. If he went back there it would presumably merely put matters off briefly. Even if the innkeeper feigned innocence and allowed him to return to his bed unmolested, he would not stay there long. The thieves had taken a very definite interest in himself and his coat, and would undoubtedly corner him there. There were no other guests to make common cause with him in defense against such predators.

He could find another inn—but perhaps not at this hour, in the snow, in Catseye. And if he went wandering about the streets, what would stop these people from following him and waylaying him at the first opportunity?

He could find a watchman and ask for protection—but he was a wanted criminal himself, out well past curfew. The thieves had no way of knowing he was a fugitive, but they did know about the curfew, and that he had a secret of some sort. They probably guessed that his secret, whatever it might be, would make him reluctant to invite official involvement. The curfew ensured that anything he did or said would be met with official suspicion.

"That coat is velvet," said the man with the knife. "It was a fine garment when it was new, but it's far from new. Handed down to you, perhaps? You had four guilders in your pockets, yet you were staying at the Elbow—"

"He had no baggage," the boy who had originally taken the coat interrupted. "Not so much as a purse."

The knife man continued, "And you have no baggage. You say you have secrets worth your life. If I were to venture a guess, my friend, I would say you are most likely a servant who stole from his employer, was caught in the act, and fled. What's in the coat, then? The family silver, perhaps?"

"I did not rob my employer," Anrel said, both annoyed and amused by the accusation.

"Still, I cannot think of any reason for an honest man with four guilders in his pocket to stay at the Emperor's Elbow. I believe you went there to hide. No one would think to look for you there."

Anrel did not reply to that.

"Kill him and take the coat so we can all get some sleep," a new voice called from the darkness.

"Hear that, friend?" the knife man said. "I am not so bloodthirsty as some of my neighbors, but I am not especially squeamish, either, and I am running out of patience."

"Then get on with it," Anrel snapped. "Try to kill me, and I will defend myself, and we will see what happens." He stretched his hand down and began to stoop slightly, preparing to grab his father's dagger.

"I would prefer to avoid that," the knife man said. "Let us see if we cannot arrive at an agreeable alternative."

"Let me go," Anrel said. "And don't follow me. That will be the end of it."

"No," the man said judiciously. "No, I do not think that would suit us. Now there are at least half a dozen of us awake and involved, and while that four guilders divided six ways will be greatly appreciated, I still have hopes for better. You have aroused both my curiosity and my cupidity. I think you came to the Elbow to hide—do you deny it?"

Anrel became aware of a faint rustling; people were moving in the surrounding gloom, people he could not see. He heard whispering, as well, a sound he had previously taken for the hiss of falling snow but now recognized as quiet conversation. He was not sure what was being said, or what these people were doing, but he doubted it bode well. "I deny nothing," he said. "Neither do I confirm it."

"Let us assume that you were, in fact, seeking a sanctuary. Has it occurred to you that we who live in the Pensioners' Quarter do so because it is *our* sanctuary?"

Startled, Anrel turned, trying to make out the other's face through the gloom. "What does that have to do with me?" he asked.

"You are a brave and levelheaded fellow," the thief said. "You have not blustered and threatened, you did not run pell-mell, you did not protest when my compatriot emptied your pocket. I think I might find a use for you, should you choose to stay here with us."

"What?"

The thief ignored Anrel's bafflement. "Tell me, was my guess right?" he asked. "Have you lived in the homes of the wealthy? Do you know their ways?"

"I lived for several years in a burgrave's home," Anrel replied cautiously.

"A burgrave? A *sorcerer*?"

"Yes, a sorcerer."

"Oh, excellent!"

"What are you *talking* about?"

"I am offering you, my friend, a place to stay, here in the Pensioners' Quarter, and gainful, if not lawful, employment."

"Doz, what are you doing?" the woman who had called Anrel mad demanded.

"Exactly what I say," the knife wielder replied. "Look at the way this man has handled himself, alone in the cold and dark, surrounded by foes! I can use a man like this."

"What about his coat?" the boy-thief demanded.

"Ah," Doz said. "*That* is the next matter to be resolved, should this fellow be interested in my offer. Are you, sir?"

Anrel wished he could see the man's face, but the faint glow of the fire behind him cast the knife wielder's features in shadow.

Could he take this offer seriously? A safe place to live and a job—that was exactly what Anrel had hoped to find in Lume. But a place in the Pensioners' Quarter, working with thieves? That had *not* been in his plans. No place in the quarter was truly safe, and no job there was entirely honest.

Still, what better choice did he have? He was here, surrounded by thieves, and they did not seem willing to let him go. Better to stay as a new recruit to their gang than as a corpse, or as a victim stripped and beaten and left lying in the snow.

And they could not watch him every minute of every day if he agreed to join them. Once he had gained their trust, once they had accepted him as one of their own, he could leave and find himself another, more respectable living.

For now it would do no harm to at least find out more of what his captors had in mind.

Rumor would have it that the inhabitants of the Pensioners' Quarter were little better than beasts, but during his student days Anrel had given the matter some thought, and noticed that the streets of the quarter were not littered with corpses—the inhabitants did not all slaughter each other, nor did they all starve to death. The numbers of thieves and scoundrels said to lurk here did not seem to dwindle over time, which meant that they had some sort of functioning society, so they were not all hopelessly stupid and bloodthirsty. Unfortunate, yes, and unquestionably outlaws, but not so ferocious or bestial they could not be bargained with.

"I might be," Anrel acknowledged.

"Then if we are to work together, we must demonstrate our trust for one another. I am called Doz, and you are . . . ?"

"Dyssan," Anrel said.

"And your coat contains . . . ?"

"I have said I will not tell you."

"But that was when we were foes. Can you not trust me with the secret now?"

"You have, as yet, done nothing to earn my trust."

"I haven't killed you," Doz pointed out.

Anrel smiled wryly to himself. "Admirable, but insufficient," he replied.

Doz sighed. "Then let us leave it for the moment. Let us find you a place to stay, and when you awake in the morning, and find that we have not killed you in your sleep, nor stolen your precious coat, why, then we may have a foundation on which to build."

Anrel considered that, then shrugged. "I confess I see no convenient alternative."

Anrel could not see the other man's face, but from the tilt of his head Anrel thought Doz was studying him. Then Doz said, "You seem a very calm fellow, Dyssan." He looked around. "I don't think we can find you a *bed,* as such, but a quiet corner out of the wind and snow, under a roof that doesn't leak much, should be attainable."

"That would suit me well enough."

"Tomorrow we will continue our discussion of your future."

"That, too, would be acceptable."

"Come, then."

He led the way toward the fire, deeper into the dreaded Pensioners' Quarter, and Anrel followed.

5

In Which Anrel Is Offered Employment

Anrel awoke the next morning and took his first look at his new lodging.

He had been led here in the dark—Doz had apparently not considered light necessary, and even in the last flurries of snow the faint glow of the city had not penetrated the depths of the Pensioners' Quarter. Anrel had been escorted through a tangle of foul-smelling alleys where he could barely avoid walking into the wall at every turn, and then through a series of unlit rooms, across creaking floors, to a chamber where Doz directed him to a corner and said, "I trust this will do."

Anrel had been unable to see any details. The room had a window, he knew that much, as that had been a visible patch of dark gray in the blackness. His assigned corner was, if not warm, at least warmer than the streets, and neither wind nor snow seemed to penetrate, which was good. Even after Doz took his leave Anrel had heard breathing, and smelled unwashed flesh, so he knew he was not alone in this place.

That, however, was the extent of his knowledge. Weary as he was, he had simply accepted it, curling up in the corner and going to sleep. He had, of course, kept his coat on and made do without a pillow; he had no intention of giving anyone another chance to steal it there in the dark.

Now the gray light of morning was filtering in the room's lone window, and Anrel was able to take in his surroundings.

There was a single door, through which he had entered, opposite the window. The window was hung with crumbling lace, and most of its dust-caked panes were cracked—Anrel was surprised they all still had glass. The furnishings consisted of a single simple bed and a small stove that stood on a slate hearth opposite the bed. The stove gave little warmth—the dampers were closed, and there was no sign of additional fuel. Still, the room was only slightly chilly.

He shared the room with four others, he discovered, three young boys and an old man, all of whom were awake.

The one bed was occupied by the old man, who appeared incapable of intelligible speech but mumbled constantly, while each of the boys had claimed a corner and collected a heap of rags for bedding. Anrel had been assigned the fourth and final corner, behind the door.

The three boys were all watching him with interest, but none of them spoke.

"Good morning," Anrel said.

No one replied. Three pairs of eyes remained fixed on him, but none of the boys spoke. The old man was staring at the ceiling and muttering something to himself.

"I'm called Dyssan," Anrel said.

"I'm Shoun," said the lad Anrel judged to be second in age, perhaps nine or ten. "That's Apolien." He jerked a thumb toward the old man on the bed.

"I'll get Doz," said the youngest. He jumped up and ran out the door.

"His name is Po," Shoun said, nodding in the direction his comrade had taken.

Anrel nodded. He judged Po to be seven or eight. That left one boy unnamed, the oldest, who Anrel thought he recognized as the thief who had stolen his coat at the Emperor's Elbow. "And you are . . . ?" he asked.

"Mieshel," the boy said softly.

"I believe we met last night," Anrel said.

"Yes," Mieshel agreed.

Anrel was debating what to say next when Shoun volunteered, "There's no chamber pot. There's a privy out back."

"Thank you," Anrel said, though he was not yet urgently in need of such a facility. The miserable swill the Elbow served as wine had not tempted him to drink deeply.

"There's a water pump in the courtyard," Shoun added.

"Thank you," Anrel repeated. "What do you lads do for food?"

"Whatever we can," Mieshel replied. "Begging, sometimes."

"We run errands sometimes," said Shoun.

"Or we steal," Mieshel said. "As you know." He flashed a brief, crooked smile.

"Well, yes," Anrel said. "But I was thinking more of who feeds you. Who cooks for you?"

"No one," Shoun said, startled. "We feed ourselves."

"When we have money, we buy food," Mieshel said. "I ate supper at the Emperor's Elbow last night—that's why old Guirion let me sleep there."

"I see," said Anrel. "And when you have no money?"

"We get a lot of food from sorcerers' servants," Mieshel said. "We do them favors, and they give us their masters' leftovers, or food that's not fresh enough for the masters."

"Not just sorcerers," Shoun added. "Rich commoners, too. And inns, and shops."

"Ah," Anrel said.

"And if that doesn't work, we don't eat," Mieshel said.

"There isn't much sometimes," Shoun agreed.

"Especially this time of year," Mieshel said.

"What about him?" Anrel asked, jerking a thumb at Apolien.

"He's not as dumb as he looks," Mieshel answered.

The other boy had nothing to add to that, it seemed. They were content to leave their elderly companion a mystery.

"Where did you live before you came here?" Anrel asked. "Or have you always lived here?"

The boys exchanged glances.

"We don't talk about that," Mieshel told him.

"That's the rule," Shoun explained. "Here in the quarter we never ask each other about where we came from, who we were, who our families were."

"For most of us it's too painful," Mieshel concluded.

"Oh," Anrel said.

With that, he found he had nothing more to say. He slouched in his corner, waiting for Doz.

The wait was not long; Po reappeared a few minutes later and scurried to his own corner, and a man who must surely be Doz stood just inside the door, looking at Anrel.

"Good morning, sir," he said.

Doz was a young man himself, perhaps no older than Anrel's own twenty-three years. Anrel had not gotten a good look at him in the darkness, and took a moment to study his host.

Like everyone Anrel had seen since arriving at the Emperor's Elbow but the innkeeper and the prostitute's patron, Doz appeared underfed. He seemed otherwise healthy enough. His long black hair was oily, as if he had not bathed recently, but was neatly combed. He wore a white linen shirt that had seen a great many better days, nondescript trousers that might have been either brown or gray originally but were now somewhere in between, and no coat, but a thick, slightly frayed blanket of brown wool was wrapped around his shoulders and pinned at his throat. A crumpled ruin of a hat sat atop his head, and his boots were bound with rags to hold the soles to the crumbling uppers.

"Good enough," Anrel acknowledged.

"Have you considered my offer of employment?"

"I fear that I have insufficient information on which to make a decision. You have not as yet told me the nature of this employment."

"And you have not yet told me why your coat is so heavy."

"I found out," Shoun said. "While he was asleep."

Anrel blinked in surprise, and turned to stare at the boy. He brushed both hands on the velvet coat; it *felt* unchanged. He thought he would have noticed if the hidden coins had been disturbed.

Doz turned to look at Shoun as well. "Did you? Good lad! And what, then, is in our guest's mysterious coat?" Before Shoun could reply, Doz added with a smile, "The boy is quite a talented pickpocket."

"Magic," Shoun said proudly.

Anrel's eyes widened.

Doz frowned. "What sort of magic?"

"*I* don't know," Shoun said. "I'm no sorcerer. But it's magic. My hands slid off every time I touched it. It looks like velvet, but it felt like cold steel."

For an instant Anrel thought the child was lying, making up some absurd tale to amuse himself, but then he remembered the ward he had tried to place, there in the hospital court in the snow. Apparently it had worked, and had lasted longer than he expected. In fact, now that his attention had been brought to it, he could sense that the ward was still in place, though weakened. He tried to reach out for magic to reinforce it, but apparently the floor here was too thick, or something else was intervening; he could not find more than a faint trickle of power.

"It didn't feel wrong last night, when I had it," Mieshel protested.

"He wasn't wearing it last night," Doz said thoughtfully.

"He was when I checked the pockets."

"You had my permission," Anrel said, startling the others.

Doz turned to him. "Then the coat *is* magical?"

"I told you I lived in a sorcerer's home for a time." That was true, but in no way did it actually answer the question.

"So you did. And that is where you acquired this coat?"

Anrel nodded. "Indeed, it is."

Doz studied him for a moment, then asked, "You stole it?"

"I did not. The burgrave of Alzur gave it to me." That was not, perhaps, the exact truth, but it was close; Uncle Dorias had paid the tailor's bill.

"You swear to this?"

Anrel frowned. "What does it matter?"

"I am trying, sir, to determine to what extent I can trust you, and whether or not you will be interested in the offer I hope to make."

"I fail to see how my coat relates to your concerns."

"Your truthfulness is obviously relevant. Also, the employment I thought to offer you is not, perhaps, entirely lawful, so an understanding of your attitude toward the property of others may also be relevant."

Anrel looked at him, then glanced around at the three boys, who had cheerfully admitted to being thieves.

"I have stolen when I thought it necessary," Anrel said, remembering his desperate flight from Naith. He had stolen a sword, a jacket, and a boat, at the very least. "However, I am not base or foolish enough to rob the sorcerer who took me into his home and treated me with respect and consideration. The coat is mine by right, and whatever magic it may have is mine, as well. My thefts were all committed *after* I left the burgrave's roof."

"Ah, *now* we're getting somewhere! Then you have played the thief on occasion?"

"I have."

"And you would be willing to do so again, should circumstances require it?"

"I would." Anrel saw no point in denying it; he had turned thief readily enough when it seemed the only way to get out of Naith alive, and he would do no differently now.

He really *wasn't* worthy of Tazia.

"You say you lived in a burgrave's home for several years," Doz continued. "How did that come about?"

Anrel glanced around the room. "These lads told me that it is not the custom in the Pensioners' Quarter to make inquiries into one's personal history."

"It is not, I confess, but your circumstances are rather unusual; will you not indulge my curiosity?"

"I was orphaned while still a small child. The burgrave took me in."

"Generous of him."

"The burgrave of Alzur is a generous man."

Doz nodded, fingering his beard thoughtfully. "And how did you come to leave this sorcerer's home? Did you simply overstay your welcome?"

Anrel shook his head. "No," he said. "I was forced to sever my ties with friends and family in that area due a misunderstanding with the local magistrates."

"Ah, I believe I have experienced such misunderstandings. But you said you were not yet a thief when you dwelt with the burgrave?"

"I was not."

"Then what was the nature of this misunderstanding?"

Anrel smiled wryly. "The magistrates had the absurd notion that I committed sedition and treason in protesting certain actions by the landgrave of Aulix."

Doz smiled back. "How very unfortunate!"

"Further, it has been said that I made my escape in a stolen boat, but I assure you, I had every intention of restoring my borrowed craft to its rightful owner, should the opportunity present itself."

"I see." Doz leaned back against the door frame. "And has the landgrave, or the boat's owner, perhaps sent representatives to discuss these matters with you?"

"Not that I am aware of, no."

"Are they aware that you have come to Lume?"

"I have no reason to think so."

"Then why did you seek out the Emperor's Elbow, when you had the money in your pocket to pay for a far better establishment?"

"I have no reason to think that I am *not* being pursued," Anrel replied. "I am perhaps, at times, overcautious."

Doz considered that for a moment, then asked, "What did you do to upset a landgrave? Or was that a fiction of the magistrates' devising?"

"Oh, it's true enough, after a fashion. I was in Naith when that troublemaker Alvos gave his speech, and I got a little carried away. I said a few things about the despicable Lord Allutar that the City Watch considered inappropriate. The part about the boat is simple fact."

"Your burgrave couldn't intercede for you?"

"The burgrave was kind to me, but I do not think his generosity extended to interceding with the magistrates. He and I did not share the same opinion of Lord Allutar, nor of the present political situation."

"Did you ask him?"

"I did not. The opportunity did not arise."

Doz nodded. "But you don't think anyone is looking for you?"

"I don't know," Anrel admitted. "I wouldn't think so."

"You understand, if you've lied about this, and someone *does* come looking for you, it's quite likely someone here in the quarter will either deliver you to them, or simply stick a knife in you."

"I am not surprised to hear it. Until such time as that happens, though, just what is it you want of me?"

"You know we are thieves," Doz said. "We prefer, however, not to rely on violence or other such crude actions. Shoun, here, is a pickpocket, while Mieshel, as you know all too well, is adept at carrying away unsecured belongings. Po is small enough to slip through unguarded openings and pass valuables out to his confederates. Apolicn—well, he has his own methods. For myself, though, my hands are not small nor quick enough to pick pockets, and I am too large to go unnoticed or squeeze through half-opened windows. I have, therefore, made a career not of simply *taking* people's money, but of convincing them to *give* it to me. I have employed a variety of ruses to that end—claiming to be a worker in various trades, or saying I need a small loan to redeem some family heirloom put up as security on a loan, and so on. However, my appearance and manner are such that I cannot expect anyone to believe I am wealthy myself, and merely momentarily embarrassed. *You,* on the other hand, with your velvet coat and elegant bearing, and your fearlessness—you could be a very useful partner in my enterprise."

"I don't understand," Anrel said. "What would you expect me to do?"

"Talk to people," Doz explained. "To the rich—sorcerers, merchants, and the like. They won't avoid you, as they do me, not if you can keep yourself clean. You can look like a wealthy man, or at worst someone down on his luck who *was* wealthy. You can distract them, or lure them in."

"I see," Anrel said. He was not entirely happy taking on such a role, but he could see how it might be useful.

"We don't need another pair of hands, not if they're attached to a mouth that needs feeding, but a man who cuts a fine figure—that we can use. And you didn't do anything stupid yesterday. Most men of your sort who find themselves in the quarter—well, they do something stupid, and wind up lying in the street with their throats slit."

"The street? The watchmen don't see?" Anrel said.

Doz snorted. "The watchmen can't be everywhere," he said. "They don't come into the quarter very often, even on their arches and walkways, and when they do, there are still places they can't see—around corners, behind pillars, inside our homes. Sometimes the best place to avoid being seen is right below a watchman's feet."

That could hardly be argued. Anrel knew well that the watch could not see what happened directly under an arch.

"Are you interested in playing roles for us?" Doz asked.

Anrel thought for a long moment before replying. He had always considered himself an honest man, but he was already a thief and an outlaw. He had no means of support, no idea how to find honest work; his training in history and law was of no use to a fugitive. Even before Valin's death he had been unable to find himself a good position, and now—well, Doz had just made him the best offer he had heard to date, and quite possibly the best he could hope for.

And he felt certain that no one from Naith or Beynos would come looking for him in the Pensioners' Quarter.

"We would split the proceeds evenly?" he asked.

Doz grinned. "That seems fair."

"No unnecessary violence? We won't hurt anyone?"

"Not unless they try to harm us," Doz agreed.

"We will make an effort to choose victims who can afford the loss?"

"Of course; those are the ones least likely to turn violent."

"I am free to leave if these plans do not work out?"

"I can scarcely watch you every minute of the day."

"You will give up your absurd interest in the coat the burgrave gave me?"

"At least until you can afford better, I very much want you to keep that coat—it makes a great contribution to your appearance, which is an essential element in our plans."

"In that case, let us give your scheme a try." He held out a hand.

Doz reached out and took it.

That was how Anrel came to the Pensioners' Quarter, which became his home for the remainder of the winter and through the spring.

6

In Which Anrel Becomes Acquainted with His New Home

Once he had accepted Doz's offer Anrel found himself once again beginning an education in Lume, but a very different one from his earlier studies. He had been taught law in the court schools; now, in the Pensioners' Quarter, he learned how to live outside the law.

He learned to play a variety of roles—the outraged brother bursting in on a whore and her customer, the disgraced cousin selling his family's glass-and-paste jewels, the drunken sorcerer entertaining a tavern crowd with sleight of hand while his compatriots robbed them.

He was too big and noticeable to become a pickpocket, but he made an excellent decoy for pickpockets. He was very believable shouting, "He went that way!" while pointing in the wrong direction.

Most of all, however, he played the part of a young man of good family who had somehow found himself without funds and who needed a guilder or two to see himself safely back home. Naturally, anyone who loaned him the money would be promised a generous reward, to be sent as soon as he was returned to his father's hearth. The tale varied with circumstances—sometimes he had been robbed, sometimes he had gambled away his allowance, sometimes he had drunk it away but was now sworn to sobriety, sometimes he had fallen in with bad company and been led astray, wasting his money on wine and women. On occasion he confessed to having become enamored of some peculiar cult and given its priests his every penny, or enamored of a whore, and given *her* his every penny in hopes of restoring her to decent society, only to have her disappoint him. Coach fare to Kallai or Azar or Sorimel would see his fortunes restored, and whoever loaned it to him would be repaid tenfold.

If coach fare was too much, perhaps threepence to send a letter? And another penny for paper?

Anrel was especially convincing when bemoaning the loss of a woman; he had merely to remember Tazia to add a large measure of verisimilitude.

The deception Anrel found most amusing, though, was to sadly confess to having been swindled out of his money, leaving him destitute.

There were more complicated schemes, as well, where Anrel would pretend to recognize an artifact as a stolen family treasure and demand recompense, or where he would insist that he was owed a debt incurred during a night of drunken debauchery.

Often Doz took part in these performances, playing the role of debt collector, or family messenger, or whatever other character might seem appropriate. He claimed half the take, however much it might be, and Anrel accepted this without argument; he considered it rent and tuition. In truth, Anrel still had enough money concealed that he scarcely missed what he paid Doz.

Anrel's clothes had become shabby enough to limit his ruses at first; he could hardly claim to have only just now fallen upon hard times when his every garment had clearly been suffering for a season or two. He therefore slipped away from Doz long enough to visit a tailor every so often, and began rebuilding his wardrobe. The very first thing he bought, other than food, was a new hat.

Whenever he found himself alone outside the Pensioners' Quarter he considered taking a room and looking for honest work, but there were few jobs to be had, and where he could give no references he was eyed with suspicion. All too often he found himself attracting the attention of the Emperor's Watch; in fact, he seemed to draw more interest from atop the watchmen's arches when he was looking for work than when he was swindling or stealing.

All the same, he could have left the quarter—but he did not. He found something appealing in the rawness of his new life, and more important, he felt as if he could contribute more to his neighbors in the quarter than he could elsewhere. Just as he learned the skills of the underworld from them, he did his best to teach them what he could of history, manners, and grammar, and whatever else he thought might prove useful.

He told himself that by bringing money to the quarter through his deceits, he made it that much less necessary for the others to resort to violence or the destruction of property. Every penny he brought in by trickery was a penny that was not taken at knifepoint, or by breaking a shop window.

His facility with paper and pen proved unexpectedly valuable; few of the inhabitants of the quarter could read or write, while Anrel was fluent not only in Walasian, but in the written form of the Old Imperial tongue, and he could get by in Ermetian, Quandish, and several other dialects. He taught anyone who wanted to learn the basics of literacy, but he also discovered and carefully developed a knack for forgery, and often found himself drafting false documents of one sort or another for his neighbors.

He learned to fight, with his fists, his feet, a knife, or a staff, or any combination of those.

His bleached hair grew out, and his natural coloring returned. Quite aside from any concerns with warmth or fashion, his new hat was needed to conceal this unseemly situation until the growth was sufficient to trim off the blond ends without leaving him bald.

And though he never mentioned it to Doz, he took lessons in magic from some of the witches living in the quarter. Not all of the witches of Lume dwelled among the city's castoffs; most had managed to maintain respectable addresses. A few, though, had been driven from their homes for one reason or another, and had eventually found themselves in the Pensioners' Quarter, where their services were in much demand, and where Anrel could receive occasional clandestine instruction in the arcane arts. These women, regardless of age, were generally happy to trade their knowledge for a few pence and a little flattery from a charming young man.

There were no male witches in the quarter save himself, or at least none who admitted to their status.

Anrel kept himself busy. He did so in part because there was so much to be learned, and the need to earn money for the people of the Pensioners' Quarter was so acute, but also in large part to distract himself from what he had lost. Building a new life kept himself from grieving too greatly for the loss of the old.

Most of all he missed Tazia Lir. Theirs had not been a great burning storybook passion, but in their time together she had become a comforting presence. Her warmth, her common sense, her beauty, and her admiration for Anrel had made her presence a pleasure like none Anrel had known before. He had intended to ask for her hand in marriage, but Reva's arrest had put those plans in abeyance, and Reva's death had snuffed them out. Tazia's absence left a hole in Anrel's life, a void that nothing seemed able to fill.

To a much lesser degree he missed his uncle, Lord Dorias, as well, and his cousin, Lady Saria. The burgrave of Alzur was hardly a great man—in fact, in many ways he was an ill-tempered old fool—but he had been the center of Anrel's life for more than a decade after his parents' deaths. And Anrel had grown up with Lady Saria; they had as complicated a relationship as any brother and sister, a mixture of love and rivalry. They had drifted apart when Anrel went off to Lume to study. Saria's easy acceptance of Lord Valin's death, and her betrothal to Lord Allutar, the man who had killed him, had put a high barrier between the cousins; still, Anrel wished he could see her again, and speak to her. He thought sometimes of writing her a letter, but letting her know he was alive might provoke her fiancé into efforts to find Anrel, and that would not do.

Writing to Lord Dorias was out of the question, as well—while such a missive might be a comfort to Anrel's uncle, it might not. Depending on the burgrave's mood when the letter arrived he might burn it unread, or hand it directly to Lord Allutar, or treat it as some sort of betrayal.

And Anrel missed Lord Valin, the fosterling Lord Dorias had raised alongside Anrel and Lady Saria, the inept sorcerer who preferred to play the advocate of the common people, the political firebrand who had antagonized Lord Allutar and gotten himself killed. Valin had been Anrel's best friend in childhood, and his death had brought the lingering remains of that childhood crumbling into disaster. Anrel still felt he owed Lord Allutar some sort of retribution for that murder; the speech in Naith had not truly balanced the scale. Valin's memory deserved a better vengeance.

There had been other friends and other losses, but those four were the ones most deeply felt, the ones that drove Anrel to learn everything he could about crime and fraud, about life in the Pensioners' Quarter, and anything else that could focus his mind on the future rather than the past.

For one thing, any consideration of the past was shadowed by the knowledge that Lord Allutar still lived, untroubled by his crimes against humanity.

Anrel learned quickly that the people of the Pensioners' Quarter had their own social structure; cooperation was highly prized, since it made a hard life easier for all involved. Those who did not cooperate, either through temperament or inability, were outcasts among outcasts, and might well find themselves left to starve, abandoned to the watch, or even quietly murdered in a corner somewhere. Those who had and shared useful skills were treated with respect, and would find themselves offered at least stale bread or sour wine after even the most unsuccessful day. If one of these worthy members of the community ran afoul of some outsider, or even the watch, he could be sure of a dozen friends aiding his escape.

Anrel soon established himself as a worthwhile member of the community, and was accepted as someone who could be relied upon, and who could rely upon his new friends.

There were also a few individuals who were, to all intents and purposes, the rulers of the Pensioners' Quarter. Doz was one of these; he had a knack for devising schemes that brought in food or money. He avoided trouble when possible, but was utterly fearless and completely ruthless should a fight break out despite him.

Another of the ruling council was Queen Bim, an old woman who knew a great deal of medicine, who had trained several generations of whores in the more esoteric skills of their unhappy trade, and who had served as midwife to every new mother in the quarter. She was a formidable creature, despite being little more than half Anrel's size.

The Judge was a one-eyed old man who had, by the look of him, once been a hulking giant; now he could barely stand, his shrunken shanks almost unable to support his still-considerable weight, but he was treated with obvious respect. He was the arbiter for disputes among the quarter's inhabitants; as a woman called Filzi explained to Anrel, "He used to settle these matters by soundly thumping anyone who disagreed with him. After a time, people stopped arguing with him—and after a longer time, they realized his decisions were usually good ones, fair and reasonable. After that, it didn't matter whether he could thump them or not."

There was Mother Baba, chief among the witches of the quarter. There were Goriden, and Kedrig vo-Kedrig, and Half-Hand Tobbi, and the Goose, and a few more—it was sometimes hard for Anrel to judge who was truly part of the ruling elite, and who was merely popular at the moment, or clever, or boastful.

Anrel learned that Mieshel's explanation of why people did not speak of their pasts was not the real reason; rather, it was because that knowing someone's background all too often provided grounds for blackmail or extortion. Often even a little information would allow a clever listener to locate a family the speaker did not want found, or to determine which upholders of the law might be interested in that person's current whereabouts. That was why no one ever asked him for a family name; when it was necessary to distinguish Anrel from the other men named Dyssan who had taken refuge in the Pensioners' Quarter, he was called Handsome Dyssan.

"Handsome," in this case, was a relative term; Anrel did not consider himself particularly attractive, but in comparison with Scarred Dyssan and Toothless Dyssan he was willing to accept the description. Certainly his mentors in witchcraft considered him presentable.

He continued to share a room with Apolien, Mieshel, Shoun, and Po, and sometimes worked with the boys, serving as their lookout or decoy, or just providing another pair of hands to help carry whatever goods they managed to acquire. More often he worked with Doz in their various deceptions intended to separate the wealthy from some of their possessions.

He did not work with Apolien; the old man worked alone. Exactly what he did Anrel was not entirely sure, but it apparently involved using some of the ancient tunnels beneath the city to gain access to places he did not belong, and fetch out unguarded valuables.

When pursuing his life of crime Anrel assiduously avoided the court schools; he did not want to risk being recognized. He also preferred to prey on strangers, rather than his former compatriots.

He avoided any sort of violence. Doz more than once had occasion to knock a man down with his fists, and every so often Mieshel or Shoun might resort to tripping or otherwise harassing pursuers, but Anrel managed to avoid involvement in these disputes.

Had he ever found himself in a situation where his new allies resorted to more permanent or damaging methods, he was unsure what he would have done. Yes, he was now a criminal in fact as well as in name, a thief as well as a witch and a seditionist, but he had no desire to physically harm anyone—except perhaps Lord Allutar, should the opportunity present itself.

It was generally believed that Doz had killed more than one man, and Anrel had no reason to doubt it, but he had never actually seen it happen, and therefore found himself able to ignore the moral issues implicit in working with a murderer.

Although he had lived four years in Lume at the court schools, his new life overlapped his old so little that he might almost have been living at the far end of the empire; he did not walk the same streets he had as a student, nor dine in the same establishments, nor converse with the same people. In fact, from the time he first entered the quarter he did not see a single face he recognized from his former existence until early spring.

And when he did, it was not a welcome encounter.

He and Doz were walking through a well-to-do neighborhood north of the Galdin, across the Varestine Bridge from the emperor's palace.

Anrel was dressed in his best clothes, playing the role of a scion of some wealthy clan, while Doz, also somewhat better attired than when they had first met, had the role of a tradesman Anrel had hired. They rounded a corner, and Anrel found himself facing an unusually fine carriage that had stopped in the street ahead.

The coachwork of this vehicle was black and midnight blue, detailed in gold and white, and the brass was polished and gleaming; the windows were glass, yet showed none of the cracks or chips that a carriage window was likely to sustain in normal usage, from the flexing of the frame or the impact of pebbles.

The design of it was unusual. Walasian noblemen generally liked their coaches to be tall and imposing and covered in fancywork, but this vehicle was sleekly elegant, with no painted landscapes, no crowns nor coronets nor crests. A small black escutcheon bearing a golden figure of some sort was mounted above the door, but that was the only such decoration. A white-haired driver sat on the bench holding the reins; he paid no attention to Anrel or Doz, and Anrel did not think he had ever seen the man before.

The tall blond man who was standing in the open door of the carriage, one booted foot on the running board and the other on the ground while he spoke to a man wearing lace and velvet, was another matter.

"Lord Blackfield," Anrel said, stopping in his tracks.

"Keep moving," Doz murmured. "Don't draw attention."

Aware of the wisdom in Doz's words, Anrel turned. "I say," he said, in conversational tones, "I believe I've forgotten the drawings."

"My lord?" Doz said.

"I must have left them at the inn; what a bother! Come on, my good man, let us fetch them at once." With that he led off at a brisk pace, turning his back to the Quandish magician's carriage.

When they had gone a hundred yards or so and were, at least for the moment, well clear of other ears, Anrel slowed his pace and said, "I'm sorry, Doz, but that Quandishman is a friend of the man I was fleeing when I came to Lume. I don't want him to see my face."

"Would he remember you?" Doz asked, glancing back.

"I don't know," Anrel replied. "He might."

"And he'd tell his friend he had seen you?"

"He might." Anrel sighed. "I don't really know. I know he disagreed with his friend on certain matters, but still—well, I prefer not to risk it."

"I'd say that's a smart attitude." Doz looked around. "Shall we try another street, then?"

"Let us do just that," Anrel agreed.

That night, as he settled onto his bedding—by this time he had managed to acquire a fairly comfortable pile of rags; bringing an actual mattress into the quarter would have been considered unacceptable ostentation—Anrel went over the brief encounter in his mind.

He did not think Lord Blackfield had seen him; the Quandishman had been busy with his conversation. There was no real danger, nothing to be done about the chance meeting, but it did set Anrel to thinking about things, people, and places he had given very little thought to of late.

Since arriving in the Pensioners' Quarter he had been far more interested in building a new life than in considering the one he had left behind. When he had given the past any thought at all it had been grief over Valin's death, grief over Reva's death, anger and revulsion at Lord Allutar, wondering about Lord Dorias and Lady Saria, and most of all, longing for Tazia and regret for how their time together had ended. He had devoted very little attention to anyone else he had known in Alzur or Naith or Lume.

It might be interesting to learn what Lord Blackfield was doing in Lume. Why was he not back home in Quand? Was he trying to convince some sorcerer in the capital to abandon the use of black magic? Where was he staying? For how long?

Anrel mentioned his interest in these topics to his roommates the following day.

It was not long after that mention that he learned, mostly from Shoun, that Lord Blackfield had taken an apartment in Dezar House, in the block where Anrel had seen him, but spent most of his time either sitting in the gallery at the Aldian Baths listening to the Grand Council's debates, or talking to the delegates when the council was not in session. The exact nature of these conversations was not detailed, but the general impression was that the Quandishman was attempting to be a voice of moderation. Whether he spoke only for himself or represented some larger group—such as the Lantern Society, or perhaps even the Gathering, Quand's own ruling body—was not known.

Anrel had, of course, heard something of the doings of the Grand Council; the entire city took an interest, since at least in theory the council ruled the empire and could do anything it pleased.

And most of what it pleased the council to do, it seemed, was talk. Delegates regularly spoke for hours at a stretch, setting forth utopian plans for restructuring the empire, or ranting about the need to return to old values and ways that had fallen into disuse, or arguing about arcane technical details in proposed legislation.

Some of these discussions escalated into arguments, and there were rumors that several of these had been settled by violence or magic. There were stories of murdered or ensorceled delegates, though details were scarce.

It was in mid-spring, not long after Anrel's glimpse of Lord Blackfield, that the committee system was introduced. Henceforth, rather than force the entire council to debate everything, committees were to be created, each devoted to a single issue, which would meet independently, and then report back to the council as a whole when a consensus had been reached. A Committee on Imperial Finance had been established to deal with the emperor's debts, and a Committee for Agriculture and Distribution was considering measures to alleviate the growing famine. Not long after, the emperor was reported to be spending much of his day, every day, closeted with the Committee on Imperial Finance.

There was a flurry of interest and hope when the news of this change reached the city streets. Surely, this new system would allow the Grand Council to accomplish more, and bring much-needed change to the empire!

Hope quickly faded, though, as the committees seemed just as prone to endless debate as the council as a whole had been.

Anrel, though he did take a casual interest in the council's doings, was far more concerned with where his next meal was coming from.

His hidden funds had been spent, little by little, much of it in providing for the less-successful residents of the Pensioners' Quarter, and the schemes he and Doz employed seemed to be bringing in less than they had at first. Worse, the shortages that had been cropping up here and there for the past few years were finally beginning to seriously affect the capital; the winter stores were exhausted, but for most of the spring fresh supplies were not pouring in with their customary speed. The price of bread soared; a loaf that would have sold for a penny in any previous year now cost as much as eightpence, and any baker who offered even the worst bread for threepence a loaf was risking a riot when his supplies ran out.

Many of the inhabitants of the Pensioners' Quarter were going to their beds hungry every night. Anrel made a point of sharing his own food with those who seemed most in need, and as a result his own belly was often empty and grumbling when he fell asleep.

Relief was expected soon, though. The Raish Valley was said to be extraordinarily fertile this year, and it was anticipated that the prodigious wheat crop would be harvested, and much of it shipped down the Raish to Naith, and then up the Galdin to Lume, before the solstice.

Fifteen days before the solstice came word that the granaries of Tereth din-Sal were full to bursting, the barges loaded and on their way.

Anrel heard this news with mixed feelings. He knew what was responsible for this bounty.

This was the blood of Urunar Kazien, the young man Lord Allutar had sacrificed to the spirits of the earth. The landgrave had cut the youth's heart out on the last autumnal equinox, and used it to summon an elemental that promised to restore the fertility of the Raish Valley. That killing had been what provoked Lord Valin into defying the landgrave, and that defiance had led to Valin's death. Valin's death had, in turn, led to Anrel's playing orator and being driven into exile. Lord Allutar Hezir had been behind the ruination of Anrel's life, and it had all begun with the condemnation of Urunar Kazien.

It would have been pleasant to attribute all his misfortunes, and the deaths of Urunar and Valin and Reva, to simple malice on Lord Allutar's part, but Allutar's black sorcery, intended to benefit the public, had worked. The earth elemental had been bound successfully, and the land was reborn. The people of Kulimir and Naith and Alzur and Beynos and Tereth din-Sal and Lume itself would have bread because a thief had died on the last autumnal equinox, and the landgrave of Aulix had used that death to work a great spell.

Hundreds would be fed—which meant Lord Valin had been wrong, and Lord Allutar had been right.

That was not a pleasant realization for Anrel, but as he looked at the hungry faces of his roommates, he could not say he would have wished otherwise.

7

In Which the Pensioners' Quarter Is Disturbed

The first grain barge from Aulix tied up at Ildir Wharf four days before the solstice. Little Po was in the crowd that gathered to watch the unloading, though he was not there to watch, but to pick pockets.

The next barge reached the dock before the first was emptied, and the third was in sight when Po decided he could not safely carry any more and headed for home. Each time a barge was spotted, the crowd would roar their approval.

"You wouldn't think that grown men would cheer for bread," Shoun remarked, when Po described the scene later while counting his take.

"It's not bread yet," Po said.

"But it will be," Mieshel answered.

"Some of it as soon as tomorrow," Anrel agreed.

"*We* won't get any for days yet," Shoun said. "Not until those first loaves have time to go stale."

"I don't think any will *last* long enough to go stale," Mieshel replied.

"Probably not," Anrel agreed. "But at least we can buy it." He gestured at the pile of coins Po had harvested from the crowd at the docks, which added up to almost two guilders.

"Or get the leftovers from the sorcerers' tables," Po said.

Mieshel shook his head. "The servants will be eating it all themselves for a while."

"It'll be days yet," Shoun agreed.

"The bakeries will be full," Anrel said.

"And charging high prices," Mieshel replied.

"At first," Anrel acknowledged. "But the price will come down."

"Eventually," Mieshel said.

"Why didn't you steal more?" Shoun asked Po, with a gesture at the stacked money. "Did someone feel your hand?"

"Of course not!" Po snapped, insulted. "But there were watchmen on the arch over Beoun Street. I knew if I stayed much longer they would come down after me. One of them followed me across the roof to the arch between Lord Athriessen's bank and the Barley Hall, and I thought he might take me, but then he stopped. I think he was making sure I didn't double back."

"You think he knew you'd been picking pockets?" Shoun asked.

"Of course he did!" Mieshel said. "The watchmen aren't *stupid,* just lazy. If he thought Po had gotten enough to be worth taking for himself, he would have been down the Barley Hall stairs in a heartbeat."

Anrel listened to this with a mixture of admiration and dismay. It was sad that boys this young were so hardened, so certain of humanity's greed and corruption—but they were so *good* at what they did! And their assessment of the watchman's actions was almost certainly accurate.

"Four days," Shoun said. "That's how long before we'll get any of the new bread."

"We can wait four days," Po said.

But it wasn't four days; the following afternoon a stir went through the Pensioners' Quarter when the word came in that No-Nose Graun had struck a deal with one of the bakers in Dragonclaw Street, and needed help to haul bread back to the quarter.

Anrel watched in amazement as half a dozen men and women returned from Dragonclaw Street carrying sacks of bread. He watched as the people of the quarter swarmed around the dry and long-broken fountain where this party stopped to distribute their burden.

He did not join the happy throng, though, because he had noticed two men of the Emperor's Watch standing on the arch across Tranquillity Street, watching the proceedings with interest.

One of the watchmen turned and left hurriedly when the first loaves of bread were pulled from one of the sacks. Anrel frowned. That was not right; ordinarily watchmen never set foot in the Pensioners' Quarter alone, not even up in the safety of their arches and walkways. Was the departing guard going to fetch more men? Why was that so urgent that he left his companion alone?

Before Anrel could mention his observation to anyone, though, a wail went up. A child's voice rose in a wordless cry of dismay. The bread distribution abruptly ceased as everyone turned to see who was crying, and what had distressed the child.

Anrel did not recognize the girl, who was surely no older than four. She was standing on the cracked rim of the fountain, clutching a chunk of bread in one dirty little hand, the other hand grabbing at the faded and stained skirt of her dress. She had taken a bite of bread, but now the crumbs fell from her mouth, down the front of her dress.

"What's wrong?" a woman, presumably the girl's mother, asked.

"It's *bad*," the girl cried.

Dozens of other people suddenly turned to look uneasily at the bread they held. Several lifted their pieces to their noses and sniffed suspiciously.

"What do you mean, bad?" the woman asked, worried.

"It tastes bad!"

"Could it be poisoned?" someone asked.

"No-Nose, who did you get this from?"

"Would they *do* that?"

"They might try to poison us, but would they waste this much bread to do it?"

Then there were several voices speaking at once, and Anrel could no longer follow what was being said—but his attention was elsewhere, in any case.

There were now five watchmen on the Tranquillity Street arch, and one of them was an archer, his bow strung and ready.

Anrel turned his gaze.

There were watchmen on the walkway along the rooftops facing Reward Street. More were appearing on the arch across Peace Street.

A loud voice drew Anrel's attention back to the crowd by the fountain. Doz had arrived and taken charge, hands raised.

"Calm down!" he ordered.

When the shouting had died away, Doz turned to the little girl and asked, "What's bad about it? How does it taste?"

"Like dirt," she said.

Doz frowned. "How do you feel? Do you feel sick?"

"I'm fine!" she said, offended. "I'm not sick. The bread is bad." She held out the chunk she had bitten.

Doz reached down, and the girl handed him her bread, then vigorously wiped her hands on her dress.

Cautiously, Doz lifted the bread to his mouth and sniffed it.

The crowd watched in silence; many of them held their breath.

Doz's frown deepened. Cautiously, he tore a little shred loose and placed it in his mouth. He chewed.

Then he spat it out, and the crowd gasped.

"She's right," he said. "It tastes like dirt."

"You mean the baker *cheated* me?" No-Nose Graun bellowed.

"I don't understand," someone said. "Is it *all* like that?"

"Maybe it's just one bad loaf!"

Crumbs flew as a dozen people tore at loaves of bread.

The watchmen were gathering into groups, Anrel noticed, and those groups were, he realized, near the various stairs that led down into the quarter—stairs that were usually blocked off by heavy iron gates.

He heard hinges creak behind him. He whirled.

There were watchmen at the top of the stair by the Golden Street arcade, and they had just opened the gate there.

"Doz," Anrel called.

"It's *all* bad!"

"I don't understand!"

"How can this be?"

"What's wrong with it?"

"*Doz!*"

Doz turned, and saw Anrel pointing at the watchmen descending the stairs.

So did several others; the noisy chaos of the bread-tasting was swiftly replaced by wary silence. People drew closer together—children ran to their mothers, women stepped behind their men, men stood shoulder to shoulder and drew weapons from their belts, from their pockets, or from beneath their garments. Knives gleamed, and clubs were raised. The older children stooped for rocks, cobbles, or chunks of brick.

At the sight of this, the watchmen abandoned stealth; orders were shouted, and they formed up into lines as they reached the streets at the foot of each stair, swords drawn but held low, points toward the ground.

"All right, you people," shouted one of the watchmen, "we don't want any trouble! We just want the thief who stole that bread."

For a moment there was stunned silence; then No-Nose Graun bellowed in outrage, "I didn't steal it! I *worked* for it!"

"Oh, of course you did," the watchman called back. "How could I *possibly* think that someone like you might have resorted to dishonest means to feed his friends?"

"I worked for it, you motherless homunculus! I earned this! Go ask the baker—Master Heileun, in Dragonclaw Street, he'll tell you! I cleaned out his cellars."

"In *Dragonclaw* Street? He paid you what, a hundred loaves of bread for a little scrubbing? That's at least ten guilders at what they charge there!"

"Are you calling me a liar?"

"A liar *and* a thief, indeed I am."

No-Nose let out a wordless roar of rage, but Doz grabbed him before he could charge the watchman.

"Officer," the Judge called from the door of his house, "might I suggest you taste the goods before making an estimate of their value?"

"Are you trying to bribe me, old man?"

"Not at all. I'm just trying to avoid a misunderstanding. Here, Shallien, take the watchman a piece of bread, would you?" He beckoned to a girl of about eleven who was clutching half a loaf of the tainted bread.

She, in turn, looked to her mother for confirmation. The mother turned to Queen Bim, who nodded.

A hundred eyes watched as Shallien walked slowly and hesitantly up the street to where the watchman stood. Then, with a final glance over her shoulder to see her mother motioning her forward, she held out the bread.

Puzzled, the watchman took it. Without taking his eyes off the crowd, he raised it to his mouth and took a healthy bite.

His expression changed, and he spat the bread out.

"If you're looking for a thief, Sir Watchman, go talk to Master Heileun," No-Nose called. "He cheated me! I worked all last night and this morning scrubbing and sweeping, and *this* is how he paid me!"

"What's wrong with it?" the watchman demanded, wiping his mouth with the back of his hand and staring at the bread he held. "It tastes like dung!"

"I don't know," No-Nose said. "The baker said it wasn't his best, but *this* . . ."

An angry murmur ran through the crowd.

"Go arrest the baker, Watchman!" a woman called.

"Shut up, you," another watchman replied.

"They probably did something to it themselves so the baker would let them have it," a third watchman suggested loudly.

"You think *we* want it when it tastes like that?"

"Why not? You eat garbage all the time!"

That was too much for someone; Anrel didn't see who, but a stone was flung at the watchman who had asked that final question, and flung hard and accurately. It caught him just below his right eye, and he went down, falling backward onto the street with a clatter of armor.

An officer shouted a command, and two dozen swords flashed up into guard position.

Stones and bricks began flying, and the scene dissolved into shouting, screaming chaos as watchmen and outcasts ran at one another.

For the third time in less than a year, Anrel found himself in the midst of a riot, but this time there was one very significant difference.

This time, he did not flee. Instead he jumped the nearest watchman and joined in the fight.

8

In Which Changes Are Made to the Capital's Architecture

The battle did not last long; the men of the Emperor's Watch were hopelessly outnumbered. The bowmen on the arches over the streets did not shoot into the melee for fear of hitting their own comrades, and because the foe was so numerous that they saw no point; the watchmen were fighting the entire population of the Pensioners' Quarter, men, women, and children alike. Most of the invaders went down almost immediately under a hail of brickbats; some managed to fend off these missiles and gather into little knots of three or four men apiece, but then could do little but try to retreat toward one of the open stairs.

Within five minutes of that first thrown rock, a score of thieves and outcasts, Anrel among them, held watchmen's swords. The only watchmen still on their feet were backing up stairways. Within ten minutes the streets were clear, the iron gates on the stairs slammed shut and locked. Anrel jabbed uselessly through the bottom gate on Golden Street one last time, then lowered his blade and turned to look over the situation.

At least a dozen watchmen were still in the streets, but down and disarmed; most had children sitting on them, holding them down, while a few had women standing over them with improvised clubs of one sort or another. None were putting up any resistance. Some of them appeared to be unconscious or dead.

Doz had chased one group of watchmen up the Tranquillity Street stair, preventing them from closing the gate at the bottom; the top gate, though, was secured. Now Doz and his men were emerging back out onto the street, talking and laughing excitedly.

"Doz!" Anrel shouted.

Doz turned. "Dyssan?"

"It's not over, Doz. They'll be back with reinforcements. Maybe sorcerers." He pointed up at the walkways; a few strategically placed archers were still in sight, but the other watchmen were either hurrying away or already gone.

"He's right," someone called.

"Let them come!" a woman shouted.

"No," Doz barked back, as he walked toward Anrel. "No, Dyssan is right."

"But there are hundreds of us!"

"There are hundreds of *them*, and they have swords and bows," Doz replied. He turned to look at the wounded guardsmen on the street.

"We should slit their throats. That would be a dozen fewer of them."

Doz shook his head. "No. Then they'd kill all of us." He looked around as he walked, then beckoned to a witch. "Keila, take a look at them, see what you can do for them."

The witch nodded, and stepped forward.

"They'll come back, whether we kill these men or not," Anrel said, as he stepped forward to meet Doz.

"Are you saying we *should* kill them?" Doz demanded, stopping his march a few feet away.

"Oh, by no means! You're absolutely right, we should do what we can for them and send them on their way; anything else would be tantamount to cutting our own throats as well as theirs. But we should also ready ourselves for another visit."

Doz looked around at the other inhabitants of the Pensioners' Quarter. "And how would you suggest we do that?"

"I don't know," Anrel admitted. He pointed up. "But they'll be coming along those walkways before nightfall, I'd wager."

Doz looked up thoughtfully at the arch across Golden Street. "They'll be exposed up there. We'll see them coming."

Anrel frowned. "Do you think they might come in on the streets, then?"

Doz shook his head. "They'd be worried about ambushes—and with good reason. They always use the walkways. I just meant they couldn't take us by surprise."

"Perhaps the women and children should seek shelter elsewhere, until this is over?"

"Where?" Queen Bim demanded. Anrel had not noticed her approach, but she was there at Doz's shoulder.

"I don't know," Anrel said.

"If we had anywhere else to go, why would we be here in the first place?" another woman demanded.

"I don't know," Anrel repeated.

"We could hide in the tunnels," Mieshel suggested. "Watchmen won't go down there."

"Neither will I," declared a woman Anrel didn't recognize. "There are *things* down there."

"The ruins on Wizards Hill?" Shoun suggested.

"That's worse than the tunnels."

"These are our *homes,* and we didn't do anything wrong!" Mother Baba said. "Why should we hide?"

"Right or wrong doesn't come into it," Doz said. "We fought the Emperor's Watch, and that means they'll come teach us a lesson." He was still gazing thoughtfully at the arch. "But you know," he added after a brief pause, "we don't need to make it easy for them." He turned and looked at the crowd. "All right, I want the witches and anyone else who knows any healing to tend to those watchmen, and then get them to the old hospital, and I want anyone who can swing a hammer to find tools." He pointed at the arch. "They've been able to keep an eye on us too easily for too long. Let's make it a little more difficult."

"What?"

"I don't understand."

A hundred voices called out questions, but Doz raised his hands for silence.

"We are going to tear down those damned arches," he said. "If the watch wants to come talk to us, they can come on the streets, like anyone else."

For a second there was silence; then a cheer broke out, like the roar of a mighty beast.

"Tear them down! Tear them down!"

"Put the watch on the streets!"

"Tear them down!"

The crowd scattered, searching for anything that could be used to smash or pry. Anrel hesitated for a only a moment, then looked at the sword in his hand. It was a shame to ruin the blade, but it wasn't a very good one to begin with; he turned and began chipping at the mortar of the staircase.

"Not here," Doz said, catching his arm. "We start with the ones that connect the quarter to the outside; once those are down, we can hammer at these at our leisure."

"Of course," Anrel said, feeling slightly foolish. "Of course."

Ten minutes later he and a dozen other men were attacking the base of the arch above the Duty Street Gate, a few feet inside the barricade that closed off that portion of the Pensioners' Quarter from the adjoining neighborhood of Catseye. Decades of neglect had made their task relatively easy; the ancient mortar crumbled away after only a few blows, giving room to set axes and crowbars solidly in place. Half a dozen men throwing their weight onto an iron bar was then enough to shift even the larger stones.

It was hard, heavy labor, nonetheless, and before long every man present was sweating and stripped down to just breeches and boots—at least, those who *had* boots. Some wrapped their blouses and shirts around the handles of their tools, to protect their hands, while others simply flung the unwanted garments aside.

Women and children did not try to join in the actual demolition, but they did fetch water for the men, and cart away stones to make room for the work to continue.

An hour or so after the Emperor's Watch had withdrawn Anrel heard the grinding of stone on stone when no one was pushing, and looked up to see the top of the arch starting to move.

"Get back!" he shouted. "Get away!"

He took his own advice, scrambling back up Duty Street with his ru-ined sword in hand. Then he turned to watch as the arch, which he knew had stood for at least a hundred years, broke apart and collapsed.

Ancient stone shattered and tumbled with a crash and a roar, and as the sound of that destruction began to subside a cheer went up.

"There are five more," a woman's voice called, but just then came a roar and a cheer from blocks away.

"Four," a man said, and most of the crowd laughed.

Anrel did not laugh; he looked at the rubble and regretted his part in bringing down this piece of history. This would make it more difficult for the emperor's men to enter the Pensioners' Quarter, but it might also make them more determined to do so. It wasn't as bad as killing the wounded watchmen would have been, but it would certainly not help mollify anyone.

"Come on!" someone shouted. "The arch by Twilight Square is still standing!"

With a cheer, most of the crowd ran in that direction, tools waving, but Anrel did not join them; instead he watched them go, then turned and marched toward the old hospital, wiping away sweat as he walked. He intended to speak with the captured watchmen to gauge their mood.

He pulled his blouse back on, and the rest of his clothes, along the way; he wanted to look like a civilized man when he questioned the captives.

He found them laid out in the courtyard of the hospital ruins. Most of them were sitting up now, their heads bandaged; a few had their arms in slings or other signs of injury. A faint scent of corruption told Anrel that some of the wounds were already infected; that was not good, but per-haps the witches might attend to it.

Several Pensioner women were gathered in the courtyard, tending to the wounded. Anrel stepped up behind one.

"Excuse me," Anrel said. "Might I have a word?"

Mother Baba looked up from the watchman she was tending. "With me?" she asked.

"No, with him."

She looked up at Anrel, looked back at the watchman, then shrugged. "If you want," she said. "This one's skull is cracked, but if he's careful he'll be fine." She stepped away to check on the next man.

Anrel knelt beside the watchman, who looked at him warily.

"Good day," Anrel said. "My name is Dyssan. Can you speak?"

"I can talk," the watchman replied. He gave no name.

"Good, good! I trust you have been well cared for?"

"I suppose."

"I'm afraid I have a favor to ask."

The man did not reply; he just stared at Anrel through slightly clouded eyes.

"Yes, well," Anrel said. "I was hoping you might give me some idea what you intend to tell your superiors when you see them."

"I wasn't planning to tell them anything," the man said.

"But won't they ask you about how you were treated? How you came to be injured?"

"They can ask, but I can't tell them anything. I don't remember what happened. I was up on the walks, and the sergeant started us toward the stair, and the next thing I know I was here, with a girl feeling the side of my head." He put a hand to the area in question. "Right here."

"Ah," Anrel said.

"That happens when you get hit hard on the head. I've seen it before. Helps if you're drunk at the time, but I wasn't, and I still can't remember it."

"I see." Anrel looked around. "Do you think anyone here *does* remember the fighting?"

"I have no idea."

"I see. Well, thank you, and I hope your recovery will be swift." He patted the man on the shoulder, then turned to the next man in the row of wounded.

That one was only semiconscious, and apparently delirious. Anrel grimaced, and proceeded to the next.

"I heard what you asked him," this third man said. "I remember just fine; I didn't get a brick to the head the way he did, I got my leg broken."

He gestured toward his right leg, which was bandaged and splinted from thigh to ankle.

"I'm sorry for your injury, sir," Anrel said.

"Not as sorry as I am."

Anrel sighed. "Probably not," he admitted.

"So what did you want?"

"I was hoping to avoid further conflict," Anrel said. "We are all loyal Walasians, faithful subjects of the empire; we should not be fighting."

"Those people should have thought of that before you started throwing rocks."

"Sir, innocent citizens were threatened and abused, falsely accused of theft and other crimes. It was very unfortunate that someone lost his temper and began throwing missiles, I fully admit that, but you can't deny there was provocation."

"What did they expect, hauling those sacks of bread through the streets? Did you really think anyone would believe that people in the Pensioners' Quarter came by them honestly? They're all thieves and beggars and whores—you know it and we know it. We don't bother them in the ordinary way of things, but when they parade all that food past hungry people . . . !"

"But we *did* come by them honestly!"

" 'We'? Who *are* you?"

Anrel realized that the man had taken him for an outsider, perhaps an investigator sent by some local official. He grimaced. "I am a resident of the Pensioners' Quarter, sir, and Master Graun earned that bread honestly."

The watchman looked at Anrel's clothes, which were reasonably clean and new and not at all typical of the Pensioners' Quarter, and shrugged. "So you say."

"Ask the baker!"

"And what do you think he'll say, if he's the one who spoiled it all? You think he'll admit he tried to palm off bad bread on you?"

That had not occurred to Anrel. He did not have a ready reply.

"Besides," the watchman continued, "what does it matter now? What's done is done, and nothing you or I might do is going to change that."

"I was not hoping to change the past, I assure you, but I do hope to prevent further conflict."

The watchman shook his head. "Too late for that," he said. "I suppose you people don't know it, but for years now the emperor has been looking for an excuse to rid the city of you once and for all. He doesn't want your sort of people in his capital. Up until now the watch always said it wasn't worth it, that trying to clean out the quarter would be too expensive and too dangerous, and that some of you weren't criminals, just poor. Now, though—you attacked us. You've sealed your own doom."

Anrel wanted to argue with that, to suggest alternatives, but he could not. Tearing down the arches was a fine gesture, but it wasn't going to stop the emperor's men from retaliating. They would find some way into the quarter whether the arches were there or not.

"I had hoped I might convince you and your compatriots to speak on our behalf," Anrel said. "We could have killed you all, if we really considered you our enemies, but instead we have done our best to care for you. Cannot that earn us some forgiveness?"

The watchman snorted. "We could speak until we can't breathe. It wouldn't help. They won't listen to us any more than they would listen to you. The Emperor's Watch was chased out of a part of the emperor's own city; that can't be allowed to stand. It doesn't matter how it happened, or why, or who was right, or who was wrong. All that matters is that the emperor's authority must be upheld."

Anrel bit his lip, nodding. "You're right," he said. "That's how the sorcerers think."

"It's how the *emperor* thinks."

"I've never met the emperor, but I've known sorcerers," Anrel said. He frowned. "Tell me, if you would—how long do you think we have before they come?"

"Not long, I'd guess. No longer than it takes for them to prepare."

"Do you think they'll come for you and the other wounded first?"

The watchman's expression changed. He had already been pale with the pain of his broken leg, but now what little color had remained drained from his face. He had been almost sneering as he spoke, but now his expression became one of wide-eyed fear.

"No," he said very quietly. "They won't. They probably take it for granted that we're all dead, that you slit our throats as we lay in the street." He looked around wildly. "We could be killed before they know we're here."

"If they have already reported your deaths, well—they might not want those reports proven wrong," Anrel suggested.

"You're right," the watchman said, grabbing at Anrel's sleeve. "You're right!"

"I'll send a note," Anrel said, pulling his arm away. "I'll tell them where you are."

The watchman looked up at him, and didn't say anything more, but Anrel could guess what he was thinking.

Would it *matter* if the Emperor's Watch knew these men were still alive? They were all too badly injured to return to active duty any time soon; perhaps it would be less of an embarrassment, more convenient, if they all simply vanished.

The watch might not in fact be that ruthless, that heartless, that careless of the lives of its own men—but what did it say about them, that this watchman was not certain of that?

And what did it say about the emperor's government, that the watch *might* be so ruthless?

"Rest," Anrel told the injured watchman. "You'll be fine. You'll see."

Then he turned and walked away, wishing he believed the lie he had just told.

9

In Which the Emperor's Watch Asserts Itself

The last of the arches connecting the walkways of the Pensioners' Quarter with the rest of the city came down while the sun was hiding behind the rooftops to the west, painting the sky above with crimson and gold. There was, as yet, no sign of the retaliation that Anrel saw as inevitable, but he had no doubt it was coming.

The watching archers had fled before the last connection fell, leaving the arches over Tranquillity and Reward and Peace deserted. A few members of the Emperor's Watch were spotted on the walkways outside the Pensioners' Quarter, observing the demolition, but they merely watched, and made no attempt to prevent the destruction of the arches. This inaction did not ease Anrel's worries.

He had written a note explaining that the wounded watchmen were in the hospital ruins, and had dispatched young Po to the watch house beside Executioner's Court to deliver it. He had no idea what effect, if any, it might have; if it served to ameliorate the coming attack in the slightest, then it was worth doing.

He had told Po not to come back that night. There was no reason for him to be involved in whatever might be coming. He made sure that others heard him give these instructions; perhaps those others would also see fit to leave the quarter and avoid disaster.

That done, he had returned home long enough to change his clothing, choosing to wear some of his best in hopes of impressing his compatriots, and then went to confer with Doz and Queen Bim and the rest of the quarter's leaders.

They accepted his warnings of a coming attack with equanimity.

"Let them come," Bim said. "We can handle it."

"You can't fight them forever," Anrel said. "They'll keep coming until you're defeated. They *need* to, to assert the emperor's authority."

"They can't defeat us," Bim insisted. "We can just hide until they give up and go home."

"Hide *where?*"

"Everywhere," Bim said with a sweeping gesture that took in the entire Pensioners' Quarter. "If they find women and children cowering in their homes, what will they do to us? Most of us are innocent bystanders, so far as they know."

Anrel stared at her.

Did she honestly think the Emperor's Watch cared about whether anyone in the quarter was guilty or innocent of any specific crimes, real or imagined? From the watch's point of view, the entire quarter had risen against them, and therefore against the emperor's own authority. Any such uprising had to be decisively put down, as quickly as possible, and anyone in the quarter was going to be treated as a rebel.

He was not sure whether women and children cowering here would be beaten, or killed, or hauled off in chains, but Anrel did not think they would be allowed to go unmolested.

He tried to explain this, but the others did not accept it.

"We have lived with the watch all our lives," the Judge said. "They know us and tolerate us, and in exchange we keep ourselves within certain limits. Today we exceeded those limits, so they will punish us, but then everything will be as it always has been."

"I don't think so," Anrel said. He started to repeat what the wounded watchman had told him, but the Judge cut him off with a gesture.

"You're young," Bim said with a shrug. "You'll learn, if you live long enough."

"We have the streets barricaded, the gates closed, and men at every barricade and gate," Doz said. "When they come we'll turn them back, at least at first, and we'll ask to parley. We'll offer apologies, we'll return the bread—we don't want to eat that foul stuff, after all, not unless we're starving. Maybe we'll let them arrest a few of our worst. And then it'll be over."

"We brought down the arches!"

"We're tired of their spying," Bim said.

"But . . ." Anrel groped unsuccessfully for words.

He had initially supported the idea of tearing down the arches, and had enthusiastically helped with the first one, at Duty Street, but now he realized it had been a mistake. Attacking the watch's own structures had been too blatant an act of resistance, and it would bring the empire's wrath down on them all.

He was certainly familiar with this sort of experience. He had made a habit of doing things on the spur of the moment, only to regret them later—most spectacularly, his speech from the First Emperor's statue in Naith. There were times when defiance of the empire and its sorcerers seemed a moral necessity, but these always came at a high cost, and when righteous outrage had subsided and a sense of practicality had returned, he always regretted having incurred that cost—but he knew he would do the same thing again, should the situation somehow repeat itself.

Still, there was no need to pay that bill with interest. The damage was inevitable, but it could be minimized. He had not stayed around Naith or Beynos to be hanged, and he did not want to stay in the Pensioners' Quarter, either—but he could not simply abandon these people who had made him welcome for so long.

"Can't you at least suggest that as many of us as possible should seek shelter elsewhere until the attack is over?" he asked, pleading. "The watch may not be in any mood for caution. Innocents may be hurt."

"There are no innocents here," Queen Bim said.

"That's what the watch believes, certainly," the Judge said.

Doz started to say something, to protest, but before he could finish a word a distant scream distracted them all.

"What was that?" someone asked.

"I don't know."

"The watch! It must be the watch!"

"They're attacking! To the barricades!"

With that, the debate was at an end, and Anrel found himself running toward the sounds of fighting—or rather, toward the sounds of whatever was happening.

It did not actually sound like fighting. There was no grunting, no shouting, no clash of steel; instead there were screams, many of them, from men as well as women and children, and the roar of shattering stone and tumbling brick, the sharp sound of breaking glass, the crackle of flame.

The sky overhead was still blue and pink and gold, but the streets were in shadow—until Anrel turned the corner onto Duty Street. Duty Street was awash in flame, the lurid orange glow a harsh contrast to the peaceful colors of the sunset. The smell of smoke, of burning wood and burning flesh, swept over him.

At first Anrel could not make out what was happening; the smoke and flame hid much of the scene, and there were people running in both directions, toward the fighting or away from it, getting in his way and blocking his view. Smoke stung his eyes, and the screams and shouts made any attempt at asking questions pointless. At last, though, he pushed through a line of fleeing men and got a good look.

The Duty Street barricade had been set ablaze and smashed apart, the fiery wreckage scattered in every direction, but it was not the men of the Emperor's Watch who had destroyed it, it was not the men of the Emperor's Watch who were now advancing slowly up Duty Street. Instead there were three looming figures, each at least fifteen feet tall, making their way into the Pensioners' Quarter over a layer of flaming debris.

They were not human. They each had two arms, two legs, and a head, but that was the extent of the resemblance. These were creatures made of fire and darkness, darkness so complete that where there were no flames they looked not so much like solid, living beings as like holes in the universe, places where the substance had been ripped from reality itself, revealing utter emptiness beneath. They had no faces at all.

"Demons," Anrel said.

He had never seen a demon before, but he had no doubt about what he saw now. He had read descriptions when he was a student—until last year's rumors about the empress and her hirelings no one had ever reported a demon in Walasia, but there were stories from the Cousins, from some of the distant lands the Ermetians traded with, and from some of the outermost reaches of the Quandish archipelagoes. There were not so much stories as mere rumors of demons, and even worse things, in the mysterious eastern lands beyond the Cousins, such as the legendary Noroda, but those could not be trusted even as much as the tales told by Quandish and Ermetian sailors.

There could be no doubt demons did exist, but not in the civilized nations. It was common knowledge that certain of the mad magicians of the Cousins had learned to summon, or perhaps create, these beings of incarnate chaos, of walking destruction, and that these magicians had on occasion sent demons to lay waste their foes in the constant internecine wars those unhappy little countries east of the empire fought among themselves. Even when the empire had involved itself in the Cousins, though, no one had ever unleashed demons on the Walasians. The Quandish and the Ermetians considered such a thing to be black magic that would carry far too much risk by its very nature, and the lords and magicians of the Cousins rightly feared the empire's response should they ever employ such horrors.

Yet here were three of these abominations in the streets of Lume, spreading fire and devastation.

This could not be anything the Emperor's Watch had done; they had no magicians of their own, and the Lords Magistrate, who provided them with sorcery when required, could not have summoned demons. *No* Walasian sorcerer could summon demons—it was forbidden by the ancient covenants that Anrel had studied before failing the trials that would have made him a sorcerer. Sorcerers could conjure lesser monsters, yes—his own parents had presumably been attempting something like that when their spell went wrong and killed them both—but not demons. That was a form of black magic Walasian sorcerers did not allow themselves.

But if Walasia's own sorcerers were not responsible, then how had these three come here?

Was the empire under attack? Had the emperor's army invaded some little land in the Cousins that chose this method to retaliate? The demons could not have come here all the way from the Cousins, word would have arrived well before they got this far and there would have been panic. Furthermore, the city walls were heavily warded; demons could not have broken through them without causing tremendous uproar, and there had been no such disturbance.

No, they must have been summoned here in Lume—but by enemy spies, perhaps? Not by the court's agents?

But why would enemies from the Cousins attack the Pensioners' Quarter, and not the emperor's palace?

They would not. The idea was absurd. The only people with any interest in attacking the Pensioners' Quarter were the emperor's own government.

The Emperor's Watch had no magic that could summon demons—but the emperor's court did. Everyone knew that the Empress Annineia had brought necromancers from the Cousins to serve as her personal bodyguards. Anrel had not wanted to believe the rumors that they had summoned demons, but surely, they had summoned these. That had to be the explanation. Nothing else was possible.

But could the emperor have permitted this atrocity in his own city? Wasn't *he* bound by the covenants?

No, Anrel realized, he wasn't. Walasian *sorcerers* were bound by the covenants; their true names were recorded on the Great List, and that list was the mechanism whereby any breach was punished.

But the emperor was no sorcerer. The Cousin necromancers weren't Walasian; neither were they bound by Quandish or Ermetian law. They were free to use whatever magic they chose.

And it appeared they had chosen demonology. That thought made Anrel feel cold and sick, but he could see no other possible explanation.

Right now, though, the demons' origins were irrelevant. The important thing was to *stop* them. Physical weapons could not harm demons, Anrel knew that; physical barriers would be ineffective as well, though they might slow the creatures. The right wards could turn demons away, at least temporarily, but Anrel's feeble knowledge of witchcraft and sorcery did not include any means of setting wards of sufficient power. He could ward off a blow, or a pickpocket, but a demon? No.

Texts he had read in the court schools implied that demons were controlled with bindings, and bindings could be broken, but would breaking the spell send the demons back to whatever realm they had come from, or merely release them from all constraint?

Besides, Anrel did not know how to break such a binding. He had learned a little theory from his schooling, but all his practical knowledge of magic came from witches. He knew how to soothe a fever, heal a wound, find the best spot to dig a well, but unbind a demon? That was far outside his very limited expertise.

Someone shoved Anrel, and he staggered to one side and looked around.

He was the only one in the street who was not moving, and the tide that had carried him this far had turned; where before he was caught between terrified people fleeing the demons' advance and eager defenders rushing to confront the monsters, now the entire current was away from those flaming abominations. The street ahead of Anrel, between himself and the demons, was rapidly emptying of people—or at least, of people still upright.

One of the demons had turned aside, and as Anrel watched it reached out and ripped a house from its foundations, sending stone and flaming wood spraying in all directions. The wood had not been burning a moment before, but anything flammable that even came *near* the demons burst into flame.

That included, horrifically, human flesh. That was the source of much of the screaming that had first alerted Anrel to the presence of these fiends—when they had smashed through the barricade they had set ablaze everyone who had been manning the defenses. Burning corpses littered the street. Worse, a few of the flaming bodies were still moving, thrashing about, some even still screaming as they burned.

This had to be stopped. This had to be stopped *now*—but how? The demons were invulnerable to everything Anrel knew.

But the people who had sent them here, the magicians from the

Cousins—*they* were human enough. If Anrel could find them and make them stop . . .

He had to get out of the Pensioners' Quarter, and find the demons' masters. He could do nothing here.

He turned and joined the fleeing throng, but at the first intersection, where most of the crowd continued to flee deeper into the quarter, he turned left; at the corner of Honor Street he turned left again.

Honor Street was deserted; this part of the quarter was more ruined than most, and largely uninhabited. Honor Street had once led out onto a plaza on the Grand Boulevard, but had been walled off long ago, making it a dead end; there was no way out of the quarter there, and Anrel knew it. Instead he turned left a third time, and made his way through a nameless, rubble-strewn alley, back toward Duty Street.

The alley ended in a small courtyard, but Anrel had expected that. He leapt up and pulled himself onto the shoulder-high wall at one side, then peered over the low roof ahead.

The demons were still advancing farther into the quarter, leaving nothing but fire and death in their wake—and as Anrel had guessed, the house that had stood between this courtyard and Duty Street was now gone, reduced to burning wreckage and broken stone.

He clambered up over the remains of the rear wall, then dropped down into the ruins. He crouched there for a moment, struggling to ignore the heat and smoke while he watched to see whether the demons had noticed him.

They gave no sign of it.

Cautiously at first, then moving more quickly as the heat and smoke grew more intense and he gained more confidence, he made his way through the debris until he emerged onto Duty Street, perhaps forty feet behind the demons.

Then he turned right and ran, away from the demons and out of the Pensioners' Quarter.

10

In Which Anrel Murau Renews His Acquaintance
with Lord Blackfield

Anrel had not given much thought to what he might find once he left the Pensioners' Quarter; he had supposed that the rest of the city would be going about its business in much the usual fashion, blithely unconcerned by the devastation being visited upon their unfortunate neighbors.

That was not the case.

Beyond the blasted remnants of the Duty Street Gate was Harbinger Court, which Anrel knew as a quiet little plaza lined with small shops. Ordinarily at this time of day a few late customers would be buying bread and wine and flowers before hurrying home for supper, a lamplighter would be pursuing his trade, and the shopkeepers who had no more trade to attend to would be standing in their doorways, preparing to close their shutters for the evening.

Tonight it was deserted; most of the shops were tightly shuttered, their proprietors nowhere to be seen. The shutters for their homes upstairs, which would ordinarily have remained open for hours, were mostly closed as well. No customers lingered, and the streetlamps were unlit.

One shop was not shuttered, though; instead it had been largely destroyed, its windows smashed, its sign torn down, shelving broken and flung across the pavement. The storefront was dark and empty, a hole in the city.

Anrel stopped and stared. That, he realized, had been Ozrai Lovan-niel's bakery. Why had that, and only that, been destroyed? Had the demons done it? There was no sign of fire, so presumably it had not been the demons—but then who, and why?

"You!" someone called, and Anrel looked up.

Several men were standing on the walkway that had once connected to the arch above the Duty Street Gate, not far from the broken end; two of them wore the uniform of the Emperor's Watch, while others were in civilian attire.

Two or three of them were wearing ceremonial robes of some sort. Could these be the magicians responsible for the attacking demons?

If so, if he could get up there, get at them . . .

But one of the watchmen was nocking an arrow, and the other was shouting, "Who are you, and what are you doing here?"

He was not going to stop any demons with an arrow through his chest; Anrel was suddenly glad he was wearing good clothes, and hoped they hadn't been dirtied too much by the smoke and ash. He called back, "My name is Dyssan Adirane; what's happening? Why are the shops closed?"

The watchmen who had spoken glanced at one of the civilians—not one of the men in robes—who muttered something. He and the watch-man spoke for a moment, during which the archer stood distressingly motionless, arrow drawn back to his ear and pointed directly at Anrel.

Then the watchman turned and called, "There's an emergency! Go home and stay out of the streets!"

Anrel knew that the natural, in-character thing to do would be to ask what kind of emergency, but he decided on caution over verisimilitude.

"Yes, sir!" he shouted back. Then he turned and trotted up a street whose name he did not recall, but which he knew would lead him to the Grand Boulevard.

Those people on the walkway had something to do with the demons, he was sure of it, but he could hardly tackle them single-handed. He turned and looked back at the Pensioners' Quarter.

Fire and smoke were billowing up into the darkening sky, hiding the three demons from sight. The Pensioners' Quarter was dying; life there had always been precarious, and now it was crumbling into ruin. Anrel hoped that most of the inhabitants had fled, and had found some way to escape. He knew several people—probably dozens, perhaps hundreds—were already dead and beyond any help, but hundreds more were still back there. He had to help them if he could.

Perhaps some of them had taken Mieshel's suggestion and taken refuge in the ancient tunnels beneath the city, remnants of the days when this city had been the capital of the Old Empire, rather than the Walasian. Would the demons find those? Would they do anything about it if they did? Anrel was unsure just how much intelligence or free will demons might have, or how much actual control the magicians who summoned them might have. He knew the homunculi that the more talented Walasian sorcerers created as servants were mere automata, following orders and incapable of true independent thought; were demons the same? If confronted with the unexpected, could they respond without guidance? Did they have some way of communicating with their masters, and of receiving fresh orders to meet changed circumstances?

Were those people on the walkway the demons' masters, or merely underlings sent to observe?

Anrel had too many questions, and not enough answers. He turned again and hurried out to the Grand Avenue, then turned right, heading for Twilight Square—he thought some of his comrades might have gotten out of the quarter there. Perhaps he could assemble a team that could return and get up to that walkway. He did not know whether that would really do any good, but he had to do *something.*

The light was fading from the sky, hastened by the pall of smoke spreading out from the Pensioners' Quarter, and the lamplighters had not been attending to their work, but he could still see well enough—the Grand Boulevard was almost deserted, and the few people he did see on the street were hurrying along, heads down, obviously eager to get out of sight. The arches that crossed the boulevard every quarter mile or so, on the other hand, were not empty; instead a man of the Emperor's Watch stood atop each and every one, his attention on the street below. Anrel had never seen that before.

Something strange was going on—not just in the Pensioners' Quarter, but all through Lume. Where was everyone? What was going on? Was this connected to the strife in the quarter, and the demon attack?

He found Twilight Square as deserted as Harbinger Court or the Grand Boulevard, and watchmen manned every arch there, as well. He had not thought the Emperor's Watch had enough men to put one atop every arch in the city, but that seemed to be what was happening, and it was clear that they were not allowing anyone to exit the quarter there.

He looked around the darkening streets, at the watchmen on the arches who seemed to be staring at him, at the thick column of orange-lit smoke billowing up from the Pensioners' Quarter, and tried to think what he should do. The world around him had gone mad. Just hours ago all had seemed to be going well—he had a home, he had friends, any pursuit by his old foes had long since vanished, and No-Nose Graun was bringing bread to feed the people of the quarter. Now his home was destroyed, his friends were scattered or dead, demons were stalking the city, and the bread had turned out to be . . . to be wrong, somehow. Anrel still did not understand just what had been done to that food, how it had been polluted.

The entire *city* seemed wrong. No streetlamps lit, watchmen every-where, everyone cowering in their homes—what had *happened*?

He needed to talk to someone, someone who lived somewhere other than the Pensioners' Quarter, someone who could tell him what was going on—but who?

He could go back to the Court of the Red Serpent and talk to Orusir tel-Panien, perhaps—but the watch had been watching the courts very closely indeed even a season ago, and Ori and the others had been afraid to talk to him.

Who else did he know in Lume? Who could he call on who would not be cowed by the Emperor's Watch?

He knew at least a few members of the Grand Council, and at last re-port the council had been in session, so they should be in Lume. There was Lord Allutar, of course—he could hardly expect any aid there—but there were also Derhin li-Parsil and Amanir tel-Kabanim, the two whose election he had advocated on the late Lord Valin's behalf in his infamous speech in Aulix Square. If he could find them, they would surely answer his questions, and probably provide him temporary shelter, but he had no idea where they lived. He could go to the Aldian Baths and try to talk his way inside, but would they still be there at this hour? The sun was well below the horizon, its glow fading from the sky; the council must have adjourned for the night by now.

The thought of the Grand Council at the Aldian Baths reminded him of something, but it took a moment for it to register. Finally, though, the name came to him: Lord Blackfield.

The Quandishman had taken rooms in Dezar House, or so Shoun had told Anrel. Anrel knew where that was. Lord Blackfield was a friend of Lord Allutar, at least after a fashion, but he had been pleasant enough to Anrel when they last spoke, and as a Quandishman he would hardly take allegations of sedition and witchcraft as seriously as a Walasian sorcerer might—he had no loyalty to the emperor himself, and might well forgive another's failing in that regard.

Anrel had avoided any contact with the Quandishman before, but his situation then had not been so perilous.

There was no reason beyond simple humanity for Lord Blackfield to help Anrel, but that might be enough; after all, his self-proclaimed mission in Walasia was to put an end to black magic, and that implied a certain reluctance to countenance cruelty.

And it wasn't as if Anrel had a great many other choices open to him. He turned his steps toward Dezar House.

By the time he arrived on the broad steps leading up to the grand front porch it was full night, though the orange glow of the burning Pensioners' Quarter lit the sky a ghastly color and the smoke hid the stars. Flakes of ash drifted down occasionally, like pale gray snow.

There could be little point in stopping the demons now; the Pensioners' Quarter was obviously beyond saving. Anrel tried to ignore that as he lifted the heavy brass knocker and let it fall. After all, he still needed somewhere to stay, someone to tell him what had happened. He struggled to compose himself, to appear calm, to look as if he belonged in this expensive neighborhood. Once upon a time he would have been at home here, as a sorcerer's son and a burgrave's nephew, but that was a good many adventures ago; now he felt thoroughly out of place.

A footman opened the door and peered out at him; Anrel essayed a small bow and tipped his hat. "Good evening, my good man," he said. "I understand Lord Blackfield is in residence?"

"Yes," the footman acknowledged warily; he did not seem impressed by Anrel's appearance, despite the good new clothes.

"I would very much like to speak to him."

"Who shall I tell him is calling?"

Anrel hesitated. He had been using various aliases for half a year now, most often Dyssan Adirane, but Lord Blackfield had been introduced to him by his real name, and would not know the others. He might recognize "Adirane" as the family name of Lord Dorias, indicating sorcerous ancestry, but he would have no reason to welcome any Dyssan Adirane.

"Anrel Murau," Anrel said. "We spoke in Alzur last year."

"Very good, sir. If you could wait on the porch, please?"

Anrel frowned; he had hoped to at least be permitted into the front parlor. Perhaps his new clothes were less stylish than he had thought, or perhaps the smoke stains and other damage from the day's events were worse than he had realized. "As you say," he replied.

There were two chairs and a bench on the porch, so at least he would not be forced to stand; he settled into the nearest chair and waited, gazing out into the street.

Even here, in this expensive area of the city, the lamps were not lit tonight. No carriages were out of their coach houses, no ladies promenading. Light spilled from a hundred windows, though; at least the shutters were not all closed, as they had been in Catseye.

Finally, though, just as Anrel was beginning to wonder whether Lord Blackfield might have sent a messenger running out the back to fetch a watchman, the door opened again and a tall old man, his snow-white hair pulled back in a long braid, leaned out. He wore unfamiliar livery in black and blue, with gold buttons.

"Master Murau?" he said. He spoke with just the slightest trace of a Quandish accent.

"Yes," Anrel said, rising.

"Lord Blackfield will see you now."

"Thank you."

Anrel followed as the Quandishman led him through a lavish entry hall, past fine marble statuary, across a magnificent Ermetian carpet, and up a broad staircase to the second floor, where he was ushered into a luxurious sitting room.

Anrel felt an odd tingle as he stepped through the door from the stairwell into the sitting room, and realized he was passing through a set of wards—powerful ones, from the feel of them, but not directed against him.

Once inside he found that the room smelled pleasantly of some faint perfume. The walls were papered in white and gold; the several chairs were upholstered in gold and green, and the various small tables were trimmed with gilt.

Lord Blackfield was standing in the center of the room, a decanter of red wine in his hand; he was impeccably dressed in a green silken coat with exquisite Lithrayn lace at throat and cuffs, over a perfectly pressed white linen shirt and fawn-colored suede breeches. A heavy signet ring gleamed on the third finger of his right hand. His blond hair was elegantly styled, not a strand out of place. He made Anrel very aware of his own smoke-stained, rumpled appearance.

He turned as Anrel entered, and picked up an empty glass. "Master Murau," he said. "Would you care to sample this vintage? It's a pleasant little thing from a village called Pordurim, somewhere in Vaun—not terribly sophisticated, but I find it suits me."

"Thank you, my lord," Anrel said as the white-haired man closed the sitting-room door behind him, leaving him alone with Lord Blackfield. "I would be happy to give it a try."

The big Quandishman poured as he spoke. "It's been some time since I saw you; have you been well?" He handed Anrel the glass and looked at him expectantly.

Anrel grimaced. "I am afraid my circumstances are sadly reduced, my lord." He took a sip of the wine.

Warmth spread through him and a magnificent taste lingered on his tongue; startled, he stared at the glass he held.

"This is *excellent* wine," he said.

"Oh, do you think so? I'm so glad to hear you say that! You Walasians with your refined palates intimidate me; I am a mere barbarian, of course, but I thought it quite a good tipple, and I am delighted to hear that my opinion is not utterly without foundation."

"Not unfounded at all," Anrel said, taking another sip. "From Vaun, you say?"

"Somewhere in the western portion of that province, I believe." He set the decanter on a nearby table, and for the first time it registered on Anrel that his host was not drinking. Thoughts of drugs and poison came immediately to mind, but he dismissed them; why would the Quandish-man poison him without first hearing what he had to say?

"Now," Lord Blackfield said, "what brings you to my door? Much as I would like to believe this a social call, I cannot quite manage it. Our previous meeting was rather brief and not under the best of circum-stances, as I recall."

"Alas, that's true," Anrel said. "I am here, my lord, because I do not know where else to go. My home for the past season and more has been burned to the ground by now, and the entire city seems to have gone mad. Brief as our acquaintance was in Alzur, you struck me as an honest and honorable man, and I hoped that you might tell me what has hap-pened to cause this chaos."

"Burned, you say?"

"Yes." Anrel hesitated before explaining further.

Before he could continue, Lord Blackfield said, "I can't imagine that you were living in a bakery, so I must conclude you had taken refuge in the Pensioners' Quarter—or is there some other disaster of which I had not yet been informed?"

"There may well be, but I have been living in the Pensioners' Quarter, yes." He started to ask what the Quandishman had meant about living in a bakery, but then he remembered Ozrai Lovanniel's ruined establishment in Harbinger Court. Had that been one manifestation of some larger phenomenon? Instead he asked more generally, "What has happened?"

The big man gazed at him thoughtfully, then gestured toward a chair. "Have a seat, Master Murau, and allow me to refill your glass. I think we may have a great deal to tell each other."

11

In Which Lord Blackfield Presents a Theory
Regarding the Cost of Black Magic

Despite Anrel's impatience Lord Blackfield diverted or ignored every question, insisting that he must first hear Anrel's own account of the day's events, as seen by an inhabitant of the Pensioners' Quarter. He sat across a small table from his guest, the wine decanter between them, and kept two glasses filled—though Anrel noticed that he filled his own far less often than he filled Anrel's.

The decanter was almost empty when Anrel finished his account to his host's satisfaction, and demanded, a little more bluntly than he intended, "Now answer *my* questions."

"Of course!" Lord Blackfield spread his hands. "Allow me one final query, and then I will do my best to satisfy your curiosity."

"A query, my lord?"

"In your travels, or in Lume, have you by any chance encountered a man by the name of Revard Saruis? I believe he is a few years older than myself, and until perhaps two years ago he dwelt in a village called Darmolir, in Kerdery."

The name Darmolir was vaguely familiar, but Revard Saruis was not. Anrel shook his head. "I am afraid the name means nothing to me, my lord. But then, I have met many men who have not chosen to give me their names of late. Why are you seeking him?"

Lord Blackfield waved a hand in dismissal. "A personal matter, nothing more. Now, ask what you will, and I will do my best to answer—and to save you the necessity of questions you might find awkward, let me first say that I hope you will be my guest tonight, and that you are welcome to remain under my roof for as long as I remain in Lume."

A wave of relief washed over Anrel. He would not be cast out into the street on this strange and hostile night. "Thank you, my lord."

"And if I may anticipate your next question, I assume you want to know what catastrophe has struck this city. I am afraid it is the price of Lord Allutar's folly—or rather, not his alone, but of all the empire's proud sorcerers."

Anrel frowned. "What do you mean, sir—my lord?" He wondered if perhaps he should have drunk less of that Vaunish vintage; since reaching Lume he had rarely been able to afford decent wine, and he feared he had lost his head for it.

"You have much of it already, sir; you have simply not put the pieces together. You know that bread has been in short supply throughout much of the empire of late; you alluded to it yourself."

"Yes, of course."

"And you know that yesterday morning, not two days ago, the first bargeloads of fresh grain from Aulix arrived in the city, rushed here by the direct order of the emperor."

"I knew the grain arrived; I hadn't known the emperor ordered it."

"Oh, yes. He fears that famine may inspire unrest, perhaps even open revolt, in the provinces, but the thought of unrest here in the capital does not merely frighten him, it *terrifies* him. In particular, he dreads what the Grand Council might do, should the populace rise against him. If the council were to side with the rebels, his position—his *personal* position— would become utterly untenable."

Anrel blinked. "I hadn't thought of that," he said.

Indeed, he had taken for granted that no matter what happened, no matter what the Grand Council might do, no matter what follies or crimes the emperor might commit, the empire would in time return to the form it had taken for centuries, with the sorcerous nobility administering it and a nonsorcerous emperor ruling. He had simply not seen any alternative. The Grand Council might theoretically have the authority to change everything, but they did not have the actual power; the nobility, the armies, and the Emperor's Watch could hardly be expected to meekly obey the council, certainly not to the point of overthrowing the emperor.

But if the council put itself at the head of a starving, outraged mob . . .

"Rest assured, His Imperial Majesty Lurias the Twelfth had thought of it. He will do anything he can to prevent a sustained revolt, and feeding the hungry mouths of Lume would do a great deal to calm the situation. He ordered that grain to be shipped with all haste, and let it be known that the barges were coming."

"How do you know this?" Anrel asked, suddenly suspicious. "Are you in the emperor's confidence?"

Lord Blackfield smiled. "Oh, no. While I am a Quandish magician, a landowner of some significance, and a hereditary Gatherman, I have nothing unique to offer His Imperial Majesty, nor have I made an effort to ingratiate myself at his court. If I had an interest in taking an active role in any government, I would surely have stayed in Ondine and taken part in my own, rather than coming here, would I not? However, there are those in the emperor's palace, and no part of the court, who don't mind talking to a harmless and amusing foreigner."

Anrel, tired and tipsy as he was, needed a few seconds to interpret this, but eventually asked, "You have spies among his servants?"

"I prefer to say that I have made the acquaintance of members of the imperial household staff, and I take pleasure in their conversation."

"You're spying for Quand!" Anrel burst out.

Blackfield grimaced, and waved dismissively. "Oh, come now, Master Murau. I make no secret of my loyalties; did I not just say I am a Gatherman? Can you truly consider it spying when I am so open about it?"

Anrel frowned. "A Gatherman?" He had learned Quandish during his four years in the court schools, and had read a great deal about Quandish history, but it took him a few seconds to make the connection.

Quand had originally been the name applied to all lands outside the Old Empire; it was simply the Old Imperial word for "outside," or "beyond the borders." Only after that empire's fall and the rise of the Walasian Empire in its place had the name come to be applied specifically to the peninsula and islands to the north and west, and then only because the many tribes and peoples in those lands had formed the Gathering—a body that consisted of a gathering of representatives from every town, tribe, and region. It had begun as a means to settle disputes among tribes without resorting to open war, but in time had taken on more and more responsibility, eventually becoming a national government. Only those places and peoples represented in the Gathering were considered Quandish; the other outlands, still far from united, were no longer distinguished from those eastern portions of the Old Empire that had rejected Walasian rule, and both the eastern outlands and the rebellious provinces were collectively known as the Cousins.

In many ways the Gathering was much like the Grand Council—a representative body that was the final authority for a nation. The difference was that where the first Walasian Grand Council had established the empire and then disbanded, the Gathering had continued to meet and govern in its own name, rather than transferring its power to a caste of sorcerers and a ruling family.

"Yes, a Gatherman," Lord Blackfield said. "I have the honor to represent the town of Blackfield, in the district of Dragonshire, to the Gathering. I assure you, the emperor's government is well aware of my identity, and has made no attempt to interfere with my collection of information."

That meant that Lord Blackfield was rather more than an ordinary sorcerer. "So you're in Walasia representing the Quandish government?"

"No, I am in Walasia representing the Lantern Society, of which I also have the honor to be a member."

"But you are in the imperial capital . . ."

"As are a great many sorcerers who use black magic, up to and including the burgrave of Lume himself. I came here on behalf of the Lantern Society, not as a Gatherman. In either role, however, I find it useful to keep abreast of events, and the best method I have found for doing so is cultivating the company of servants and tradesmen—while I am sure these worthies are as capable of keeping secrets as anyone, they see no need to keep *other people's* secrets, and are often all too glad to tell me what they have learned in observing their supposed betters. Sorcerers and officials who would never dare speak of certain matters to one another will happily chatter about them with their staff, or in the shops they visit."

"And the palace servants told you that the emperor was rushing that grain here to prevent unrest?"

"Indeed they did."

That made perfect sense, and there was no reason for Anrel to argue the point further. "Very well, then," he said. "What does that have to do with today's events, or with black magic?"

Lord Blackfield interlaced his fingers, and touched his index fingers to his lower lip. "Can you not guess?" he asked. "The grain arrived directly from the Raish Valley in Aulix and was rushed to the bakers, so that they might restock their shelves with the bread that would fill the empty bellies of Lume. That was all as the emperor expected and desired. But—did you taste any of that bread your No-Nose Graun brought to the Pensioners' Quarter?"

"No," Anrel said. "I didn't taste it myself, but something was wrong with it; everyone who tasted it agreed. It was tainted somehow. That baker in Dragonclaw Street must have done something wrong, and thought he could salvage something from the ruin by selling No-Nose the spoiled bread."

Lord Blackfield shook his head. "The baker did nothing wrong."

"But the bread was foul!"

"Because the flour from which it was made was befouled."

"How? Did someone poison one of the barges, perhaps? Ermetian agents, or some madman from the Cousins? Since you're telling me this, I conclude it was not Quand's doing . . ."

"Not Quand's, nor Ermetia's, nor any foreign power's—Walasia did this to itself. It was not the barges that were polluted, but the earth in which the wheat grew."

Despite his wine-muddled head, Anrel suddenly understood. "The Raish Valley—you said this was the result of Lord Allutar's folly. You meant the black sorcery he performed last year, to restore the fertility of the Raish Valley."

"Indeed I do."

"The spell went wrong?" Anrel shuddered; he remembered all too well what could happen when a sorcerer's spell went wrong. Another possibility occurred to him. "Could Urunar Kazien have done this somehow, when he was dying? An act of revenge?"

Lord Blackfield shook his head again. "That poor boy had no idea how to affect the spell, and no power to do so. Nor, before you ask, did your friend Lord Valin have anything to do with it. This is simply a natural consequence of black magic when applied with insufficient safeguards. Do you think we of the Lantern Society want to eliminate black magic merely because we are a collection of high-minded idealists? No, we sound a warning because we see dangers that others refuse to acknowledge. Back in Alzur you heard me tell Lord Allutar there would be costs beyond Master Kazien's life; I spoke the honest truth, though Allutar refused to recognize it."

"I had thought you meant that he was harming his soul, and would pay for it in the afterlife," Anrel exclaimed. "I had no idea you meant worldly consequences like this!"

"Oh, I have no doubt that when Allutar Hezir faces his ancestors he will have much to answer for, and I did indeed intend that interpretation. I fear that experience has taught me and my companions that vague warnings of unforeseen results will elicit only contempt, while a threat to one's prospects in the afterlife may at least cause some hesitation. Every sorcerer who would attempt black magic thinks himself far too clever to be caught in such a trap as this disaster in the Raish Valley."

"But can you not provide examples?"

"Of course we can! Some sorcerers even listen, and choose not to pursue their darker spells. Most, though, simply say they are not such fools as the people we describe, and will not be caught in such mishaps." He sighed. "Very few of those mishaps have consequences on such a scale as this. Lord Allutar's little escapade might well bring down your emperor."

Anrel tried to grasp that idea, and found it hard to encompass. "But . . . how did it go wrong? Allutar said that he used Urunar's death to summon an earth elemental that bestowed greater fertility on the soil of the Raish Valley."

"Precisely. That soil yielded forth a crop of unnatural size—but Lord Allutar had failed to concern himself with anything but the quantity. A natural crop draws its life from the Mother, from her essence in the earth; *this* crop drew its life from this artificial elemental that your landgrave bound to that soil. The elemental is not the Mother; it is not even born of the Mother. It is, rather, a creature made from blood and death, and that blood and death poisoned everything that drew life from it."

"Then the bread is poisoned?"

Lord Blackfield hesitated. "Perhaps that was not the best word to use," he said. "I do not think that eating the bread will harm you—but I doubt it will nourish you, either. It is not so much a toxin as a deception, empty of life." He shook his head. "I confess, I do not know its nature with any certainty. This was not a spell that has been often used, nor has it been properly studied. I can only guess at its ramifications."

Anrel considered this, his mind still hazy with wine and weariness. There was a certain bitter satisfaction in knowing that Lord Allutar, the man who had caused so much misery in Anrel's own life, was responsible for this disaster. "And *all* the bread baked with the Raish wheat is bad?"

"Yes. At least half the bakeries in Lume produced the same foul stuff that No-Nose Graun brought to the Pensioners' Quarter."

"What happened?"

Lord Blackfield sighed. "I do not pretend to know all the details of every incident, but there were disturbances throughout the city. Like your friends, most of those who tasted the bread thought the bakers were trying to cheat them somehow. Bakers were beaten, their shops destroyed. Every man of the Emperor's Watch was called out to restore order, and order was restored, but only by clearing the streets. The cannon on the emperor's palace were loaded and aimed, though thank the Mother and the Father they were not fired into the crowds. Only in the Pensioners' Quarter, though, was the watch defeated, and only in the quarter were arches torn down; I assume that was why it was only in the quarter that the emperor's mercenaries from the Cousins unleashed demons."

"I see," Anrel said unsteadily.

The *emperor's* mercenaries. Anrel did not doubt that Lord Blackfield knew what he was saying, and that it had been the Walasian emperor himself, and not the Ermetian-born empress, who had ordered the demons to be summoned. His Imperial Majesty, Lurias XII, had set demons upon his own people.

That made Lord Allutar's crimes seem petty by comparison.

"You look unwell, Master Murau, and it strikes me that I have been an absolutely *abominable* host!" the Quandishman exclaimed. "I have given you wine, but not a thing to eat!" He reached up and tugged at a cord; a bell jingled somewhere. "I'll have Harban fetch us some supper, shall I? I assure you, there will be no Raish wheat in it. My cook, Mistress Uillea, uses only the finest ingredients in her creations."

"Thank you," Anrel said. A bite to eat would be very welcome; he had had nothing since breakfast.

He sat quietly, trying to gather his thoughts, as Lord Blackfield went to the door of the sitting room and exchanged a few words with his white-braided servant. When the Quandishman had done that he returned to the little table and resumed his seat, but said nothing, allowing Anrel the time to consider everything he had been told.

After several minutes, Anrel said, "The famine—not the tainted grain, but the shortages we have suffered in recent years. Is it all natural?"

"Do you mean, is it the result of black magic?"

"Yes."

Lord Blackfield shook his head. "I do not believe it is. Your Walasian sorcerers have not been as careless as all that. Callous as they may be, few use black magic with any frequency, and I do not believe any but Lord Allutar has attempted anything of that nature, and on such a scale, heretofore." He shrugged. "Though I could, of course, be wrong. I am not omniscient."

"But sorcerers have been using magic to increase their crops for as long as I can recall, even if it was not *black* sorcery. Might that have had some effect?"

"It might," the Quandishman acknowledged. "They may have coaxed more from the Mother than she wanted to give, and left that much less for subsequent years. My learned Ermetian comrade in the Lantern

Society, Kerren of Algard, has propounded such a theory at tedious length, but we have little evidence for it." He sighed. "And, I must concede, none against it."

"Is there any way to undo the damage?"

"We do not even know whether there *is* damage."

"I meant to the Raish Valley."

"Ah! Of course. Well, Lord Allutar can dismiss his elemental at any time, and that will put an end to the artificial fertility. Whether the land's natural bounty will be immediately restored, or whether it will require years to return, I cannot say, nor, I believe, can any man."

Anrel shuddered. "And the city—what will happen here in Lume, do you suppose?"

"I would suppose that the Emperor's Watch will maintain order for the present—reports of the demons' rampage in the Pensioners' Quarter will undoubtedly aid them in their efforts. In time, more natural and wholesome crops will reach the mills and bakeries and grocers, and life will return to normal."

"I hope—"

Anrel's reply was interrupted by a knock at the door. Lord Blackfield strode over and swung it open, admitting his servant, who bore an immense and heavily laden silver tray. Lord Blackfield snatched this from the older man's hands and whisked it to a table—not the small side table where he and Anrel had been drinking, but a larger one toward the back of the sitting room.

Then he turned to his guest and said, "Master Murau, if you would do me the honor of joining me for supper?"

Anrel doubted there was any honor in his presence, but he did not let that stop him.

"I would be delighted," he said.

12

In Which Anrel Dines with Lord Blackfield

For the most part the food, while plentiful and varied, was simple, hearty fare, somewhat unfamiliar in content and preparation. Anrel supposed it was the result of Quandish cookery. Whatever its origins, the meal was entirely satisfactory.

Of course, Anrel knew his standards might well be lower than they once were; it had been half a year since he had regularly eaten well. Nivain Lir and her daughters had been decent cooks but could not afford the best ingredients, and in the Pensioners' Quarter anything that one could keep down was considered good enough.

When the edge had been taken off his appetite and he was content to nibble a little here and there, rather than devouring everything on his plate, Anrel looked up and said, "It's most generous of you to make me welcome in this fashion, my lord."

"Ah, it's nothing, I assure you."

"On the contrary, it was quite presumptuous of me to arrive here unheralded. We barely know each other, and we have almost nothing in common."

"Oh, I think you misjudge. I should say we have several similarities. After all, when we first met, were we not both hoping to convince Lord Allutar not to put young Urunar Kazien to death?"

Anrel grimaced. "In truth, my lord, I was there in hopes of keeping

Lord Valin out of trouble, not because I thought I could save Master Kazien." He shook his head. "I regret to say I failed."

"Oh?" The Quandishman dabbed at his mouth with a napkin. "Has misfortune befallen Lord Valin?"

Anrel winced. "Lord Valin is dead, my lord." He had somehow assumed Lord Blackfield had known all about it, but why would he? The unfortunate killing of a very minor sorcerer in a village in Aulix was hardly the stuff of international gossip.

Lord Blackfield dropped the napkin. "How dreadful! I had been told as much before, but could not believe it. How did it happen, pray?"

Anrel proceeded to tell his host the sorry history of how Lord Allutar had deliberately misinterpreted Valin's insults as a challenge to trial by combat, a trial to ascertain whether Allutar would remain landgrave of Aulix or be replaced by Valin. He described the grotesquely mismatched contest that had ended in Valin's death.

"I see," Lord Blackfield said. "And—forgive me if I am rude, and do not feel you are under any obligation to answer so impertinent a question— does this have something to do with how you came to be here in Lume, and a resident of the Pensioners' Quarter?"

"Yes," Anrel replied. He hesitated, unsure what more to say; it wasn't really any of Lord Blackfield's business, and admitting that he, Anrel Murau, was the infamous Alvos of Naith, might be unwise. After all, the Quandishman had no reason to protect him, and might well take the opportunity to curry favor with the emperor by turning him over to the authorities.

Seeing his hesitation, Lord Blackfield said, "You need not say anything incriminating, Master Murau, but I assure you, anything you *do* say will be held in the strictest confidence. You have my word as a Gatherman and as a sorcerer."

That was reassuring, but Anrel still did not feel any need to be specific. "Let us just say, then, that after Lord Valin's death I said certain things in public that the magistrates considered highly inappropriate."

Lord Blackfield sipped wine, then said, "Might it be that you said these things in, perhaps, Aulix Square, in Naith?"

That guess surprised Anrel; he had not thought he was being so obvious. "It might," he admitted. Having come this far, he saw little point in lying. He was at the Quandishman's mercy.

"And did you perhaps, while speaking, give another name?"

"I did."

"Did you speak again with that name in Sharam?"

Startled, Anrel said, "I have never been to Sharam."

"Ah, that wasn't you? But were you perhaps present at a hanging in Beynos this past winter?"

"Indeed, I was."

Lord Blackfield set his wineglass down. "You know, when I heard that this mysterious Alvos had denounced Lord Allutar for an unjust death, I had guessed that he might be Lord Valin, speaking of Urunar Kazien's death. When you first told me your friend was dead I did you the courtesy of believing you spoke the truth, but assumed that he had died subsequently—perhaps apprehended by the authorities and quietly slain, the killing kept quiet to avoid stirring up public sentiment, or perhaps in some more commonplace manner. But when you told me how he had actually died, I suspected the truth. Thank you for trusting me with it."

"You said you had heard he was dead?"

"Yes. Certain acquaintances of mine had said so, but I had guessed they were misleading me in an attempt to protect him. There are those who would take great pleasure in hanging Alvos of Naith, but there's nothing to gain in hanging a man who is already dead, so I thought the story of his death might have been put about to forestall further efforts at his capture. I thought he might yet live, and if so, I would be interested in speaking with him. One reason I told Harban to admit you was that I thought you might be here as Lord Valin's representative."

"In a way, I am exactly that," Anrel said. "As Alvos I gave voice to *his* beliefs, which were never my own."

"Really? How droll!" Lord Blackfield picked up a sweet from the tray and popped it into his mouth. "Then you did not believe those impassioned words you spoke that have inspired such unrest?"

"I did not," Anrel said. "Valin believed that a new order could be created in which every man would be master of his own destiny, and sorcerers would be the servants of the nation, rather than its masters, but I considered this idealistic nonsense. Without magic, how would the government enforce its edicts? And if they are not rewarded with power and status, why would sorcerers use their magic for the public welfare?" He shook his head. "I know that you Quandish have no such arrangement, and that you seem to have managed, but I do not pretend to understand *how* you have managed, nor do I think your systems, if such chaos can be called systems, would work for us here in Walasia."

Only after the words had left his mouth did Anrel realize how insulting they might sound, and he tensed as he awaited his host's response.

"Quand is not the only place to reject the rule of magicians," Lord Blackfield pointed out calmly with no sign of having taken offense.

"You mean Ermetia? Where they have two separate governments, one for sorcerers, and one for commoners? I have never understood how *that* system survives, either—why has the Council Arcane not destroyed the Council Terrestrial, overthrown the king, and assumed control?"

"From what they tell me, they have no *desire* to control the mundane government," Lord Blackfield replied. "Consider, Master Murau—does your uncle, Lord Dorias, *want* to administer Alzur? Not every sorcerer seeks earthly power."

"For the most part, Walasian sorcerers do," Anrel retorted. "Indeed, my uncle very much enjoys the authority he holds; it is merely the accompanying responsibility he would prefer to avoid."

"Do you think he would choose to serve as burgrave, if he did not already hold the post?"

"He could resign, my lord, yet he has not done so. The taste of power is sweet."

Blackfield leaned back in his chair. "You have dismissed Quand and Ermetia as inexplicable; what of the rest of the Bound Lands?"

"The Cousins?" Anrel snorted derisively. "Surely, you cannot be putting forth *that* madhouse as a model of anything but disaster! For that matter, half of them *are* ruled by magicians!"

"But half are not, and they are not noticeably less successful, on average."

"But they are not the empire. For almost six hundred years, we have been ruled by sorcerers—and before that, the Old Empire was ruled by wizards. It's all we have ever known here."

Lord Blackfield sighed. "Does that mean nothing else is possible?"

"It means that this system suits us."

"And has nothing shaken your certainty on that count?"

Anrel hesitated. He remembered the tainted bread, the flaming demons, the mob in Beynos, the mob in Aulix Square.

Lord Blackfield leaned forward across the table. "Would you like to know an interesting thing, Master Murau?"

"My lord?"

"Did you know there are fewer sorcerers in the empire than there are in Quand?"

Anrel frowned. "But the empire is—" He stopped in midsentence, suddenly unsure of his facts. "Isn't the empire far larger?"

"Less so than it once was, thanks to our brave Quandish pioneers in our overseas colonies, but yes, I believe the empire is still significantly larger, in both land and population, than Quand. Yet we have more sorcerers than you do. Do you know why?"

"I have no idea—assuming you are correct."

"Because in the Walasian Empire, sorcerers invariably marry sorceresses—if they marry at all. After all, for a noble to marry a commoner would be . . . *inconvenient,* in certain regards. In mixed marriages not all the children will inherit the ability to use magic, and it can be embarrassing for, say, a burgrave to find his sons unable to inherit, for lack of magic. So your sorcerers grow ever more inbred, and because many are too busy with other matters to want to raise children, they have small families—after all, a sorceress cannot be got with child against her will; even the feeblest magician can manage that much. Thus, even while the empire's population grows, the number of sorcerers stays constant, or even shrinks."

"I have never heard this before," Anrel answered warily.

"Why would you? I am not sure whether anyone in the empire is really aware of it. I assume the keepers of the Great List know the present tally of names to be no more now than it was a century ago, but do they draw any conclusions from this, or even bother to mention it to any-one?"

"I don't know," Anrel said.

"In Quand, on the other hand, there are no restrictions on who a sor-cerer might wed, and while sorceresses can and sometimes do limit the size of their families, sorcerers married to non-magicians often raise large broods. A sorcerer is considered quite a catch for most girls, and his magic can help ensure a healthy family."

"But the children won't all be sorcerers! Even here, occasionally a sorcerer's child will fail the trials . . ."

"As you did?"

Anrel fell silent, unsure whether Lord Blackfield's question might im-ply the Quandishman knew that Anrel had failed the trial deliberately.

"Yes," Lord Blackfield continued. "About half the children fail to in-herit any gift for magic—but even so, the *other* half has been sufficient to keep our population of sorcerers growing, both in absolute numbers and as a percentage of our population. We have plenty of sorcerers for our purposes. Meanwhile, the empire is trying to administer a growing population with fewer and fewer sorcerers—and when a magician *does* turn up outside of the established noble families, he is either labeled a witch and hanged, or if allowed to be acknowledged and trained as a sorcerer, he is often still treated as a nuisance, a minor embarrassment, as Lord Valin was."

Anrel found himself growing unreasonably annoyed at this foreigner describing flaws in the Walasian system. "What is your point, my lord?"

"My point? Why, that your empire cannot sustain itself indefinitely if it persists in its present policies. You say that it has operated this way for almost six hundred years, and you are quite correct, but that does not mean it can continue this way forever. Cracks are beginning to show, Master Murau—the famine, the Raish wheat, the demons in the Pensioners' Quarter, even Lord Valin's death, these are not signs of a healthy nation."

"I suppose you think we would be better off adopting the Quandish system, and merging the Grand Council with the Gathering?" Anrel replied angrily.

"No." Lord Blackfield shook his head. "No, while I am proud of my own nation, you are quite right when you say the empire is different. I would not welcome a merger. It is not my place to dictate what the Walasian people should do, how you should rule yourselves. I merely hope to offer what counsel I can, so that whatever changes may come will do no more harm than they must."

There was really little Anrel could say to this. For a moment conversation paused, replaced by a contemplative silence as both men picked at their remaining food. At last, though, Anrel broke the silence by asking, "You said you had been told Lord Valin was dead—by whom?"

"Why, by two of Naith's representatives on the Grand Council—perhaps you know them? Derhin li-Parsil and Amanir tel-Kabanim. I understand that Delegate li-Parsil attributes his election to a certain speech."

"I have made their acquaintance," Anrel acknowledged. "I cannot say I knew them well. They were Lord Valin's friends, more than my own."

"I have the impression, my dear Master Murau, that they would be pleased to see you again, and to be assured that you are alive and well."

"Meeting with me might not be wise," Anrel replied. "I am, after all, a notorious criminal."

Lord Blackfield stroked his close-trimmed beard. "Ah, you may have a point. I do not know the legal details of the situation."

"You are certainly free to assure them of my good health."

"Then I will do that." The Quandishman hesitated, then said, "If you will forgive my impertinence, Master Murau, may I ask what your intentions are? As I have said, I am delighted to have you as my guest, but I wonder whether you have made plans for the future."

Anrel grimaced. "In truth, my lord, I have not. I have, for the most part, been too greatly concerned with remaining alive and free to give much thought to any long-term plans. I have no prospects for a career, at present, and as for family—well, there was a young woman, but I am afraid I have lost her forever." He winced inwardly at the memory of Tazia, but forced himself to continue. "After all, even should some miracle bring her to Lume and we chance to meet again, what do I have to offer her? I have been living among thieves and beggars, and can hardly ask her to dwell there with me."

"Will you be returning to the Pensioners' Quarter, then?"

"My lord, I am not certain the Pensioners' Quarter still exists." He shook his head. "And even if the damage proves to be only superficial, I took up residence there more out of necessity than by choice. I would very much prefer to find another home—but I do not know where I might accomplish this."

"Of course." Lord Blackfield cleared his throat. "Where my previous question was impertinent, I am afraid my next verges on the downright indelicate. Do you have any means of support?"

Anrel sighed deeply. "I do not really know. Before I was branded a criminal I had certain resources, but their present status is unknown to me. I am sole heir to my parents' estate—not the land, of course, since my name is not on the Great List I cannot own land, but their other property has been held in trust for me, and that had provided a modest income while I lived in Alzur. My uncle, Lord Dorias, supported me, even to the extent of paying for my education at the court schools, so the income from my legacy has remained largely untouched, but I cannot see any way to collect it while a fugitive—and that assumes it has not been declared forfeit to the state, in recompense for my supposed crimes. Nor was it any great fortune, in any case; I spent those four years in study partly for the joy of learning, but equally in hopes of a career as a clerk to the provincial government in Naith that would supplement my inheritance."

"I take it you do not see an administrative career in your future."

"Not so long as I am branded a seditionist."

"How have you provided for yourself since fleeing Naith?"

"By theft and fraud, for the most part," Anrel admitted. "I am not proud of that, but I did what I thought necessary."

"I take it you would prefer not to resume that line of work."

"Indeed." While his stay in the Pensioners' Quarter had not been so dreadful as he might once have anticipated, neither had it been particularly pleasant, and the day's events could only have made his circumstances there worse. He was more than ready to move on, to reinvent himself again.

Lord Blackfield considered that for a moment, then placed both palms on the table and rose to his feet, pushing back his chair. "Well," he said, "I do not think we can solve all the world's problems tonight. You must be weary, after your adventurous day; shall I have Harban show you to your room?"

"That would be most kind of you, my lord." Anrel drained the last of his wine, then stood. "There is one more thing I would like to ask you, though."

"Oh? What would that be? If you want the name of my tailor, I'm afraid his shop is in Ondine, on the far side of the Dragonlands, but I do know a fellow in Silk Street who does a very decent job."

Anrel smiled. "No, my lord, I am not yet ready to further replenish my wardrobe. You have been apologetic about asking me some very basic questions tonight, though you had every right to inquire into my situation, given that I had arrived uninvited on your doorstep and imposed upon your hospitality, so I hope you will forgive me asking one at least as rude as any of your own."

"You intrigue me, sir! What would this question be?"

"Simply, why?"

Lord Blackfield cocked his head to one side. "Why what?"

"Why are you being so kind to me? Your generosity has been entirely unreasonable. I am a confessed criminal, a virtual stranger, who presented himself unannounced, in disarray and none too clean, yet you have taken me into your home, answered my questions, and fed me most sumptuously. You have treated me like an honored guest, rather than an intruder, and have shown no sign of delivering me to the authorities, though my presence here might endanger you. You are a sorcerer and a Gatherman, a Quandish lord, clearly a man of wealth and education, yet you have treated me in every way like an equal. Why?"

The Quandishman's expression turned serious. "A thoughtful question, sir, and one that deserves an honest answer, but to answer fully would take half the night, and we both need our rest. I will say this much—we are both the children of the Mother and the Father, and whatever differences in rank or station we may have are the doing of our human fellows, not our divine ancestors. I believe that every man, woman, and child should be judged by his actions, and not by his name or other accidents of birth, and I try to live in accordance with that belief. The world is a harsh enough place without adding any unnecessary harshness of our own. But I said you deserved honesty, so I will not pretend that my reasons are entirely unselfish; I expected you to provide me with information I may find useful, and you have indeed done so. I might have gotten it from you while treating you with disdain, but it was surely more pleasant for both of us to exchange information while conversing like the equals we are in the eyes of our ancient ancestors, rather than in some sordid game of threats and bargains. I remembered you from our brief encounters in Alzur, and you struck me there as a sensible and presentable young man; why should I not enjoy your society, then? Yes, you have fallen on hard times, while I have flourished, but that means nothing, really, except that I can well afford any generosity I have shown you. I have merely treated you as I would like to treat everyone, as I would prefer to be treated myself were I in your position."

"You have my heartfelt thanks for that treatment, my lord," Anrel said.

The Quandishman waved a hand in dismissal. "Now, sir, let us be off to our rest, and if you think of further questions tonight, pray, ask them in the morning."

Anrel bowed in response, then turned and found the white-haired servant, Harban, standing in the open door.

"This way, Master Murau," Harban said with a bow just slightly deeper than Anrel's own, and a gesture toward the hallway beyond the door.

"Thank you," Anrel said.

He glanced back as he left the room, and saw Lord Blackfield still standing behind the supper table, stroking his chin thoughtfully.

13

In Which Anrel Enjoys a Quiet Morning

Anrel awoke feeling utterly relaxed and thoroughly rested for the first time in a season. This had been his first night in a real bed since fleeing Beynos, and an excellent bed it was. He lay there for several minutes, enjoying the cool smoothness of the linen sheets and admiring the gleaming whiteness of the bedchamber ceiling. Nothing in the Pensioners' Quarter was ever so clean as that painted plaster.

He was in no great hurry to rise and begin the day; there was nothing he particularly needed to do, and after the magnificent supper and plentiful wine Lord Blackfield had provided the night before he felt no need for a quick breakfast. Eventually he knew he would have to get up and be about his business, whatever business that might be, but he allowed himself to savor the moment.

At last, though, memories and guilt began to seep in, dissolving his contentment. His home in the Pensioners' Quarter was probably destroyed, and most of his meager belongings with it. He hoped that his friends—Po, Shoun, Mieshel, Doz, Bim, Mother Baba, even Apolien— had all survived the demonic attack, but he did not know; he had no idea how many people had died at the hands of those monsters, or in the fires they had started. He remembered the bodies sprawled in Duty Street, but he had not seen most of their faces; the ones he had recognized had been mere acquaintances, he had seen none he would call friends.

Still, they had been his countrymen, and they had been killed by demons, demons that had surely been summoned by the Cousiner magicians in the emperor's employ. They had been betrayed and murdered by their own government.

And he really had no idea how extensive the damage was. How much of the Pensioners' Quarter was still standing? How many of its inhabitants still lived?

The emperor had done this—or if the rumors were true, perhaps the empress, or some underling, but certainly the emperor had permitted it.

There was a popular myth among the commoners of Walasia that the emperor's purpose was to keep the excesses of the nobility in check, that the emperor was required to not be a magician himself so that he would always remember the needs of ordinary citizens and defend them against the sorcerers. The Great List gave the emperor the ability to render any sorcerer powerless, and the widespread belief was that he would use this to prevent sorcerers from abusing commoners too blatantly.

Sorcerers, on the other hand, believed that the emperor's role was to keep any one sorcerer, or any one faction, from gaining power over the others, and that his position had nothing to do with protecting commoners.

It seemed to Anrel that the attack on the Pensioners' Quarter demonstrated that the sorcerers' theory was closer to the truth. This emperor plainly had no great love for the lowliest citizens of his empire.

This emperor was, in fact, a disgrace to his position. He had turned foreign magicians loose on loyal Walasians. Anrel found himself more sympathetic than ever before to the idea that the empire's whole system of government needed to be replaced.

Overall, though, he still believed that so radical a change was not worth the risk. Replacing Lurias with his brother Sharal, or with a regency in the name of his infant son, would probably be enough to restore sanity and order to the empire—though it would not restore the Pensioners' Quarter, nor restore the dead to life.

As for his own role in the disaster, Anrel hesitated to assess that. Some might argue that he had been a coward to evade the demons and flee the quarter as he had, and indeed, a part of his own heart seemed to believe this, but rationally he told himself that he had done what he could. He had intended to stop the demons by stopping the magicians who had summoned them, but he had been unable to do so alone, and he had been unable to find any help. Nothing would have been accomplished by an attempt to stop the demons directly, or by climbing a stair to the walkway above Harbinger Court and attacking the magicians there; the result would most likely have been his own death or incarceration.

That assumed he could have climbed such a stair in the first place; the iron gates at the top and bottom of every stair had undoubtedly been locked, and despite his recent training in many of the criminal arts he was not a skilled lock-breaker.

Perhaps he could have helped others escape from the quarter, but really, everyone there knew the streets as well as he did. He suspected that the surviving residents of the quarter were now scattered all through Lume.

No, rationally, he had done the best he could, even if in the end he accomplished nothing but delivering himself to this delightful bed. The guilt that nagged at him was unjustified.

Knowing that did not make it go away, of course, but it allowed him to keep it under restraint.

He wondered whether there was anything he could do to remedy his errors of the evening before. Was there some way he could help the survivors of the quarter? Some way he could ensure that the emperor never again unleashed such horrors on his own people?

And at root, the cause of all the catastrophic events was Lord Allutar's arrogance, and his sacrifice of Urunar Kazien's life to fuel black magic. It was that spell that had poisoned the fields of the Raish Valley, and triggered yesterday's events. It was Master Kazien's death that had driven Lord Valin to denounce Lord Allutar and provoke his own death. It was, in turn, Lord Valin's death that had led to Anrel's own speeches in Naith and Beynos.

Lord Allutar had killed Urunar Kazien, and Lord Valin, and Reva Lir, to maintain and enhance his own position. He had cheated half the city of Lume of their daily bread, and brought on riots and disaster.

Anrel had considered Urunar's death an acceptable cost of maintaining the traditional order. He had deplored and protested Valin's death, but only on a personal basis; he had not thought it meant Allutar did not deserve his position as landgrave of Aulix. But ruining the grain harvest—*that* was a grave failure in Lord Allutar's performance of his duties, and one that had led not to one death, but indirectly to dozens.

But what could be done about it? Once appointed, landgraves served for life, unless either successfully challenged by another sorcerer, or deposed by the emperor.

Or, perhaps, removed by the Grand Council. Anrel mused on that for a moment.

Lord Blackfield had said that Derhin and Amanir were on the council. Could they introduce some motion to censure Allutar, perhaps?

Anrel shook his head. Even if they did introduce such a measure, it wouldn't pass. Half the council was made up of sorcerers or their appointees who would surely vote to protect one of their own. No, Lord Allutar's misdeeds would go unpunished.

Unless, of course, Anrel found some way to punish him. Anrel had no idea what that might be, but he certainly wouldn't find it lying in bed; he sat up and swung his legs over the side of the bed.

As if he had been waiting for this signal Lord Blackfield's manservant appeared in the door of the room, a bundle in his arms.

"Your pardon, Master Murau," he said. "I took the liberty of having your clothes cleaned, and ordering a few items."

"Thank you—Harban, is it?" Anrel accepted the bundle.

"Yes, sir."

"Do you know whether Lord Blackfield is expecting me to join him for breakfast?"

"Lord Blackfield breakfasted some time ago, sir, and has gone out."

"Oh, has he?" Anrel glanced at the nearest window, trying to judge the time. He had assumed he had awoken at his usual early hour, but perhaps the fine bed had coaxed him into more than his usual amount of sleep.

"Indeed."

"Did he leave any instructions concerning me?"

"Your breakfast will be ready momentarily, sir, and Lord Blackfield would consider it a favor, should you leave the house before his return, if you would inform me before you go."

"Thank you."

Harban bowed, and left the room.

Anrel dressed himself quickly, and took a good look out the window at the streets and the sky. The streets were still not as crowded as their norm, but neither were they as deserted as they had been at yesterday's dusk.

The sky was streaked with smoke, more than seemed entirely appropriate for a warm day, and Anrel guessed that the Pensioners' Quarter was still smoldering. He *hoped* it was the Pensioners' Quarter, and not some other part of the city.

And as Harban's remarks had implied, the angle of the sunlight through the smoke showed that Anrel had slept much later than his usual custom.

Well, he told himself, he was up now. He straightened his coat.

This was not his old, much-abused brown velvet coat; that was lost forever in the ruins of the Pensioners' Quarter. This was a dove-gray garment he had bought perhaps a quarter season ago, to help him pass for a wealthy man. Upon casual inspection it gave every appearance of being a fine and costly garment, but a closer look would reveal that it had no lining, that the lapels had no backing, and that the fabric was not of the first quality. The cuffs were made to look as if a generous bunch of lace had been tucked back into them, when in fact there was only a narrow strip of real lace, and the rest a bit of well-worn rag.

Still, it served him well enough.

His breeches were of much better manufacture; he had decided to pay the cost of real quality there, so that they might last, rather than make do with some further sham. As Harban had said, they had been freshly laundered, the smoke stains sponged away, yet were not even damp; someone must have been busy.

Anrel's blouse was adequate, if not particularly fine; it, too, was a recent acquisition. The lace-edged handkerchief in his pocket was new, as well. Thus attired, Anrel could pass for a wealthy man; he had demonstrated as much. Doz had been pleased with this outfit, and despite the previous day's abuse, Harban or some other servant had restored it to its original glory.

Thus reminded of Doz, Anrel hoped very much that the other man was alive and well, and that they would meet again, but he was glad Doz was not there. Doz would probably want to pocket a few valuables and then head home to the quarter; Anrel, on the other hand, preferred to remain Lord Blackfield's guest for several days yet, if he could. He wanted to get another perspective on Lume, to see it as a wealthy for-eigner would, rather than as a Walasian swindler and thief, or as a stu-dent at the court schools.

He wondered where Lord Blackfield had gone, what business he was about. Might the Quandishman be courting some Walasian lady, perhaps?

No, Anrel told himself, that was unlikely, and that it had been the first possibility that came to mind said more about his own streak of roman-ticism, and perhaps how badly he missed Tazia, than about anything Lord Blackfield might do. Wherever Lord Blackfield was, it was his own business, and not Anrel's.

It might be useful, though, to have some rough idea of when to ex-pect his host to return. If Lord Blackfield was going to walk in at any mo-ment, then Anrel's plans would be rather different than if he knew the Quandishman would be out all day.

Either way, though, the first order of business would be that breakfast Harban had mentioned. He turned away from the window and headed for the door.

Although he had seen some of Lord Blackfield's rooms the night be-fore, he was startled to discover that the residence had several more he had *not* seen, one of which was a breakfast room with magnificently large, clear windows that gave a grand view of the gardens behind Dezar House, and even a glimpse of the Galdin River. Harban saw to it that Anrel was seated alone at a table much larger than a single person needed, in a position where he could gaze out the window as he ate.

The actual breakfast was delightful—honey-glazed ham, an assort-ment of fruit, and odd, eggy little cakes unlike anything Anrel had pre-viously tasted. Whatever they were, they were clearly not made from Raish Valley flour; they were delicious.

Harban refused to admit to any knowledge whatsoever of his employer's plans, but when pressed, did admit that Anrel probably had at least an hour or two before Lord Blackfield returned.

He also explained that Lord Blackfield rented the entire second floor of Dezar House, while the ground floor held four small apartments, one of which was vacant at present, and the top floor comprised several small suites that were all leased by a pair of brothers, but were inhabited at any given time by whichever women the brothers had installed there—not merely their own current mistresses, but other women who had a need for such accommodations. Lord Blackfield trusted that Anrel would not trouble any of his neighbors.

Armed with this information Anrel was able to talk his way into the Quandishman's library, where he settled down to improve his own mastery of the Quandish tongue by working his way through the memoirs of an anonymous traveler who had apparently spent half the previous century wandering the world.

At first he struggled with the unfamiliar language—not only was his Quandish, never as fluent as he might have liked in the first place, somewhat rusty, but the author affected a deliberately archaic style. After an hour or so, though, Anrel found himself settling into it, and losing himself in the narrative.

The descriptions of the Quandish countryside were almost certainly flavored by patriotism and perhaps nostalgia, but were so charming that for the first time in his life Anrel found himself seriously tempted to visit that strange, fogbound country. The account of crossing the Dragonlands from Redcliff to Kallai was thrilling, though that was as much the author's style as the events he described; when Anrel finished that chapter he realized that in fact, the traveler had never been in real danger at any point, and the few dragons he had seen had all been at a safe distance.

The descriptions of the Walasian countryside and people, in Kerdery and Aulix, were far less flattering than the author's report on his homeland, but that was to be expected. If Anrel had the chronology right, the author's adventures there had taken place only five or six years after the War of the Kite, a conflict in which Quand and the empire had fought each other to a bloody stalemate. Some lingering animosity was hardly surprising.

What's more, it became clear that the author had been an officer in the Quandish army, and had served in the War of the Kite—one of the reasons for his journey was to revisit some of the sites where he had fought. His account of meeting one of his former foes in a tavern in Kuriel, an encounter that left both men in tears, was heartrending.

By the time he reached the author's account of his audience before His Imperial Majesty Lurias IX Anrel was utterly rapt, and it came as a shock to hear Lord Blackfield's voice, jarring him out of the traveler's tale.

"I see you have found my great-grandfather's memoirs," the Quandishman said. "I should warn you, family legend says that the old man was fond of embellishing his adventures. I would not put too much faith in anything he says."

Anrel looked up from the book, taking a second to gather his wits, then said, "True or not, your ancestor told a fine tale."

"Oh, indeed he did, and the general outlines of it are definitely factual. It is only the details that were . . . enhanced."

"I see."

"I had not realized you read Quandish."

"I did spend four years in the court schools; I have some mastery of Quandish, Ermetian, and the Old Imperial common tongue, as well as a smattering of three or four of the Cousiner dialects."

"Quite the scholar, then," Lord Blackfield said in perfect Ermetian— the Algard dialect, Anrel thought it was.

"I have some learning," he replied in the same tongue. Then, in Quandish, he asked, "Have you completed your business for the day?"

"More or less," the Quandishman replied in Walasian.

Anrel glanced at the library's windows and realized he had read all the morning and part of the afternoon away. "Would it be rude to ask what your business was?"

"Master Murau, my only business, wherever I may go and whatever I may do in your empire, is simply to do whatever I can to stave off the disaster I see looming before you and your countrymen, or at the very least to lessen its impact. My every action is directed toward that end."

"Disaster?" Anrel took another look out the window, and realized he could again see smoke rising—not the everyday smoke of forge and hearth, but the thick and wild smoke of burning buildings.

And unless he was completely disoriented, this room did not face the Pensioners' Quarter.

"Disaster," Lord Blackfield repeated. "The empire is nearly bankrupt, your people are starving and at war with one another, the sorcerous nobility is using magic at the slightest whim regardless of cost or effect and seems to ignore anything unpleasant, and the government as a whole seems determined to commit suicide. How can that *not* lead to disaster?"

"I don't know," Anrel admitted, reluctantly closing his book as he stared out at the smoke.

Lord Blackfield's gaze followed his guest's. "Indeed, the disaster has begun, and you saw it for yourself. Lord Allutar has effectively poisoned the capital's bread. The emperor has loosed demons upon his own people, and burned part of his own city. The Grand Council and the emperor and the nobility are all at cross-purposes, refusing to cooperate to restore order. Do you not consider that disastrous?"

"I confess, it does sound disastrous," Anrel agreed, setting the book on a table. He could scarcely argue the point after what he had seen the day before.

"There are complications of which you are probably not aware," Lord Blackfield continued. "The Emperor's Watch is divided—some are unhappy that they are working with mercenary magicians from the Cousins against their own countrymen, and are on the verge of defying their own officers. The City Watch has reportedly been set to spying on them, but their loyalty is also suspect. The Grand Council spent most of this morning arguing over who was to blame for yesterday's fighting, and for the tainted grain, and beyond that they did nothing to attend to the situation. There has been no provision for compensation for those who paid for worthless bread or flour, or for the farmers who grew that ruinous crop. Nothing has been done for the innocents driven from their homes or businesses. Who is to blame, who will pay—they argue about *that*, but do nothing to repair the damage."

"What would you have them do?" Anrel asked, turning to look his host in the eye. "It is not the Grand Council's responsibility, surely— shouldn't the burgrave of Lume take charge of the situation?"

"The burgrave of Lume, Lord Koril Mevidier, is a member of the Grand Council, and has specifically relinquished any responsibility in this, saying that those who caused the problems should rectify them." Anrel thought he heard a note of contempt in Lord Blackfield's voice.

"Ah," Anrel said. "And who does *he* say is responsible?"

"He blames three people," Lord Blackfield said. "He blames Lord Allutar for ruining the wheat, and he blames the emperor for turning his watchmen and his Cousiner magicians loose on the city."

"That's two," Anrel said. "Who is the third?"

Lord Blackfield looked down at him and smiled wryly.

"You," he said.

14

In Which Anrel Considers His Culpability
in the Capital's Misfortunes

"*Me?*" Anrel asked, astonished. "How would the burgrave of Lume know anything of me?"

"Lord Koril knows nothing of Anrel Murau," Lord Blackfield replied, "but he is quite familiar with the reported activities of Alvos of Naith."

"Oh." Anrel blinked.

"Lord Koril is convinced that if the mysterious Alvos had not stirred up popular discontent, Lord Allutar's ghastly error would have been seen as an isolated mishap. If Alvos had not spoken, no one would have dared defy the Emperor's Watch, and a few unfortunate incidents would not have escalated to the level of summoning demons to lay waste to a portion of Lume. If Alvos had never been heard, the Grand Council would be united and able to effectively confront the issues that trouble the empire."

"That's absurd," Anrel said. "I did not *create* discontent; I merely gave it a voice."

"Do you think that so insignificant, then?"

Anrel did not reply immediately; instead he weighed the facts, considered the question carefully, and came to a conclusion he did not like at all.

He *had* contributed to the crisis. Intentionally or not, he had added to the chaos.

"If I had not spoken, someone else might have," he said, trying to find a way to disclaim responsibility. "After all, others spoke in the name of Alvos, all over the empire. Earlier you mentioned someone in Sharam; that was not me. Only in Naith and Beynos was *I* the one who used that name."

Even as the words left his mouth, he regretted them. He knew he sounded like a child trying to spread blame for his mischief, and thereby lessen the portion that would fall on him.

"But you were the first," the Quandishman said mildly. "You were the one who inspired the others."

"Another might have done so," Anrel said before he could stop himself.

"And another sorcerer might have attempted the fertility spell Lord Allutar used. That does not diminish his responsibility, nor does it diminish yours. Another *might* have done it, but you *did*."

Anrel knew he could deny it no further, but he still felt compelled to defend himself. "I did not think this would . . . I did not intend—" He stopped. Saying what he had *not* done would not help. He sighed. "I meant only to embarrass Lord Allutar, and to see that Valin's murder did not profit him."

"I think it is Urunar Kazien's death that is going to ruin him," Lord Blackfield remarked. "*You,* on the other hand, may be responsible for far more extensive damage."

"But all I did was tell people to choose their own delegates for the Grand Council, and not let the sorcerers control it!"

"Hmm." Lord Blackfield tapped his cheek. "Is that all? The reports have you saying rather more than that."

Flustered, Anrel said, "I don't . . . I don't remember my exact words . . ."

"No one does, and undoubtedly the tale has grown in the telling. Some would have it that you spelled out a detailed plan for overthrowing the present system of government and instituting a paradise of equality and prosperity."

"I did no such thing! That's ridiculous. That's not even remotely possible."

"Well, we agree on that much."

Anrel turned and stared out the window again, at the smoke rising from somewhere east of the emperor's palace. "You said you were working to stave off disaster," he said. "Could you be a little more specific?"

"I have been trying to talk sense to those in a position to influence the course of events," he said. "Today, for example, I spoke at length with Delegate li-Parsil, in hopes he might steer the debate in the Grand Council in productive directions."

"Derhin li-Parsil?"

"The very man. You might be interested to know that his account of your speech in Naith does not differ greatly from your own, and is quite free of any descriptions of an egalitarian paradise." The Quandishman sighed. "I regret to say that his compatriot, Delegate tel-Kabanim, is not as restrained."

"From what little I saw of those two, Derhin was always the more sensible," Anrel said.

"That is why I spoke with him, rather than some of the other delegates."

"Of course. And what did you recommend he do, then, to mitigate the disaster that has befallen the empire?"

"I suggested he take immediate steps to reconcile the various elements of the empire—do what he can to reassure the emperor that the Grand Council has no intention of overthrowing him, see to it that good food is brought to the city as quickly as possible and that this is seen to be a joint effort by the council and the emperor, and give no credence to either the radicals who would bring down the entire system, nor the reactionaries who would happily kill countless Walasians if it would ensure their continuance in power."

Anrel nodded. "That sounds sensible," he acknowledged, though privately he thought that overthrowing the emperor and seating his brother might be better.

"Alas, Delegate li-Parsil had doubts about whether these modest goals could actually be attained. He believes that the radicals and the nobles may be so far apart now that peace cannot be made between them. Your name came up in that discussion, just as it did when I spoke with Lord

Koril—Delegate li-Parsil wondered what would happen to any peace that might be arranged if you were to reappear and speak against it."

"But I wouldn't!" Anrel exclaimed.

"Ah, but how is the esteemed delegate to know that? Unlike many of the radicals, you have not published letters explaining your position. You have appeared without warning in two cities—I would have said three, but you deny the one in Sharam—and spoken eloquently, sparking riots in both cases. The possibility that you might appear in the capital and take some unexpected position has been the cause of great concern among the delegates."

"But I *wouldn't*," Anrel repeated. "I have no interest in politics. I spoke only on behalf of my friends, one living and one dead at the time, and both now dead."

"But how is anyone to know that, when you have not *said* so?"

Anrel had no answer for that.

"In fact, Master Murau, I have taken a liberty I hope you will forgive me," the Quandishman said. "I told Delegate li-Parsil that I knew your whereabouts, and could deliver a message, should he wish to do so."

"Oh," Anrel said, startled. He blinked. "Did he give you a message?"

"He did. I felt we should discuss certain other matters, as we just have, before I delivered it."

"I see. What is it, then?"

"Frankly, Master Murau, Delegate li-Parsil does not entirely trust me. I am, after all, a foreigner, and an official of a sometimes hostile government. He has therefore asked me to tell you that he would like to arrange a meeting, so that he might speak with you directly."

"Oh," Anrel said again. He frowned. "But how am I to know he doesn't intend to deliver me to the authorities to be hanged?"

Lord Blackfield smiled. "I see you do not trust him any more than he trusts me. I had thought you two were friends."

"Acquaintances," Anrel said. "He was Valin's friend, and I was Valin's friend, but Derhin and I scarcely knew each other. Their friendship had developed while I was studying in Lume."

"Yet you entreated the people of Naith to choose him as their delegate."

"Because in Lord Valin's absence, he was the closest available approximation. I would not have chosen him myself; I was speaking on Valin's behalf, not my own."

"Does Delegate li-Parsil know that?"

Anrel grimaced. "I have no idea."

"If my opinion means anything, I doubt very much that he intends to betray you."

In fact, Anrel had a great deal of respect for Lord Blackfield's opinion; the Quandishman seemed a sensible, if overly idealistic, person. Still, gambling his own life on Derhin li-Parsil's good faith was not something to be done lightly. "You said he fears what I might do, what I might say in another speech," Anrel said. "Surely, sending me to the gallows in Executioner's Court would put an end to his concerns in that regard."

"Indeed it would, but I do not think that is his intention."

Anrel looked out the window again. He did not like to think of himself as a coward, but neither did he care to take foolish risks.

"If I may," Lord Blackfield said, "there are methods I could suggest that would make it very difficult for him to deliver you to anyone."

Anrel cast him a sideways glance. "I think, my lord, that you are altogether too knowledgeable in certain areas. Such a mastery of intrigue hardly suits a traveler who only seeks to talk a little sense to our sorcerers."

"I am a Gatherman, you will recall, and a hereditary one. Politics is subject to intrigue everywhere, and I learned the skills of the trade at my father's knee."

"But here in Walasia, of course you have no part in any such devices."

"Of course not." He smiled wryly.

Anrel turned back to the window. "If you can arrange it so that we can meet safely," he said, "I would be willing to participate, though in truth, I don't know what Derhin wants of me. I am no one of significance."

"You are the mortal manifestation of a legend, Master Murau. As yourself you may indeed be of no particular importance, but Alvos is a hero of the people. Heroes are useful—and dangerous."

Anrel stared at the drifting smoke. "I scarcely feel dangerous," he said. "Or, for that matter, heroic."

"Others often see us rather differently than we see ourselves."

"Indeed." He turned away from the window and looked at Lord Blackfield. "You, for example—how do you see yourself, my lord?"

"Me?" The Quandishman hesitated; Anrel had the impression he had been about to give a flippant answer, but then thought better of it. He said seriously, "I see myself, Master Murau, as a man upon whom the Father and the Mother have bestowed a great many unasked for gifts— magic, wealth, health, a noble birth—of which I struggle to be worthy."

Anrel nodded. "When first I met you, in Alzur, I thought you an idealistic fool."

Lord Blackfield smiled wryly. "Many people seem to think that."

"Having spoken with you here in Lume, though, I have revised my opinion—I no longer know *what* to think, but I cannot call you a fool."

The Quandishman bowed in acknowledgment. "I am flattered to have risen in your esteem."

"You'll arrange a meeting?"

"Would tomorrow suit you?"

"It would indeed." Anrel grimaced. "After all, what else do I have to occupy my time? I am, at the moment, unemployed and homeless, with neither friends nor family to help me, and prevented from pursuing most ordinary activities by the inconvenience of being under sentence of death. Anything that might distract me from these unhappy circumstances, as your admirable ancestor's book has, is very welcome."

"Pray tell me, dear guest, that I do not actually detect a note of bitterness! You have a home here with me for the present, and I hope that someday you may consider me a friend. This sedition nonsense is a mere temporary obstacle, I am sure. After all, are you not meeting with a government official tomorrow?"

Anrel cocked his head. He had not considered that aspect. "I am, am I not? Do you think that Derhin might be able to arrange a pardon of some sort?"

"One can hope that he might."

"Indeed."

"And if no pardon or parole is forthcoming, I scarcely think it means you must spend your entire life as a fugitive. Sedition is not a crime in Quand, and most certainly sedition directed at the Walasian Empire will not trouble anyone in my homeland."

Anrel blinked up at his host. "Are you suggesting I might flee the empire entirely, and take refuge in your homeland?"

"I believe I am, yes. Is the idea so utterly outrageous, then?"

"I have no means of reaching Quand; I cannot afford passage by sea. Perhaps Ermetia or the Cousins would be more practical—"

"Oh, nonsense, Master Murau! You can reach Quand quite nicely by riding thither in my coach. I would welcome the company."

"Across the Dragonlands? I thought only sorcerers could do that."

"I *am* a sorcerer. If you thought I could not bring others with me, how do you think Harban came here?"

"Ah," Anrel said, feeling foolish.

"A young scholar, thoroughly conversant in Walasian history, might well find employment in Ondine," Lord Blackfield continued. "There are those who take an interest in our largest neighbor, but who prefer not to venture across the border in person."

"I . . . do not think that would suit me," Anrel replied slowly. "I am a loyal Walasian, whatever I may think of certain officials, or even of our present emperor. To serve a foreign and sometimes hostile government— that seems to me far more treasonous than anything I said in Naith or Beynos."

"I understand." Lord Blackfield nodded. "Indeed, I sympathize. Still, I would think a place might be found that you would deem acceptable."

"Much as I appreciate your interest and consideration, my lord, I am not sure I could be happy in a foreign land."

"Well, then, perhaps a new name and identity, and a home in some corner of the empire where the odds of encountering anyone who might recognize your face are minuscule? Pordurim, perhaps—that village in Vaun that produced the lovely wine we drank yesterday. I have arranged such things before."

Startled, Anrel said, "You have?"

Lord Blackfield smiled. "Why, yes—a few seasons back, when certain persons were accused of a crime I felt could not possibly have been their doing, I arranged for them to relocate."

Anrel scarcely knew what to make of this admission—or perhaps it was not so much an admission as a boast. "Do you make a *habit* of flouting imperial law, then?"

"I would not say a *habit,* sir, but I do not shirk from doing so when I feel justice is better served by my methods than the empire's."

"And you have done this with impunity?"

"Say rather, I do not believe anyone in authority is aware of my actions."

"If you have helped fugitives to disappear, how can the officials involved not be aware that something is amiss?"

The Quandishman spread his hands. "Oh, I am sure they know things have not gone as expected."

"And you have no fear that they might connect these misfortunes to you?"

"I am a sorcerer, Master Murau, and a good one."

Anrel blinked at what seemed an irrelevance. "I do not see how that can ensure your safety from discovery."

Lord Blackfield sighed. "I can work a glamour, sir. I can bind perceptions, or memories. For the most part, if I do not wish to be seen, I am not. If I do not wish my presence to be remembered, it is not. If I want someone to see me as a bent old woman, or a beardless child, why, then, that is how I will be seen!"

"But that . . . I have never heard of . . . Isn't a glamour a difficult spell?"

"Oh, fair to middling difficult, yes. As I have said, I am a powerful sorcerer."

Anrel had known Lord Blackfield was a sorcerer, but had not realized his magical skills were as great as that. The witches Anrel had known had considered glamours to be far beyond their own abilities, and Uncle Dorias had certainly never attempted one. "I had not known anyone in Quand could work magic of that sort," he said.

One side of Lord Blackfield's mouth rose wryly. "Well, we would hardly *tell* you, would we?"

"I suppose not," Anrel acknowledged. "You surprise me, my lord, and you once again make me suspicious of your motives."

Lord Blackfield sighed. "I wish no one harm, Master Murau—not you, nor any of your friends, nor for that matter, any of your enemies. I came to Walasia on behalf of the Lantern Society, just as I have said. The society was created to discourage the use of dark sorcery—to cast a light into dark places, as the name suggests, in an attempt to make our world a better place. That is what brought me into the empire; I intended merely to visit with sorcerers and try to dissuade them from using black magic. When I arrived, though, I found signs of impending catastrophe on every side—famine, oppression, injustice. I could not ignore these wrongs. I have sought to alleviate them; I freely admit that I have pursued justice and mercy, rather than law and order. I cannot stop the coming disaster, whatever form it may take, but I hope I may be able to lessen its severity and perhaps spare a few individuals from its fury."

"So you have aided criminals in escaping."

"No, sir, I have aided *innocents* in escaping. I have been quite selective."

"You did not save Urunar Kazien."

"He was not innocent of the crime for which he died, nor was he yet at liberty when his circumstances came to my attention."

"I suppose not." Anrel stared at his host for a long moment. "I did just what they say I did," he said at last.

"You spoke out against injustice. I cannot consider that a crime, no matter what your magistrates may say."

"I have committed other crimes to survive, many of them. I cannot claim innocence."

The Quandishman shrugged. "No one is entirely innocent. I believe you to be a good man at heart. You spoke out in honor of a friend, and in an attempt to save a life, not for your own benefit."

That was true, but somehow did not seem to entirely satisfy Anrel's objections. He had spent the past season deceiving, swindling, and robbing Lume's wealthier citizens. Did that count for nothing?

But then, Lord Blackfield did not actually *know* what Anrel had done during his stay in the Pensioners' Quarter, and Anrel felt no need to tell him. He asked, "So you would spirit me out of the country, or hide me away in some village somewhere?"

"If you wished it, yes."

"Thank you, my lord," Anrel said, meaning it. "But let us wait and see what Derhin has to say before we make any hasty decisions."

"Of course." The Quandishman bowed. "I will leave you to your book, then."

He turned, and left the room.

Anrel stared after him, and did not pick up the book again for several minutes.

15

In Which Anrel Speaks with a Delegate
to the Grand Council

Anrel watched as the blindfolded Derhin was led into the room, and his hands untied.

Anrel was sitting at a table in an upstairs room above a ruined bakery—the baker and his family had fled the city, at least for the moment, and his abandoned home made as good a meeting place as any. The mob had done considerable damage to the apartment, as well as to the shop, but the table and two chairs remained intact. Anrel found it amazing that the entire building had not been burned to the ground— though there was a faint whiff of smoke that implied someone had made the attempt. Why the flames had not spread Anrel did not know, and did not much care; it was enough that the place was still here, and suitable for this meeting.

Harban had fetched Derhin hither, his wrists bound and his eyes covered so that he would not know where he was being brought. Anrel had arrived earlier and had prepared the room, making sure the doors were closed and the windows covered so that there would be no clue to their location.

Now Derhin li-Parsil stood quietly as Lord Blackfield's manservant unwound the rope from the delegate's wrists. Harban stuffed the cord into one of the pockets in his brown woolen coat, then reached up and removed the black leather blindfold, as well.

Derhim blinked; the room was dim with the shutters and curtains closed, but still brighter than what he had seen on the way here. He took a second to focus; then his gaze fell on Anrel.

"Delegate li-Parsil," Anrel said. "It's been some time, hasn't it? Congratulations on your election to the Grand Council."

"Anrel Murau," Derhin said, eyeing him warily. "Or should I say, Alvos the orator?"

Anrel shrugged. "Either name will serve. I understand you wished to speak with me?"

"I did. I do."

"Sit," Anrel said, gesturing at the other unbroken chair. "Let us talk."

"Thank you," Derhin said, taking his seat and keeping his gaze on Anrel's face.

Harban cleared his throat to catch Anrel's attention; Anrel looked up, and said, "Thank you, sir. If you could wait outside, please?"

Harban essayed a quick bow, then slipped quietly out the door to the stairwell.

When he had gone, and the door had clicked shut, Derhin glanced around the room. "Is this where you are living?" he asked.

"No," Anrel said. "This is somewhere we could meet safely, nothing more. After today I doubt I will ever again set foot in this room."

"Ah, I see." Derhin hesitated.

"Come, sir," Anrel said. "You asked for this meeting; surely you have something to say? Questions to ask, news to impart, requests to make, orders to give?"

Derhin grimaced. "Yes, well, in truth, I was partly motivated by a desire to see whether our Quandish friend was telling the truth when he said he had seen you."

"He was," Anrel said. "I can understand, though, how you might wonder about his veracity. I have never caught him in a lie, nor had good reason to doubt what he says, but somehow he does not inspire great confidence in his truthfulness. One often has the impression he is leaving out important details."

"My own thoughts, exactly!" Derhin smiled.

"I cannot believe, though, that you agreed to be bound and blind-folded and transported through half of Lume merely to test a man's honesty. Surely, you had some other goal?"

"I wanted to see you," Derhin said. "To see that you are indeed still alive and well. You do know you are a legend, I assume."

"I have been told as much, yes—but really, Alvos is the legend, and I am merely the man, Anrel Murau."

"Of course, of course." Derhin nodded understanding. "Still, this is as close as I can come to meeting the legend."

Anrel did not reply; he was not comfortable with his legendary status. After a moment's silence, he asked, "You had no other questions?"

"Oh, I have a thousand questions!" Derhin exclaimed. "So many I scarcely know where to begin."

"Begin wherever you please; I have all day." Anrel settled back comfortably in his chair.

Derhin paused for a moment, apparently choosing his approach, then asked, "Why are you in Lume? With every watchman in the empire looking for you, why would you come to the capital? I thought you must have fled to the Cousins. When Lord Blackfield claimed to have spoken with you, at first I thought he meant you had sought sanctuary in Quand."

"I am a loyal Walasian, Delegate, whatever some sorcerers and their lackeys might claim," Anrel said, his chin held high. Then he lowered it and cocked his head. "Besides, I knew people here, and I know no one in the Cousins, or in Quand. I studied in Lume for four years, remember?"

"Then you have not come here to carry out some grand revolutionary scheme?"

"Unless staying alive and free is a scheme, I'm afraid not."

"And your speech in Naith—was *that* part of some larger design?"

Anrel sighed. "Would that it were," he said. "I might look like less of a fool." He shook his head. "Lord Allutar killed Lord Valin to silence him; I was determined that Allutar would not profit by his crime, and there-fore Valin's words must be heard. That was all. I gave no thought to the consequences, for either Lord Allutar, or myself, or the empire; I merely wanted Valin's words to be heard."

Derhin stroked his beard, then said, "You told the people of Naith to elect *me* as their delegate."

"I advised them to do so, yes."

"Why?"

"Because your beliefs, as you described them in that wine garden in Aulix Square, more closely matched Valin's own than did those of anyone else I could name."

"That was all?"

"That was all. I hardly knew you or Amanir, but no one else I knew in Aulix had taken up anything like Valin's positions. I knew some suitable firebrands in Lume, but I was speaking in Naith."

"So there was no intention to . . . to use us, once we were elected?"

"Use you? In what manner?" Anrel shook his head. "No, I had no hidden motive or secret agenda." He hesitated. "Though now that you mention it, I understand that several members of the Grand Council feel that Alvos in some way contributed to their election."

"Yes."

"Then—might it be possible for the Grand Council to grant me a pardon? I would very much like to go home to Alzur, see my uncle, and return to my old life."

"I—don't know," Derhin said. He bit his lip. "No, that isn't the truth. I *do* know. I'm sorry, sir; it isn't possible."

"You are certain? I could give my parole to refrain from political activity."

"I'm certain. I know the alliances and loyalties in the Grand Council all too well. To grant you absolution—well, you see, in the early days, when we still had high hopes for what we might accomplish, we set forth rules, and we are now too divided to alter any of those rules. Certain actions require more than a simple majority. Granting any sort of pardon or parole requires the approval of three-fourths of the entire council, and these days it is almost impossible to get three-fourths to vote, let alone all vote the same way." He grimaced. "It was feared that anything less than a three-fourths majority would encourage corruption, that wealthy criminals might purchase pardons, or that we might grant pardons for our own political gain—which, frankly, would seem to be exactly what you are asking of me."

"What? No, no—I want nothing more to do with politics. I want only to be allowed to live openly again."

"But do you not think there would be political consequences were it to become widely known that I had arranged a pardon for the infamous, the brilliant, the mysterious, the legendary Alvos?"

"I had not given the matter any thought," Anrel admitted. "Which was, I suppose, dreadfully naive of me."

"I would say it was, yes." Derhin stared across the table. "You know, Master Murau, I find it hard to believe that you are truly as apolitical as you claim. You are *Alvos,* after all, who gave fiery speeches in half the cities of the empire."

"I did not," Anrel said sharply. "I gave only two, in Naith and Beynos."

"It was not you who spoke in Ferrith?"

"No."

"I knew most were imposters, but I had thought that one genuine."

"No. Naith and Beynos, nowhere else."

"Not in, perhaps, the Pensioners' Quarter?"

Anrel frowned. "I will not deny I spent time in the Pensioners' Quarter, and was there the day before yesterday when demons set it ablaze, but I gave no speeches there."

"But you were there?"

"Yes."

"Then it's true? The watch sent *demons* into the quarter?"

"Of course it's true," Anrel said, startled. "Was there any doubt?"

"There are those who claim it was men with torches, perhaps men under a glamour, who set the fires and burned out the beggars and whores."

"No," Anrel said. "Three demons. That was no glamour. And when I departed I saw the magicians who had summoned them, standing on the walkway above Harbinger Court."

"You will swear to this?"

"If you wish; it is the truth."

"Would you swear to it before the Grand Council?"

Anrel glowered at him. "Have you not just explained that I cannot be pardoned? I am under sentence of death for sedition; I cannot appear before the council."

"Of course, I understand; I was foolish to ask. But to have Alvos himself, *Alvos*, swear that the emperor's men used demons . . ."

"I do not see why I would be believed if other witnesses are not; surely, there are a hundred observers who could tell you what they saw."

"There are . . . those who claim to be survivors, yes. Most are reluctant to speak."

The implications of the word "survivors" did not please Anrel. He felt suddenly guilty that he had not, in the day and a half since the attack, ventured back into the quarter to assess the damage and see what he might do to help. He had been seduced by the amenities and peace of Lord Blackfield's home, the return to the leisurely and comfortable life he had known as his uncle's fosterling, and he had neglected the duties he owed his friends.

"I am sorry to hear that," Anrel said.

"The officers of the Emperor's Watch reported that one man seemed to be the leader of the mob there. I wondered whether that might have been you."

"No. That was—" Anrel caught himself before he gave Doz's name— even though it was not his real name, it might be enough to track him down. Anrel had quite enough on his conscience without endangering another friend. "That was someone else."

Derhin observed the pause, and said, "You know who it was."

"Yes. I know him. He once held a knife to my back." He hoped that would be sufficiently misleading to keep Derhin from pressing for more information.

"Do you know his name?"

Anrel shrugged. "He used a dozen names in the time I knew him." He did not mention that most of these were in service to the various swindles that he and Doz had conducted as partners.

"Do you think you could locate him, to testify before the Grand Council?"

"I have no idea," Anrel said truthfully—his ability to locate Doz would depend on what and who remained in the Pensioners' Quarter, and he had not yet learned what the situation there might be.

That was not where he had thought Derhin's questions were leading, however. He had assumed that Derhin wanted to turn Doz over to the magistrates.

"Why do you ask?" he said.

"Because," Derhin replied, "we are looking for . . ." He paused, then glanced at the door where Harban had departed.

"He may well be listening," Anrel said, guessing the delegate's thoughts, "but what if he is? He is a Quandish manservant."

"He may well gossip with Walasians, though." He sighed. "But I don't suppose it can be hidden for long, not when hundreds of delegates have been involved in the debate. Anrel, *someone* must pay for the crimes that have been committed against the Walasian people. Many of the nobles want to find a scapegoat among the commoners—*you,* as Alvos, would serve nicely, or this mysterious leader in the Pensioners' Quarter. Most of us, though, do not believe that would be just—and more important, we do not believe it would help. The people of Lume are angry, Anrel, and they are not angry with *you,* or with the thieves and beggars, or now that word has spread of what really happened, with the bakers or bargemen. They are angry with the sorcerers who ruined the Raish Valley grain harvest, with the magistrates who allowed it, with the officials who rushed the grain to Lume without noticing its polluted nature, with the watchmen who fought them in the streets, with the foreign magicians who unleashed demons on their fellow Walasians. They are *furious,* and they demand retribution. Some of the sorcerers on the council have tried to soothe the city with spells, but such is the popular rage that this magic is like sprinkling a handful of water on a raging bonfire. The emperor has refused to take action—his representative to the council told us yesterday, in so many words, that His Majesty considers the matter settled, a misunderstanding that is now past and nothing more. The burgrave of Lume has said it is none of his concern—the grain was not grown within his walls, nor did he order it shipped hither, nor did he have any say in the actions of the Emperor's Watch, while the City Watch was not involved. The captains of the Emperor's Watch say they were merely doing as they were ordered. The Lords Magistrate say they can do nothing. Only the Grand Council is in a position to act, and willing to do so—but we are not yet determined upon what action to take. If we had someone the people would accept as a reliable witness who would swear that demons were turned upon Walasian citizens, then we could demand that the foreign magicians be punished, and that would be better than nothing. If the people believed the whole thing to be a plot of the Ermetian king, or of some sorcerous conspiracy in the Cousins, then we might find enough peace to restore order and calm."

"But it *wasn't* the Ermetians or a sorcerous conspiracy, was it?"

"No." Derhin grimaced. "At least, I don't think so. Some delegates may well believe that it was, but I do not. I think our own government was responsible, not through malice, but through carelessness."

Anrel gazed at Derhin thoughtfully. "If the mob wants blood, can you not give them blood? Who *was* responsible?"

"I think you *know* who was, at root, responsible."

"Humor me, if you would be so kind. Tell me their names."

Derhin sighed. "The demons were summoned by the magicians that the emperor himself had hired at the request of the empress. We believe the magicians were acting on the emperor's own orders. The Emperor's Watch, as well, was acting on either the emperor's orders, or orders given by one of his appointed officers. The grain was rushed to Lume at the emperor's personal instigation. Every official, every watchman, every sorcerer involved acted at the emperor's behest."

"Can you not say as much to the people?"

"Anrel, he is the *emperor*."

"And you are a delegate of the Grand Council, which has the authority to remove the emperor."

"Anrel, be serious. In theory, yes, we have the authority to do whatever we please, but we do not have the *power* to do so. The Emperor's Watch does not answer to the Grand Council. The mercenaries from Ermetia and the Cousins, both soldiers and sorcerers, do not answer to the Grand Council. The sorcerers and their underlings, the guards and watches and armies, do not answer to the Grand Council. If we declare Lurias to no longer be emperor he will declare the Grand Council disbanded, and the Emperor's Watch will enforce his decree, not ours, regardless of what the law might say."

Anrel was tempted to argue, but he did not; he knew that Derhin was right. "Can you not explain to the emperor that the mob demands a sacrifice? Can he not let them have a few underlings to hang?"

Derhin glanced at the door again. "I should not tell you this."

Anrel shrugged. "Then don't. I am here at your request; I have no hold on you."

"Oh, you most certainly *do* have a hold upon me, Alvos," Derhin replied, leaning forward. "Without you I would not be a delegate. Without you the Grand Council would be the emperor's puppet, and from what I have seen of His Imperial Majesty's work so far, I fear that might well have meant the empire's downfall. We owe you a great deal."

"But not a pardon," Anrel replied bitterly.

"No," Derhin said, sitting up again. "Not a pardon. Not now. Perhaps someday."

"I am owed an uncollectible debt, then."

"Yes. I admit it; you are. You are a sensible man; I saw that back in Naith. You understand."

"If I were a sensible man, I would have no *need* for a pardon."

Derhin smiled crookedly. "Perhaps," he said. "Nonetheless, we are here, I am in your debt, and I would appreciate your counsel."

"My *counsel*? Delegate li-Parsil, I am merely an outlaw clerk, a student of law and history who failed to find an appointment."

"You are a man my late friend Lord Valin trusted and considered a close friend."

Anrel could not deny that; he stared at Derhin in silent frustration for a few seconds, then said, "Please yourself, then, but let it be upon your own head."

"We have sent envoys to the emperor," Derhin said. "We have told him that this was *not* a mere misunderstanding, it is *not* past, and it is *not* settled. We have asked him to deliver to the magistrates, or to the council, the foreign magicians and whatever officials were responsible for distributing polluted wheat. So far, he has refused to listen."

"That is unfortunate."

"Yes."

"Can you not have them arrested without the emperor's involvement?"

"The emperor has said he will not permit it, that they were acting upon his own orders and are not to be punished for obeying him."

"The emperor is a fool," Anrel replied. There had been times he would not have stated it so bluntly, but he was already condemned for sedition; what further harm could it do to speak plainly?

"I have been aware of that for some time now," Derhin said, "but in this case he may have some reason for his reluctance. You know it is traditional to allow the condemned to make final statements; if everyone we hang says he was acting upon the emperor's orders, that will not enhance His Imperial Majesty's situation."

"True. Could those final statements be prevented, perhaps? Threats made against the families of the condemned to ensure silence?"

Derhin stared at him. "By the Mother, Anrel! Threaten innocents? Women and children?"

Anrel gazed back calmly. "Lord Valin was an idealist; I am not. Even so, I am not suggesting such threats be carried out, only that they be made. Harming innocents would not benefit the government; it would instead provoke the populace. If no one but the condemned is aware that such threats were made, though, then the knowledge will pass harmlessly into the afterlife with them."

Derhin's shocked expression faded only slightly. "I don't . . . I don't believe such a thing has been suggested."

"You might bring it up, then. How much have you offered the emperor for your scapegoats?"

Derhin blinked. "What?"

"Well, you want him to do something he doesn't want to do. In such a case, you must offer payment for his cooperation."

"Oh," Derhin said. His expression turned thoughtful. "I had not thought of it in those terms. We had told him that he needed to act to appease the people of Lume, but I don't believe we have offered anything more in return."

"He probably does not consider the common people a real danger."

"As you said, he is a fool."

"You will continue your negotiations with him, then?"

"I am sure we will."

For a moment the two men sat silently, contemplating each other across the table. Then Anrel said, "There is another name you have not mentioned in this matter."

He had resisted mentioning this until now, despite the obvious temptation. Here, at last, was a chance to see Lord Allutar brought to trial—not for murder, as Anrel would have preferred, but for the misuse of sorcery and endangering the common welfare. Valin and Reva would be avenged, albeit not as directly as Anrel might have hoped.

"Oh?"

"You made a reference to sorcerers who polluted the Raish Valley farmlands, but you surely know that was the doing of one man, not several."

"Was it? I have heard rumors . . ."

"Yes. The landgrave of Aulix. Lord Allutar Hezir."

"How do you know that?"

That stopped Anrel for a moment. How *did* he know?

Lord Blackfield had said that Allutar's fertility spell was responsible for the pollution, but did Anrel actually *know* that to be the case?

He frowned, trying to compose a reply.

"It doesn't matter," Derhin said before Anrel could answer. "We can't touch Lord Allutar in any case."

"What? Why *not*?"

"Because he is a member of the Grand Council."

"What?"

"Have I not mentioned that? Has no one told you? Delegates to the Grand Council are granted a full pardon for any and all crimes they may have committed prior to their election. It became necessary to enact such a decree to prevent a constant stream of accusations and attempts to discredit or depose delegates—in the early days, just after the winter solstice, some factions developed a tactic of having opposing delegates arrested on purely fictional charges just long enough to prevent them from voting on certain matters. The blanket pardon put an end to it. Delegates are now answerable only to the council itself, not to any lesser authorities or magistrates."

The audacity of this staggered Anrel. "That's . . . that's very convenient," he said.

"It was necessary," Derhin replied. "At any rate, Lord Allutar cast his fertility spell before his election, so he has a pardon that we cannot withdraw without casting the council into renewed chaos. Even assuming that any magistrate would find a landgrave guilty of a crime for trying to improve his land's wheat yield—and we both know how outrageous an assumption that is—we cannot make any such charge."

"So of those guilty of malfeasance in the recent events, *all* of them are protected by either the emperor, or by the Grand Council itself."

"I am afraid that is indeed the case."

"That's ridiculous."

"Nonetheless, it is the case."

Anrel glanced at the shuttered windows, and sighed deeply. "Delegate li-Parsil," he said, "I am beginning to think that the empire *deserves* the disasters facing it."

"Only the Mother and the Father can say whether that is so, Master Murau," Derhin replied. "But I fear you may be right."

16

In Which Anrel Visits Several Parts
of the Imperial Capital

The remainder of the conversation achieved nothing of any great significance; Anrel told Derhin something of a few of his exploits and inquired after the health of Amanir tel-Kabanim, while Derhin told Anrel a great deal about the work and workings of the Grand Council since it had first convened. At last, though, both ran out of questions, and they agreed to separate.

Anrel waited while Harban once again blindfolded Derhin, bound his hands, and led him out to Lord Blackfield's coach, and once he heard the rattle of harness and creak of the wheels, Anrel descended to street level himself and set out on foot—not for Dezar House, but for the Pensioners' Quarter.

The damage was far worse than he had expected; anything that might burn had burned, and not a single structure in the quarter still had a roof. Even most of the walls of stone and brick had fallen; bricks had cracked and crumbled in the intense heat, and mortar had burned away. Blackened corpses still lay in the rubble here and there. The major streets had largely been cleared of rubble, but for the most part the watchmen and laborers had not yet ventured into the still-smoldering ruins on either side.

Ordinarily after two days in the summer heat the stench of those bodies would be horrific, but these were so badly scorched that the smell of decay was almost undetectable.

The smell of smoke, on the other hand, was overpowering.

Anrel avoided the workmen clearing the wreckage as best he could; there were half a dozen teams moving through the streets, hauling away debris. Each of these groups was composed of three watchmen and half a dozen laborers, and Anrel did not want any contact with watchmen—though these wore the deep red of the City Watch, rather than the green of the Emperor's Watch.

Except for those crews, the only signs of life were insects—ants and buzzing flies. Even the rats had not yet returned.

This devastation was at the emperor's orders, and according to Derhin, His Imperial Majesty considered it a mere incident, over and done with. Anrel wondered whether His Imperial Majesty had *seen* just what his hired magicians had done, seen it with his own eyes.

He made his way through the once-familiar streets now rendered strange, and found his way to his own erstwhile home on Tranquillity Street.

The house, once home to a dozen people, was now not even a shell, but merely a collection of fragmentary walls in a sea of ash and charcoal. Anrel took some comfort in the fact that he could see no evidence of human remains; apparently all his housemates had escaped.

Or perhaps they had died in the streets, but at any rate they had not been caught in their beds. He had not thought that any of the three boys would have allowed themselves to be trapped here, but the old man, Apolien—well, who knew what he might have done? He had always been incomprehensible. And there had been the people in the other rooms—a mother and two daughters in one, a husband and wife in another, a pair of brothers and their adopted son in a third.

Where had they all gone? Surely, they had not all perished; where were they, then? Some might still be hiding in the ancient tunnels, but most had probably scattered through the city, hiding in alleys, perhaps taking shelter under the watchmen's arches—every thief and beggar knew that the best place to hide from the watch was in the shadows under their very feet.

But they might come back to see what had become of their former home, just as he had. He leaned over a ruined wall and picked up a blackened scrap of iron from Apolien's bed frame, then scratched a quick message in thieves' cipher into the soot covering the wall, the plaster that showed through the letters standing out whitely against the black.

It read simply, DYSSAN—DEZAR HOUSE. He thought that would be enough so that anyone looking for him would find him. They would need to figure out that he was staying on the second floor with Lord Blackfield, and not with any of the other residents above or below, but he did not think that would be a real obstacle.

That done, he turned and walked away. There was nothing left for him here.

He arrived back in Lord Blackfield's rooms in time for supper, and the Quandishman questioned him as they dined, eager for every detail of both his conversation with Derhin and his visit to the Pensioners' Quarter.

"If you will pardon the indelicacy, Master Murau," Lord Blackfield said when Anrel had finished his account, "I take it that for the past season or two you have been making your living outside the law."

"It is difficult for a wanted criminal to do otherwise," Anrel replied.

"Do you intend to resume your life of crime?"

"Not if I can avoid it, my lord."

"Yet you returned to the Pensioners' Quarter, and looked for your former comrades in your illicit enterprises."

"Say rather, my lord, that I looked for my friends and neighbors."

"Of course, of course; how terribly rude of me! And I am sure that I do not need to tell you that I would consider it most inappropriate should you participate in any sort of thievery or other misbehavior while living here as my guest."

Annoyed, Anrel said, "My lord, while I stay here, I have food and shelter far superior to anything I might obtain by other means. I have no *reason* to resume my old habits."

"Of course! But you may not yet have considered a possibility. I take it you left a message of some sort, telling your former neighbors where they might find you?"

Anrel had not mentioned the note he had scratched on the wall, but it was not an unreasonable inference from some of his remarks. "I did," he acknowledged.

"Naturally, and I would hardly expect otherwise. However, I want to impress upon you that you must make it absolutely clear to any of your friends who might visit that any pilferage or other damage to my household is not acceptable. Remind them that while I may not be a noble of the Walasian Empire, I am nonetheless a sorcerer. I know how to place wards upon my belongings, and I feel no need to rely on watchmen to protect my home or my person."

"Of course, my lord!" The possibility that Mieshel or Doz or Po might think it clever to steal a few choice little treasures from Lord Blackfield had occurred to him, and Anrel knew it was a legitimate concern, but he thought he could keep any visitors in line.

"Also, if you don't mind, I might be interested in meeting some of your old comrades. I might be able to find employment for some of them."

Startled, Anrel said, "I will mention this, my lord."

"Thank you. Now, might I interest you in a little wine? I have a case of red newly arrived from Lithrayn . . ."

The following day was the solstice; there was obviously no possibility of visiting the Adirane family land, so Anrel accompanied Lord Blackfield and Harban to one of the public shrines on New Altar Street, and said his quarterly prayers to the Mother and the Father, thanking them for his survival and for his good fortune in finding a place with the Quandishman, and pleading for mercy for Reva Lir's soul.

He thought about Tazia with longing, but said nothing about her at the shrine. Whatever her fate might be, he felt he had no say in it after so thoroughly failing her sister.

It was midmorning two days later, as Anrel was stepping out onto the street, that he heard a hiss and turned to find Shoun leaning against the corner of the porch. The boy's face was smeared with soot, and his clothes, never good to begin with, had several visible tears.

Anrel beckoned to the lad. "Walk with me," he said.

With a quick glance around, Shoun scurried to Anrel's side, and the two of them strolled side by side along the boulevard. They were so obviously mismatched that they drew stares from a few pedestrians and the driver of a passing coach, but Anrel ignored this.

"It's good to see you," Anrel said, as they rounded a corner onto a less-traveled street. "I was worried."

"I was lucky," Shoun said.

"What about Mieshel and Po?"

"They're safe, too. Mieshel and I went out through the alley behind Victory Square together, and we found Po later."

"Where are you staying?"

Shoun looked mistrustfully along the tree-lined street, and said, "Around."

Anrel had lived in the Pensioners' Quarter long enough to know what that meant; if the boys had found a new home, the answer would have been, "We have a place."

"What about you?" Shoun asked, looking up at him. "You look well."

"I am," Anrel said. "I took a chance on an old acquaintance, and he took me in."

Shoun looked straight ahead again. "You were luckier than we were, then."

"I was," Anrel agreed. "I was very fortunate indeed."

"I saw your note."

"I wanted to know what had become of everyone."

Shoun shrugged. "We're getting by."

"Do you know about anyone else?"

"I see some of them around."

Anrel looked up as they approached a watchmen's arch; no one was visible atop it just now. "I suppose they're staying out of sight, if one doesn't know where to look."

"Mostly."

"It doesn't sound as if you trust me."

Shoun cast him a look. "I came to find you, didn't I?"

"Yes, you did, but you aren't *entirely* sure it isn't some sort of trap, are you?"

"Is it?"

Anrel shook his head. "No. Thank you for coming."

They walked on, under the arch, where Anrel stopped, glanced around to make sure no one else was in sight, and bent down to whisper to the boy.

"Listen, Shoun," he said. "I'm staying with a Quandish lord—I met him in Alzur last year, and after the fire he took me in. He claims he's a do-gooder visiting Lume to try to help out, but I think he may really be a Quandish spy of some sort. He's made friends with some of the delegates to the Grand Council, he has connections in high places, but he says he's interested in meeting some of the others from the Pensioners' Quarter—some people like you. I think he may be hiring people to spy for him. Now, if you want, I can introduce you to him. He probably won't take you in the way he did me, it wouldn't look right, but he may be willing to pay you to do things for him. Are you interested?"

Shoun blinked, then stared at Anrel as if he had gone mad. "Of *course* I'm interested!"

"He may want you to spy for Quand. You're Walasian."

"I'm not stupid, Dyssan, and I'm not a traitor, either. I can run his errands without being disloyal. If he asks me to do something wrong, I'll just disappear."

Anrel straightened up. "Good enough, then." He looked around, judging the hour from the shadows. "He's at the Aldian Baths right now, listening to the Grand Council argue, but he'll be home for supper. Come to the servants' entrance at Dezar House when the sun reaches the rooftops, and we'll arrange something—either I'll meet you, or Lord Blackfield's man Harban will. He's an old Quandishman with a white braid. Bring a friend or two if you want—but no more than two, this first time. If the job doesn't work out, at the very least I'll see you're fed."

"Before sunset, back door at Dezar House. Good."

"Now, I was planning to go down to the Promenade and see how the city is faring. You're welcome to join me, but if there's anything else you want to attend to . . ."

"I do believe my schedule could accommodate you," Shoun said, smiling for the first time since Anrel had spotted him by the porch.

Together the two made their way down to the banks of the Galdin, and along the waterfront toward the emperor's palace, continuing to ignore the stares they drew. As they came in sight of the palace Anrel studied the ramparts, and noticed something that looked odd.

"The cannon," he said, pointing. "I remember them as being a brighter red. Perhaps the light . . . ?"

"They were fired into the crowd during the riots," Shoun told him. "The smoke stained them."

That was what Anrel had feared. He had not heard them, so far as he knew—not that he knew what cannon sounded like, but the stories said they roared like thunder, and he had not noticed anything fitting that description. Of course he had been far away, and the sound might well have been lost in the chaos of the fire.

He had learned as a student that it was the Walasian custom to paint new cannon red so that their crews could judge how much use they had seen by how much of the barrel was stained black with smoke, and could adjust their handling appropriately. A new cannon might have poor welds or other flaws, and might well explode when it was first fired; likewise, an old and heavily used cannon might have eroded away enough of its metal that it, too, might burst. Therefore either pure red or pure black cannon were considered untrustworthy and handled with caution, while one that was half red and half black was deemed experienced, but sturdy and safe.

The cannon on the palace walls had always been bright, pure red—until now.

"You saw that? You saw them fired?"

Shoun shook his head. "No. But it's all over the city."

Anrel knew that did not mean the tale was true, but the darkened mouths of the cannon certainly provided good evidence. He shuddered. As if demons were not enough, the emperor had apparently turned guns on his own people. What was *wrong* with the man? Did he not understand what he was doing?

The sorcerers, the nobles, were supposed to keep order among the common people; that was not the emperor's responsibility. While the Emperor's Watch was indeed used to watch over the capital, since the city's own burgrave simply couldn't afford to safeguard so large a population without that assistance, it was certainly not the job of foreign magicians or palace guards to interfere.

Had any of the nobility addressed the matter? There was supposed to be a balance between the emperor and the nobles—the sorcerers had their magic, so that they could restrain the emperor and his soldiers if necessary, while the emperor had the Great List that could strip any treasonous sorcerer of that magic.

But it had only been a few days, and the existence of the Grand Council probably complicated the situation.

Anrel had never believed that the Grand Council could accomplish anything useful; he had always taken it for granted that a way would be found to pay off or repudiate the empire's debts, that the famine would end either through better weather or magical intervention, and that everything would then return to what it had always been.

Now, after seeing the demons, and the cannon, and the vandalized bakeries, and the ruined bread, he was not sure. *Could* the empire go on as before after this?

But then, order had been restored after the wars. That had all been before he was born, but he had read about it in his student days. The wars with Ermetia or in the Cousins had not seriously strained anything but the imperial finances, but the Quandish Wars had seen two invasions of Walasia that had laid waste to broad swathes of the empire.

Yet the empire had recovered, had flourished, and now traded with Quand and allowed Quandishmen like Lord Blackfield to wander freely.

Perhaps this crisis would pass, as the wars had, and order *would* be restored.

Anrel wondered whether that would really be a good thing.

17

In Which Anrel Learns Something of Imperial Politics

Lord Blackfield returned home earlier than Anrel had expected; the afternoon was scarcely half over when the big Quandishman flung open the door and stalked into the sitting room, his expression stormy.

"Good afternoon, my lord," Anrel said, looking up from his current book.

"Oh, it is anything *but* good, Master Murau!" Lord Blackfield roared, flinging his hat at the wall.

Then, as if a bubble had burst, his obvious rage vanished, and he was as calm as ever, standing coolly in the center of the room, his hands folded behind his back, his eyebrows slightly raised.

"*Do* excuse me," he said. "I can't imagine what I was thinking, bellowing like that and flinging my hat about. What would my haberdasher say if he saw me treating his work so callously? I'm sure the poor fellow would be reduced to tears by such inconsideration—quite unforgivable, don't you think?"

Anrel blinked. "I'm sure he could find it in his heart to forgive you, my lord, if you had sufficient provocation."

Lord Blackfield smiled. "Why, by the Father and Mother, I believe you're right—he's a gentle soul, all in all, far kinder than *I* am. And I cannot deny that I *have* been provoked, in large part by an individual with whom I understand you to be acquainted—a delegate by the name of Amanir tel-Kabanim."

"I know him slightly," Anrel said warily.

"Do you know what he has done, then?" The faintest glimmer of suppressed fury flickered in the Quandishman's eyes.

"Not at all, my lord. I took a stroll by the river this morning, but have otherwise spent most of the day in this very room, taking advantage of your library, utterly without news from the outside world. What has Amanir done that has irked you so?"

"Let me first explain, sir, that as is my custom, I betook myself to the baths to listen to the Grand Council's deliberations. I do this so that after the conclusion of business, or before the start of the next day's labors, I might talk to the delegates in full knowledge of what has been discussed, and counsel them in hopes of preventing needless strife. I have spoken with Delegate tel-Kabanim more than once, and he is familiar with my views, and has claimed to be in sympathy with them."

"I have understood this to be your habit, yes," Anrel said.

Lord Blackfield took a deep breath, and said, "This morning it was necessary to *fight* my way to the baths, as a great unruly mob had gathered outside, and when I reached the doors I found my path barred by soldiers of the City Watch, who told me that they had orders to admit no one but the delegates and their guests. I protested that I was indeed a guest, of Delegate li-Parsil, and a messenger was sent, and the delegate was kind enough to confirm that I was welcome within. I was admitted, and took up my accustomed place in the gallery above the central gathering, but by that time the crowd without had taken up a chant, shouted in unison by a thousand or more voices, calling over and over, 'Bring us Allutar's blood! Bring us Allutar's blood!'"

"Oh," Anrel said. "*Oh.*"

"And that confounded fool, tel-Kabanim, took up the chant on the floor of the Grand Council!"

"*What?*"

Lord Blackfield nodded, and held out a hand toward Anrel. "You see? So much for his protestations of supporting my efforts at peacemaking!"

"Indeed, my lord."

Lord Blackfield let his hand fall. "Fortunately today's chairman, Lord

Guirdon, called upon him not for silence, which I suspect would have provoked outright revolt, but to present the case against Lord Allutar and offer suggestions as to how the matter might best be handled."

"Ah."

"That inspired quite an instructive and productive morning, really," Lord Blackfield said, dropping into a chair. "It was made clear that Lord Allutar, and he alone, was indeed responsible for the ruination of the Raish Valley wheat fields—that is no longer mere rumor or speculation, but acknowledged fact. It was further made explicit that he cannot be subjected to any legal penalty for that action—the Grand Council has granted all its members pardon for all actions taken prior to their election, no matter what those actions might be, or what repercussions they may have had. Suggestions that this decision might be rescinded stirred lively debate, but were defeated in the end.

"It was then proposed, by tel-Kabanim and his compatriots, that the Grand Council devise some arbitrary penalty for Lord Allutar regardless of the law, since after all the council is *above* the law, but that . . . well, the debate degenerated into shouting at that point, and it took some time for Lord Guirdon to restore order." He glanced at Anrel. "Have you followed much of the council's actions?"

"No," Anrel admitted. "I spoke with Derhin, but I cannot say I have paid close attention."

"Well, you may know that there are several factions within the council, named for where in the ruins their members gather before the general meetings. The Hots hold forth in the pool the ancients heated with fires in the room below, the Beaters in the room we believe to have been used for massages, and so on. Amanir tel-Kabanim is one of the loudest of the Hots, commoners who blame all the empire's ills on the misuse of sorcery, while Lord Allutar is a leader of the Cloakroom, sorcerers who lay everything at the emperor's feet and would solve the empire's problems by deposing Lurias and replacing him with his brother Sharal, then confiscating enough of the imperial family's property to pay off the empire's debts. No matter what the subject, you can rest assured that anything any member of the Hots might propose will be blocked by the Cloakroom, while every suggestion from the Cloakroom, no matter how benign, will run afoul of the Hots. Everyone knows this, so anything that truly needs to be done is introduced by one of the more moderate groups, so that the Hots and the Cloakroom can vote for or against it on its own merits. There are also committees dealing with various matters, so that they might be handled more expeditiously than they would be through the Grand Council as a whole."

"I see," Anrel said.

"Once order was restored, a compromise was put forth whereby a committee would be created that would investigate the entire matter—the ruined grain, the riots, the destruction of the Pensioners' Quarter, everything—and would then report back to the Grand Council. Our friend tel-Kabanim rose up and denounced this idea in no uncertain terms, maintaining that this would at best delay any prospects for justice, and at worst would allow the council to ignore the whole thing indefinitely. And when it appeared that the vote might go against him, he led the Hots, all of them, out of the chamber and onto the street, where they led the crowd in fresh chants of 'Bring us Allutar!' At that point it became clear that no further business would be conducted today, and Lord Guirdon declared the council adjourned, and I returned here—but it required a cordon of watchmen to see me safely out of the baths, through that chanting mob to my coach." He sighed deeply. "*Most* distressing!"

"I wonder how Lord Allutar was able to depart safely. Are there enough watchmen in Lume to protect him from such a mob?"

"Oh, there are hidden ways in and out of the baths," Lord Blackfield said with a dismissive gesture. He leaned back in his chair, letting his head fall back. "They are, of course, reserved for the delegates, and heavily warded."

"Of course." Anrel pursed his lips, then said, "Though it is by no means of the significance of your own report, I may have a bit of news that might brighten your day a little."

"Oh?" The Quandishman raised his head.

"You said you wished to meet some of my acquaintances from the Pensioners' Quarter, and I have taken the liberty of inviting one of them for supper. I suggested he might bring a friend or two, but I cannot say whether he will."

"Splendid!" Lord Blackfield sat upright, clapping his hands together. "That's excellent, Master Murau! When shall we expect them?"

"Perhaps an hour before sunset, at the rear entrance," Anrel replied. He held up a hand to forestall protest. "I know that it is hardly appropriate to ask a guest to come that way, but given the boy's appearance I thought it wise to make an exception in this case, to avoid unwelcome attention." He did not mention specifically how he and Shoun had drawn stares on their walk, but was prepared to do so if the Quandishman argued.

"Ah, I see," Lord Blackfield said. "An acceptable precaution, I think. Thank you."

Anrel nodded an acknowledgment. "I should mention that he is quite young. A boy, in fact."

"That does not trouble me in the slightest, I assure you."

"I did not commit you to any particular circumstances, though I did promise they would be fed."

Lord Blackfield flung his arms wide. "Then they shall dine with us!"

"I had hoped you would say so, my lord." While a meeting of such different classes might have its awkward aspects, Anrel thought it would be very educational for both sides.

For a moment, then, neither man spoke, as Lord Blackfield sat back in his chair, and Anrel marked his place and set aside his book. Then a thought occurred to him, and he asked, "So Amanir is one of the appropriately named Hots?"

"Indeed he is."

"What of Derhin li-Parsil? Is he, too, a Hot?"

"Li-Parsil? No, he has more sense than that. He is, at least for the moment, in the Atrium—a fairly moderate faction that believes fundamental changes are necessary, but looks for compromise, peace, and gradual transitions, rather than a complete and immediate overthrow of the present system." The Quandishman sighed. "I fear that he is not entirely happy with some of his fellows in that group, though, and that he may soon switch his allegiance to a more radical party."

"I see," Anrel said. "And if you were a delegate, rather than a foreign visitor, what faction would *you* choose?"

Startled, Lord Blackfield said, "Oh, don't ask me that!"

"I am afraid I already have."

"Master Murau, I am not a Walasian. I am not entitled to an opinion on how your nation should govern itself. I only wish to see bloodshed and misery kept to a minimum. For that reason I would certainly support neither the Hots nor the Cloakroom, as they both seem willing and eager to inflict harm upon those who disagree with them, but I cannot choose among the others."

"You would not find the Atrium intolerable?"

"No, not intolerable, but neither do I agree with them upon every particular, and the same could be said of several others."

Anrel nodded. He hesitated, debated saying more, then reached for his book again.

Some time later Anrel descended to the rear entrance to await Shoun's return, and found Shoun, Mieshel, and Po had already arrived, and were sitting in the little yard behind Dezar House, engrossed in a game of pebble toss. Anrel did not interrupt immediately, but watched as Po attempted a tricky ricochet off the bottom step, trying to knock Shoun's stone away. Unsurprisingly, his shot missed, leaving the way open for Mieshel's next throw to fall in no more than two inches from the line.

Anrel cleared his throat.

"We saw you, Dyssan," Shoun said without looking up.

"We wanted to finish the game," Po said.

"It's my shot," Shoun said, and with a quick snap of the wrist he sent his stone skittering forward until it stopped dead even with Mieshel's.

"A draw?" Mieshel said.

"Good enough," Shoun agreed.

Po frowned, but did not protest. All three boys pocketed their pebbles, then turned to face Anrel.

He looked them over thoughtfully. All three were dirty, their clothes in sad condition, but they seemed to have made an effort to make themselves presentable—their faces had been wiped, however ineffectually, and their clothes appeared to have been brushed, the worst tears pinned closed. Po had even managed to find a battered gray cap that partially disguised the sorry condition of his tangled hair.

Ordinarily Anrel would never have brought them into a respectable man's home in this condition, but Lord Blackfield was not an ordinary householder. Once inside the Quandishman's rooms, protected by his wards, they would be away from prying eyes. Anrel took a quick glance at the watch's walkway, running along a rooftop some fifty yards to the east, and saw no one, but he knew a watchman might come along at any moment.

"This way," he said, beckoning them in and up the stairs, hoping they would not encounter anyone from any of the other households in Dezar House. At this hour the rear stair saw little use, but the possibility of a meeting existed, and Anrel had no idea how he would explain the presence of the three urchins.

Fortunately, they reached the second floor undetected. There he paused and looked them over again.

"I'm not sure whether I need to tell you this or not, but I think I had better, just in case," he said. "Our host, Lord Blackfield, is a sorcerer. He is also a friend of mine. You will not take anything that belongs to him without permission, no matter how tempting—not only would you be stealing from a friend of mine, but you don't know what wards he has in place, or what he'd do if he caught you. Is that clear?"

"It's clear to me," Shoun said.

Mieshel looked at Po.

"I won't touch anything!" the youngest protested. "Not even if he's left guilders lying everywhere!"

"Good," Anrel said. Then he turned and knocked on the back door of Lord Blackfield's suite.

Harban opened it immediately and nodded to him. "Master Murau," he said. "And are these our dinner guests?"

"Yes, Harban," Anrel replied. "This is Mieshel, and Shoun, and Po."

Mieshel bobbed his head, and Po took off his cap, but Shoun held out a hand. "Pleased to meet you, sir," he said.

Harban shook the proffered hand solemnly, then said, "The pleasure is mine. Lord Blackfield is awaiting you all in the sitting room, and I do not recommend making him wait, but if I might offer a suggestion, I think you all might want my assistance in cleaning up before we dine."

Mieshel cast Anrel a startled glance. "Dine?"

"Lord Blackfield has asked that you do him the honor of joining him for dinner," Anrel said.

Po suddenly looked very nervous.

"I told you he'd feed us," Shoun said.

"But you didn't say we'd be eating *with* him!" Po answered.

Shoun glared at the younger boy.

"We'll be fine," Mieshel said. He glanced at Harban. "They seem very nice."

"Thank you, sir," Harban said. "This way?"

Together, the five of them walked through the wards, and down the passage to the sitting room where Lord Blackfield awaited them.

18

In Which Anrel Refuses an Offer of Employment

"Another slice?" Lord Blackfield said, holding out a platter of ham.

Ordinarily, of course, Harban would have been offering the meat from behind each guest's shoulder, but Lord Blackfield had noticed that the boys—or at any rate Mieshel and Po—did not seem entirely comfortable being served in such a fashion, and had ordered that the serving dishes be left upon the table, so that the diners might help themselves.

He had also seen to it that the foods provided were simple ones, nothing that would present too great a challenge to an untrained palate. Anrel wondered whether Mistress Uillea had been irked by this limitation upon her skills.

"Thank you," Mieshel said as he speared a slice with his fork. Given how rarely he had ever had the opportunity to use one, he wielded the implement well.

Shoun, too, took another serving, but Po shook his head; Anrel thought he was too awed to take proper advantage of this opportunity to stuff himself, but perhaps his small belly was simply already full.

Harban had done a good job of tidying the boys up, given how little time he had; he had managed to get all three faces and all six hands surprisingly clean, had removed Po's cap entirely over the boy's loud objections and brushed the hair beneath into a semblance of order, and had even managed to provide Mieshel with a clean, whole blouse that fit him reasonably well, replacing the ragged mess he had arrived in.

So far, everything had gone well. Lord Blackfield had introduced himself to his guests and learned their names; there had been a slightly awkward moment when he inquired about their surnames, but Anrel had explained that no one in the quarter used them, and the Quandishman had let the matter drop.

Then Harban had swept them off to be cleaned, and ten minutes later the entire party had gone in to dinner.

So far the conversation had been restricted to the meal, the weather, and other such trivial pleasantries, but now, as Lord Blackfield set aside the platter of meat, he said, "Shall we get down to business?"

Po looked up at the Quandishman, and Mieshel alternated between his host and his food, but Shoun threw Anrel a quick glance before saying, "Whatever you like, my l—lord." He stumbled slightly over the unfamiliar honorific.

"While you are here as my guests, and are under no obligation to do anything but enjoy your supper, I do confess to an ulterior motive," Lord Blackfield said. "I am hoping to hire someone—or perhaps two or three someones—for certain duties here in Lume, and I believe you three might be suitable."

"What duties, my lord?" Shoun asked before stuffing another forkful of ham into his mouth.

"Well, that's a little difficult to explain. I am looking for someone who will keep me informed of any news that may be circulating in the streets in such a way that it would not ordinarily reach a man of my station. As I'm sure you understand, this calls for an individual of good judgment—someone who will know what I want to hear, and what can safely be ignored as of no interest. This person might also be called upon to serve as a messenger on occasion, and perhaps run other errands for me. An ability to go places that not everyone can go would be greatly valued. The ability to listen to conversations without being noticed, and report their contents accurately even if it seems meaningless or irrelevant, would also be welcome. A certain degree of self-confidence is required, but I think, after watching the three of you here, that will not be an issue—I am quite aware that my table is as foreign to you as the jungles of some Ermetian mystery land, and you have all acquitted yourselves well here."

"You want a runner with a good ear," Mieshel said. "That's what we'd call it in the Pensioners' Quarter."

Lord Blackfield stared at him for a moment, then let out a bark of laughter. "I daresay," he said. "A runner with a good ear—of course you'd have a name for it! Indeed, I believe that's precisely what I am seeking, a runner with a good ear."

"You're new at this, my lord?" Shoun asked.

Lord Blackfield turned to the middle boy. "Not entirely, lad, not entirely. I've had my equivalents of runners with good ears here and there in Quand and scattered around the empire, but never on the streets of Lume. You three, if you take the job, will be my first here."

"What's it pay, my lord?" Shoun asked. Mieshel cast him an annoyed glance, as if he thought the younger boy was usurping his prerogative as the eldest.

Lord Blackfield glanced quickly around all three faces—no, all four, as he included Anrel as well as the boys.

Anrel had an idea what the going rate for this sort of service was, but he was not about to tell Lord Blackfield that and ruin the boys' negotiations. He kept his expression carefully blank.

"I was thinking a penny a day, to start," the Quandishman said.

Mieshel opened his mouth, but before he could speak, Lord Blackfield added, "Each."

Po looked from Shoun to Mieshel, clearly struggling not to say anything lest he somehow ruin this opportunity.

"For that, of course, I would expect you to stop by at least every sixth day," Blackfield continued. "If I am not readily available, you would report to Harban, or perhaps Master Murau." He nodded at Anrel.

"They know me as Dyssan, my lord," Anrel said.

"Ah, of course. Dyssan, then." He nodded. "You would deliver not merely any news you may have heard, but also a report on what you judge the mood of the city to be—are the people happy or miserable, angry or resigned to their fate? Do they blame their miseries on themselves, or the Father, or the emperor, or the burgrave, or the Grand Council? That sort of thing."

"I understand," Mieshel said.

170

"We can do that," Shoun said.

"Also, I am looking for a Kerderian fellow by the name of Revard Saruis, from a place called Darmolir. He is getting on in years, but I'm afraid I can give little more description than that. Any news of him will earn you an extra penny or two."

"Revard Saruis." Mieshel nodded.

Anrel recalled that Lord Blackfield had asked him about this Master Saruis, as well. He wondered what the Quandishman's interest in him was.

"You haven't heard of him?" Lord Blackfield asked.

Mieshel, Shoun, and Po exchanged glances. "No, my lord," Shoun said.

"Ah, well," the Quandishman said. "There would be additional payments for any additional duties, of course, and you would always be free to refuse a given assignment, though should that happen I would not take it amiss if you suggested someone who might undertake it in your stead."

Po did not seem to follow this sentence and started to ask a question, but Mieshel shushed him quickly. "Fair enough," Shoun said.

"Should you ever find yourself without any other recourse, and your funds, for whatever reason, insufficient to feed you, you will always find a meal here—though probably not a dinner like this so much as a little something from the servants' table, handed to you at the back door. Should you ever need shelter, or a way out of the city, I will do my best to arrange it, but do not expect to be welcome guests here."

Anrel hardly thought that last needed to be said, and judging by the expressions on the other faces, Mieshel and Shoun had considered it unnecessary, as well. Po, on the other hand, appeared disappointed.

"And finally, while I'm sure this is obvious, I am going to say it all the same, so that you cannot ever claim ignorance. This is all confidential. You are not to ever mention to your friends, or for that matter to anyone else, that you know me, that you have spoken with me, that you are in my employ."

"Of course, my lord!" Shoun said.

"Runners with good ears and closed mouths," Mieshel said. "I'm good for that, my lord."

"How long is this for?" Po asked.

"For as long as I am in Lume," Lord Blackfield replied. *"Whenever* I am in Lume—if I leave and return, we will pick up where we left off. Does that suit you?"

Po threw Shoun a wary glance, then nodded. "Yes, my lord."

"Good. Then you're hired. Mieshel?"

"I'm good for it."

"That's two. Shoun?"

"I would be honored, my lord." The boy made a sketchy attempt at a bow, complicated by the fact that he was seated at the table.

"Excellent! Then let us see what confections Harban and Mistress Uillea have for us to round out our meal."

Harban and Mistress Uillea proved to have a glittering pink and white sugar cake, which was quickly devoured. As it was consumed Lord Blackfield began questioning the boys about the mood in the streets, taking their first reports; Anrel listened with interest.

If what he heard was accurate then the people of Lume were even more unhappy than he had realized, and placed the blame for their unhappiness on two parties—the emperor, and the sorcerers responsible for the famine. It seemed to be taken as an established fact that the mistakes of sorcerers were indeed responsible for all the crop failures of recent years, and not just the ruined harvest in the Raish Valley. Anrel did not know how much truth there was in this, but it was clearly widely accepted.

There were rumors that Lume was not the only place that had experienced outbreaks of violence in recent days, though Anrel was unsure how much credence to give these reports, either.

The last dishes had been cleared, Po and Mieshel had run out of news, and Shoun was struggling to find a few more tidbits to report, when a knock sounded somewhere. Anrel glanced up as Harban slipped out of the dining room, and a moment later he heard low voices, followed by departing footsteps and the click of a latch.

Then Harban stepped back into the room and coughed quietly. Shoun stopped in midsentence—Anrel thought he looked relieved, as the sentence had not seemed to be going anywhere useful. Lord Blackfield turned and looked at his servant.

"My lord, Delegate li-Parsil is downstairs and wishes to see you," Harban said. "He says it's urgent."

Lord Blackfield turned to Anrel. He said nothing, merely gave his guest a questioning look.

"I think perhaps I should take these boys out the back way," Anrel said.

The Quandishman nodded. He rose, and offered Mieshel his hand. "Your company has been a delight, sir, and I look forward to working with you—come back for your first report the day after tomorrow. Harban, see that each of these young men has sixpence as an advance on his salary, and then go bring up the delegate."

"Yes, my lord."

Coins appeared in Harban's hand as if by magic, and were swiftly distributed; as they were, Lord Blackfield shook Shoun's hand and told him, "I expect to see you four days from now. Come to the rear entrance and Harban will admit you."

Harban, having paid the three, somehow manifested Po's cap out of thin air and placed it on the boy's head. Then he vanished as Lord Blackfield squeezed Po's hand. "Six days from now."

"Yes, my lord," Po said in a squeaky whisper, clutching his coins tightly with one hand and straightening his hat with the other.

Then Anrel gathered the three boys and herded them out; he glanced back as he did, and saw Lord Blackfield opening his wine cabinet.

Night had fallen, and the courtyard and alley were dark; Anrel hesitated before sending his former roommates out into the gloom. A thought struck him.

He did not want Derhin to know he was living as Lord Blackfield's guest, so he did not want to reenter the rooms until Derhin had left, but he had no idea how long that might be. What's more, he did not want to watch the front door himself; Derhin might spot him and recognize him when he emerged, and in general, someone standing around watching the front of Dezar House might well attract unwelcome notice.

That could wait, though. "Do you know where you're going?" he asked.

The boys exchanged glances. "No," Mieshel admitted.

Anrel frowned. He did not like the idea of sending the boys out onto the streets for the night, but he did not really see any practical alternative. Each of them had sixpence, a tenth of a guilder—perhaps they could find a room for that much.

But then what would they do tomorrow? No, they would have to make do, as they had for the past several days, ever since the Pensioners' Quarter burned. There was nothing Anrel could do for them. . . .

Well, almost nothing. He had a few pence of his own, carefully hoarded. Perhaps he could do something to add a little more money to their meager store—not enough to matter, really, but a little.

"Listen, I want to know when Lord Blackfield's guest leaves—Delegate li-Parsil. I'll pay a penny for one of you to watch the front door and let me know when he emerges."

The three looked at one another; then Shoun said, "I'll do it. Mieshel can keep an eye on Po."

"I don't need anyone watching me," Po protested.

"You have me anyway," Mieshel said. "Come on." Then he looked at Shoun. "Same as last night?"

"Unless you know somewhere better."

"Same place it is. See you later, then. Come on, Po. Good night, Dyssan. Give Lord Blackfield our thanks."

"Of course." Anrel bowed, and watched as Po and Mieshel trotted off into the night, Mieshel's hand-me-down clean white blouse gleaming. Then Anrel turned to Shoun. "I'll wait here," he said. "You go watch. Try not to let him see you."

Shoun gave Anrel a look that he could read even in the dim glow from the shuttered windows, a look that plainly said he was an idiot to think Shoun needed to be told to stay out of sight; then the boy slipped away into the darkness.

Anrel watched him go, then sat down on the rear stoop, wondering what Derhin wanted with Lord Blackfield.

He also wondered what he would do with himself. Living as the Quandishman's guest was all very well, but he could hardly stay on indefinitely. He had spent a season as a swindler and thief, but he had no desire to return to that line of work, even if he could—and he had rarely worked alone, in any case, but usually with a partner. With no way to find Doz, or another partner he trusted, and with their homes in smoking ruin, Anrel did not see how he could resume his criminal career.

Before his arrival in Lume he had spent a season as a witch in training, but he knew from conversations with Mother Baba and others that he would not be welcome in that trade; Lume had its own witches who did not feel any need for additional competition.

Before *that* he had been a student, living off his uncle's generosity and his inheritance, neither of which could he draw on now that he was an outlaw.

No, none of his previous occupations would serve. He would need to find an entirely new career. But what?

He had no money to invest—at least, no money he could reach. He had no personal connections to draw upon, or at any rate none for which he saw any obvious utility. His skills, such as they were, had their uses, but did not immediately suggest a profession he could pursue while under sentence of death. He had intended to become a lawyer or clerk, but neither of those was open to someone who had been condemned to hang.

He had not yet come up with any new options when he heard a hiss and found Shoun peering at him from the alley.

"He's gone," the boy said.

"Thank you," Anrel said. He stood up and fished in his pocket for the promised penny.

"Didn't stay long."

Anrel had to some extent lost track of time, but now he realized that the boy was right. "No, he didn't, did he?" He found what he was after, and tossed the coin to Shoun, who caught it in midair.

"See you another time, Dyssan," Shoun said, and then he vanished into the night.

Anrel stood for a moment staring at the spot where the boy had been, then turned and headed back up the stairs.

He found Lord Blackfield in the sitting room, comfortably settled in his favorite chair, a glass of wine in his hand and his head tipped back as he contemplated the ceiling. He lifted his head to look at Anrel.

"Join me in a glass, Master Murau?"

"I would be delighted, my lord."

A moment later Anrel was seated as well, sipping a pleasant Lithrayn red.

"I'm sure you're wondering what the delegate wanted," Lord Blackfield said.

"I am," Anrel admitted.

"He was hoping I could tell him where his friend, Delegate tel-Kabanim, might be."

Anrel looked puzzled. "Amanir tel-Kabanim?"

"The very one, yes. The man we spoke of earlier. It seems our Hot friend received word from Lord Allutar requesting a meeting—Delegate li-Parsil says that the note was carefully phrased to imply that the landgrave wished to discuss terms of a surrender, though it did not say so in so many words. Tel-Kabanim agreed to meet him, against the advice of li-Parsil and others, and went off this afternoon for this private discussion, and hasn't been seen since."

That did not sound encouraging. "Why come to you, my lord?"

"Li-Parsil had thought I might have served as a neutral party in arranging the meeting. Rest assured, I did not. I had my own plans for this evening, as you know."

"Indeed."

"He also thought that perhaps, as a sorcerer, I might have some magic that could locate his friend. I regret to say that I do not, and I told him as much. If I had known I would want to locate tel-Kabanim I could have placed a spell upon him that would lead me to him, but I did not know that and did not prepare such a spell. If I had some bit of him—a lock of his hair, for example—I could use that to locate him, but I do not. If I knew his true name, I could find him, but to the best of my knowledge he does not *have* a true name, since he is no magician."

"I understand."

Lord Blackfield stared at Anrel for a moment, then said, "You know Lord Allutar—what do *you* think he's up to?"

"My lord?"

"Do you think he intends to surrender himself for a trial of some sort, as the Hots demand?"

"No, of course not," Anrel replied without thinking.

"Then why request a meeting?"

"To destroy Amanir," Anrel answered immediately. "Or at any rate, to remove him as a threat. Through blackmail, perhaps. Lord Allutar is a great believer in silencing his foes, and is not particularly scrupulous about his methods."

Lord Blackfield nodded. "That was my own opinion, as well, but you've known Allutar Hezir longer than I have."

"Unfortunately, I have."

"Have you any guess as to what method he might employ to ensure an end to tel-Kabanim's harassment?"

Anrel shrugged. "Whatever he believes he can get away with."

"Enchantment?"

"Oh, certainly. Or worse."

"Spells can be broken."

"I wouldn't know."

"You are the son of a sorcerer, are you not?"

Startled, Anrel acknowledged, "Yes, I am. I had not realized you were aware of it."

"I try to stay abreast of the news, as I would think my conversation with tonight's dinner guests demonstrated."

Anrel nodded. "Of course, my lord."

Lord Blackfield gazed silently at him for a moment, then said, "Not all my informants live on the streets," he said.

"You did say as much at supper, my lord, and you have previously mentioned talking to servants in the emperor's palace."

"I can find uses for a wide variety of information."

"I could scarcely doubt it," Anrel replied, slightly puzzled by this remark.

"I am offering you employment, Master Murau."

"You . . . what?" Anrel blinked.

"You seem to have friends in many quarters, from the alleys of Lume to the Grand Council."

"I . . . I suppose I do, my lord."

"That can be a valuable resource. I know you are no street urchin, to be paid in pennies; I would pay you a half guilder a day for your services as my agent."

Anrel stared at him. He had just been despairing of his employment situation, and here was this generous offer, dropped into his lap. It was as if the Mother and Father were looking after him.

But generous as the offer was, and desperate as his situation might be, Anrel was in no hurry to accept it.

"I would be spying for Quand," he said.

"You would be spying for *me*," Lord Blackfield corrected him.

"Nonetheless, I would be spying."

Lord Blackfield frowned. "I fear I have let my fondness for a clever turn of phrase lead this discussion in an unfortunate direction. The services I hope for need not be considered spying, surely?"

"You wish me to gather information and then deliver it to you, regardless of whether its source intended it for you, do you not?"

"I . . . well, yes."

"That's spying."

"Very well, then, it's spying. For me, for half a guilder a day."

Anrel shook his head. "I owe you a debt, my lord, for taking me in when my home burned, for treating me as an honored guest, and for a thousand other considerations. I think I must consider you a friend, as well, for I have very much enjoyed my stay here. For these reasons I assure you that I will happily pass along information I think will interest you, should the occasion arise and my ethics allow it; you need not pay me for it, as I already owe you so much. That said, I am not ready to formalize our association and declare myself to be in your employ. I prefer not to place myself under any further obligation to you. I believe you to be an honest and honorable man with only the very best intentions, but the fact remains that you are a Quandish Gatherman, and I am a loyal subject of the Walasian Empire, and we are both caught up in political affairs, one way or another. You have chosen to involve yourself in the Lantern Society and the doings of the Grand Council, and I have inadvertently made myself infamous as Alvos, the orator of Naith. It may be that our loyalties and circumstances will force us into conflict. I would hope that our friendship might survive such mischance, but I would not put the additional weight of employment upon it."

Lord Blackfield set his wineglass down and stared at Anrel. "Mother and Father, Master Murau, but you surprise me! I would hardly expect such scruples in a man who by his own admission has been earning his bread by theft and deception, but I cannot help but admire them. I am honored that you consider me your friend, and I hope to remain worthy of that honor."

"Thank you, my lord."

"Mind you, I am not accepting your decision as final and irrevocable. The offer will remain open for the present; should you reconsider, simply say so."

"I will keep that in mind." Anrel began to find his host's scrutiny uncomfortable; he set his own glass down. "If you will pardon me, my lord, it has been a long and eventful day."

"Indeed it has. Sleep well, Master Murau."

With that, the two men rose and went their separate ways, and as Anrel prepared for bed he found himself grimacing at what he had done. Although every word he had spoken in explaining his reasoning was true, the facts were that he needed an income, and Lord Blackfield had offered him one, yet he had refused it. Could he really *afford* such scruples? He had spent a season as a thief, and a season as a witch; would a season or two as a spy be any worse?

Well, he would give the matter serious thought for a few days, and see what he conclusions he might reach. Perhaps another, more acceptable opportunity might fall into his lap, just as this one had.

He hoped that the three boys were safe.

And he wondered what had become of Amanir. Surely, despite the obvious provocation, even Lord Allutar would not simply murder him, not after so openly arranging a meeting. Perhaps the delegate would be found alive and well, come morning.

But knowing Lord Allutar, Anrel doubted it.

19

In Which Anrel Is Offered Unexpected
Political Advancement

Lord Blackfield had already left for the baths when Anrel rose the next day, and Anrel once again took refuge in the Quandishman's library. There he mused on whether he might somehow make a living reading books, since that was what he found himself doing every day of late. He could not think of how that might be managed.

But then he realized that he was reading a book in colloquial Quandish—an account of a shipwreck in the northern isles of the Quandish Archipelago—and it occurred to him that there were not so very many people in the empire who could do that. Might he perhaps find work as a translator? If he found these Quandish travelogues so enthralling, might not other Walasian readers enjoy them, and pay for the privilege?

This might even be an occupation he could pursue more or less anonymously, so that his death sentence would not be an insuperable problem. If he could find a reliable publisher, perhaps use someone he trusted as a go-between . . .

This, he felt, was a very promising notion, so promising that he found himself distracted from his book. He knew very little about the book trade beyond the fact that as a student he had thought his texts too expensive, but surely, he could learn. A single new copy of a book might sell for a guilder, or even more; he wondered how much of that money found its way back to the author or translator. Did the publisher pay the author a lump sum, or was the money dependent upon how many copies sold?

As a translator, would he need to share his proceeds with the original Quandish authors? He had no idea what the law had to say on the subject, if it said anything at all.

How long would it take to translate a book?

This was intriguing, and offered the first viable alternative he had come up with to working as Lord Blackfield's spy, so that after some further meditation he decided it was time to visit one of the bookshops off the east end of the Promenade, near the courts, and ask a few questions. He gathered himself up, informed Harban of his destination, and set out.

He discovered that booksellers and publishers were all very willing to discuss their trade, but that no one was sure whether there would be a market for translations from Quandish. A few seemed startled to learn that there *were* books written in Quandish; the thought had apparently never occurred to them. After all, Quand was outside the Bound Lands, and therefore assumed to be rather barbaric; one didn't ordinarily think of barbarians as literate. Quand was associated with foggy forests, rocky coasts, and rain-swept moors, not with books.

When all was said and done, Anrel was not sure whether he had found himself a viable career or not. He returned to Dezar House in midafternoon with his head full of information about typesetting costs, print runs, royalty schedules, and the like, through streets that seemed alternately unnaturally quiet or full of angry voices. He was so focused on his newfound knowledge of publishing that it took him some time to realize that something must have happened to disturb the city, but that obvious conclusion had been reached well before he climbed the stairs to Lord Blackfield's rooms.

He wondered what had caused this fresh unrest, and hoped it was not Amanir's murder. Amanir had been Valin's friend, and for that reason, if no other, Anrel hoped he was still alive and well somewhere.

He paused on the landing as two of the women who lived on the third floor came hurrying down the stair past him, chatting excitedly and ignoring him completely. He bowed politely but said nothing as they passed, and they seemed utterly unaware of his existence.

He wondered whether they had noticed how disturbed the city's atmosphere was, or whether they were as oblivious to the concerns of the common people as they were to his presence. He hoped they would be safe, that none of the anger he had heard would be directed at them.

When they were gone he opened the door to find Lord Blackfield already home, settled in the sitting room, staring out the window at the boulevard.

"Good afternoon, my lord," Anrel said with a nod.

"Master Murau," Lord Blackfield acknowledged. "Have you heard the news?"

Anrel glanced out the window as well, but saw nothing he had not already observed. He stepped inside and closed the door. "What news is that, my lord?"

"Delegate Amanir tel-Kabanim hanged himself this morning."

Anrel's mouth tasted suddenly sour.

"Hanged himself?" he asked.

"Yes."

"How did it happen?" Anrel suspected he knew a part of the answer already.

"It would seem he had arrived at the baths during the night, and brought a rope with him," Lord Blackfield said. "He rigged a noose from one of the exposed beams above the pool that gave the Hots their name, and when his friends arrived this morning they found him standing atop the headless statue of Mother Earth, staring at nothing, with the rope around his neck. He ignored their greetings, their expressions of delight that he was alive, and their entreaties to explain what he was doing. They tried to talk him into removing the noose, but he screamed out something about how they were defying the natural order, then stepped off the broken stump of the Mother's neck—and the rope then broke *his* neck, so although his companions cut him down as quickly as they could, he was quite dead."

"Horrible!" Anrel said, the image of poor Reva Lir hanging from the Beynos bridge filling his thoughts.

"Naturally, the Hots accused Lord Allutar of killing him, but a dozen of the Cloakroom swore that Allutar had been with them all night at an infamous brothel in Old Altar Street."

"But . . . surely, Amanir *was* enchanted, to hang himself thus!"

"So the Hots say, but the Cloakroom argues that he had merely finished the process of going mad. There was no trace of sorcery lingering on the body, but then, there wouldn't be, if a properly constructed binding was used." Lord Blackfield sighed. "Allutar himself has said nothing, as yet."

"If he admitted the crime, would his pardon protect him?"

"I think not; as I understand it, the pardon was for all crimes committed before election to the council. Anything subsequent to election would be subject to the relevant laws. What those laws might be in a case like this, however, I cannot say."

Anrel frowned. "He is landgrave of Aulix, and Amanir was a commoner from Aulix. Lord Allutar might claim that Amanir's death was within his right to dispense justice."

"Tel-Kabanim was openly calling for Lord Allutar's head, but I know of no other offense he might have committed. Was that a crime justifying summary execution under imperial law?"

"That might well qualify as sedition," Anrel said. "Lord Allutar would be within his rights to hang a man for sedition back in Aulix."

"Or for incitement to riot, perhaps? Tel-Kabanim helped rouse the crowd outside the baths."

"Perhaps. But that would be in Aulix. Here in Lume, Lord Allutar's authority is questionable, at best."

"Then it would be murder, if he killed tel-Kabanim."

"That would be for the courts to decide; Allutar would probably plead unpardonable provocation, or perhaps self-defense. As a landgrave he would be tried before either the Lords Magistrate or the emperor himself, not in the burgrave's courts, and I am unsure what laws would apply."

"Ah, the niceties of imperial government are beyond me. Would his membership in the Grand Council have any effect?"

Anrel puzzled over that for a moment, then said, "If the Grand Council said so, yes. Otherwise, I think not."

"This all assumes that Lord Allutar did indeed compel tel-Kabanim to hang himself. Might it have been some other sorcerer?"

"Oh, I suppose so," Anrel admitted, "but Lord Allutar certainly had the greatest motive, the putative authority, and the sorcerous skill, and allegedly arranged to meet with Amanir last night. I would think that solid evidence."

"Indeed." The Quandishman stroked his beard. "Not just any sorcerer can make a man hang himself."

The image of Reva lingered. Anrel said, "Lord Allutar has done it before, of course."

Lord Blackfield blinked. "Has he?"

"Well, he enchanted a woman to hang herself, at any rate. He did so in Beynos—the witch Reva Lir put her own head in the noose and jumped from a bridge, rather than wait for the hangman, while under Lord Allutar's spell."

"Ah."

"I find—" Anrel began, but then he was interrupted by a banging behind him, and several voices arguing. Then many rapid footsteps came battering up the stairs beyond the sitting room door, and a moment later a fist hammered upon it.

Lord Blackfield was on his feet before Anrel could react, pushing him aside, behind the door and out of sight. The Quandishman opened the door as the pounding renewed.

"Yes?" he demanded.

Two voices spoke at once; Anrel recognized one as the landlady's footman who regularly answered the front door, and the other was also familiar, though he did not place it immediately.

"I'm sorry, my lord, I tried to stop them," the footman said.

At the same time the other voice said, "Lord Blackfield, we must speak with you at once."

"Thank you, Kalnes, that will be all," Lord Blackfield said. "I will speak with these men."

"Very good, my lord," the footman said, and Anrel heard his footsteps as he retreated back down the stairs.

"Now, Master li-Parsil, how may I help you?"

That was the other voice! Anrel felt foolish for not recognizing it immediately, though there was an unfamiliar note of hoarseness.

"Lord Blackfield," Derhin said, "I am here on behalf of my fellow delegates."

From his concealed position Anrel could not see what was happening, but he imagined Lord Blackfield had bowed in acknowledgment.

"I see several familiar faces," the Quandishman said. "If I am not mistaken, these are all members of that faction known as the Hots—except yourself, of course, Master li-Parsil."

"He said you knew where to find Alvos," an unfamiliar voice called.

"Where is he?" demanded another.

"Yes, these are the Hots," Derhin said. "Or at any rate, the *surviving* Hots."

"I heard about poor Master tel-Kabanim," Lord Blackfield replied.

"Bring us to Alvos!" someone shouted.

"You have been observing the council for half a season," Derhin said. "You know how precariously balanced it is."

"I know that it is divided into a plethora of factions, sir. I have observed miserably little balance."

"Yes, well, Amanir's death has thrown it even further out of balance. His absence leaves Naith underrepresented, and the Hots without a spokesman."

"So I understand."

"These delegates behind me—we were grieving together over the loss of my old friend, and the issue of how he might best be replaced arose."

"Is he to be replaced, then?"

"He *must* be!" a new voice roared. "We will not allow Lord Allutar's perfidy to be rewarded!"

Anrel's heart beat faster at the sound of that, as he remembered his own determination to ensure Lord Valin's voice had not been stilled. Lord Allutar had made the same mistake again, killing a man to silence him, not realizing that there were others who would give voice to the dead man's words.

"Alvos!" someone called.

"Alvos!" several shouted in unison.

"Yes," Derhin said, sounding somewhat unsure of himself. "They all agreed that if they could only find the famous Alvos he would be the ideal replacement for Amanir. And I . . . I mentioned that I had spoken to Alvos recently, and that you knew how to reach him."

"I see," Lord Blackfield said. He paused, then said, "I might be able to get a message to the man who called himself Alvos back in Naith."

"Well, do it, then!"

"Tell him!"

"We want Alvos!"

"Bring him to us!"

Anrel could stand it no longer. This might be the occasion when he could avenge all the harm Lord Allutar had done. This was a chance to thrust himself into a position where he could accomplish something. He had never before concerned himself with politics and affairs of state beyond their effects on himself and his family and friends, thinking it all above an ordinary young man like himself, but now it seemed that the Mother and Father were giving him an opportunity to be more, to *do* more. He stepped around the door and stood beside Lord Blackfield.

"I am Alvos," he said, "and I am here!"

He found himself looking out on a crowd of more than a dozen men, mostly young, filling the hallway and crowding the top few steps of the staircase. Derhin stood at their head; his eyes were red, and his expression strained. The smell of sour wine hung over them all.

"Anrel," Derhin said softly. Anrel met his gaze.

Those eyes were very red, and wet. Anrel thought Derhin must have been weeping—and why not, when his best friend had died? Anrel could not think of anything to say in the face of such a loss. He knew that no words had been any comfort to him when Valin had died, and Derhin's emotions must be similar.

For a moment no one else spoke; then one of the delegates demanded, "Is that Alvos?"

"It is," Derhin said.

"Can you doubt it?" Anrel asked, turning his attention from Derhin to the others. "You came seeking me, in the name of justice; would the

Father so disappoint you as to provide an imposter? I am the man who spoke from the statue of the First Emperor in Aulix Square. I am the man who implored the people of Naith to send Master li-Parsil and his late companion to Lume as their delegates to the Grand Council. I am Alvos. What would you have of me?"

"Vengeance!" someone called.

"And how am I to give you that? I am only a man, not a magician nor a miracle."

"Lead us!"

"We need you on the council!"

"Anrel," Derhin said, "we want you to take Amanir's seat on the Grand Council."

Anrel hesitated for a moment. He had heard them say they wanted him to take Amanir's place, and he had assumed they wanted him to make a speech somewhere denouncing Lord Allutar, picking up where Amanir had left off. He would be more than willing to do that. But to actually take a seat on the Grand Council? That was more than he had expected.

They were waiting for his reply, though, so he demanded, "And how is this to be achieved? Is there a means to replace delegates who can no longer serve? What would it accomplish?"

Derhin looked over his shoulder at the crowd, then turned and leaned close to Anrel and Lord Blackfield. "May we discuss this?" he murmured. "Not this whole drunken crowd, but myself and perhaps two or three of my more sober companions?"

"Of course," Anrel whispered. "At least—" He turned. "My lord? Might we trouble you for the use of a room?"

"By all means," Lord Blackfield murmured.

Anrel straightened. "My friends," he announced, addressing the crowd beyond the door, "I will consider your request—but there is a time and a place for everything, and this is not the time for any discussion of myself, or of the future. Our friend died today—a worthy man, an honorable man, a loyal son of the empire and a proud Walasian, dead at his own hand, if perhaps not of his own will. Let us pause and remember him, and mourn our loss. There is no need to press headlong into an uncertain future; tomorrow will be soon enough for that. For now, I ask you all to go forth and honor the memory of Amanir tel-Kabanim. Drink to his spirit and pray for his soul, and remember his deeds, his kindness, his generosity, his enthusiasm, his hope for the future of our nation. Give him this one night before concerning yourselves with his successor. I will be here in the morning, and we can speak then of what role I may have, if any, in carrying on Amanir's legacy. I thank you for the honor you do me by thinking I am worthy to follow in his foot-steps, but let us not rush into any rash decisions. Go, remember Amanir, and compose yourselves for the long struggle ahead!"

"To Amanir!" Lord Blackfield said, raising a wineglass—Anrel had no idea how he had contrived to have one in his hand, but he did, and now brought it up in salute, then drained it in a gulp.

"To Amanir!" Derhin repeated, raising a fist.

"To Amanir!" chorused the others.

Then Anrel stepped back into the sitting room. Lord Blackfield fol-lowed him, and closed the door—but he did not latch it, but instead stood ready, handle in his hand, listening.

For a moment there was a confused muttering, then one by one An-rel could hear footsteps retreating down the staircase. After a moment the front door could be heard to close, and then silence fell.

Lord Blackfield opened the door again, and ushered Derhin and two others in.

"Anrel Murau, Lord Blackfield," Derhin said as the Quandishman closed the door solidly, "this is Zarein Lorsa, delegate from Kallai, and this is Pariel Gluth, delegate from Holmissa."

"An honor to meet you," Anrel said, taking Delegate Lorsa's hand and bowing. Then he turned to Delegate Gluth. "And you, sir."

"Master . . . Murau, did he say?" Lorsa asked.

"Yes."

"Alvos is not your real name?"

"No; it was an identity I created on the spur of the moment when I spoke in Aulix Square. I had no idea that name would gain such infamy."

"How do you *do* that, sir?" Gluth asked.

"I'm sorry," Anrel said. "Do what?"

"Speak like that! It wasn't your words—oh, they were chosen well enough, but they were not so very exceptional. It was something about how you spoke them. You took a drunken mob that had every intention of carrying you off on their shoulders to confront Lord Allutar, and turned them into a respectful party of mourners. By all accounts your speech in Naith had a similar magic. Hardly anyone agrees on what you said, but everyone who was there swears it was brilliant. How did you *do* that?"

"I . . . I don't know," Anrel said, taken aback. "I spoke as well as I could, and tried to put my heart into my words, but beyond that, I have no more idea of what I did than do you."

"A natural flair for oratory," Lord Blackfield said. "A very useful gift, when properly applied."

"And one we very much hope to use, Master Murau," Delegate Lorsa said. "Shall we discuss the matter?"

"By all means," Anrel said. "By all means."

20

In Which Anrel Prepares to Assume His New Duties

The conversation lasted well into the evening, continuing through a fine supper where the three delegates were guests.

Anrel learned that there was a process by which delegates unable to continue in office could be replaced, but it was somewhat vague. Delegates could specify who was to succeed them, but such inheritance had to be confirmed, and in any case Amanir tel-Kabanim had never named an heir. Where no successor had been chosen by the deceased, it fell to the representative closest in origin to appoint a provisional successor. Since Amanir had been one of the two commoners elected by the people of Naith, it was presumably the responsibility of the other, Derhin, to make that selection.

"It's a good thing Naith is the provincial capital, so there were two of us," Derhin said. "Otherwise it would be up to the burgrave's man to choose Amanir's replacement, and I don't think Lord Oris would name anyone the Hots would accept."

"Lord Oris?"

"A petty official at the College of Sorcerers," Derhin explained. "The burgrave of Naith appointed him to the council."

Derhin's choice, however, was only provisional. He would need the approval of at least one-fourth of the Grand Council—not a majority, in recognition of the differing interests of different parts of the empire, but enough to show that the appointment was not utterly bizarre and unreasonable. Once that was obtained, officials and delegates of the city or region he was to represent could demand an election confirming his appointment—as Lord Allutar and quite possibly Lord Oris or the burgrave of Naith might well do.

"We can get the confirmation in the council," Lorsa said, "but an election may reverse it, so your term may not last very long."

"I think he would survive an election," Derhin said. "He would be a full delegate in the interim, in any case."

In addition to the mechanism by which he might become a delegate, there were two other major issues that Anrel wanted to discuss.

One was how agreeing to serve on the Grand Council would benefit him personally, and that was quickly answered—as a delegate, he would be pardoned for all his previous crimes, not merely the sedition charges, or assaulting and robbing the watchman in Naith, but his various crimes committed during his residence in the Pensioners' Quarter.

Furthermore, he would be provided with room and board by the burgrave of Naith. He would join Derhin at the burgrave's town house on Lourn Street—Lord Oris, despite having been appointed by the burgrave, was not resident there, but was instead staying with his sister, Lady Vimia, who had lived in Lume by her own choice for several years.

As a delegate Anrel would also receive a small stipend from the provincial government of Aulix, and there were also other, less official sources of income available to delegates. He would no longer be dependent on Lord Blackfield's hospitality, and would never again have to resort to theft or fraud simply to eat.

Those were very tempting reasons to accept the offered post, but there was another, equally important matter.

"What would be expected of me?" he asked.

That portion of the discussion was what filled most of the evening. It seemed the Hots wanted a new spokesman to replace their late leader. Anrel would be there to represent Naith and Aulix, but it was also assumed that he would take on a significant role with the Hots—and that was a problem, because Anrel did not in fact agree with many of their positions.

"Surely, you cannot deny that the sorcerers are responsible for most of the empire's problems!" Gluth exclaimed, when Anrel first expressed his doubts about Hot doctrine.

"Most?" Anrel shook his head. "A great many of them, certainly, but most? I am not convinced. I think ordinary people are fully as capable of error as sorcerers." He held up a hand as Gluth started to protest. "But that is not what I see as the greatest difficulty with your plans. As I understand it, you want to sweep the sorcerers from power, and replace them with commoners—or at any rate, people who are commoners now, people who cannot wield magic."

"Yes," Gluth said. "They have had their chance!"

"And what is to become of the sorcerers, then? Do you think they will yield up their power without a struggle? Do you think they will not use sorcery to retake that power?"

"Those who do not accept the new order must be shown their error," Lorsa said.

"Would you cast them into prison, then? Do you think prison can hold a sorcerer?"

"There are ways to suppress a sorcerer's magic, are there not?" Lorsa asked. He glanced at Lord Blackfield, then turned back to Anrel. "Does not the emperor have the means to deal with rebellious nobles?"

"He has the Great List, of course," Anrel said. "But you are proposing to overthrow *all* the sorcerers, not just a handful."

"Would the Great List not serve to neutralize them all?"

"I suppose it would, if you found someone other than a sorcerer who could use it, but it would take time, and power—"

"We can afford the time."

Anrel shook his head. "What of our defenses against invasion? We need magic to protect the empire from its foes."

"No longer," Lorsa said. "We have cannon now, and they do not."

It was Anrel's turn to glance at Lord Blackfield before speaking to Lorsa; the Quandishman was looking carefully blank. "Do you think we can keep our methods of manufacturing cannon secret indefinitely?" Anrel asked. In truth, he suspected that Quand could already produce cannon if its people felt any need for them, and he was quite sure from his readings of history that Ermetia could, if not necessarily up to the technical standards of the Walasian weapons.

"Not forever," Lorsa said, "but long enough to raise up a generation of magicians who are loyal to the empire, rather than only to themselves."

"And what will you do with sorcerers, or for that matter anyone, who doesn't agree?"

"They will be outlaws, and will be punished accordingly. Since there are alleged to be practical difficulties in hanging sorcerers, those who resist will be burned at the stake, as rebels were in the empire's early days." His voice rose. "Our new empire will be cleansed in fire and blood, and made strong as forged iron!"

Anrel shook his head. "I cannot agree with that. Aside from any moral issues, considering only the pragmatic, you will not forge unity so much as resentment in the survivors, in the friends and families of those you kill."

"They will be swept aside," Lorsa insisted.

Anrel stared at him, then turned to Gluth.

"Delegate Lorsa's beliefs are perhaps a little extreme," Gluth said calmly. "Surely, it won't be necessary to shed any significant quantity of blood—the sorcerers will recognize the futility of their cause, the sheer numbers that oppose them, and will yield peacefully. Why, many of them will probably welcome relief from their administrative duties!"

Anrel remembered his uncle Dorias; he could hardly deny that the burgrave of Alzur would be at least slightly relieved to give up his post, and surely Lord Dorias was not unique. Anrel hesitated.

The debate continued, and in the end neither side convinced the other, but other issues emerged.

If Anrel refused the appointment then another man would eventually be found for the job, but at present there was no other candidate under consideration, nor could anyone think of any who would be as enthusiastically received as Alvos. The Hots would be leaderless and voiceless for a time, and that might allow the Cloakroom to strengthen their position. Lord Allutar might well escape any penalty for Amanir's murder.

If Anrel accepted the appointment, he need not stay with the Hots indefinitely. Once he had led the campaign to punish Allutar, he would be free to shift his allegiance to some other faction—the Beaters, perhaps, or the Atrium. What the Hots wanted from him was not so much his leadership, nor a long-term commitment, but a few days' use of his talent for oratory. They needed a spokesman in their campaign to see Lord Allutar brought down, and they could hardly hope for better than Alvos.

"Remember, Anrel, I am not among the Hots," Derhin said, "and I am the one who is to name Amanir's successor. I am not going to demand that my choice hold all the same positions poor Amanir did. I have agreed that his heir should speak for him, and for the Hots, in the matter of Lord Allutar's responsibility for his death, and we are all agreed on that. Beyond that, you will be free to follow your conscience."

That was, in the end, what decided Anrel. A pardon, room and board, and the chance to denounce Lord Allutar yet again—not, this time, to a powerless crowd of commoners, but to the Grand Council—was enough incentive to overcome any lingering doubts.

"I will accept the appointment," he said at last.

And with that settled, it was agreed that he would accompany Derhin to his official lodgings in Lourn Street, so that the two might walk to the baths together on the morrow for Anrel's presentation to the Grand Council.

Lorsa and Gluth went their own way, and then Anrel took his leave of Lord Blackfield while Derhin waited at the door.

"My lord," he said, "I cannot begin to express my gratitude for all you have done for me."

"Nonsense, Master Murau," the Quandishman replied. "The pleasure has been entirely my own—a guest as amiable as yourself is a treasure not easily come by! I trust you will enjoy your new home and your new post, and that you will serve your empire wisely. I think I know you well enough to be certain you will not give in to some of the follies Delegate Lorsa espouses, and the Grand Council can certainly use another voice of sanity and moderation."

"I will do my best," Anrel assured him.

"Then be off with you, and I will watch from the gallery tomorrow to see how good that proves to be!"

With that, Anrel joined Derhin, and the two men made their way down the stairs and through the entry hall, then down from the porch to the boulevard. As they ambled through the shadowy streets, from one flickering lamp to the next, they discussed what Anrel should expect in the morning. There would be procedural matters, and then Derhin would be called upon to speak; he would present Anrel, but Anrel would not at that time say anything beyond a sentence or two indicating his willingness to serve.

Then the council would vote on his confirmation. After that, assuming his appointment had been accepted, there would be a few congratulatory speeches, and then, at last, he would be called upon to address the council.

That was when he would unleash his very best oratory in denouncing Lord Allutar as Amanir's killer, and demanding justice.

"By law, nothing said in the council can be considered seditious or treasonous," Derhin told him, "so say whatever you feel is right."

Anrel nodded.

The town house in Lourn Street was significantly older and less elegant than Lord Blackfield's rented rooms, and there was no faithful Harban there to assist them, nor a Mistress Uillea to feed them, but it was comfortable enough, and the two men had the entire house to themselves. Anrel's assigned room was considerably larger than Lord Blackfield's guest chamber, though it smelled of must rather than fresh linen, and Anrel settled into it happily, looking around at the faded tapestries and wondering how long this would be his home.

He wished he had something else to wear, though; he had found no trace of his other clothes in the ruins of the Pensioners' Quarter, and his garments were beginning to suffer from use. He promised himself that when he received his first stipend payment he would visit the tailors in Satchel Court at the first opportunity, and start assembling a wardrobe once again.

With that in mind, he undressed and went to bed.

He was awakened with a start by Derhin's hand on his shoulder. He had slept so soundly that the remainder of the night had seemed to pass in an instant, and the morning light pouring through the curtains had appeared as abruptly as if a steel shutter had been flung open. He did not dawdle, though, and in moments he was up and dressed and joining Derhin in the kitchen.

Breakfast was a dismal affair compared with the pleasant morning meals he had shared with Lord Blackfield, as Derhin was not much of a cook nor interested in becoming one. Derhin also proved much less of a conversationalist than Lord Blackfield. They made no effort to take their meal to the breakfast room, but simply ate in the kitchen, leaning against the cabinets.

Despite this rude beginning to the day, in short order Anrel was awake, clothed, fed, and on his way to the baths at Derhin's side.

Anrel had heard of the Aldian Baths many times, but had never seen them before. Until the calling of the Grand Council they had been just one more set of little-used Old Empire ruins cluttering up the capital's landscape, like the Garz Hill Towers or the Forbidden Street, and he had never had any reason to approach them. Unlike the Diel Courts they had not been restored and returned to everyday use, nor had they been, like the Wizard Gate, the subject of centuries of drunken student pranks.

Now he gazed ahead with intense interest as they neared the baths, eager to see where the council met.

The first thing he noticed, though, was not the baths themselves, but the crowds in the street. Men, women, and even a few children stood shoulder to shoulder, filling the street's width for more than a hundred yards, shouting slogans and shaking fists. Some of the slogans were intelligible; others were not. "Bring us Allutar!" and "Allutar's blood!" were common. "Down with the emperor!" was clear. It took Anrel a moment to puzzle out "No foreign magicians!" as it was often accompanied or overlapped by the simpler "No magicians!"

This was the first time since the burning of the Pensioners' Quarter that he had encountered such a mob firsthand. He had heard about several, but he had not *seen* them, and the reality had a visceral impact that even the more lurid descriptions had lacked. These people were angry, and they were dangerous.

And these were not the beggars, whores, thieves, and witches of the Pensioners' Quarter, but ordinary citizens—many were dressed better than Anrel, with his unlined coat and false cuffs, was. These were tradesmen and craftsmen and housewives, commoners of every description, calling for the blood of a landgrave, or even for the overthrow of the emperor himself.

What's more, men in the green and gold uniforms of the Emperor's Watch were standing here and there around the edges of the crowd, or observing from the nearest arches, and doing nothing at all to silence the shouting.

For the first time Anrel really understood that drastic changes to the empire's governance were not merely possible, but had already begun. A year ago, when he had still been a student in Lume, a gathering like this would not have been tolerated, and watchmen would not have stood idly by while Walasians shouted, "Down with the emperor!"

A thought struck him. "Why are they *here*, instead of the emperor's palace?" he asked Derhin.

Derhin's mouth twisted wryly. "Two reasons," he said. "No, three. First, they can hardly expect the emperor to overthrow himself, while the Grand Council might at least make the attempt. Second, if they want Lord Allutar's head, well, Lord Allutar is a delegate here, not a courtier at the palace. And finally, we have no cannon on the ramparts."

Anrel had no answer to that.

A few seconds later they rounded a gentle curve in the street, and Anrel got his first look at the baths. The main building was largely intact, but was surrounded by scattered heaps of bricks and stone where other structures had crumbled completely, so that the baths seemed to be rising from a broad expanse of rubble.

The central facade had once been a grand expanse of marble, adorned with columns and statuary; now much of the marble facing was gone, revealing the dull brown brick beneath. Only two columns still stood, supporting nothing, and most of the niches were empty. The few remaining figures were all missing limbs or heads or half a torso.

"Come on," Derhin said, beckoning Anrel to one side.

Startled, Anrel followed, and found himself being led past a large watchman into a sort of aisle, separated from the crowd in the street by a low wooden railing. Watchmen stood guard along the railing, one every twenty or thirty feet, and ahead of him Anrel could see a few other people hurrying toward the entrance to the baths.

"Delegate!" someone shouted, inches from his ear. "Delegate! Do your duty, and give us Lord Allutar!"

"Kill the sorcerers!" someone else bellowed from a few feet away.

After that the voice of the crowd became an undifferentiated roar, and Anrel could no longer make out any words at all. Derhin hustled him forward, past hands grabbing at him, and a moment later he found himself led around a corner and thrust through an empty doorway into the baths.

21

In Which Anrel Accepts His Position

The interior of the building was surprisingly bright and airy, and it took a moment before Anrel realized that that was because the windows were all empty frames, without glass, bar, or shutter, and parts of the roof had fallen in, leaving some areas open to the clear blue sky of a beautiful morning.

Meeting here in the winter could not have been pleasant, he thought, though he could see from the smoke stains on the remaining ceilings that there had been some provision of heat.

He and Derhin were in an entry hall; they had not come in through the front, but through a small side door, so that the grand doors were on their right, most of the building's interior was on their left, and directly ahead was a particolor stone archway leading into a good-sized room. Anrel could see figures moving in that room, and hear voices.

"That's the cloakroom," Derhin said, pointing at the arch. "You would be very unwise to set foot in there."

"Thank you," Anrel said as he looked around.

The floor on which they stood was mostly white tile, though there were elaborate patterns in blue and green around the edges, and many tiles were missing. The wall to the right had once been a magnificent concoction of tile, marble, and gilding, but large areas were now bare brown brick, so that the original grand design could only be guessed at. There were three sets of doors, all of bronze-bound wood, though the bronze was now green and crumbling, and the wood black with age. The side doors were of roughly normal height, perhaps seven feet tall, but the central pair was easily twelve feet tall, and sunlight leaked through a few holes near the top where the wood had rotted through, or perhaps been eaten by worms or insects.

It seemed very unlikely that any of those doors could still be opened, which suited Anrel well; he could still hear the shouting mob beyond.

The most remarkable feature of that wall and its six doors, though, was that Anrel could sense a very faint tingle of magic there—someone had placed a ward on those doors a long, long time ago, and it still held, to some extent. That was probably why the doors were still there, while the one through which they had entered was utterly gone. It might also explain why these ruins had sometimes been said to be haunted.

Odd, he thought, that some ancient magician had put so powerful a ward on the front doors, but not on the rest of the building.

Then he turned left, at Derhin's urging, and looked at the baths.

There was an open expanse of once-tiled floor stretching forty feet or so between two double rows of columns, leading to a huge domed space—the central bath, where the Grand Council met. The floor of the gigantic circular bath was about five feet below the surrounding floor, with steps leading down into it on every side, but it was utterly dry and deserted now, much of its white tile lining cracked and broken. Men and a few women were standing here and there, talking quietly, but no one had set foot in the sunken area yet. A few individuals were present who wore odd red and white sashes diagonally, over one shoulder and down to the waist; these people all seemed to be hurrying somewhere.

Derhin noticed where Anrel's attention had fallen, and said, "The sashes indicate our staff. We have some forty or so people who run our errands, fetch us food and drink, carry messages, and so forth."

"I see," Anrel said. He continued studying the architecture.

To either side of the entry hall, beyond the rows of columns, stairs led up to a gallery that encircled the base of the dome, twenty feet above the main floor, and looked down on that empty pool. That was presumably the gallery from which Lord Blackfield watched the proceedings. A few observers were up there now, looking down.

On either side of the dome, arcades opened into other rooms, and beyond it was a sunny courtyard. A small section of the roof had fallen in above that forty-foot entryway leading to the central bath, letting sun in there as well, but the dome itself appeared to be intact, and there was no rubble to be seen anywhere; presumably it had been cleared away when the building was first put to use by the council.

"That's the atrium, on the far side," Derhin explained, pointing at the courtyard. "The massage area is on the left, the towel room over there, the changing rooms down that way. The hot baths—well, I think you should stay with me until your appointment is confirmed, but the hot baths are past the main pool on the right, to one side of the atrium."

"Thank you," Anrel said again.

He followed Derhin through the entry hall, around the central bath, and out into the atrium, where flagstone paths had sunk so deeply into the turf they were almost lost. About a dozen men and two women stood chatting, and Derhin joined them, introducing Anrel. The names and places of origin were recited so quickly that Anrel did not remember any of them five minutes later.

He was startled that none of them seemed particularly interested in him; indeed, he felt somewhat slighted. Then he realized that Derhin had introduced him by his real name, and while he had said that Anrel had come from Naith, he had not explained who he was or why he was there. He stood and listened as they discussed what to expect from the Hots, from the Cloakroom, from the emperor's representatives, in response to Amanir's death and the accusations the Hots were hurling at Lord Allutar.

"And you, Master Murau," an older man said, turning to Anrel. "What do you think of all this?"

"I find it very interesting," Anrel said.

"I suppose you've come to report on your delegate's actions, to assure the people of Naith that they are being well represented?" another man asked.

Anrel cleared his throat and looked at Derhin.

"I'm afraid you have misunderstood," Derhin said. "Anrel is the new delegate from Naith, replacing poor Amanir."

A dozen heads suddenly snapped around, and two dozen eyes focused on the stranger.

"Here?" one of them asked. "With us?"

"His final loyalties are not yet determined," Derhin replied. "He has agreed to speak for the Hots on certain matters in Amanir's stead, but he does not fully accept their positions."

"But will he . . . That is . . ."

"His loyalties are not yet determined," Derhin repeated. "He is here with us because I am the one presenting him for confirmation. Once confirmed, he will join the Hots until he has given the speech he has promised them. After that, it will be his own choice."

"I do not yet understand the various beliefs well enough to have joined any specific faction," Anrel said. "I intend to listen with interest to today's deliberations."

"Of course! Good sense, young fellow," the older man said.

"Thank you, sir."

Anrel might have said more, but he was interrupted by a voice calling from somewhere behind him.

"Hear me, delegates of the empire's people!" the speaker cried. Anrel turned.

"Hear me!" the voice continued. "The Grand Council of the Walasians is hereby called to order! Let every person delegated to speak for their community gather!"

"That means us," the older man said, clapping Anrel on the shoulder. "Come on."

Anrel joined the men and women of the Atrium as they marched into the great domed chamber and descended the steps into the ruined pool. Derhin led him across the broken tiles to a position almost directly below a raised platform at one side, a platform that Anrel had not noticed before.

A man in a green and gold robe stood on the platform. When the delegates had all climbed down into the empty bath, while observers were still jockeying for position on the surrounding floor or in the gallery above, the robed man lifted a carved white rod and proclaimed, "I was chosen as today's first speaker, and as such I hereby declare the Grand

Council of the Walasians convened for this fourth day of summer in the five hundred and eighty-ninth year of the Walasian Empire, which is the twenty-fourth year of the reign of His Imperial Majesty Lurias Imbredar, twelfth of that name. Is there any objection?"

No one spoke out, though a few voices murmured quietly.

After a brief pause, the speaker continued, "I remind the Grand Council that we are charged by our people with determining the course of their governance, and that we are not bound by past law or custom, but empowered to create what law pleases us. Through us the Walasian people speak their will, and assert their authority throughout the empire. A great responsibility has been placed upon us. If there are any here who feel themselves unfit to accept this responsibility, let them speak now, that we may release them from their obligations."

He paused again, and again, no one spoke.

"This is the one hundred and eighty-fifth day since the gathering of this Grand Council, and the one hundred and sixty-third session of deliberation. As today's first speaker I hereby propose that we provisionally accept all actions and decisions of the prior one hundred and sixty-two sessions that have not previously been rescinded. All in favor?"

Hundreds of voices said, "Aye!" in approximate unison, startling Anrel.

"Opposed?"

Perhaps two or three voices said, "Nay!"

"The proposal has been accepted. Business will continue from previous sessions, rather than starting anew. Let it be so recorded." He waved the white rod.

"That much is all recited every day," Derhin whispered in Anrel's ear.

"I now ask the delegates whether every province of the empire is duly represented, in accordance with the summons that created this Grand Council. Is the full delegation of the province of Demerren in attendance?"

"It is," someone answered from the floor.

"Is the full delegation of the province of Hallin in attendance?"

"It is."

The speaker ran through the list of provinces, one by one, until at last he said, "Is the full delegation of the province of Aulix in attendance?"

"It is not, sir!" Derhin responded instantly.

"Identify yourself, sir!"

"I am Derhin li-Parsil, delegate from Naith in Aulix. My compatriot from Naith, Amanir tel-Kabanim is not present, nor will he be." Derhin's voice shook as he spoke these last few words—trembling with grief or rage, Anrel supposed.

"The council recognizes the delegate from Naith, and asks that he explain his compatriot's absence."

Derhin immediately marched up the steps, circled around the platform, and strode up to stand beside the speaker, who bowed and retreated, leaving Derhin alone on the platform.

"As you all know, Amanir tel-Kabanim will never again address this gathering. He hanged himself yesterday morning." He paused after those words, his hands clutched into fists, then swallowed hard before continuing, "As his fellow delegate from Naith it falls to me to name a provisional replacement, and I have made my choice." He took a deep breath, then continued, "I could talk at length about the horror of poor Amanir's death, about the suspicious circumstances surrounding it, about the need to find a suitable heir swiftly, about the delicacy required in selecting that heir so that I might properly balance the demands of Amanir's townspeople back in Naith, the demands of his friends in this council, and a dozen other factors. I will not. Our empire is in a state of crisis, and we have no time to waste on such matters. You all know most of what I might tell you, and no worthwhile purpose would be served by such a recitation. Instead I will say that fate—or perhaps the Mother and Father of us all—delivered to me the ideal individual to take up Amanir's place in this honorable gathering. He is a man most of you, perhaps all of you, know by reputation, though that reputation now owes as much to myth as to fact. His given name is Anrel Murau; no true name is recorded in the Great List, for although he attempted the sorcery trials, he did not succeed in them. You all know him, however, by another name, a name he gave himself when he addressed the crowds in Aulix Square in our home city of Naith, and that he used again in

Beynos. It is a name claimed by others on occasion, but this man, Anrel Murau, is the originator and the original. Members of the Grand Council, I hereby name as heir to Amanir tel-Kabanim the man known to you all as Alvos, the orator of Naith."

Anrel had already started toward the steps, but he stumbled and almost fell, startled by the roar that Derhin's final words provoked. Hundreds of voices were shouting, bellowing, questioning. Then he got his feet back under him and trotted quickly up and around and onto the platform, where he stood silently beside Derhin.

"Members of the Grand Council," Derhin shouted, trying to be heard over the chaos, "I present Anrel Murau, known as Alvos!"

"How do we know it's really him?" someone called out.

"I give you my word as a delegate and a Walasian that this is the man who spoke in Aulix Square and asked the people of Naith to elect Amanir and myself to this council!" Derhin called back.

"Alvos! Alvos! Alvos!" someone began to chant; Anrel thought he recognized the speaker as one of the Hots who had come to Lord Blackfield's rooms the previous night.

Derhin turned to Anrel. "Anrel Murau," he said, "do you accept this appointment to serve as a delegate to the Grand Council, to represent the people of Naith, and to do your best to guide the future of the empire?"

"I do accept this charge," Anrel replied, speaking loudly and clearly. "If the council allows, I will serve to the best of my ability."

The assembled delegates applauded—or at any rate, most of them did; Anrel heard a few objections and catcalls amid the cheers. That was hardly surprising. The noise continued for several seconds while the speaker remounted the podium; Derhin and Anrel stepped back to make way for him. He raised his hands for silence, and gradually the crowd quieted.

"I call upon the delegates to vote upon Delegate li-Parsil's nomination of a successor for the late Amanir tel-Kabanim!" he shouted. "In the interests of celerity, I ask for approval by acclamation. Those in favor, say aye!"

Hundreds of voices shouted in reply.

"Those opposed, say nay!"

Dozens of voices—perhaps hundreds, Anrel could not be certain—responded. The volume was unquestionably less than had been the roar of approval. A new round of applause broke out.

Bellowing to be heard, the speaker proclaimed, "Since provisional acceptance requires approval from only one-fourth of this body, I hereby declare Anrel Murau to be the new delegate from Naith."

The applause—and an admixture of jeers and protests—continued for a moment, and as it gradually faded one voice began to stand out.

"Master Speaker! Master Speaker!" someone was calling.

"I recognize the noble delegate from Naith."

Anrel followed the speaker's pointing finger and saw a well-dressed man of middle years, tall and slim.

"Lord Oris," Derhim murmured in Anrel's ear.

"I must insist upon a proper election!" Lord Oris shouted.

"That is your privilege," the speaker replied. "As a friend of the burgrave of Naith, I trust you can arrange the matter, Lord Oris?"

Lord Oris seemed discomfited by this immediate acquiescence. "I . . . yes," he said.

"Then Anrel Murau will serve until such time as the results of the election are known to us. Delegate Murau, do you wish your name to be entered in this election Lord Oris proposes?"

"I do," Anrel replied.

"Then let it be done." The speaker took a deep breath, and said, "Let me say a few words now to congratulate the newest member of the Grand Council, and instruct him in a few of the expectations he must now face."

Anrel raised his chin and tried to look interested as the speeches began.

22

In Which Anrel Proposes a Compromise

The speeches rambled on for almost an hour. The speaker, whose name Anrel still had not learned, spoke in grand generalities of the council's heritage and promise. He was followed by Derhin, whose speech was to all intents and purposes a eulogy for both Amanir and Lord Valin, mentioning Anrel only in passing. Lord Oris then spoke about the beauty and importance of the city of Naith and the province of Aulix, and concluded with the hope that Anrel would be worthy of them, while making it clear that Oris himself doubted that Anrel could achieve such a height.

Then there was a stir as someone made his way toward the platform, and Anrel was startled to see Lord Allutar mounting the steps.

"Master Murau," Lord Allutar said with a nod.

"My lord," Anrel acknowledged.

Then Lord Allutar turned to address the delegates.

"Members of the council, I stand before you to congratulate this young man on what he has accomplished today. Through the influence of his foolhardy friends and the clever manipulation of public sentiment, Master Murau has found his way onto the Grand Council, and has thereby earned a pardon for any crimes he might have committed before today. An hour ago he was under sentence of death for sedition, inciting riots, assault upon an officer of the peace, innumerable counts of theft, conspiring with witches, and undoubtedly other offenses of which I am blissfully unaware. To dismiss all that with a few well-chosen words, a friend's assistance, and a round of applause—that's quite remarkable, and I must confess my admiration for his audacity. I must also admit to relief on a purely personal level. As some of you may know, I am affianced to Lady Saria Adirane, daughter of the burgrave of Alzur. What you may not realize is that Master Murau is Lady Saria's cousin. It is indeed a relief to know I will be marrying into the family of a delegate to the Grand Council, rather than rendering myself kin to a traitorous thief and brigand."

The crowd stirred at that; Anrel's familial connections were obviously news to most of them. Anrel saw that by mentioning this link, Lord Allutar was using his own infamy as the despoiler of the Raish Valley to taint Anrel and undercut Anrel's standing with the Hots and other populist factions. He was also making sure that everyone present knew that Anrel had a base personal motive for accepting appointment to the council.

That was, Anrel thought, probably far more effective than open opposition.

"I have known Master Murau for some time," Lord Allutar continued, "and I know him to be a man of learning, a man of sense, a man who values his friends above his own political principles. I trust his actions as a member of the Grand Council will continue to be guided by expedience and personal loyalties, rather than any great passion for justice or deep moral convictions."

A stunned silence had fallen over the crowd; Lord Allutar turned to Anrel and smiled sardonically. "Master Murau, I believe it is now time for you to address your compatriots in this body."

Anrel stepped forward. "Thank you, Lord Allutar," he said. He turned to face the crowd, and took a deep breath as he looked at the upturned faces in the great pool, and at the watchers in the gallery above. He thought he spotted Lord Blackfield, but was not entirely sure.

This was different from his speeches in Naith and Beynos. Here he was not addressing a random group of citizens, but the Grand Council. There would be no riot—but his words might have effects much more widespread and lasting.

He had planned out much of what he intended to say, but now, after hearing Lord Allutar's speech, he quickly modified it to suit the situation. "I am afraid I must correct you in one matter," he began. "Yes, my cousin is your fiancée, to my dismay. Yes, I am glad to be free of the outrageous charges against me—I am always pleased when common sense vanquishes folly. I am also pleased that I am pardoned for those thefts and other offenses I did indeed commit in order to survive as a fugitive, and I hope that now I am able to live openly again I will eventually be able to make recompense for them. You were correct in those particulars, my lord." He paused, and turned his head to look at Lord Allutar.

The landgrave met his gaze calmly.

"However," Anrel proclaimed, "when you speak of my personal loyalties overriding my passion for justice, you malign me. You sorely misjudge me." He turned back to the crowd in the great round pool. "It is a passion for justice that has always driven me. It was my passion for justice that compelled me to speak out in Aulix Square against your own injustices, Lord Allutar. It was my passion for justice that drove me to speak again in Beynos, and that forced me from my comfortable home in Alzur. It is a passion for justice that has brought me here today. I am here in *pursuit* of justice, my friends and fellow Walasians. I seek justice for my predecessor, Amanir tel-Kabanim, who I believe you, Lord Allutar Hezir, murdered by sorcerous means. I seek justice for Lord Valin li-Tarbek, who I *know* you murdered—who died in my arms with his chest torn open by your magic. I seek justice for a young woman named Reva Lir, who harmed no one, yet who you hanged for witchcraft over the vigorous objections of the people of Beynos, using your sorcery to ensure that she put her own head in the noose—just as did Amanir tel-Kabanim. I *know* you can make an innocent hang himself, my lord—I saw you do it in Beynos. Can I doubt that you did the same here in Lume? We have witnesses who can swear that Amanir went to meet with you the night before his death; was that when you ensorceled him? Was that when you condemned him to die?"

"You have no evidence of any such thing," Allutar replied, addressing Anrel rather than the crowd. "Amanir tel-Kabanim died by his own hand. I was not even present."

Anrel stared at him for a second, tempted to argue, but he resisted the temptation. This was not a trial, and he was not a prosecutor. He was making a broader point than merely accusing Lord Allutar of murdering a delegate.

And in fact, the landgrave was right; he had no evidence.

"I seek justice for those three deaths," he said, "and for a fourth, as well. I seek justice for Urunar Kazien, my lord, who you executed for petty theft because you needed his blood for a certain black sorcery—the spell that so polluted the fields of the Raish Valley that crops grown there are inedible. That young man died for *nothing*, my lord, and his death brought only corruption and hunger."

For the first time, Allutar looked visibly angry. Anrel did not pause in his speech.

"I seek justice for the people of the Pensioners' Quarter," he shouted, "who were burned out of their homes, many of them burned to death in the streets, for daring to protest when they were sold your tainted wheat! I seek justice for *all* the ordinary citizens of the Walasian Empire who have been betrayed and abused by their rulers! I am indeed driven by a passion for justice, Lord Allutar. Without justice we are nothing more than beasts. It is in pursuit of justice that I stand here now and ask the Grand Council to do what was once unthinkable, and place real restraints upon the sorcerers who rule the empire, who do not concern themselves with justice, and who place their own interests above the welfare of the empire. I know that nothing Lord Allutar has done is necessarily a crime under the laws of the empire, I know that the deaths he caused were within his rights as landgrave, I know that his ruination of the fields of the Raish Valley was permitted. I *know* all that, fellow delegates, but I say to you all that we must have justice even when the law does not demand it, even when the law *denies* it. I say that the sorcerers must be brought to account for their offenses against our common humanity. Under the laws we have accepted for centuries there is no provision for such an accounting, but we, we who are gathered here today, we are *the Grand Council*. We *are* the empire. We are the font from which the law derives. We can bring the sorcerers who have done so much damage to the empire to justice."

He looked out over the crowd and saw a sea of rapt faces—once again, his talent for oratory had won out.

"We can, and we *must*," he said. "I am new to this body, and not yet familiar with its workings, so I do not know precisely what the next step might be, but I call upon you all to *take* that step without further delay! We have the authority to demand an accounting of the wrongs the sorcerers have committed over the years—can we not do so? Can we not look at what has been done, and say, regardless of the law, that this act was wrong, while that one was right? That this one was harmless, while that one was so dangerous that only a fool would attempt it? Can we not point out where our nobles have been so negligent of the public safety that their actions constitute a crime in fact, if not in law? I understand that the council as a whole would be too unwieldy to investigate every detail, but can we not appoint a committee to study what has been done, so that those who thought themselves above the law might nonetheless face *real* justice, the justice they have so long evaded?"

That drew shouts of protest from several directions—from sorcerers, Anrel did not doubt.

"I do *not* call for the overthrow of our system of government," Anrel continued. "I know that there are those among you who want such a revolution, and that some of them are among those who most wanted to see me here, in poor Amanir's place, but I do not want the council to take any action so extreme. To do so would be the equivalent of burning down a house to rid it of fleas. No, our sorcerers and their magic are vital to the empire, and these sorcerers have experience in governance that the rest of us do not. I ask only that we no longer place them beyond the reach of justice. Heretofore, commoners have had no real recourse when wronged by their superiors, for it was those very superiors who held the power we call, all too inaccurately, high and low justice. Our magistrates, for the most part, serve at the pleasure of our landgraves and burgraves and margraves, and naturally take the side of those sorcerers in every dispute, fairly or not. Can we not create a body that will restrain those few sorcerers who abuse the trust and the power we have given them?" He waved toward the closed doors. "You have all heard the crowds out there calling out for justice—can we not at least *try* to give them what they demand?"

At that, Lord Allutar spoke up. "You would give me to the mob? You would allow that rabble to dictate to us?" His voice shook with rage.

"*No,* my lord, I would not!" Anrel replied, turning to face the land-grave. "Rather, I would insist that a calm and rational study of the situation be made, and appropriate actions be taken, so that the mob out there does not take justice into its own hands. If *we* do not act, *they will,* sooner or later. We must present them with a satisfactory resolution before their patience is exhausted, or we will *all* suffer for it!"

"So you would make the nobility of the empire answer to some *committee*?" Anrel had rarely heard anyone put so much hatred and disdain into a single word.

"Yes, my lord, I would," he replied calmly.

"And what of those who are responsible for the present disorder who are *not* sorcerers? Will you investigate them as well, and bring them to face what you call justice?"

Anrel spread his hands. "Why not? Justice must be evenhanded, or it is not justice."

That was clearly not the answer Lord Allutar had expected.

"You would have no objection to bringing to order those who have incited riots in, say, Naith and Beynos?"

A sudden silence fell as the entire Grand Council watched Lord Allutar and Anrel Murau glare at each other.

Anrel, like everyone else, knew exactly what Lord Allutar was saying. He knew that he was being presented with a choice—to back down, and let both Lord Allutar and himself escape, or to stand firm and be pulled down with his foe.

He had never really thought of himself as suicidal, but to stand on principle now could be nothing else.

He had promised himself that he would stop taking action without considering the consequences, that he would think about what it would mean to do what he thought should be, *must* be done. And so he thought, as he had promised he would. He imagined his life cut short at the end of a hempen rope, as Reva's had been. He imagined dying ignominiously—but knowing that Allutar would die, as well.

That was not so very terrible that he could not face it. He already faced a future in which he would never see Tazia again, and if he backed down he knew that the entire empire faced a future of chaos and disorder, a future in which the sorcerers would do all they could to cling to power, regardless of how much damage it did to their homeland. If he pressed his case the empire might yet be saved, the nobility purged, the mob satisfied, and order restored. If it cost his life, then the price was high, but could be borne.

And in the end, none of that mattered. He had been caught up in his own words. He knew that at another time he might think very differently, but here and now, at this moment, the passion for justice he had roused in his own breast took precedence over everything else. If justice demanded his death, then he must die—better to die than to forsake justice.

"I have faith in the good sense of my fellow councillors," Anrel replied at last. "Yes, I would accept a committee to investigate commoners, if that is what we must have to establish a committee for the regulation of sorcery."

"But of course, members of this council would be exempt?"

There was the offer again, another chance to save himself, but only by saving Lord Allutar—and in the process, ruining the whole thing. Many of the worst criminals in all the empire's nobility were here, in this great chamber, and they could not be allowed to go free and use their absent brethren as scapegoats.

Anrel met Lord Allutar's gaze. "Why, no, my lord. I think that would render the entire exercise pointless. While we would retain our general immunity, I think any crimes or improprieties that contributed to the present crisis must be dealt with, no matter who committed them. Yes, this would mean that you and I must both face justice. I am prepared to accept the consequences of my actions, Lord Allutar. Are *you*?"

Allutar stared at him as if he could not believe what he was hearing. "Your pardon is scarcely an hour old, yet you would already renounce it?"

"For the good of the empire, my lord, yes, I would."

"You're mad, Murau!"

"I do not think I am, my lord."

"Delegates!" the speaker said, stepping between them. "Delegates, you have made your positions clear. Let us now consider your proposals."

"They aren't clear to *me*," someone shouted from below.

"Nor me!"

"My fellow Walasians," Derhin called, "let us hear specific proposals that we might debate!"

The speaker grimaced, then turned to Anrel. "Master Murau, do you have a proposal to make?"

"I do, sir. I propose the creation of a Committee for the Regulation of Sorcery, backed by the full authority of the Grand Council and charged with the responsibility for investigating the misuse of magic, past and present, regardless of whether it was technically allowed under the law of the time, and establishing guidelines that all sorcerers must follow in the future. I say this committee must be given the power to impose appropriate penalties for such misuse, regardless of the rank or station of the guilty party."

"And I," Lord Allutar shouted in response, "propose the creation of a Committee for the Restoration of Order, backed by whatever authority this council may truly possess and charged with investigating the causes of the recent unrest, and punishing those responsible, whosoever they might be—assuming, of course, that they are not sorcerers, for Master Murau's committee will be dealing with *those*." He looked out over the crowd. "You will not lay all the blame upon us. It was not sorcery that burned bakeries and rioted in the streets of Lume. It was no sorcerer who fired cannon into the streets and enraged the crowds."

"Good!" Anrel said.

Lord Allutar stared at him, dumbfounded.

"I am aware that my predecessor opposed a proposal somewhat similar to Lord Allutar's," Anrel said. "I believe he was wrong to do so. He said it would be used to delay justice and obfuscate the truth. I have more faith in this council than that—I believe that *both* committees must be established, and quickly! We must be seen to be impartial in our actions—and we must be seen to *act*. These dual committees will show the empire that we are not favoring one side over another, and that we *are* taking action, regardless of the cost to ourselves."

"We have two proposals," the speaker said unhappily.

"We have *one* proposal," Anrel interrupted. "That *both* committees be created."

"No, sir," Allutar snapped. "We have *two* proposals—yours, whatever it may be, and mine, which is only that we create a Committee for the Restoration of Order to find and punish those responsible for the recent unrest."

"We have two proposals," the speaker repeated. "Let us consider Delegate Murau's first . . ."

With that, the debate began, and although it lasted for almost three hours, Anrel never doubted the outcome. The Hots and other rabid commoner factions supported the two committees because they wanted a Committee for the Regulation of Sorcery, and would accept the other to get it; likewise, the sorcerers were eager to see a Committee for the Restoration of Order, especially once it was made clear that it would indeed have the authority to question the emperor himself, and they would tolerate the Committee for the Regulation of Sorcery to get it. Both groups saw that this would go a good way toward appeasing the mobs, and bringing a semblance of peace and order to the capital.

In both cases, most of the delegates did not see that they themselves would be at risk; after all, *they* had not incited any riots or poisoned any farmland.

And among the nobles they asked themselves what power a Committee for the Regulation of Sorcery could really have. All magic was in the hands of sorcerers. The sorcerers told themselves that they had nothing to fear.

Lord Allutar made that explicit at one point during the debate when he leaned over and murmured to Anrel, "You realize that you may yet hang, while they cannot harm me?"

"We will see," Anrel murmured back.

"You are putting your own neck in the noose for nothing."

"I am acting for the good of the empire," Anrel retorted.

"I will tell your cousin you said that."

Lord Allutar's proposal for a single committee was brought up, but was rejected in fairly short order—the Hots wanted an investigation of *all* the evils sorcerers had committed, not just those that had contributed to the present crisis, and there was a general feeling that a single committee would be overwhelmed by the scope of their task.

So in the end, as Anrel had expected, both committees were voted into existence, though it was by no means unanimous. Lord Allutar argued vehemently but uselessly against them, and managed to sway a portion of the Cloakroom, while scattered others voted against the idea for their own reasons, but in the end a solid majority approved the proposal.

And in the end, to no one's surprise, Anrel was appointed to the Committee for the Regulation of Sorcery, though Zarein Lorsa was named chairman. Anrel did not recognize most of the other names. No sorcerers were nominated for that committee, since they could hardly be impartial in establishing rules for their fellow nobles. All in all, a score and a half of delegates were appointed, all of them commoners, with at least one representative for each of the sixteen provinces.

Anrel had reservations about appointing an extremist like Lorsa to chair the committee, but he said nothing. The other members of the committee would surely restrain the Hots.

Lord Allutar was *not* named to the Committee for the Restoration of Order, to his annoyance; he placed his name in nomination, but was voted down. As several people pointed out, the mob outside was demanding his blood; placing him in any new position of authority would be a foolish defiance of the popular will. Most of that committee was made up of sorcerers, but a few commoners, some three of the two dozen members, were included for the sake of appearances.

And when that was settled, the assembly voted itself a recess for luncheon.

Before Anrel could find Lord Blackfield among the observers, or speak to Derhin about lunch plans, Zarein Lorsa came up beside him and grabbed his arm.

"Come with us," he said. "There's no time to waste. I've sent a man to bring us food, so we can speak without interruption."

Anrel blinked at him, startled.

"The committee is meeting immediately," Lorsa explained. "Before the sorcerers can find a way to interfere."

"The committee . . . ?"

"Yes. The Committee for the Regulation of Sorcery. As its chairman, I am calling a meeting. I will not tolerate delay. This way, sir." He pulled at Anrel's arm.

Anrel had not expected this level of enthusiasm, but he could hardly argue; he followed as Lorsa led him through the crowd, gathering other committee members along the way.

23

In Which Anrel Makes a Dangerous Suggestion

At the insistence of its chairman the Committee for the Regulation of Sorcery, comprised of some thirty delegates, met initially in what had once been the heated baths. One rather naive committee member asked whether this might inconvenience the Hots, and the laughter of the others set him blushing angrily.

"The other committee is meeting in the cloakroom," someone told him, not unkindly. "This isn't a coincidence."

"But I'm not a Hot!" the committee member protested.

"Most of the committee isn't," he was told, "but our chairman is one of the leaders of the Hots, half a dozen of his closest companions are here, and the other Hots are very eager to hear what we have to say."

"Shouldn't we be meeting in secret, though?"

It was Anrel who asked, "Why? The entire *point* of this committee is to show the people of the empire that we are doing something about their complaints. There may be occasion when certain things should be kept private, but we should at least *try* to keep our actions open, shouldn't we?"

"Exactly!" Lorsa proclaimed. "Enough of secrecy and deception! The people deserve to see how we deal with the tyrants who have oppressed them." He turned to Anrel and continued, "I want to thank you, Delegate Murau, for accepting poor Amanir's position and presenting our case so effectively. I do not know that we could have established this committee without you."

"Zarein," Delegate Gluth murmured, "I think you underestimate what Delegate Murau has done."

"Oh?" Lorsa turned to his friend. "In what way?"

"Not only could we not have created this committee without Murau's help, we could not have created it without allowing the creation of the other committee—we didn't have the votes, not unless we gave them something in exchange."

"Yes?"

"What we gave them, Zarein, was Master Murau's life. He agreed to set aside his immunity as a member of the Grand Council if the Committee for the Restoration of Order demands it. As a result, he will most likely be hanged for sedition—and he allowed this, knowing as much."

Lorsa's head snapped around to stare at Anrel. "They would not *dare*," he said. "Alvos is a hero of the people!"

"And soon to be a martyr," someone Anrel did not recognize said. "That was plain to us all. Did you not see it, Delegate Lorsa?"

"We can *use* a martyr," Gluth said. "I would never have asked it of anyone, but Murau has volunteered for the role."

"I saw no alternative," Anrel said. "There was no other way to bring this committee into existence, and without it Lord Allutar would never be brought to justice. Indeed, this committee may be the salvation of the Walasian Empire."

"This committee is useless," another man said. "It's a sham. We will investigate, and issue rulings, and what will come of it? Nothing. The sorcerers will ignore us. And what can we do against them? We have no magic of our own, no soldiers—what can we do if one of them defies us?"

"Delegate Murau and I discussed that the other night," Lorsa replied. "Are you all familiar with the Great List?"

"Only the emperor can use the Great List," a committee member replied.

"No, only the emperor *has* the Great List," Lorsa said. "Any magician can use it—is that not so, Delegate Murau?"

"I believe so," Anrel replied.

"What do *you* know of magic?" someone demanded.

"My parents were sorcerers," Anrel said. "I grew up in the household of the burgrave of Alzur."

"One of *them!*"

"No, no," Lorsa said. "He is no sorcerer, and has no love for them, despite his parentage. Is that not so, Murau?"

"It is," Anrel agreed.

"Then if we were to somehow gain access to the Great List, Delegate Murau, could you use it?"

Anrel looked for the speaker, but could not identify him. "No, sir," he said. "I could not. I failed the trials when I was twelve; I am no sorcerer." He did not mention that he had failed deliberately, nor did he say anything about his brief training in witchcraft—these did not strike him as people who would look kindly on witches.

And in fact, he had never learned the use of true names. He had not actually lied.

"Then who *would* use it?"

"Any sorcerer," Anrel said. "You might offer some noble amnesty for his crimes in exchange for his assistance in this."

"Or we might follow the emperor's example, and hire a magician from the Cousins," Gluth suggested. "There are several possibilities."

"But we do not *have* this list!"

"We have the full authority of the Grand Council," Anrel said. "In theory, we can require the Emperor to allow us access to it. We can note down the names we need—most particularly, Lord Allutar's true name—and then proceed from there."

"In *theory*," Gluth said.

"In practice," Anrel said, "I am sure we can find something to offer His Imperial Majesty to obtain his cooperation. Consider the existence of our sister committee, and who sits on it—is it not true that the Cloakroom considers *the emperor himself* to be responsible for the recent unrest? Is the Committee for the Restoration of Order not charged with identifying and punishing those responsible? Is that committee not staffed with several powerful sorcerers who might well be capable of enforcing an edict against even the emperor?"

"Despite the Emperor's Watch and his foreign mercenary magicians? I do not think they could . . ."

"That would be treason!"

"I don't believe . . ."

"It's madness!"

The discussion collapsed into chaos for a few moments until Lorsa was able, by sheer volume, to shout it down and restore order. When he had finally obtained relative calm, he said, "Perhaps we are not all in full accord as to what would best serve the empire, but permit me to set forth a course of action, step by step, and see how far we can proceed before disagreeing."

There was a murmur of acceptance.

"The Committee for the Regulation of Sorcery has been created by the Grand Council for the purpose of investigating the misuse of magic."

No one objected to that.

"The most egregious recent misuse of magic was the pollution of the farmlands of the Raish Valley."

Again, no protest.

"It is generally believed that this pollution was the result of black sorcery performed by Lord Allutar Hezir, landgrave of Aulix, in an attempt to increase the yield of those lands."

Still, no one argued.

"The people of Lume are calling for Lord Allutar's blood, and if nothing is done to appease them, we can expect more violence."

That one set a few feet to shuffling, and eyes to glancing warily about, but no one spoke up.

"Therefore, we must assign a high priority to questioning Lord Allutar regarding his actions last year."

"But we can't . . ."

"He won't . . ."

Lorsa held up his hands for silence. "I have said nothing about *how* this task is to be undertaken," he said. "I have merely said that we should give it a high priority. Can anyone argue with that?"

Again, silence fell.

"Now, you have all heard Allutar speak. Many of you have dealt with him on occasion. Is there anyone here who thinks he would cooperate with us voluntarily?"

That drew mutters, and someone called, "He might."

"If only to mock us," someone else added.

"What can we do if he *doesn't*?"

"So this, then," Lorsa said, "is where we first encounter difficulties. Leaving aside the question of whether he *will,* does everyone here think that Allutar Hezir *should* cooperate?"

The chorus of agreement was slow and hesitant, but it came in time. No one denied the premise.

"And if, *if* a means could be found to *compel* his cooperation, should we not use it?"

Again, feet shuffled and eyes darted about uneasily, but again, the entire committee clearly agreed, however reluctantly.

One man spoke up, though. "But only against Lord Allutar," he said.

"At least for now," another added.

Anrel glanced about, studying the faces. Many of the committee members were uneasy, and he understood that; all their lives they had been taught that sorcerers were above the ordinary laws, subject only to the rulings of the emperor or their fellow magicians, yet here these ordinary men and women were talking about *forcing* sorcerers to testify, perhaps to incriminate themselves. It was a frightening prospect.

Perhaps more worrisome to Anrel than the uneasy expressions, though, were the eager ones—including Lorsa's, when he occasionally allowed his emotions to show. Some of these people clearly wanted revenge against the sorcerers for past slights; they were not interested in investigation, but in retribution.

That urge must be kept in check, Anrel thought, or the committee could do severe damage.

"Then let us send two or three of our esteemed members to negotiate with the emperor's men," Lorsa said. "It may be that we can obtain access to the Great List simply by asking, and thereby learn Allutar's true name. After all, surely His Imperial Majesty has no great love for the landgrave of Aulix, the man whose ruined wheat caused so much strife here in the capital! Surely, the Great List would not exist at all if there weren't occasion for its use, and isn't this such an occasion?"

"I'll go," Anrel said. He had little left to lose, should the negotiations go badly.

Lorsa frowned, and shook his head. "No, Delegate Murau, I don't think that would be wise. We all know of your connections to Allutar Hezir, and who knows what word might have reached the emperor's court about your identity as Alvos? I think we should send someone with a better claim to be dispassionate." He grimaced. "I am afraid I am no more suitable than yourself. Perhaps . . ." He looked at the committee. "Perhaps Delegate Savar?" He pointed at a dark-haired young man with a long face and intense eyes.

"It would be an honor, sir," Savar replied with a bow.

"And . . . Delegate tel-Olz?"

That was an older man, his hair streaked with gray. He shook his head. "I would rather not, Master Lorsa," he said.

"Well, I won't insist. Delegate Guirdosia, then?"

He, too, accepted.

"One more, please," Savar called as Lorsa hesitated. "In case Master Guirdosia and I disagree about some detail, a third vote to break the tie?"

"As you wish. Delegate Essarnyn?"

"Delighted to be of service."

It was at that point that the promised luncheon finally arrived, and business was put aside for a moment as bread, cheese, carrots, and wine were distributed. Anrel noticed that Lorsa gathered Savar, Guirdosia, and Essarnyn to him, presumably to discuss their mission. Anrel was debating whether to eavesdrop when Pariel Gluth tapped him on the arm.

"Master Murau," he said.

"Master Gluth," Anrel acknowledged.

"I meant what I said about martyring yourself," Gluth said without further preamble. "If you are having second thoughts, it isn't too late to flee. You have done your full duty and then some today; I am not at all sure we could have ever have made such progress without you. I would not fault you if you chose to vanish; it's too late now to undo these committees, and I think we can now deal with Lord Allutar without you."

"I appreciate your concern," Anrel replied. "However, I have not come this far only to turn and flee; I will see through what I have started. Delegate Lorsa is . . . intemperate, and I fear that he may go too far and bring what we have begun today to disaster. I hope to be a moderating influence."

"Ah, I see." Gluth glanced at Lorsa, who was speaking with quiet intensity to Fulsio Essarnyn. "You may have a point."

"Still, I am not suicidal; I would prefer not to be a literal martyr. Should you hear anything you think I should know, please do inform me."

"Of course."

Gluth turned away, and Anrel watched him go.

He thought he understood Lorsa—he was an idealist like Lord Valin, but one who had turned fanatic, allowing his righteous wrath and revolutionary fervor to overcome everything else. Gluth, though, puzzled Anrel; he seemed so calm and rational, yet he was one of the Hots, devoted to overthrowing the old order. He spoke of the value of martyrdom, but then suggested Anrel avoid it. If he was an idealist, he had nonetheless somehow managed to retain a pragmatic streak. This mix of moderation and extremism was not something Anrel could easily grasp.

Well, it didn't matter what motivated Pariel Gluth. What mattered was guiding the empire through the present crisis and into a peaceful and prosperous future. To accomplish that the Grand Council would need to see the sorcerers brought to heel, and the revolutionaries silenced. The mob would need to be appeased, and the emperor's debts retired.

And then, with order restored, the Grand Council would dissolve itself, and everything could return to normal.

Anrel hoped he would survive long enough to see it.

24

In Which Anrel Is Reunited with an Old Friend

The Grand Council's afternoon session was devoted to debates on any number of topics. The Committee on Imperial Finance gave a report that said, in essence, that the situation was exactly what everyone knew it to be—the imperial court's debts could not be paid unless a new source of funds was found, the nobles controlled every possible source under present law, and they were unwilling to yield up any of that money. All attempts to change the law so that the emperor could levy new taxes or increase existing ones were being blocked—the Grand Council invariably fell half a dozen votes short of passing the necessary resolution.

"You realize that will probably change at last," Gluth whispered in Anrel's ear. "The Committee for the Regulation of Sorcery ought to be able to sway a dozen sorcerers' votes."

Startled, Anrel looked at him.

"Had you not thought of that?" Gluth asked with a cold little smile. "That possibility may convince the emperor to give us access to the Great List."

Anrel had not thought of that, nor could he think of anything intelligent to say in response. Once again, he found himself marveling at Delegate Gluth's turn of mind.

The Committee on Agriculture and Distribution presented a very brief and very depressing report—they were trying to find some way to determine whether sorcery had permanently damaged the empire's croplands, and envoys were negotiating with merchants in Ermetia, Quand, Azuria, and Skarl for grain imports, but as yet none of these efforts had produced any results. Several provinces were already running out of food.

There were reports from towns and cities around the empire, as well, brought by friends and family of various delegates, and Anrel was dismayed to learn that the recent violence had not been restricted to the capital. Bakeries and granaries in the Raish Valley had been burned, and several communities had seen rioting and arson. Several sorcerers who were thought to be involved in black magic, or who had taken a suspicious interest in increasing crop yields, had been driven from their homes, or had their estates burned in their absence. Many of these nobles had taken refuge in Lume, and while they were hardly likely to join the mob in the street calling for Lord Allutar's blood, they were certainly not feeling conciliatory.

Finally, Anrel was surprised to learn that most of the neighborhoods in Lume were forming their own militia. It seemed few people still trusted the Emperor's Watch, overstretched as it was, to defend the city against itself and keep crime under control; in fact, some of the people who spoke seemed to consider the watch part of the problem, one more thing to be defended against, and given what he had seen in the Pensioners' Quarter, Anrel was not inclined to argue with that position.

Instead of relying on the watch the heads of household in the various neighborhoods were forming their own miniature councils, more or less after the model of the Grand Council, and each of these had named a warden to be in charge of maintaining order in that neighborhood and defending it against intruders. The Grand Council had apparently known about this, and even encouraged it.

"Our reliance on the sorcerers has made us weak," Lorsa explained when Anrel commented on these developments. "We need to rely on ourselves, on the common people of the empire."

"The sorcerers themselves mistrust the emperor enough that they're happy to allow it," Gluth added.

And when Anrel wondered why he had not heard about this before,

Gluth suggested that perhaps living with a wealthy foreigner in rented quarters was not the best way to stay in touch with the doings of ordinary Walasians.

After that the reports and discussions began to wind down, and at last the speaker named his successor, who would conduct business the following day, and adjourned the session.

Anrel found Derhin, and the two men left the baths together by the same door they had entered that morning, as did dozens of others.

Anrel was startled to discover that the crowds were still standing in the street—or perhaps this was a different crowd; he did not pretend to recognize anyone. They were not chanting as the delegates filed out; most watched silently, though a few called questions or taunts.

"Have you decided how to save the empire yet?"

"Will your arguing fill our children's bellies, Delegates? Why aren't you home working on your farms?"

"It's been two seasons—have you accomplished *anything* yet?"

"Down with Lord Allutar!"

"Down with the emperor!"

Anrel paid little attention; he was walking with his eyes down, thinking over the day's events. Then a new cry arose.

"That's him! That's Alvos!"

Startled, Anrel looked up to see someone pointing at him.

"Alvos!"

"Alvos!"

"Alvos! Alvos! Alvos!"

Much of the crowd began to cheer; others booed. "Traitor!"

"Fraud!"

"Come on," Derhin said, tugging at Anrel's arm.

Anrel did not answer, but he picked up his pace. The two men did not run; that would invite pursuit. Instead they walked briskly.

"You said there are hidden ways out," Anrel said. "Perhaps we should have used one of them."

"I prefer not to skulk about like a criminal," Derhin said with a glance over his shoulder. "You may have a point, though."

Watchmen were holding the crowd back as more delegates exited.

More shouting had broken out, though Anrel could not make out what this round was about, and some members of the throng were shoving one another. Something was thrown—Anrel had a glimpse of something dark and fist-sized flying through the air, but he could not be sure what it was; a rotten fruit, perhaps, though it was hard to imagine anyone would waste food in the present climate.

He and Derhin rounded the first corner, and the din behind them was muffled. They did not slow, though; in fact, at the second corner first Derhin and then Anrel broke into a trot, which they maintained for several blocks. Only when they came to the corner of Lourn Street did they drop back to a casual walk.

"I . . . had not expected that," Anrel said, as they ambled toward the burgrave of Naith's town house.

"Expected what?" Derhin asked.

"The shouting mob, the cheering, the . . . the scheming."

Derhin glanced at him. "You should have," he said.

"I suppose I should," Anrel agreed. That ended the brief exchange; they walked the final few yards in silence, and entered their temporary home without comment.

Remembering breakfast, Anrel did not wait for Derhin to make any supper preparations, but set about feeding himself, which suited both men. The food had all been provided by Derhin, but he told Anrel to help himself; they could worry about repayment later.

Cold salt beef, good hard cheese, and a bottle of inexpensive red wine made an adequate meal for Anrel. Derhin made do with yesterday's bread and some of the cheese, and drank his share of the wine. They had both finished eating and were sitting in the drawing room, sipping the last of the wine, when Anrel heard a knock.

"What was that?" he said.

"What?"

Anrel did not answer, but listened.

The knock sounded again. This time Derhin heard it as well. "There's someone at the door," he said.

"Are you expecting anyone?" Anrel asked.

"No, are you?"

"Who even knows I'm here?"

"Lord Blackfield, of course, and several of the Hots," Derhin replied. "It's hardly a secret."

Anrel got to his feet. "Then I should see who it is," he said.

Derhin quickly rose, as well. "No, *I* should," he said. "*You* are the legendary Alvos, and it could easily be some madman who imagines you his enemy."

"But I . . ." But Anrel was addressing Derhin's back; the other man was already on his way out of the drawing room.

Anrel followed, but hung back a few feet. Much as he hated to admit it, Derhin had a point about his fame—or infamy, depending on how one viewed it. A few days ago he would never have hesitated to speak for himself, but the crowds shouting for him outside the Baths had shaken his confidence.

A third knock sounded as Derhin approached the front door. He swung the door in a few inches and peered out at the street, which annoyed Anrel; he could not see anything of who or what might be on the stoop. He moved slowly forward, intending to look for himself.

"Yes?" Derhin said.

A woman's voice asked hesitantly, "Does . . . does Anrel Murau live here?"

Anrel stopped dead. That voice . . .

"May I ask—" Derhin began, but before he could complete his question he was interrupted by a shout from Anrel.

"*Tazia?*"

"Anrel?"

"Tazia!" Anrel ran forward and snatched the door handle out of Derhin's hand, pulling the door wide.

There on the doorstep was Tazia Lir—but not quite as he remembered her. She had lost weight; her face was drawn, and her dress, one he remembered, was much the worse for wear, but still, it was unmistakably Tazia. At the sight of him a worried expression vanished, replaced by an adoring smile. "Anrel!"

That smile, and her unexpected presence, swept away doubts that had troubled Anrel ever since he had seen Tazia's sister die on the bridge in Beynos. He had thought that his failure to save Reva would have crushed any affection Tazia might have had toward him, that the fury her father had directed toward Anrel for not agreeing to die in Reva's place might create an insurmountable barrier between them. He had feared that Tazia might not have approved of his rabble-rousing speech, might have been angry that he had not taken a better approach, that he had appealed to the crowd rather than to Lord Allutar or Lord Diosin.

Her happy face erased any such concern. Anrel's arms encircled her, and she enthusiastically returned his embrace.

For a moment no one spoke; the unexpected joy of her presence left Anrel unable to find words, and he felt no need for them in any case. The feel of her warm body against his, the scent of her hair, the sound of her breath were all he wanted and more than he could have asked. The pressure of her hands on his back and her cheek against his own said more than the finest speech anyone had ever given. Any worries about his future or the fate of the empire vanished, at least for that moment.

Then Derhin said dryly, "I take it you know her, Anrel. By all means, then, let us invite her in."

Tazia raised her face from his shoulder and leaned away, looking up to meet his eyes. "Yes, of course," Anrel said, releasing her. "Come in, come in! Are you hungry? Could I get you something to drink, perhaps?"

"I don't . . . perhaps a little . . ." She sounded breathless, though Anrel had not held her as tightly as he might have liked.

"We'll open another bottle," Anrel said, taking her hand and leading her over the threshold. "And there's still some of the cheese."

Derhin stepped past them and leaned out the door to give the street outside a careful look, then closed the door securely behind the happy couple and followed them to the drawing room, where Anrel gently guided Tazia into the best chair. When she was seated Anrel remembered enough of his manners to turn to Derhin.

"Derhin," he said, "allow me to present Mistress Tazia Lir. Tazia, this is Derhin li-Parsil, delegate to the Grand Council representing the commoners of Naith." That said, his gaze returned to the face of his beloved, and he stared into her eyes, smiling foolishly.

Derhin bowed. "I am delighted to make your acquaintance, mistress."

"Thank you, Master li-Parsil," Tazia said, bobbing her head, though she was looking at Anrel, and not Derhin, as she spoke.

"I'll fetch a fresh bottle, shall I?" Derhin said.

"Thank you," Anrel answered.

As Derhin turned and headed for the kitchen, Anrel tore his gaze away long enough to find himself a chair and settle into it. He turned back to Tazia and asked, "What are you doing in Lume? I thought this was the one place your family wouldn't go!"

Tazia gazed at him helplessly. "I scarcely know where to begin," she said. "We've been here half a year, looking for you!"

"For *me*?" Anrel made no attempt to conceal his astonishment. "And . . . 'we'? You're *all* here?"

"Mother, and Perynis, and I," Tazia said.

The omission of her father was obviously significant, but Anrel did not care to guess just what it meant. "Tell me all of it," he said. "From the day . . . in Beynos . . ." He hesitated, unsure how to safely refer to her sister's death.

"The day Reva was hanged," Tazia said, the last trace of her smile vanishing.

"Yes," Anrel said, almost choking on the word as he remembered the horror and despair of that morning.

"We were there," Tazia said. "We saw you dive off the bridge."

"I saw you in the crowd," Anrel said. "I didn't . . . I couldn't reach you." The explanation sounded feeble even as he gave it.

Tazia waved that away. "Of course not. You were busy trying to save Reva, and when that didn't work you did what you had to to save yourself."

"I'm sorry—" he began, but Tazia cut him off.

"You have nothing to apologize for, Anrel," she said. "That was a brave and gallant thing you did."

Anrel stared at her, not comprehending how she could forgive him. "But I failed," he said. "Your sister—Reva died, despite all I could do. Lord Allutar had enchanted her. Or Lord Diosin, I don't really know which, but I assume it was Allutar."

"It doesn't matter," Tazia said, reaching out to take his hand again. "You tried. You did all you could. We understood that." She grimaced. "Well, Mother and Perynis and I understood it. Father . . . Father did not. He said you had deserted us in our hour of need, and that you could have saved Reva if you had gone along with his scheme to trade your life for hers."

"I don't—" Anrel began.

Tazia put a finger to his lips, silencing him.

"You couldn't," she said. "I know that. Lord Allutar had no intention of letting her live, no matter what you did, not when she had had the effrontery to try to cast a spell on *him*."

"What happened?" he asked when she took her finger away. "After I dove from the bridge, I mean."

"There was a riot," she said. "You probably knew that."

"I heard," Anrel acknowledged as Derhin reappeared with wine and cheese.

"The burgrave's home, and Lord Allutar's house on Bridge Street Hill, were burned, and a few other buildings," she said as Derhin set the plate of cheese on a handy table.

"Burned?" Anrel said, stunned.

"Was this in Beynos?" Derhin asked. "Or Alzur?"

Startled, Anrel glanced at him as Tazia replied, "Beynos."

Derhin nodded, and pulled a corkscrew from his pocket.

"We were frightened, but we were angry, too," Tazia said. "Mother was weeping, grieving for Reva, and wanted no part of any more violence, but Father was furious, so Perynis and I made our way out of the crowd and took Mother back to the inn, while Father joined the mob rampaging up Bridge Street. He didn't come back to the Boar's Head for a day and a half, and when he did he was stinking drunk." Her tone made it plain that she did not approve.

"He had just lost his eldest daughter," Anrel said.

"Yes," Tazia said. "But it meant that for a day and a half the three of us were huddled in that room above the stables, lonely and terrified, with no idea whether he was dead or alive, no knowledge of whether *you* were dead or alive, no way to know what had become of Reva's body, whether we would be able to give her a proper burial and commend her soul to the Mother. It was unspeakable. If you ever committed any offense against my family, Anrel, it was then, in doing nothing to let us know what had become of you."

"I *couldn't*," Anrel protested. "To return to Beynos—I would have been arrested and hanged. And I thought you would hate me for not saving your sister; I could not imagine you would be generous enough to forgive me that failure."

"I know," Tazia said, her expression softening. "I know. But at the time, even while I knew there was nothing you could safely do, I hated you for not doing it anyway, for deserting us there."

"I'm sorry," Anrel said, his heart aching in his chest. "I am so very sorry."

"Of course you are, but you have no reason to be," she said, reaching over to caress his cheek.

"What happened then?" Derhin asked as he poured wine.

"Father did come back eventually," Tazia said. "Mother wanted to know what had become of Reva's body, but all *he* wanted to know was where Reva's money was. We all knew she had been saving up to go out on her own, perhaps find a husband—she had chafed under Father's rule for years, and had been hoarding every penny, and now that she was gone, he said that money was *his,* and he wanted it.

"Mother tried to say that was the wine talking, that the money wasn't important, but he would not speak of anything else. So she said that the money should be split between Perynis and myself, to dower us, that Reva would have wanted that, and Father bellowed at her . . ."

Tazia swallowed, and fell silent for a moment. Neither man spoke; Derhin stopped pouring, and they waited for her to continue.

"Father had shouted at us all often enough," Tazia said at last, her voice a trifle unsteady. "For as long as I can remember, we all lived in fear of his temper, when he would shout at us and insult us, and perhaps slap us if we provoked him. Mother had always protected us from the worst of it. She had always been able to soothe him, but after that day and a half alone at the inn, grieving for Reva, she could not restrain herself. She shouted back, and called him a monster, a callous beast, a miser, a whoremonger, treating us all as if we were nothing more than slaves, or less than slaves. She said he would never have Reva's money while any of the rest of us still lived."

Anrel saw tears welling in Tazia's eyes. He leaned in his chair and reached for her, dreading what she was about to say.

"He beat her bloody," Tazia said, pulling her hair back from her face with both hands. "I tried to stop him, and he knocked me aside as if I was nothing. Perynis did not try to help us; she was smarter than that. She ran for help, while Mother and I kept him from following her. I don't know what she told the men downstairs, but they came running in, with Master Kabrig in the lead with a club in his hand, and they took Father down, and dragged him from the room. He was still shouting drunken threats." She took a deep, shuddering breath and dropped her hands. "We wanted to flee immediately, to get away before he could return, but Mother's arm was broken and she was dazed from the blows to her head, so we stayed long enough to heal her—well, to help her heal herself, she was always the best of us at healing magic."

"Magic?" Derhin threw Anrel a glance.

"Witchcraft," Anrel told him.

"It took most of a day, and that was long enough for Father to sober up," Tazia said. "Master Kabrig came to tell us that Father had been turned away from the inn, and that he had said he would be back with the City Watch to claim what was his. We could stay there no longer. There was no telling whose side the watchmen might take, especially if Father told them we were witches. So Master Kabrig saw us safe to the city gate, and we set out for Kolizand, thinking we would find friends there."

"Your customers," Anrel said. "The people you had healed of the fever."

"Yes. But they had heard that rioters had destroyed half of Beynos at the behest of a witch, and they gave us no welcome. We tried to explain the truth, but they would have none of it."

"Of course not," Anrel said bitterly.

"What's more, we worried that we had left a trail in the snow and mud that Father could follow—there were few on the road at that time of year. So we did not stay in Kolizand. We turned toward Lume, just as you had, to hide among the throngs here. And we had hopes of finding you, if you still lived. We asked in the courts where you told us you had lived as a student, so we knew you had reached Lume alive, but we could hear no word of where you had gone when your old neighbors turned you away."

"By my second night in the capital I had taken refuge in the Pensioners' Quarter," Anrel said.

Tazia nodded. "We thought perhaps you might be there, but we did not dare come looking for you in that lawless place, and we had no idea what name you might be using. Instead we rented a room in Catseye at first, and then found work as domestics."

"Domestics? Servants?"

She nodded again. "What other skills did we have that we dared to use? To find even that work we used witchery to persuade our new employers to hire us, rather than more experienced or more compliant women."

"Compliant?" Then Anrel realized what she meant; wealthy men often found serving wenches convenient for more than cooking and cleaning. "Oh."

"We have been living quietly here in Lume ever since," Tazia said. "We have taken no part in any of the politics, any of the riots—well, Perynis was caught up in the crowd that looted a bakery, but nothing else. We wanted nothing but to stay out of trouble and out of sight. But then today we heard that Alvos the orator had been made a member of the Grand Council, and we knew it must be you—no, we *hoped* it was you, but feared it was some imposter. I asked after you, and encouraged cooperation with a few gentle spells, and . . . and here I am, and it *is* you, and I am so, *so* very glad to see you!"

And with that she flung herself from her chair into Anrel's arms, weeping with joy.

25

In Which Anrel Receives Unhappy News

Tazia's visit lasted for roughly another hour, in which she provided more details of her family's misfortunes, and listened avidly to Anrel's and even Derhin's accounts of what they had done. At last, though, she rose. "It's getting dark," she said. "I should go."

"The streets are not safe for a woman alone," Derhin agreed. "Which is a disgrace to the empire."

"I would be happy to accompany you, to see you safe to your family's bosom," Anrel said. "Or perhaps . . ." He glanced at Derhin.

"Perhaps what?" Derhin asked.

"I am not certain I should suggest this," Anrel said. "I am not at all sure of the finances or the proprieties; if either of you feels it inappropriate, do not hesitate to say so. It occurs to me, though, that perhaps we could employ a housekeeper here. Or even a staff of three."

"I don't . . . I . . ." Derhin blinked, and did not finish his sentence.

Seeing his discomfort, Anrel said, "Well, let us not be hasty, in any case." He dismissed the matter with a wave. "I will walk Mistress Lir home, and if she and her mother and sister would care to consider working here, we can discuss it another day."

"I think we will give it every consideration," Tazia said, smiling. "Though you do understand, I trust, that we are not as compliant as some hired women."

"I would hardly think otherwise!" Anrel replied, smiling back.

He did indeed escort her back to her home in Catseye, where she shared a shabby attic room with her younger sister. Tazia informed Anrel that their mother Nivain was employed in a somewhat better household, and had a room there, but the two sisters worked for the manager of a row of tenements, and their accommodations were far from luxurious.

When Tazia opened the door at the top of the stairs Anrel was standing behind her, and Perynis, looking up from where she sat at her sister's return, spotted him immediately. She let out a squeal and sat bolt upright.

"You found him! It's really him!"

"Yes," Tazia said, and Anrel thought she blushed, though it was hard to be sure in the orange glow of the single lamp above the steps.

"Come in, come in!" Perynis called, beckoning

"We aren't allowed to have men in our room . . ." Tazia's voice trailed off uncertainly.

"Oh, but he's a delegate to the Grand Council!" Perynis said, getting to her feet. "Surely, that exempts him from ordinary rules!"

Tazia looked helplessly at Anrel.

"I'm afraid I cannot stay," he said, sparing her any temptation to impropriety, "but you are both most welcome to come visit me tomorrow— or perhaps more than visit."

"More?" Perynis looked from Anrel to Tazia and back.

"I'll let Tazia explain," Anrel said. Then with a wave, he turned and hurried back down the stairs before he could change his mind, his heart filled almost to bursting with a fiery stew of emotion. He was overcome with delight at seeing Tazia again, frustrated that he must part from her even briefly, pleased to see Perynis alive and well, furious at Tazia's account of their father's actions, distraught that they were reduced to near poverty, relieved that neither woman seemed to hold any ill will toward him despite his failure to save poor Reva, and wildly eager with anticipation of seeing Tazia again, and perhaps pursuing the courtship he had long thought impossible.

He could scarcely think, his mind awhirl as he trotted through the streets.

Back at the town house on Lourn Street he found himself barraged with questions—very politely—by Derhin. Anrel gradually explained to him the entire tale of how he had fallen in with the Lir family, and what had become of their eldest daughter.

"This is why I was so certain that Lord Allutar was responsible for Amanir's death," he explained. "I had seen him hang someone before."

"Ghastly!" Derhin said with a shudder. "That poor girl!"

Between them they finished another bottle of wine, and then retired for the night.

In the morning they returned to the Aldian Baths for Anrel's second day as a member of the Grand Council. The speaker of the day was not as good at the job as his immediate predecessor, and several discussions wandered off topic or descended into shouting matches. By midday everyone was obviously weary of it, so the afternoon was dedicated to committee meetings, rather than continuing the general assembly.

The Committee for the Regulation of Sorcery met once again in the old heated pool, where Delegates Savar, Guirdosia, and Essarnyn reported on their initial contacts with the emperor's staff. The first meeting, the previous evening, had gone well; they were awaiting word on an audience with the emperor himself, and were optimistic about their prospects. His Imperial Majesty had met with the Committee on Imperial Finance several times over the past season, so there was certainly precedent in their favor. Whether an audience would be granted for just the three of them, or for the entire committee, remained unclear—if an audience happened at all.

In other business, the committee began compiling a list of sorcerers who should be investigated; almost every one of the thirty members had a name to put forth. Anrel did not mention anyone; his only complaints were against Lord Allutar, who headed the list by unanimous agreement.

The most common reason for adding a name was a suspicion that the sorcerer in question had been practicing black magic, which prompted Anrel to suggest that the committee might do well to speak with members of the Lantern Society.

That was met by a moment of puzzled silence.

"Who?" someone asked at last.

"The Lantern Society," Anrel said. "It is an organization of magicians from Quand and Ermetia who have been campaigning against the use of black magic. They had hoped to convince the empire to ban such practices."

Another, more hostile silence met this explanation.

"Foreigners, trying to tell Walasians what to do?" Delegate tel-Olz asked.

Anrel saw his mistake, and tried to ameliorate it. "They offered neither threats nor promises, but only advice," he said. "The Lantern Society magician I spoke to, a Quandish sorcerer, said that they believed black magic invariably held hidden dangers, and sought only to help make their Walasian comrades aware of the risks. And now we know, from what befell the Raish Valley, that black sorcery *does* carry risks we had not realized. It would seem that the Lantern Society was right."

"If you believe your informant, perhaps," Gluth murmured.

"Why would he lie? I have reason to believe this particular Quandishman to be a good and generous man."

"And can you be sure he is not in the pay of his nation's government, sent to spy on us and subvert *our* government?" Lorsa demanded.

Anrel hesitated.

He did not want to lie, and any brief recounting of the truth would not help him—Lord Blackfield *was* a Quandish Gatherman, after all, and he *had* recruited spies here in Lume.

"I have no reason to believe he wishes the empire ill," he said at last.

"He is Quandish, and we are Walasian," tel-Olz said. "Isn't that enough?"

"We are not at war with Quand," Anrel said.

"We have been in my lifetime, and I suspect we will be again before many years have passed," tel-Olz replied.

"These people, this Lantern Society, may be at the root of all our problems," said a man Anrel did not recognize. "What if they somehow *changed* Lord Allutar's spell, and that was why it went wrong? What if they have been damaging our farms all along?"

"I hardly think they could do anything of the sort without our own sorcerers noticing," Anrel said. "Magic leaves traces, does it not?"

"But what if they never worked magic of their own, but only distorted good Walasian spells?"

Anrel had no answer for that; he simply didn't know enough about sorcery. Since there were, by design, no sorcerers on the committee, and the observers were mostly Hots who had made sorcerers feel distinctly unwelcome in the room, no one else present knew whether it was possible, either.

The discussion continued, but Anrel, disturbed by the course it had taken, made his way out to the edge of the bath and did not take part for a time.

He was standing there, elbows behind him, leaning on the side of the bath, when Delegate Gluth came up beside him. For a moment neither spoke, but then Gluth said, "This Quandish magician you know, the representative of the Lantern Society—that would be Barzal, Lord Blackfield, I suppose?"

"Yes," Anrel admitted.

"And he was most generous with you, so naturally you would be reluctant to think ill of him."

"I sought him out in the first place not because I knew him to be generous, but because I believed him a good man," Anrel said. "Yes, he has been extraordinarily kind to me."

"You don't believe he is acting against the interests of the empire?"

"Delegate, I no longer know what the best interests of the empire *are*," Anrel said gloomily. "I believe Lord Blackfield genuinely wishes harm to no one, and that he seeks to maintain peace—or rather, given the present state of the empire, to restore peace. He sought to dissuade Lord Allutar from using the execution of Urunar Kazien in a spell, not because he knew precisely what the spell would do, but only because he did not trust any sort of magic based on blood or death."

Gluth nodded. "Was Barzal of Blackfield present when Allutar Hezir carried out this execution?"

"No, he was not," Anrel said angrily. He knew that Gluth was implying Lord Blackfield had tampered with the spell.

"Are you certain of that? Were *you* present?"

"No," Anrel admitted reluctantly. "I was celebrating the solstice with my family."

"Ah, your family. The unfortunate Lord Dorias and his daughter, I suppose."

"Unfortunate?" Startled, Anrel turned to look Gluth in the eye.

"Had you not heard?" Gluth said, meeting his gaze calmly. "The home of Lord Dorias Adirane, then burgrave of Alzur, was burned to the ground by irate townsfolk when he made the mistake of trying to defend Allutar Hezir's estate. He and his daughter have taken refuge in the Adirane family property here in Lume."

Anrel stared at the other man in astonishment, then asked, "*Then* burgrave? Do you say he is burgrave no longer?"

"No, no," the other said, smiling faintly. "To the best of my knowledge he retains the title, for the present."

Anrel found it infuriating that Gluth maintained an imperturbable calm while making these vicious implications, but forced himself to contain his rage and restrict his response to the simplest facts. "But you say he is here in Lume?"

"So I am given to understand, yes."

"His house in Alzur was burned? My *home* was burned?" Anrel was surprised at how painful the thought was. He had never expected to dwell there again, had not really expected to ever again set foot across its threshold, but the idea that the Adirane manor had been burned still hurt him badly.

"Your uncle's home in which you were suffered to reside, yes."

Anrel glared at him.

He had spent more than half his life in that house, which had stood for almost four centuries, and which had been in the Adirane family for well over a hundred years. To have this miserable little man speak so casually of its destruction was almost unbearable.

Perhaps the reports were exaggerated. Perhaps it was merely damaged. After all, its outer walls were solid stone. Even so, the thought of those lovely old polished wood floors and paneled walls ruined by fire and smoke was horrible. The books, the carpets, the tapestries . . .

And the people. "Was anyone hurt?" he asked. "My uncle maintained a staff of six."

"I am not aware of any injuries," Gluth replied.

"Thank the Father for that, then."

"You seem untroubled by your uncle's attempt to aid Allutar," Gluth said.

"My cousin is betrothed to Lord Allutar," Anrel said calmly. He had regained control of his temper. "I would scarcely expect my uncle to be entirely heedless of his daughter's future happiness. Besides, burning down a house hardly seems an appropriate way to punish Lord Allutar for his crimes. Would it not be better to take that house away from him and give it to someone more deserving? Maybe one of those he has wronged. Transform it into a hospital, perhaps, or an orphanage."

"An interesting suggestion." Gluth smiled a tight little smile. "Alas, too late to be of any use."

"Unfortunate."

"Yes." Gluth eyed Anrel consideringly. "I confess, Delegate Murau, that you puzzle me sometimes. I am accustomed to men who have chosen a side and adhere to its every tenet, which you do not seem to have done. You seem determined to see Allutar Hezir brought to justice, yet you will speak no ill of his allies, and you appear to regret actions his own people have taken against him."

"I do not like disorder," Anrel said. "I want to see Lord Allutar punished, yes, but punished in accordance with the law. Wanton destruction should not be encouraged, no matter the excuse."

"I see. And you seem to put a great deal of trust in this Quandish sorcerer, while claiming to be a loyal Walasian."

"I *am* a loyal Walasian," Anrel said. "That does not mean I must consider every foreigner a scoundrel and villain, or every Walasian a paragon. We are all human, Walasian and Quandish alike, and I judge Lord Blackfield to be a good man, worthy of my trust."

"Let us hope you are correct in that assessment—but forgive me if I do not take it as proven."

"You are, of course, free to form your own estimate of his character."

"Of course." For a moment the two men were silent; then Gluth said, "Delegate li-Parsil tells me you were a student in the court schools."

Anrel nodded. "Four years."

"Then I take it you can write a fair hand."

"I suppose I can, yes."

"We may have a use for your services soon."

"Oh? Who is 'we'?"

"The committee."

"Taking notes? I had thought someone had already assumed that chore."

"Oh, Master Fuilier is recording our proceedings. No, I meant something else entirely."

"What would that be?"

"Copying the Great List."

Anrel blinked. "What?"

"Oh, not the entirety! I assume it is a massive document, and most of it would be useless to us. But I believe we might find a portion of it useful."

"I had thought . . . why would we need any of it copied? We want Lord Allutar's true name, of course, and perhaps a handful of others we choose to investigate, but noting those down should hardly tax the skills of whichever of our representatives is given access."

"Indeed—but I think we may find it advantageous to obtain a little more information than that, while we have the chance."

"I suppose we might," Anrel admitted. "But we would need the emperor's permission, surely, and as I understand the ancient pact, he should not give that permission. *He* is to be the sole keeper of the list."

"That was the old agreement, yes, but we are the Grand Council, Delegate Murau. We are free to change the terms of the pact should we believe it will benefit the empire."

Anrel stared at him, unable to think of a response.

Gluth stared back for a few seconds, then turned away.

"We will call upon you when the time comes, Delegate Murau," he said. "Do not disappoint us."

"I will hope to avoid it," Anrel murmured.

He watched, puzzled and wary, as Gluth moved away to speak to someone else.

26

In Which Anrel's Services Are Called Upon

On the fifth day after Anrel's appointment to the Grand Council negotiations between the three representatives of the Committee for the Regulation of Sorcery and the emperor's court were said to be progressing nicely, but all details were held in secret, even from the remainder of the committee. Zarein Lorsa seemed to be reasonably satisfied, at any rate, with what his three envoys told him.

Not that he allowed that to temper his speeches, which remained fiery—so fiery that even some of the other Hots were clearly uncomfortable with his open denunciations of various sorcerers.

Anrel was not comfortable with *any* of the Hots, and had retreated to the Atrium for the morning conferences. He still remained active on the Committee for the Regulation of Sorcery, though, where he tried to restrain Lorsa's wilder enthusiasms.

Nivain Lir was still hesitating over the propriety of allowing her daughters to take up employment in the home of two unmarried young men, and whether or not she wanted to remain in her own present position as housekeeper to a prosperous wine merchant and his family, so Anrel and Derhin still tended to their own needs in the town house on Lourn Street.

The Committee for the Restoration of Order was said to be collaborating with the burgrave of Lume in compiling a list of individuals to be questioned, and a list of actions to be taken. Everyone knew that Anrel's name headed that first list, but it was taken for granted that nothing but planning would be done until everything had been properly prepared and the Grand Council as a whole had received a report of the committee's intentions.

The remainder of the Grand Council was continuing its endless debate of various schemes for revising the empire's governance, and listening to reports of disasters great and small. A sense of urgency was building, though—where before various plans had been suggested that would take years, or even decades, to implement, most proposals now were targeted at a mere season or two in the future. It was now acknowledged that simply finding and storing enough food to make it through the next winter without widespread starvation might be a more important issue than the emperor's debts.

On the advice of Derhin li-Parsil and Pariel Gluth, Anrel had had no further contact with Lord Blackfield; associating with a Quandish sorcerer and suspected spy was deemed too dangerous to his reputation. The glorious Alvos could not be permit himself to be tainted by familiarity with such people.

Due to her employment and her mother's reservations, Anrel had seen much less of Tazia than he had hoped. Perynis had been equally absent, but that was of far less concern to him. He had also lost all contact with the various unfortunates and scoundrels he had known during his residence in the Pensioners' Quarter; he believed that Mieshel, Shoun, and Po were reporting regularly to Lord Blackfield, but Anrel had cut that connection, and he still had no idea what had befallen Doz or the rest.

He wished he knew more of their circumstances. He wished that he could spend his time in Tazia's company, rather than at the Aldian Baths listening to speeches and arguments; he wished he could see more of Lord Blackfield than an occasional glimpse of him in the gallery. He wished he knew that Doz and Mieshel and Shoun and Po were all safe and well. He wished he knew how Lord Dorias and Lady Saria were faring. He saw Lord Allutar at the baths, and was tempted to ask after his fiancée, but thought better of it—any discussion with the landgrave was likely to turn ugly very quickly.

Anrel was not comfortable with many of his fellow delegates, in fact, while others were not comfortable with him—the legendary Alvos did not fit easily into their society.

As a result, he sometimes felt himself to be very much alone and at loose ends when the Grand Council was not actually in session, and on that fifth day, after the Council adjourned in midafternoon, he resolved to do something about his relative isolation.

He had hoped that Lord Dorias and Lady Saria might track him down, as Tazia had, but as yet there had been no indication that they were making any such attempt, so he decided that he would save them the trouble, and obtained their address from Delegate Gluth, along with directions on how to reach it. Tazia would be working for another two or three hours, and Derhin was lingering in the atrium with his friends, so Anrel set out alone to find his uncle.

The Adirane town house was on Wizard's Hill Court in the Old Heart, just down the slope from the Forbidden Street—a much older neighborhood than either Dezar House or Lourn Street, but one that was still very respectable. Old Heart had, as the name suggested, once been the core of the city, but that had been long, long ago, centuries before the Old Empire fell. Now it was a quiet backwater, and Wizard's Hill was one of the older, quieter neighborhoods therein.

Anrel had been to Adirane House only once before, very briefly, when his uncle had brought him to Lume to be enrolled in the court schools, and he had not paid any particular attention to its location at the time, so he had not remembered how to find it. He followed Pariel Gluth's directions carefully, making his way along the narrow, cobbled streets of Old Heart, walking under the watch's arches and past statues worn faceless by centuries of rain and wind.

These streets did look familiar from that one prior visit, but Anrel did not remember any specific landmarks, and relied on the delegate's guidance.

There were few people on the streets, and those he did see seemed to eye him warily before hurrying on about their business. The only coach he saw passed him without incident.

The directions brought him at last to an entry that he was fairly certain led into Wizard's Hill Court; it was sufficiently familiar from that brief visit five years ago that he was sure the directions he had followed had been accurate. He glanced up and saw no watchman standing on the arch above this entry, but as he started forward a man in a black coat and hat stepped out of a doorway and put an arm on his sleeve.

Startled, Anrel turned.

"What is your business here, sir?" the man in the black coat asked, his voice firm.

Anrel was very tempted to say, "None of yours," but he resisted. "Why do you ask?" he said instead.

"Because I am the warden for this block, and I do not recognize you." He pointed to a badge of red cloth sewn to the lapel of his coat, with the word WARDEN embroidered on it in yellow.

Anrel looked at the warden a little more closely, and saw that he had a cudgel thrust in his belt. The hand that had touched Anrel's sleeve was hovering near it.

"My apologies, sir," Anrel said. "I did not recognize you, either. My name is Anrel Murau, and I am a relative of the Adirane family. I have heard that my uncle is in residence at number two Wizard's Hill Court, and I had thought to pay him a visit."

The warden pursed his lips as he considered this, then glanced up and down the street. Then he looked up at the empty rampart atop the arch, then back at Anrel.

"Allow me to accompany you as far as the door, sir," he said.

That was hardly an unreasonable request, and Anrel certainly wanted no trouble. "Of course," he said.

That settled, the two men walked under the arch side by side into Wizard's Hill Court.

The court was circular, and the circle was entirely paved, with not a trace of greenery showing through the stones. Six houses fronted on the court, and the Adirane property was second on the left—although no numbers were visible, and his memory was not necessarily completely reliable, Anrel was absolutely certain he had found the correct address when he saw the escutcheon over the big black front door. It bore the same incomprehensible design he had so often seen over the fireplace in his uncle's study. When he was thirteen Anrel had asked Lord Dorias to explain the heraldry of that blazon, and Dorias had admitted its significance was long lost. The burgrave had been sure that the sinuous curve across the top was meant to be a vine of some sort, and not, as Anrel had first thought, a dragon's tail, but Uncle Dorias had said that Anrel's theory that the angular thing on the left was a book of some sort was as good a guess as any, and no one in living memory had ever been able to make any sense of the interlaced lines on the right.

With a glance at the warden, who waited on the cobbles, Anrel marched up the three granite steps to the door and lifted the heavy brass knocker.

A moment later the door opened a crack, and a familiar face looked out—Ollith Tuir, one of Lord Dorias's footmen, looking somewhat more haggard than Anrel remembered him. "Yes?" he said.

"Ollith!" Anrel said, smiling. "I'm here to see my uncle."

The footman looked at the visitor's face and blinked. He hesitated. Finally he said uncertainly, "Master Murau?"

"Yes."

"I will see if Lord Dorias is in," Ollith said. He closed the door again.

That was a chillier reception than Anrel had expected. He stood on the step, surprised and puzzled, and waited. Three steps behind him the warden waited, as well. Anrel threw him a glance, but said nothing—he could not think of anything to say that would not have sounded stupid and empty.

Then the door opened again. "Lord Dorias is not at home, Master Murau," Ollith said. "If you feel you have urgent business with him, you may leave a message."

Anrel's mouth opened, then closed. He blinked. "Ollith, I . . ."

He caught himself.

Anrel had known Ollith Tuir since Anrel's arrival in Alzur at the age of four. They had never been friends, as their respective roles did not allow it, but Anrel had always thought Ollith liked him and thought well of him. To be treated as an unwelcome stranger by this man was surprisingly painful, but there was no reason to embarrass himself.

And his uncle was refusing to see him; that hurt, too.

But it was no reason to forget his manners. "Of course," he said. "Please tell Lord Dorias that I was here, and that I would be delighted to call upon him again at his convenience. He and Lady Saria would also be very welcome to call at my own residence, at the burgrave of Naith's town house in Lourn Street. Number twelve. I understand that their home in Alzur has burned, and I had hoped to express my sincere condolences, and offer whatever aid I may. I have been appointed a member of the Grand Council, and if that connection might be of service to them, I would be happy to use it as they direct." He paused, cleared his throat, then continued, "I realize that I have not communicated with my uncle, nor with my cousin, for more than half a year, and I tender my profound apologies for that extended silence, but my circumstances were such that it was not practical to make contact. If there is some other way in which I have displeased Lord Dorias, I do hope he will see fit to explain my failings to me, so that I might have an opportunity to set right whatever I have done wrong."

"I will inform Lord Dorias, Master Murau," the footman said with some visible discomfort.

"Thank you, Ollith. I'm very sorry to trouble you with such a message, and that I had not prepared a note, but I had not expected my uncle to be out. Perhaps if I were to stop by again in a few days . . . ?"

"I do not think Lord Dorias will be at home, Master Murau."

"Ah." Anrel blinked; his eyes seemed suddenly moist. "Thank you." He turned away, and found the warden watching and listening.

The door closed behind him, and he heard Ollith throw the bolt. That sound felt like a knife in his back; he hunched his shoulders and trudged down the steps.

The warden watched him curiously as he descended, then said, "A member of the Grand Council?"

"Yes," Anrel said. "Representing the commoners of Naith. I was appointed a few days ago, after the death of Amanir tel-Kabanim." He started walking slowly toward the exit from the court, trying to hold himself straight and strong despite the weight of his disappointment.

"One of the Hots, then?" the warden asked, falling in beside him.

Anrel threw him a glance, startled by the man's familiarity with the council's doings.

But then, he was a warden; he would be keeping up on the news as best he could, and Amanir's apparent suicide had certainly been news. His knowledge was not really surprising at all. "I am uncommitted, as yet," Anrel said. "I have been gathering in the atrium for the moment."

The warden nodded. "But you are representing the commoners of Naith, when the burgrave of Alzur's your uncle?"

This time, Anrel was not caught off guard by the warden's knowledge. Naturally, he would know something of the neighborhood he was charged with protecting, and would know that Lord Dorias was burgrave of Alzur.

"I failed the sorcery trials when I was a boy," Anrel explained. "I'm a commoner, my family notwithstanding."

"Ah. And your uncle won't see you."

"Apparently not."

"You understand, sir, that if Lord Dorias tells me you aren't welcome here, I will have to respect his wishes."

"Will you?"

"It's my duty as a warden, sir. I am charged with maintaining the peace in my district, and keeping out undesirables." He let out a sound that was half laugh, half sigh. "Though it's hard to think of a delegate to the Grand Council as an undesirable!"

Anrel turned and gazed thoughtfully at the other man. "And who charged you with these duties?"

"The district council, sir."

"And who gave them the authority to do this?"

The warden seemed startled by the question. "Why, the Grand Council, wasn't it?"

"Perhaps it was," Anrel said. "I am only newly appointed, after all." He sighed. They were passing under the watch arch; he looked up at the stonework.

It looked very solid, but he remembered how the arches around the Pensioners' Quarter had been pulled down by a few determined men with simple tools. It was always easier to destroy than to build. The people of the empire, led by the Grand Council, seemed determined to tear down their old government; he hoped they were building something better in its place.

At least this warden was evidence that they *were* building something. Whether it was better remained to be seen.

The two men emerged onto the main street, and walked together in silence for another hundred yards, to a corner where the warden stopped.

"This is the end of my district," he said. "Good luck in reconciling with your uncle, Delegate Murau."

"Thank you," Anrel said. He shook the man's hand, then continued alone, aware that the warden was watching him. He wondered whether that was mere casual interest, or to be sure that he did not double back and cause trouble.

He did not turn back to assuage his curiosity; better to let the warden go about his business.

Retracing his steps was easier than finding Wizard's Hill Court had been, and it seemed only a few minutes later that Anrel turned into Lourn Street, and found a rather scruffy messenger, wearing the red and white sash that indicated someone in the Grand Council's employ, waiting on the steps of the town house he and Derhin shared. The man was slouched against a pillar, but straightened up as Anrel approached.

"May I help you?" Anrel asked.

"Are you Anrel Murau?" the messenger demanded.

"I am," Anrel said.

"Then fetch your best pen and ink, and come with me."

Anrel frowned. "Oh? Why should I?" The man seemed very rude for a messenger.

"Because Delegate Lorsa sent me for you more than an hour past."

"Ah." Perhaps the apparent rudeness was really impatience; the messenger had probably expected to find Anrel at home, and had not anticipated a wait. This summons was presumably a committee matter of some sort, and as such not an appointment Anrel cared to miss, regardless of the messenger's behavior. "I'll just be a moment," he said.

He hurried inside the town house, and took a moment to wash his face before borrowing Derhin's lap desk and its contents—he had none of his own, as yet—and emerging onto the street once again.

The messenger was still waiting. "Come on," he said, turning to lead the way.

Anrel fell into step at the messenger's heel and asked, "Where are we going?"

The messenger threw him a disbelieving glance. "The emperor's palace, of course."

"Ah," Anrel said with a nod. He remembered Gluth's warning that his services as a scribe might be called upon when the Committee for the Regulation of Sorcery was granted access to the Great List.

It seemed that call had come.

"Of course," he said and quickened his pace.

27

In Which Anrel's Penmanship Is Put to Use

The messenger led Anrel through the streets and along the Promenade, where the afternoon shadows were lengthening and the crowds, none too numerous to begin with, were thinning. A few people turned to stare at the messenger's red and white sash, but most, concerned with their own affairs, ignored the pair. The drivers of the three coaches they encountered paid no attention.

The palace was guarded these days by the Emperor's Watch—not merely the regular watchmen on the ramparts and on the arches connecting the palace to the rest of the network of walkways, but watchmen patrolling the perimeter at street level, ambling along each with a hand on the hilt of his sword, making sure that no one approached the doors or windows too closely. The messenger made a sign to one of these patrols as he led Anrel toward the palace; the watchman returned the sign and let the two pass unhindered.

As they passed the guard Anrel felt a slight resistance that had nothing to do with the Emperor's Watch; they were passing through wards. He had never sensed any wards around the palace when he had been a student, but times were more troubled now; it was no great surprise that the Emperor had chosen to add a little magical protection to the men and walls that guarded him and his family. Anrel wondered just what the nature of the wards might be—did they alert some magician inside the palace? Did they keep certain people from approaching at all?

The messenger gave no sign he was aware of any wards, so Anrel did not mention them. He followed quietly as the messenger escorted him along the palace wall to a small door half hidden beneath the ramparts, only a few feet from the sheer drop into the river. There Anrel's guide knocked twice, then stepped aside.

After only the briefest pause the door opened. An unfamiliar face peered out at the new arrivals.

"Anrel Murau," the messenger said.

"And more than time," the other replied. He swung the door wide, and gestured. "This way, Delegate Murau. The others are all wait-ing."

Anrel did not bother to reply, but with Derhin's writing desk under his arm he stepped through another layer of warding spells into the shad-owy interior, where he found himself in a narrow stone corridor. The door slammed shut behind him, closing out the sinking sun; there were no windows or other openings, and the only light came from a small lantern held by the man who had admitted him.

The messenger had been left outside; his job, it seemed, was done.

Anrel's new escort raised the lantern to illuminate the stone walls, and led the way down the short passage.

The corridor ended in a massive iron-bound door that stood open, admitting them into a small chamber; Anrel was hustled through this, down another passage, through a succession of other rooms, up a curv-ing stone stair, through more rooms, and finally shown into what ap-peared to be a library, where bookshelves lined two walls and two large tables occupied much of the floor space. Several good oil lamps pro-vided a warm glow, but again, as in the passages that had brought him here, there were no windows.

Several men were gathered around the tables. Anrel recognized five of them immediately as his fellow delegates from the Committee for the Regulation of Sorcery—Lorsa, Gluth, Guirdosia, Savar, and Essarnyn—but the others were strangers. Three of them were dressed in green and gold imperial livery, and one of these three held a large ring of keys, which he was jingling nervously.

"Ah, Delegate Alvos!" Lorsa said. "At last you appear!"

"My apologies," Anrel said. "I was not expecting your summons, and was seeing to some personal business."

"I trust it has been concluded, and you are able to devote your entire attention to the task at hand?"

"I believe so, yes."

"Then let us begin!" He turned to the man with the keys. "Master Seneschal, if you would be so kind?"

The green-clad man with the keys bowed, then marched across the room to a bookcase, where he fitted a large iron key into a hole in the wooden frame. He turned the key, and something clicked loudly; then he pulled at the frame. The entire bookcase swung out from the wall, revealing another room behind it—a dim, windowless, and rather dusty room with bare stone walls. A table and a single chair stood in the center, with an unlit lamp upon the table, and shelves that covered the farthest wall held dozens of heavy volumes in similar bindings.

"The Great List," the seneschal announced, stepping aside.

This was not at all what Anrel had pictured when he had imagined the actual list. He had thought of it as a few sheets of paper—but of course, he realized, it couldn't be. There were hundreds, or more likely thousands or even tens of thousands, of sorcerers in the empire.

Still, that did not account for an entire *room*.

"Where?" Lorsa said.

"Why, *there*, Master Lorsa," the seneschal said, waving toward the shelves of books.

Lorsa frowned, but before he could say anything more Anrel stepped forward. "May I?" he asked the seneschal.

The seneschal glanced at Lorsa, then said, "The emperor instructed me to grant up to half a dozen members of your committee complete access to the list, on condition that not a single volume shall be taken out of that room, that nothing in the list room shall be damaged or altered in any way, and that none of the true names recorded herein shall be spoken aloud within the palace walls. You are a member of the committee, Master . . . Alvos?"

"My name is Anrel Murau," Anrel said with a sour glance at Lorsa. "Yes, I am a member of the Committee for the Regulation of Sorcery."

"Then I am ordered to allow you into the list room." He gestured for Anrel to proceed.

"Thank you," Anrel said, stepping into the little room. He could sense magic everywhere here, but he was not certain whether it was yet another layer of wards, or something else. He beckoned to the man with the lantern. "Could you light that for me?" He pointed to the lamp.

"*No*, sir!" the seneschal barked, before the lantern-bearer could respond. "He is not one of the permitted committee members!"

Startled, Anrel blinked, then said, "Of course. My apologies. Delegate Savar, would you please light the lamp?"

Savar stepped forward and took the lantern from the other, while Anrel set Derhin's writing desk on the table, then crossed the little inner room and lifted down the first volume from the left-hand end of the top shelf.

"Be careful," the seneschal called. "The older volumes are quite fragile."

Indeed, the book Anrel had chosen was so old that the cover gave beneath his fingers, leaving brown smudges and raising a small cloud of fine, powdery dust. Seeing its condition, he did not try to open it, but did look at the faint, faded label on its front cover.

The ink had faded to near invisibility, and the calligraphy and spelling were extremely archaic, but he could make it out.

THE TRUE NAMES & SECRET HISTORIES OF THE WALASIAN SORCERERS, FROM THE FALL OF THE EMPIRE TO—

That much was all in a single hand, but then a final phrase, "the Present Day," had been crossed out, and someone else had lettered in "the Fifteenth Year of the Reign of the First Walasian Emperor."

Anrel stared at that for a moment, then carefully slid the book back into place on the top shelf, hoping he had not damaged it irretrievably. He stepped to the right and found the final volume on the bottom shelf, and pulled that out, instead.

THE GREAT LIST OF THE TRUE NAMES OF THE SORCERERS OF THE WALASIAN EMPIRE, VOLUME 168: 20TH YEAR OF THE REIGN OF LURIAS XII TO— The label was unfinished, with a blank space where someone might eventually write the date of its completion.

Anrel turned and set the book on the table, where Savar had managed to light the lamp. He opened the volume.

Most of it was blank; a few pages at the front held neat little entries. Anrel chose one at random and read aloud, "Thirty-third Day of Summer, 22nd Year of the Emperor's Reign, at the College of Sorcerers in Naith in the Province of Aulix, Candidate Evier Kalith completed trials before the Lords Magistrate, Lord Neriam Kadara presiding, succeeding in nineteen of twenty-two attempts in divers wards and bindings. The true name—" At the last instant he remembered the seneschal's instructions that no true names were to be spoken aloud, and stopped. He also remembered another reason not to say it, a reason that had nothing to do with the emperor's whims—or perhaps, the reason the emperor had set that restriction in the first place. The true name was there on the page—Tal Deg Ved Zara—but Anrel did not say it; instead he made a sort of humming noise, then continued reading. "—was bestowed upon Lady Evier, and will bind her hereafter." He looked up. "This is indeed the Great List, Delegate Lorsa." He gestured at the shelves. "*All* of it, back to the founding of the empire."

The other delegates stared at him as his words sank in. Lorsa frowned. "How are we to find the ones we want in all *that?*"

"The entries are in chronological order, according to when the report of each sorcerer's completion of the trials was received here," Anrel explained, looking over the page. "Most sorcerers complete the trials at the age of twelve. I assume that everyone in the first, oh, hundred and fifty volumes or so must be dead of old age by now; we need concern ourselves only with these last few."

Even as he spoke, Anrel wondered at the numbers. The empire was five hundred and eighty-eight—no, eighty-*nine* years old. One hundred and sixty-eight volumes in five hundred and eighty-nine years worked out to an average of between three and four years a volume, yet this last volume, covering four years, was still mostly blank. What had filled all those thousands of pages?

Lord Blackfield had told him that the number of sorcerers in the empire was declining; had it declined *that* much?

Perhaps earlier volumes contained additional information; after all, that first one had said it contained true names *and* secret histories.

"Excellent," Lorsa said. "Seneschal, you and your men may leave us."

"No, sir. We must see that the emperor's instructions are followed."

Lorsa looked at him, obviously annoyed, but before he could speak, Gluth cut him off.

"Master Seneschal," he said, "You need to see what we do, correct?"

"Yes."

"But you do not need to hear what we say."

"No," the seneschal admitted with obvious reluctance.

"Then let you and your men take up positions at the far end of the library, and observe us from there. We will leave the entry open and as unobstructed as we can manage, and if we wish to speak of matters that do not concern you, we will whisper."

The seneschal hesitated, then nodded. "As you say," he said and with a gesture he sent the other two men in green and gold to the far end of the outer room, then joined them there. All three turned to watch.

Lorsa clapped Gluth on the shoulder, and together the two of them stepped into the secret room where the list was stored. Gluth dragged one of the library chairs with him.

"Now," Lorsa said to Anrel in a hoarse voice he probably intended as a whisper, "Fetch the ones we need. Set them on the table, and let us get on with the task at hand!"

Anrel retrieved volume 167, then 166, as he asked quietly, "What *is* the task at hand, then?"

"Why, copying out the true name of every living sorcerer," Lorsa said with a glance at the seneschal. "We have no need of the details about trials and bindings. The names will suffice."

"*All* of them?" Anrel said. "But I had thought you had only a few you wanted to investigate."

Lorsa looked at him pityingly. "Delegate Murau," he said in a better approximation of a whisper, "I had thought you a man of sense. We may never have this opportunity again—the emperor may change his mind, or even, may the Father prevent it, die, and leave the throne to a less cooperative successor. Even if we have but a handful of sorcerers we want to question *now,* there may be occasion in the future to confront others. Let us seize the opportunity to gain what small advantage against our oppressors that we can, *while* we can."

During this exchange Guirdosia and Essarnyn had stepped cautiously into the list room, bringing chairs and writing supplies with them. Each set his writing box upon the table and got out pens and paper. Savar and Gluth followed suit.

Anrel hesitated, and as he did, Guirdosia reached out and took volume 166 from his hands. "I'll start with this one," he said.

Anrel started to object, then looked at Lorsa and released the book. He watched as Guirdosia opened it, flipped past the title page and a few introductory notes, and then set it down with the first page of names.

"Some of these are dead," Guirdosia said, pointing.

Lorsa glanced over, and Anrel peered at the page; sure enough, at the bottom of the first entry someone had written in, "Deceased of natural causes, 13 Winter, 21st year of Lurias XII."

"We have no need of those," Lorsa said. "Record only those still alive."

Guirdosia nodded, dipped his pen, and began copying the names in the second listing.

"We must all of us make haste," Gluth said, opening volume 167 and glancing at the seneschal. "I will take the left-hand pages in this volume; Savar, you will take the right."

"I have the right here," Guirdosia said. "Essarnyn, would you essay the left?"

That left Lorsa and Anrel with volume 168. "My hand is not strong," Lorsa said. "Do you think, Master Murau, you can manage this volume alone?"

Remembering that two-thirds of the pages were blank, Anrel thought he could easily manage this one in the time it would take each of the other pairs to finish their tasks, but he hesitated. "This book is only for the past four years," he said. "Those listed here would most likely be no more than seventeen years of age; need we concern ourselves with them?"

"The merest kitten will grow fangs and claws in time," Lorsa said. "Let us be prepared."

Reluctantly, Anrel sat down and began copying.

After a moment, as he turned a page, he paused and looked around. Four of the others were scribbling busily; Lorsa was standing by, his hands clasped behind his back, trying unsuccessfully to look interested.

Gluth noticed Anrel's gaze; he leaned over and whispered, "If you wonder why Lorsa does not help us, rest assured, he is willing enough, but his education is lacking—he can barely read, and his writing is all but illegible."

Anrel nodded, and looked at Gluth's own papers. Gluth wrote a fine, steady hand, without a smear or smudge to be seen, a little smaller and less elegant than Anrel's own, but very clear. Savar and Guirdosia also wrote well; Essarnyn's work was not readily visible.

None of them seemed troubled in the least by the work they were doing, but Anrel could not overcome his own reservations. The knowledge contained in these pages could ruin hundreds of lives; the merest half-fraudulent witch, given a sorcerer's true name, could strip away the sorcerer's magical birthright and bind him to her will.

Anrel had no great love for most sorcerers, but he recognized this as powerful and dangerous information, and he did not want to entrust it to someone like Zarein Lorsa. Lorsa was a fanatic, a man who loathed sorcery and sorcerers, and these names would give him power over hundreds of them. He could destroy any sorcerer he chose, or use the threat of such destruction to blackmail one.

And not merely some theoretical sorcerer, either—somewhere in these books were the true names of Anrel's uncle and cousin.

What had the emperor been thinking, agreeing to give the committee access to the Great List?

He had probably been thinking he was ingratiating himself with the Grand Council, and arranging for Lord Allutar, and perhaps a few other scapegoats, to be sacrificed to calm the populace. Anrel doubted it had ever occurred to the emperor that Lorsa might want far more than that.

Anrel could only conclude that the emperor was a fool—but then, he had suspected as much for some time.

Was there some way, perhaps, that Anrel might protect a few people? He could miscopy names—but he was only recording the true names of children; one of the others would find the listings for Lord Dorias Adirane and Lady Saria Adirane.

He copied out name after name as he tried to devise some way to ensure that his family, and perhaps some of the other sorcerers he had known and liked over the years, were not accurately recorded.

He could come up with nothing, no stratagem to arrange it so that he, and no one else, would copy their names.

They had been writing for more than an hour, and Anrel, despite writing as slowly as he dared, was nearing the end of the filled portion of volume 168, when he was interrupted by a sudden shout.

"I have him!"

28

In Which Anrel Learns His Foe's Secret

Anrel looked up, startled, to see Essarnyn pointing at a page, grinning broadly. "I have him!" he repeated. "Allutar Hezir, succeeded in twenty-four of twenty-four attempts!"

"What is his true name?" Lorsa said, turning to look.

"Don't read it aloud!" Anrel warned.

The others turned to look at him.

"Why not?" Essarnyn asked.

Guirdosia glanced at the three men in imperial livery, standing out of earshot. "They won't hear us."

"*He'll* hear you," Anrel said.

"What?"

"He'll hear you," Anrel repeated. "Lord Allutar."

"But he's nowhere near us, surely," Guirdosia said. "Why would he be in the palace?"

"He's probably not in the palace. It doesn't matter where he is," Anrel said. "He's a sorcerer, and it's his *true name*. He will know when it has been spoken, no matter where or by whom. It's a part of him."

"Most interesting, if true," Gluth said.

"What does it *matter* if he hears us?" Lorsa said. "We have his true name! We have complete power over him!"

"Not without a magician who can work a binding," Anrel replied. "And if he knows someone has learned his true name, he may be able to create defenses—I don't know what or how, I'm no sorcerer, but there might be a way. Why give him a warning, and a chance to prepare?"

Lorsa's brow knitted; Anrel met his gaze, but neither of them spoke.

"Just write it down, then," Gluth directed Essarnyn. "Delegate Murau has a point. We will have it when we need it; no need to alert our foe."

"No, let him know his days are numbered!" Lorsa protested. "Let him taste the fear, just as those who have felt his heavy hand have known fear."

"Surely, Delegate Lorsa," Gluth said mildly, "it is better to forego the pleasure of his fearful anticipation if it makes it all the more certain that when the time comes, and our spell descends upon him like a bolt from the heavens, he will have no possibility of dodging the blow."

"I'll write it down," Essarnyn said, matching his actions to his words. "And circle it, so that it may be found easily."

The others watched as he dipped his pen and carefully recorded the syllables of Lord Allutar's true name, then drew a neat ring around them.

Then Gluth clapped his hands and said, "Come now, Delegates, we are not here merely to counter one man, but to restrain an entire class. Let us get on with our work!"

At the far end of the library, the seneschal cleared his throat. "Excuse me," he called, "but how much longer do you intend to be at this? Surely, you have found what you were after by now."

Startled, Lorsa turned to face him. "Why, I think we will be some time yet," he said. "I can't say exactly."

"I don't believe that is acceptable," the seneschal replied. "The emperor ordered me to give you access to the list, and I have done so, but he did not say I must allow you unlimited time. I think I have been quite generous in saying nothing until now, but we are at the point when I must insist you inform me how much longer this will take."

Lorsa looked at the others; Gluth looked at volume 167 and said, "Another hour. Give us another hour, and we will be content."

"There, Master Seneschal," Lorsa said. "You have your answer— another hour, and you may send us on our way."

"Thank you," the seneschal replied. "I can give you another hour, but not a moment longer."

With that settled, the five scribes returned to their work. Instead of continuing to work as slowly as he dared, though, Anrel hastily finished up volume 168, deliberately reversing syllables in every remaining true name he recorded—he did not think anyone had the right to bind the souls of boys and girls of thirteen.

When he had completed that, he joined Essarnyn and Guirdosia on volume 166, and again, from that point on he deliberately introduced errors in every entry he copied—with the need for speed, he was fairly sure that no one would check his work.

He looked for any Adiranes, but did not see them.

They finished volume 166 with perhaps a quarter hour remaining, and pulled volume 165 from the shelf, to see whether any of the elders listed therein might still be alive. Several were. By this point Anrel and Essarnyn had run out of paper, even after squeezing more entries into every available margin, but Guirdosia still had a few sheets, which he shared out.

They had not finished with volume 165 when the seneschal called time, but they had made a good start, and the three later volumes were complete. Under the seneschal's watchful eye the four volumes were returned to their proper places on the shelves; then the six members of the Committee for the Regulation of Sorcery gathered up their writing utensils and their stacks of paper, and allowed themselves to be shown out of the list room, dragging their chairs behind them, leaving only the single table, chair, and lamp. On his way out Gluth extinguished the lamp's flame, returning the room to the state in which they had first seen it.

When everyone and everything had been cleared out the emperor's men swung the bookcase back into position, and the seneschal locked it.

"Good night, masters," the seneschal said, bowing. "My men will see you out."

Ten minutes later the six delegates and their associates were on the Promenade, outside the line of watchmen, clutching their writing boxes and sheaves of paper. The sun had set, and the sky above the river was deep indigo, fading to black, but torches blazed on the palace ramparts.

"Now, friends," Lorsa said, "give me your work, and I will see to it that it is put to the best use." He took the bundle of papers from Essarnyn's hand as he spoke.

One by one, with varying degrees of reluctance, the others surrendered their lists to the committee's chairman.

"What are you going to do with them?" Guirdosia asked.

"I am going to have copies made," Lorsa said. "Indeed, if any of you would care to aid in that, your assistance would be most welcome, but I would think your hands must be tired."

"I would advise organizing the material," Gluth said. "At present, these lists are a jumble, very roughly arranged by age; I would recommend a geographical list, or perhaps ordered by rank or family. The time may come when we cannot spare a minute to shuffle through these pages seeking a particular name; a properly ordered list might be essential."

"Excellent, Delegate," Lorsa agreed.

"I would be happy to assist with that."

Lorsa clapped Gluth on the shoulder. "Come with me, then. We will let these other fine men go to their well-earned supper while we devote ourselves further to the task of freeing the empire from these magical parasites."

The two of them turned away, leaving the other delegates standing there. The aides had already drifted off.

"But what are they going to *do* with the list, after they copy it?" Guirdosia asked. "He didn't say!"

"Perhaps it's best if we don't know," Savar replied.

"They'll use it to make sure any sorcerer we question will answer us," Essarnyn said. "What *else* could they do with it?"

Anrel could have answered that with a dozen possibilities, none of which he liked. He was beginning to think that he had made a very grave error in agreeing to serve on the Grand Council. Giving the speech that led to the creation of the Committee for the Regulation of Sorcery was even worse. He had long thought that the council was doomed to be ineffectual, to accomplish nothing significant; now he *hoped* it was. That list could make the committee, if not the council as a whole, very dangerous indeed.

It could make Zarein Lorsa, in particular, very dangerous.

But it was too late now to stop it; the list was made, and in Lorsa's hands, and despite Anrel's best efforts, most of it was accurate.

Surely, someone should be warned—but who?

"Well, whatever it's for, we have done our part," Guirdosia said. "I'm going home. I wish you all a good night, fellow delegates." With a tip of his hat, he set off down the Promenade.

Anrel glanced at the other two, wishing he knew them better, knew whether he could trust them—but he did not. For all he knew, they might think a scheme to destroy every sorcerer in the Empire would be a fine and glorious thing. He could not share his concerns with these men. He needed to talk to someone, but not his fellow committee members.

"Good night," he said, touching the brim of his hat.

Then he, too, turned and departed, bound for Lourn Street.

29

In Which Anrel Receives a Letter

The next day's council meeting was uneventful, in large part because certain delegates were not in attendance. Among the Hots, Lorsa and Gluth were noticeable for their absence. In the cloakroom most of the delegation from Lume itself had failed to arrive. No explanations were given.

There were always a few people who could not be at any given session, but the number was unusually large on this occasion, and the missing voices included several who were normally among the louder and more insistent. The result was a relatively brief session in which nothing of note was accomplished.

Anrel sat on the steps of the great pool and listened to the reports, speeches, and debate, but he did not address the council himself; he felt he had said quite enough already. He was uneasy, to say the least, about the previous night's exploits; what did the Committee for the Regulation of Sorcery intend to do with those names?

Or really, what did the Hots intend? There could be little doubt that Lorsa, Gluth, and their fellows were solidly in control of the committee, and therefore in control of the names they had copied from the Great List.

Anrel wished there was someone he could talk to about this, someone who would understand his concerns, but he could not think of such a person. Every member of the Grand Council was pursuing his own agenda, and would see the news of the copying of the Great List through the lens of that agenda, while others, such as Tazia, lacked a grasp of the politics involved.

Lord Blackfield might have provided a sympathetic ear, but as a foreigner he could not be trusted with the knowledge that the Hots now knew the true names of hundreds of sorcerers. If Quandish or Ermetian spies were to obtain a copy of the list, the empire would be almost helpless before an invasion.

The longer he sat there, listening to his countrymen droning on, the more Anrel regretted his role in the creation of Lorsa's list. This might be the worst thing he had ever done, worse than his speeches in Naith and Beynos, worse than allowing Valin to die, worse than any of the crimes he had committed when he lived in the Pensioners' Quarter.

As he walked back home at Derhin's side, Anrel wondered whether he should resign his position on the council. He did not feel he was doing any good as a delegate; on the contrary, the list aside, he seemed to have inadvertently given Lorsa and the Hots encouragement that might lead to fresh disasters. He glanced at Derhin, almost ready to speak of his concerns, then decided to hold his peace a little longer. At the very least, he wanted to know what Lorsa and Gluth had been doing that had prevented their attendance—he had never before seen either of them miss a day. The abbreviated Lume delegation was another mystery. Some of them were members of the Committee for the Restoration of Order, and he expected someone representing that committee to arrest him, sooner or later; could their absence mean they were preparing a strike?

They would probably not dare to arrest the notorious Alvos right there in the Aldian Baths, but he half expected to see watchmen waiting for him on Lourn Street.

There were no watchmen, and he and Derhin entered without hindrance.

They had been home for scarcely a quarter hour, though, when Anrel heard a knock at the door. Hoping to see Tazia, he hastened to answer it, and instead found a messenger holding a letter.

"Delegate Anrel Murau?" he asked.

"Yes," Anrel replied, startled.

"This is for you." He handed Anrel the letter, then turned away. By the time Anrel had gathered his wits sufficiently to ask any questions, the man was twenty feet away and there seemed little point in calling him back.

Puzzled, Anrel stepped back inside, unfolded the letter, and began reading.

He recognized his uncle's handwriting immediately, but was surprised by the lack of any of the customary greetings. The letter read,

Anrel:

I am given to understand that you came to my door the other day hoping to speak with me. I am writing to ask you not to make any further attempt to intrude; you are not welcome here.

It pains me to do this, but I have no choice. Your actions have made it clear that you have no respect for me, or for the rule of law and the good order of the empire.

When my sister died I took you in, and raised you as if you were my own son. When you failed the trials I was bitterly disappointed, but I allowed you to remain in my home, and I like to think I continued to treat you honorably, with respect and affection. When it became clear that you would never be a sorcerer I sent you, at my own considerable expense, to study in the court schools of Lume so that you could find a position suitable to a commoner born of a noble family.

Perhaps it was the foolish ideas that circulate at such schools that poisoned your mind against me; I cannot know. Whatever the cause, from the time of your return you behaved abominably, encouraging the late Lord Valin in his mad follies, attempting to dissuade my daughter from a most suitable marriage, and conspiring with that Quandish scoundrel. When Lord Allutar protested your actions, you goaded Valin into challenging him, forcing Lord Allutar to kill the poor lad.

Unsatisfied with encompassing the death of a man you had claimed was your friend, you then preached treason and sedition in the provincial capital. You assaulted and robbed a watchman, commandeered a canal boat, stole a farmer's fishing boat, and in general pursued a career of reckless, unbridled criminality, of which the only benefit was that I needed no longer concern myself with you, since you had vanished from civilized society.

At first your actions pained me, as much for the heartache they must surely have inflicted on my daughter, your cousin Saria, as for their effect on my own emotions. In time, though, I realized that I was well rid of you. I cannot guess why you have acted as you have; your parents were fine people, but either you have willfully denied your own blood, or you are not truly their son at all, but some changeling. I have, in my darker moments, wondered whether you might be responsible for their deaths — perhaps my true nephew died as well, all those years ago, and the monster that killed them assumed his form.

But no, it is probably merely human evil, such as we have seen all too much of in the past year, that drives you.

Do you know what befell us after you left? The mobs you inspired to rebellion in Naith spread the poison to Alzur, where our own people, who should have loved us, burned our home and drove us out, forcing us to flee. Alzur is now in the hands of mutinous commoners calling themselves "wardens," while we are exiled here, awaiting an audience with His Imperial Majesty, in hopes that he can spare a company of soldiers to root the traitors from their holes and hang them all.

And what should we hear, upon our arrival in Lume, but that you, too, are within the city walls, and what's more, you have somehow arranged to take a seat on this supposed "Grand Council," where you can once again spew your venom upon susceptible ears.

All that is of a piece with your prior behavior, of course, and should by now come as no surprise, but I confess I am surprised that even you would have the effrontery to stand on my doorstep and ask to see me, as if you were a decent person paying a social call.

Perhaps you thought I had not comprehended the depths of your depravity, that I might allow our alleged shared blood to influence me to overlook your actions; rest assured that while my eyes are not as sharp as they once were, I can still see the truth when it is thrust under my nose. You are not welcome in Wizard's Hill Court, nor within the pale of Alzur. That you have received a pardon does not make your crimes go away. The law may forgive you, but I will not.

Do not reply to this letter, nor attempt any further contact with me; it will be refused. Do not dishonor us further by pretending to an apology you cannot mean and I cannot accept. I must, to my shame, acknowledge you as my kin, but neither law nor custom requires me to tolerate your presence.

Dorias Adirane, Burgrave of Alzur

As Anrel read this unpleasant missive his chest seemed to tighten and his heart to sink heavily; he felt physically ill.

He knew, though, that there was no point in arguing, either in person or by letter; Uncle Dorias had never been willing to listen to anyone once his mind was made up.

"A letter?"

Derhin's voice startled Anrel; he turned to see the other man standing in the passage.

"Anrel, what is it?" Derhin asked when he saw Anrel's face. "Your face is white, and your hand is trembling!"

Anrel started to speak, but could not. He stopped, swallowed, and forced himself to calm.

"My uncle," he said. "He takes issue with my actions."

"From the look of you, he does more than that!"

"He takes issue *strongly*," Anrel said.

Derhin hesitated, then said, "Come have a drink. It will calm your nerves."

"Thank you," Anrel said. "I think you're right." He followed Derhin to the dining room, where the wine cabinet yielded up a dark, sweet Lithrayn red.

An hour later the letter had been safely tucked into Anrel's blouse, and the better part of three bottles of various wines from Lithrayn had been emptied into Anrel's belly. Derhin had not abstained, by any means, but Anrel had clearly needed the larger share of each bottle.

They had spoken on a variety of subjects, but Anrel had not told Derhin the contents of the letter, so it was something of a surprise when he finally said, without preamble, "He puts the worst possible light on *everything*."

"Who does?" Derhin asked a bit muzzily.

"Uncle Dorias. I always knew he was prone to seeing things in his own way, but in this letter he blames me for *everything*, no matter who was actually at fault."

Derhin shrugged. "It's convenient, having a single target for all blame. Zarein Lorsa blames sorcerers for everything, Lord Koulis blames the emperor for everything, the mob blames Lord Allutar for everything—it's convenient."

"It is not *just*."

"No," Derhin agreed sadly. "Merely convenient."

"And who do *you* blame for everything?"

"Oh, I think there is quite enough for all of us to have a share."

"That's generous of you."

Derhin looked at Anrel. "Who do *you* blame?"

"I will claim my share, no question about it," Anrel replied. "I have done a great deal of harm, though that was never my intention. And Lord Allutar, too, has earned a good portion of despite. The emperor cannot be entirely excused. Indeed, I can think of no one who is wholly innocent. Perhaps you're right, in saying we all deserve it."

"Well, there you are, then—we are all at fault. But what's to be done about it?"

"Stop laying blame," Anrel answered immediately. "Try to atone for our errors, if we can."

"A noble ambition, certainly, but not one easily achieved." Derhin straightened in his chair. "Would you stop laying blame entirely, then, and hold no one responsible for his actions? Would you forgive Lord Allutar for Valin's death, or the poisoned grain? Is there any way in which he could atone for such wrongs?"

Anrel put his hand to his breast, over the letter. "He could at least have the grace to *try*," he said. "If he were to acknowledge that he had done wrong, that would be a start."

Derhin's reply was somewhere between a grunt and a snort, his chin sinking to his chest. Upon hearing himself, he jerked upright again, and announced, "I am going to bed. I will see you in the morning, Anrel."

"Good night, Derhin," Anrel said as he sat and stared at the empty bottles on the table.

A moment later, alone in the room, he repeated, "If he were to acknowledge that he had done wrong, that would be a start."

He was not thinking about Lord Allutar, though; he was thinking about his uncle and himself.

Lord Dorias had said not to make any attempt at an apology, and Anrel intended to honor that request, in part because as he thought back over his actions, he could think of nothing he should apologize to his uncle *for*. He had done no wrong to Lord Dorias. He had not, as the letter accused, urged Valin to his death; he had tried to prevent it. He had not encouraged Valin in his folly. He had not conspired with Lord Blackfield—not in Alzur or Naith, at any rate. He had not made any serious effort to dissuade Lady Saria from marrying Lord Allutar. His hand had certainly not held the torch that set the Adirane home ablaze.

Yes, he had given voice to Valin's seditious notions, but was that an offense against Lord Dorias? Yes, he had done whatever was necessary to escape from Naith, but again, why should that require an apology?

Perhaps he might contrive a nonspecific apology, saying that he regretted any dishonor or opprobrium he might have brought upon the Adirane name—but his uncle had told him not to apologize, so he would not.

No, any reconciliation must come about through his uncle's actions, rather than his own.

But perhaps he could somehow contrive to get word to the Adiranes that their true names were now in the hands of Zarein Lorsa, the hottest of the Hots. A warning was not an apology, and however hostile Lord Dorias might be, he deserved a warning.

Anrel decided immediately that he could not send a letter; if he knew his uncle, any such letter would be burned unread the moment his handwriting was recognized. Nor did he want to entrust such a message to an ordinary messenger—who could say where the political loyalties of such a person might lie? His warning might wind up in entirely the wrong hands.

Perhaps one of the boys from the Pensioners' Quarter who were now in Lord Blackfield's employ? No, Lord Dorias would not admit them. He would recognize them as the guttersnipes they were, and refuse them entry lest they steal the silver.

Lord Blackfield himself was out of the question; even had he been willing to trust his former host with the information, not only would it be unspeakably presumptuous to ask him, but Lord Dorias was not likely to trust anything a Quandishman might say, particularly not a Quandishman with whom his nephew had *conspired*.

Conspired to do *what*? Anrel wondered. The letter didn't say.

Then he shook his head and returned to more important matters. Who could he send to speak to Lord Dorias?

One of Anrel's fellow delegates to the Grand Council? No, that was preposterous—the other members of the Committee for the Regulation of Sorcery seemed to be very solidly in favor of Lorsa's plan to use the Great List to bring the empire's nobility to heel, and who could he trust who was *not* on the committee? Derhin, perhaps, but no one else.

Derhin—but no, that would not do. Derhin, too, might think Lorsa's scheme a good one, and probably had no great love for Lord Dorias, who had done so little to defend his fosterling, Derhin's friend, from death at Lord Allutar's hands.

Perhaps Tazia?

That thought gave Anrel pause. Unlike all the previous notions, no objection sprang immediately to mind. Lord Dorias had a weakness, common in men of all ages, for pretty girls; he would not turn Tazia away without giving her a chance to speak.

Anrel frowned. He was, he knew, somewhat drunk, and perhaps there was some obvious flaw in the idea that the wine was hiding.

He would not act on it immediately, then—for one thing, calling on Tazia and Perynis at this hour would be inappropriate. If he could still see no argument against it by the light of morning, though, he would give it a try.

With that decided, he got unsteadily to his feet and after a moment's uncertainty as to exactly which direction he needed to go, he headed for bed.

30

In Which Anrel Receives a Warning

Morning was well advanced when Anrel arose; he had not made a late night of it, by any means, but it had been a long and tiring day that ended with a significant quantity of wine. Although he remembered his decision of the night before—a pleasant surprise, under the circumstances—there was no time to act upon it if he was to have any hope at all of being at the baths when the Grand Council's daily session was called to order. Besides, Tazia and Perynis were probably already begun on the day's labors.

There was no sign of Derhin; whether this was because he was still asleep, or because he had already left on the day's business, Anrel did not know and did not investigate. The empty wine bottles still stood on the table where he had left them, but that signified little; Derhin might well have left them there as Anrel's responsibility.

He did not eat a proper breakfast, any more than he had eaten a proper supper the night before, but he did wolf down enough bread and cheese to quiet his belly before setting out for the Baths.

Since he was alone this time he did not walk openly along the street to the front of the Baths, but instead followed the directions he had been given that took him down an alley to a tunnel that supposedly led under the surrounding ruins and emerged in one of the unused and unidentified back rooms.

He cautiously descended the steep stone stairs at one side of the alley, and found the tunnel just as described. The underground passage was gloomy, but not utterly dark—gratings in the pavements above let in enough daylight for Anrel to see where he was going.

One feature his informants had failed to mention, though, was the prickly sensation of dread and foreboding that washed over him as he passed under the outer wall of the baths. He was unsure whether this was a ward someone had placed to keep thieves and beggars from wandering into the council's chambers, or some lingering remnant of old magic; it didn't *feel* like any ward he had ever encountered, but that proved little.

The Aldian Baths were said to be haunted, and whatever it was he felt at that point would certainly fit with such a belief.

The fear faded quickly, though, as he pressed on, and he found himself with a choice of stairs leading up. He chose one at random; it brought him up into a dim gray room with a single door.

When Anrel opened that door he emerged into the atrium, which was deserted; the council was already assembled in the central bath. He hastened to join them.

The day's speaker was introducing the chairman of the Committee on Imperial Finance for yet another report, presumably to tell the council once again that nothing had changed; seeing that, Anrel slowed his pace. There was no need to rush.

He had therefore not yet reached the steps down into the pool when Pariel Gluth spotted him and hurried to his side.

"Delegate Murau," he said quietly.

"Delegate Gluth," Anrel acknowledged. "A pleasure to see you here today. You were missed yesterday."

Gluth smiled a tight little smile. "I'm sure. Could you spare me a moment, though, before we join the council as a whole?"

Puzzled, Anrel said, "Of course." He followed Gluth to the side, to a small alcove where they could see the edge of the main gathering, but where they had a modest degree of privacy.

"You have been of great service to us," Gluth said when they had reached the back of the alcove. "I felt it only fair, therefore, to warn you."

"Warn me of what?" Anrel asked uneasily.

"Some of us on the committee took action yesterday to facilitate matters," Gluth said. "It has long been clear that the Grand Council as a whole is simply too large and unwieldy, and too varied in its composition, to be effective, while the committees are too specialized and for the most part too timid to do what needs to be done."

"I had noticed that the council has not been particularly efficient in bringing about an earthly paradise," Anrel answered dryly.

"Indeed," Gluth said, his humorless little smile widening very slightly. "Therefore, certain forward-minded individuals have taken it upon themselves—or perhaps I should say, ourselves—to act in the council's stead in certain matters."

Anrel was in no mood for subtlety. "Forgive me, Delegate, but what are you talking about? When you say I have been of service to you, of whom are we speaking?"

Gluth's smile vanished. "Some of us from the Committee for the Regulation of Sorcery spent most of yesterday in conference with members of the Committee for the Restoration of Order, and with the burgrave of Lume, and with the chief wardens of the city," he explained. "We have developed a plan of action to resolve certain matters, and move the empire forward into a more progressive future. In the course of negotiations each faction made certain concessions to facilitate cooperation."

That, Anrel presumed, explained who Gluth represented, but not the nature of any warning. He was about to say so when Gluth continued, "*You*, Delegate Murau, were one of those concessions."

"What?" The single word was startled out of him.

"Starting this morning the Joint Committee, with the assistance of the burgrave and his men, will be assuming temporary control of the city of Lume," Gluth told him. "The city will be sealed off—indeed, the orders have already been sent to the gates—and all those suspected of treason will be brought before tribunals for questioning. *All* those suspected, regardless of rank or affiliation. Each party provided a list of suspects. The representatives of the Committee for the Regulation of Sorcery produced a list of some forty-three sorcerers who are to be arrested and tried, while the spokesmen for the Committee for the

Restoration of Order put forth fifty-six names, most of them officials or hirelings of the imperial court. One of those fifty-six names is your own, Anrel Murau."

Anrel stared at his informant. "So you agreed to let them arrest me?" he said. "Then why are you telling me this?"

"You have been very useful to the progressive factions, as I said," Gluth said. "While we cannot protect you, and have agreed to sacrifice you for the greater good, we are not ungrateful. I am therefore giving you this warning so that you will have a chance to put your affairs in order, and say your farewells."

"And if I do more than that? If, perhaps, I manage to elude capture?"

"I would not be unduly dismayed," Gluth said, again smiling his tight little smile. "While a martyr can be valuable, a hero of the people who has vanished into the alleys and tunnels also has a certain romantic appeal that will most likely rouse the enthusiasm of the populace. Our alliance with the Committee for the Restoration of Order is unlikely to be permanent, and the time may come when we have uses for such a legendary figure."

"I see." Anrel glanced out at the council, apparently carrying on with the day's tedious business in the usual fashion, and wondered whether he could really believe what Delegate Gluth was telling him.

Gluth cleared his throat. "You might also want to know that at the burgrave's suggestion, to facilitate the maintenance of order, all foreigners have been instructed to leave the city by sunset tonight, or face arrest. You will not be able to take shelter with your Quandish friend. A messenger has been sent to inform him of this—him, and perhaps two hundred other assorted foreigners, not counting any who may be in the employ of the imperial court. Those last will be dealt with separately. We have no need for foreign spies and agitators while we are purging the capital of traitors."

"Of course not," Anrel agreed. He saw that Gluth was still gazing intently at him, and added, "Is that all, then, or is there more?"

"That is the entire extent of the warning. I wish you the best of luck, Delegate Murau. Will you be joining us in the great chamber, then, or do you think you might prefer to forego this session?"

"I am not . . ."

Anrel's answer was drowned out by a tremendous roar from the gathered council.

"Ah," Gluth said. "The first announcement has been made."

"What?" Anrel turned to stare out at the main chamber.

"The Committee on Imperial Finance has just revealed that the impasse has finally been broken—the empire's debts are to be paid from the confiscated property of convicted traitors." He smiled crookedly. "Delegate Arnuir, the chairman of that committee, has been waiting half a season to have something to say that our fellows wanted to hear; I am sure he took great pleasure in presenting the news as dramatically as possible. When he has completed his explanation, Lord Huizal, of the Committee for the Restoration of Order, will be speaking next, naming the first suspects, and the arrests will begin immediately thereafter. If you intend to leave, friend Murau, you had best leave *now*."

"Thank you," Anrel said, shaken. He no longer seriously doubted Gluth's warning.

He hesitated a fraction of a second longer, though, as he considered what he would do. He had two choices, stay or go.

If he stayed, he would almost certainly die. No matter how great an orator he might be—and he did not think himself as talented as others seemed to—he doubted he could sway the council. His fate had been decided; his enemies wanted him dead, and his allies were willing to sacrifice him, make him a martyr in their campaign to reform the empire. His death would help cement the power of what Gluth called the Joint Committee. Any ideas he might have had about what the council should do, any influence he might have had as a member of the Committee for the Regulation of Sorcery, would be forgotten; his life would be nothing but a payment in the political transactions of the *real* powers.

If he fled, he would be giving up his established life and starting anew. He would be a fugitive once again, a traitor under sentence of death. He might be caught and killed at any time—but he would have a chance. He had been a fugitive before, yet he still lived.

And this time he might be able to remain in contact with Tazia.

Without another word he turned and hastened out of the alcove, back toward the tunnel by which he had arrived just moments before. He crossed the atrium to the room where he had emerged, closed the door behind him, and hurried down the steps. Once he was completely out of sight, alone in the tunnel, he broke into a run.

He was not sure he believed *everything* Gluth had told him, but he had no doubt there was a basis of truth in it. For one thing, as he fled, he could hear Lorsa's distinctive voice thundering from the floor of the great pool, "Fellow Walasians, today we will at last begin to cleanse the empire with the blood of its foes!"

Anrel knew that he was one of those foes, but with any luck, thanks to Gluth's warning, his blood would not be spilled.

Lord Allutar, on the other hand, was assuredly another such foe, and his blood very well might be a part of that cleansing. This was not quite the revenge Anrel had hoped for, but it would do.

He found himself taking surprisingly little satisfaction from his enemy's doom as he ran through the tunnel.

A rush of dread flickered through him as he passed out of the Baths, but he ignored it as he fled and tried to think what he should do, where he should go. He could not stay in the burgrave of Naith's town house, obviously, and Gluth had just warned him he could not expect any help from Lord Blackfield this time. If the gates were closed, as Gluth had said, getting out of the city would be difficult—not impossible, as he might be able to stow away on a boat, but difficult, and it would require planning.

Though where could he go, if he left Lume? He no longer had a home anywhere outside the walls. He had no trusted friends who might shelter him, and not enough money to buy anyone's silence.

No, at least for the present he would need to find a refuge *within* the walls. Gluth had spoken of alleys and tunnels, and certainly plenty of those existed, but Anrel did not know his way around them. Although many of the former residents of the Pensioners' Quarter made good use of the tunnels, until today Anrel had never been one of those people. Venturing blindly into the maze beneath the city was a hazardous undertaking; the rumors of monsters and magic lurking below the streets, however exaggerated they might have become, almost certainly had some basis in fact.

Anrel knew that a few hardy souls were beginning to resettle in the burned-out remains of the Pensioners' Quarter, but Anrel was not eager to join them, and besides, if anyone was seriously searching for him, that would be one of the first places they would look.

He could not hope for concealment in the student courts now any more than he had when he first arrived in Lume.

Lurking in alleys was hardly an appealing prospect, but Anrel could see little alternative. At least he might still be able to meet with Tazia occasionally; he would not endanger her by seeing her often, but surely they might risk an encounter or two.

He would probably have time to gather his few possessions from the town house before going into hiding; his would-be captors would expect him to be at the baths, and would not head for Lourn Street until after they discovered his absence.

Accordingly, when he emerged from the tunnel he turned his steps in that direction, walking briskly; a running man might attract the attention of wardens or watchmen.

He stopped dead, though when he rounded the corner onto Lourn Street.

There was a coach in front of the town house, a coach paneled in dark blue and black trimmed with white and gold, and built in a foreign style. Anrel recognized it immediately. It appeared that he would have an opportunity to say farewell to Lord Blackfield after all.

Either that, or it was a trap of some sort. He could not rule out that possibility. He approached the carriage warily.

Lord Blackfield's man Harban was in the driver's seat, a battered black hat pulled down to his ears, his white braid trailing down his back. He turned, spotted Anrel, and tipped his hat. Then he rapped on the roof of the coach.

One of the glass windows slid down, and Lord Blackfield's face appeared. "Master Murau!" he called. "A word with you, if you please."

"Of course, my lord," Anrel said, stepping up. The door of the carriage swung open, and Lord Blackfield's hand reached out for him, fine lace at the cuff.

Anrel accepted this help, and a moment later the two men were seated facing each other as the coach began rolling forward.

"Rest assured, sir, I am not abducting you," the Quandishman said. "I think we will draw less attention if we are moving, though, and at the present time I think that drawing attention would be most unfortunate."

"We are in full agreement, my lord," Anrel replied.

"You have heard, perhaps, that all foreigners are being expelled from Lume? We are to be without the walls by sunset, on penalty of—well, they did not actually say, but the penalties were implied to be dire indeed. You knew about this?"

"Yes, I knew. I was informed perhaps half an hour ago. I am honored, my lord, that you troubled yourself to come by to wish me farewell, under the circumstances."

"I came by to offer you something more than a farewell, Master Murau. I have reason to believe that you are in danger here."

He looked as if he might have more to say, but Anrel interrupted, "As do I. In fairness, I must warn you that my presence in your carriage may be a danger to *you,* as well."

The big Quandishman dismissed that with a wave of his hand. "Oh, do not trouble yourself about that, sir! I assure you, I am entirely capable of coping with whatever dangers you may bring with you. No, I have come to offer *you* a way out of Walasia."

Anrel blinked. "What?"

"I am inviting you to join me for the journey to Quand, Master Murau, and to be my guest in Ondine for as long as it suits you to stay."

"I . . . I am honored, my lord," Anrel said, as he tried to gather his wits. He had almost never seriously considered the possibility of fleeing the Empire entirely; what would he have done, as an outcast in a foreign land? What he knew of the Cousins did not render them particularly attractive, and Walasians were not generally very welcome in Quand or Ermetia. But to stay in the Quandish capital as a Gatherman's guest was a far more pleasant prospect than anything he had previously imagined.

There were still drawbacks, of course, severe ones.

"You have demonstrated yourself to be a resourceful young man," Lord Blackfield said, before Anrel had entirely decided on a response. "I do not know whether your talent for oratory will translate into Quandish, but I believe you have sufficient other skills to earn your keep, should you fear you might abuse my hospitality. Not that *I* am concerned about such things, as I assure you, even the most protracted stay would be no great imposition, but I think it might trouble *you*."

"My lord," Anrel said slowly, "your generosity must surely do you credit in the eyes of the Mother of us all, and your soul's reward in the next world will undoubtedly dwarf the riches you possess in this one, but I cannot accept."

Lord Blackfield cocked his head to one side. "Whyever not?"

"To begin with, my lord, I am already a fugitive—my pardon has been withdrawn, and I am to be arrested by representatives of the Committee for the Restoration of Order at the first opportunity. That is why I am not at the baths at this very moment, in my role as a delegate to the Grand Council. I am told that the city gates are already closed, and I will not be permitted to leave."

"Oh, I know *that*," Lord Blackfield said, dismissing it with an airy wave. "The messenger who delivered the letter from the burgrave, ordering me out of Lume, told me that he would be taking orders to the gatekeepers to seal off the capital. But as a foreign dignitary, you see, I am to be given free passage out of the city, even when no Walasian is allowed to pass."

"They will undoubtedly look in this coach, though, and see me, and detain me," Anrel said. "My presence might well endanger you, perhaps void your guarantee of passage."

The Quandishman waved that away as well. "You forget, Master Murau, that I am a sorcerer, and very practiced in seemings, glamours, and deceptions. You will to all appearances be a member of my staff, and not a Walasian at all."

Anrel *had* momentarily forgotten that; he had to admit it made the offer more practical, but there were still other factors to consider.

"There are those here in Lume I cannot bear to leave behind," he said. "I will go nowhere without them."

The Quandishman blinked at him in astonishment. "Father and Mother, Anrel, who *do* you mean? When you came to me in Dezar House not half a season ago, you said you had no one else to turn to!"

"Indeed, I did not, but since then I have learned of others recently arrived in Lume. Most important, Mistress Tazia Lir, my beloved, who I hope to make my wife one day, is here."

Lord Blackfield stared at him for a moment, a smile spreading across his face. "Oh, magnificent, Master Murau!" the Quandishman exclaimed at last. "My congratulations upon finding her, and may your hopes soon be realized! Of course you shall not leave her behind; you must bring her with us!"

Anrel's mouth opened, then closed again.

Why not? Tazia had little to keep her here in Lume; in Quand, where magic was not restricted to the nobility, she could presumably work openly as a witch, rather than settle for domestic labor.

But she was Walasian, born and bred. The empire was her homeland, and Quand a foreign mystery.

"I cannot speak for her without consulting her, my lord," he said.

"No, of course you cannot," Lord Blackfield agreed. "Let us go and speak with her, then, and see what she says."

"She has . . . she has her mother and a sister to think of, my lord."

Lord Blackfield's blandly cheerful expression faltered at that. "Four of you?" he said. "Well, I could certainly have managed a staff of four had I wanted to—five, counting Harban. I think we might still manage it. Fortunately, Mistress Uillea has chosen to remain in Lume."

"And . . ." Anrel swallowed. "And there is my uncle, my lord."

"Lord Dorias?" The Quandishman actually frowned at that. "What does he have to do with anything?"

"He and my cousin Saria are here in Lume, my lord, at the Adirane town house in Wizard's Hill Court. Their home in Alzur was burned, and they fled to Lume."

"Well, what of it?"

"Lady Saria is betrothed to Lord Allutar, and Uncle Dorias has spoken in Lord Allutar's defense. I am sure you know how unpopular Lord Allutar has been of late; his name is first on the list of those the Committee for the Regulation of Sorcery wishes to condemn, and I have no doubt that his friends and associates may be questioned. What's more, I know that the chairman of the committee has obtained their true names. I fear they are in grave danger if they remain in the capital."

"Indeed? Their true names are known?" The Quandishman's expression was unreadable.

"The committee was granted access to the Great List," Anrel explained.

"Were they? How did *that* happen?"

Anrel did not feel like explaining the foul bargain the emperor had made. He said, "The Grand Council has ultimate authority in the empire, my lord."

"In theory, but I had not expected it to be accepted in such a manner! Well, well. That does seem to put them at risk, if you are sure of your facts."

"Quite sure, my lord."

"That makes seven, then." Lord Blackfield sighed. "I fear the coach will be most unpleasantly crowded, and even for my sorcery, convincing the guards at the gate to let so many pass unhindered may prove a challenge."

"I know," Anrel said miserably. "I cannot ask you to put yourself at risk—but I cannot simply abandon any of them. It may well be that Nivain and Perynis Lir will choose to remain in Lume, or that my uncle and cousin will refuse my aid, but I cannot in good conscience fail to consider any of them. It is *your* coach and safe-conduct, my lord; I have no right to inconvenience you in any way."

"Oh, don't be so dismayed," the Quandishman said. "I can never resist a noble gesture. Let us see who is interested, and who is not, and take it from there, shall we?"

"I . . . I don't know what to say."

"*I* say, let us meet somewhere in, oh, two or three hours—that will give you time to speak to them all?"

"I think so, my lord."

"Good. It will give *me* time to prepare a few spells. Where shall we meet, then? Your beloved's residence, perhaps?"

"No," Anrel said as he quickly reviewed the logistics. "My uncle's town house, in Wizard's Hill Court."

Lord Blackfield nodded, then glanced up at the sun, or where the sun would have been if it were not obscured by clouds just then. "Wizard's Hill Court, in three hours' time, then," he said. "If you are not there I will not wait long, though, and I will not look for you elsewhere. I have my doubts about whether they will truly give me until sundown, and I would prefer not to test it any more closely than I must."

"I will be there, my lord."

"I certainly hope so." With that he leaned back and tapped the roof of the carriage with his walking stick. Anrel heard Harban call to the horses, and the coach came to a stop.

They had looped around, and were once again only a few yards from the burgrave of Naith's town house. Anrel swung open the door of the coach and clambered out, then turned and watched as the carriage rolled away.

When it reached the corner he turned, and hurried into the town house to retrieve his few belongings. There was no time to waste.

31

In Which Anrel Sends Tazia on an Errand

Tazia and Perynis were not in their attic room; when they did not answer his knock Anrel threw himself against the door and burst it open. The cheap old lock provided little resistance.

When a quick glance confirmed their absence Anrel closed the door again and hurried through the hallways and stairwells of the tenement in search of them. He was beginning to worry that they might be off on some errand that would keep them away for hours when he heard a woman's laughter.

He followed the sound, and found Tazia and Perynis kneeling in a corridor, rags in hand; they had obviously been scrubbing at the floor, which bore a large purple stain upon the gray planking and reeked of sour wine. Tazia had apparently been telling jokes, as Perynis was leaning against the wall, trying unsuccessfully to stop giggling. She happened to be facing Anrel, however, while Tazia was not, so it was Perynis who saw him first and exclaimed, "Master Murau!" That, at last, seemed to calm her laughter, and she sprang to her feet.

Tazia's head whirled, and she almost fell sideways; turning so swiftly while on one's knees was awkward, to say the least. "Anrel!" she said.

Anrel nodded. "I am delighted to see you both," he said.

"What brings you here, at this hour?" Tazia asked.

"Urgent news," he said. "And an opportunity."

Tazia tossed her rags into the bucket the pair had been using, then got to her feet. "What news?" she asked.

Anrel had not taken the time to work out how to explain the situation, and he was unsure whether either woman paid any attention to politics. "The Grand Council," he began, "or rather, the more extreme elements of the Grand Council—" He stopped, took a breath, and started over. "I have learned," he said, "that some members of the Grand Council intend to close off the capital, seal the gates and guard the river, and then arrest everyone they consider responsible for the recent turmoil—*everyone,* on all sides."

Perynis looked blank; Tazia produced a puzzled frown.

"That includes Lord Allutar," Anrel explained. "He will finally be brought to justice for his crimes."

"Then that's *good* news!" Perynis said, smiling.

Tazia, however, had read Anrel's expression. "Go on," she said.

"That also includes the infamous rabble-rouser Alvos," Anrel said. "I am to be brought before a tribunal, questioned, and in all probability hanged."

"Oh," Perynis said.

"But you're here, and still free," Tazia said, her gaze fixed on his face.

"There are those who would prefer me to escape," he said. "I was given a warning. It is very likely, though, that there are watchmen or wardens looking for me even now."

"Will you be going into hiding, then?" Tazia asked. "Will we still be able to meet with you?"

"That brings us to the opportunity," Anrel replied. "My Quandish friend, Lord Blackfield, has been ordered to leave the city, but has been given until sundown to do so. He has offered to take me with him to Quand—I will ride in his coach and pretend to be one of his servants, and he will use his sorcery to make this ruse difficult to detect."

Tazia's expression hardened. "Then have you come to say farewell?"

Anrel's heart seemed to stop at those words. "No, no, my dearest," he said hastily. "You misunderstand me entirely. I have come to invite you to *join* me."

Tazia's mouth opened, then closed.

"Witchcraft is legal in Quand," Anrel said. "You could live openly and honorably as an honest businesswoman—and if you will give your consent, beloved, as my wife. There is room in the coach for both of us."

"I don't . . . I . . ."

"Oh, you *must* go!" Perynis said, almost squeaking. She sprang to her feet and embraced her sister. "Go to Quand and marry Anrel!"

"But I can't . . . I . . . what about Mother?"

"Oh, we'll be fine," Perynis said.

"Perynis," Anrel said, as Tazia continued to hesitate.

"Yes?" Perynis said, startled.

"There might be room for you and your mother, as well."

The younger woman's eyes lit up. "Truly?" she said.

"It's Quand," Tazia warned. "We would be foreigners. We don't speak Quandish. We would know no one at all."

"You know *me*," Anrel reminded her.

"No one except Anrel and each other," Tazia amended.

"And who did you know in Lume when you arrived here?"

"No one," Tazia acknowledged. "But we spoke the language, and knew the customs. In Quand we will be strangers, outcasts."

"At first," Anrel admitted.

"I—" Tazia began, but Anrel held up a hand.

"I am not going to require you to make your decision here and now," he said. "Neither of you. There is more I must explain first."

"Go on," Tazia said, as Perynis nodded.

"There are two others I hope to save," Anrel said. "My uncle, Lord Dorias, and my cousin, Lady Saria."

"Sorcerers?" Tazia asked.

"Yes," Anrel said. "They are sorcerers, and I believe they are in danger because they are sorcerers, and because they are associated with Lord Allutar. Indeed, Lady Saria is betrothed to Lord Allutar."

Anrel could hear Perynis suck in her breath at that. Tazia simply stared at him.

"They are my family," Anrel said. "My uncle took me in when my parents died, and Saria was almost a sister to me when we were children.

I owe them whatever aid I can give them, no matter how much I detest my cousin's fiancé and my uncle's politics."

"Can your Quandish friend really save so many?" Perynis asked.

"I don't know," Anrel said. "I don't think *he* knows, either. The more people in the coach, the greater the chance the ruse will be penetrated and all of us captured. If you feel the risk excessive, and prefer to remain in Lume, I would certainly not think any the less of you—*your* names are not on the Grand Council's lists. On the other hand, that may mean that even should our masquerade be detected, you might be permitted to go free."

The two sisters exchanged glances.

"There's more," Anrel said.

Both turned their attention back to him.

"My uncle has disowned me," Anrel said. "He has believed Lord Allutar's version of events, rather than my own, and has taken positions even more extreme than Allutar's own in faulting me for everything that has gone wrong for him in the past year. *I* cannot approach him to warn him, or to offer him safe passage in Lord Blackfield's coach; he will not speak to me or allow me in his home."

"Then why do you mention him at all?" Tazia demanded.

"Because I still owe it to him to try to warn him and save him," Anrel said. "Therefore, Tazia, I ask you, will you please act as my emissary in this matter? Will you go to him, and tell him that the Committee for the Regulation of Sorcery has learned his true name, and is likely to arrest him for conspiring with Lord Allutar? Will you tell him that Lord Blackfield has offered him and his daughter passage out of the city, to Quand?"

Tazia frowned. "You ask a great deal, Anrel," she said.

"I do," Anrel said. "I know. And if you refuse, I will accept that without question, and it will not alter what I am about to promise you."

"Promise me?"

"I promise you, Tazia, that whatever you decide—to go to Quand, or to remain in Lume; to play the envoy for my uncle, or to leave him to his own devices—whatever you may choose, I will not leave you. Not again. When I left you in Beynos, thinking you must hate me for allowing

Reva's death—of all the mistakes I have made in my life, everything I have done wrong, everything I have failed to do, that is the one I regret most deeply, and the one I cannot bear to repeat. If you choose to go to Quand, I will go with you. If you choose to remain in Lume, I will remain in hiding in Lume. I have already said that I would gladly make you my wife in Quand; rest assured, I would gladly marry you no matter where we might be. Whatever you ask of me, I shall endeavor to deliver—though I pray to the Mother and the Father that you will never ask one thing of me, and that is not to see you further. I love you, Tazia, and would be with you always, if you will allow it."

"Oh," Tazia said breathlessly.

Anrel turned to her sister, who was staring at him, wide-eyed. "Perynis," he said, "If you will allow it, I would like to accompany you to find your mother, so that we might offer her passage to Quand. If Tazia refuses to speak to my uncle then of course she must come with us, but I hope she will agree to present my message to Lord Dorias while we speak with Nivain."

Perynis nodded, still staring.

"Lord Dorias and Lady Saria live at number two, Wizard's Hill Court," Anrel said. "Lord Blackfield's carriage will be in Wizard's Hill Court in about two and a half hours, and will depart thence directly for Quand, with whichever of us have chosen to go. Any who are not there when the carriage departs—well, there is no second chance; I cannot imagine that Lord Blackfield will ever return to Lume. I hope that you and I, Perynis, will bring your mother safe to that meeting, and that Tazia will coax my uncle and my cousin out of their house to Lord Blackfield's coach."

"Oh," Perynis said.

"I will try, Anrel," Tazia said. "I will be there, whether your uncle speaks to me or not."

"Then let us be about it!"

They stopped at the sisters' room to fetch those possessions they could not bear to leave, then departed the tenement, Tazia heading for Wizard's Hill Court while Anrel and Perynis turned their steps toward the wine merchant's home where Nivain lived and worked.

They had scarcely gone a hundred paces when Perynis asked, "Who are *they?*" She pointed at a dozen figures who were moving purposefully down the avenue. Other people were hurrying out of their way.

Anrel turned to look, then hastened his step. "Come on," he said, taking Perynis's arm and guiding her down a side street.

He could not be absolutely certain, but he had a very good idea who those men were. One in the front of the group wore a black coat and hat, with a red badge visible on his chest; the others wore an assortment of attire, but each man—and they were all men—had a red band tied around his left arm between elbow and shoulder. Each of them also bore a weapon—mostly cudgels and clubs, but Anrel saw the glint of steel; at least one of them was carrying an unsheathed sword.

The leader was almost certainly a warden, while the others were most likely deputies he had recruited, and Anrel guessed that they were on their way to arrest someone on the council's list. He had no interest in providing them with a fresh target.

The two of them had covered most of the distance to the wine merchant's house when they rounded a corner and found themselves looking at another such group, but these men had obviously already found their prey. Four of them were half dragging, half carrying a man in a paisley velvet jacket. Their captive was moaning; one side of his head was smeared with blood, and the shoulder of his jacket was stained dark red as well.

The warden walked at the front of the group, looking straight ahead, while the deputies who were not hauling the prisoner appeared grimly wary, their weapons still out and ready. Perhaps, Anrel thought, they expected someone to attempt a rescue.

Under other circumstances he might have considered intervening himself, but not now, not when his name was already on the wardens' list, not when Tazia would be expecting him in Wizard's Hill Court, not when he had Perynis with him. Instead he once again pulled the girl aside, out of the warden's path, and waited in the shadow of a balcony while the ferocious little company marched past.

Anrel and Perynis were by no means the only people who stepped aside and watched the warden's company go by; in fact, all normal activity on the street seemed suspended in a fifty-foot radius around the warden and his prisoner, and the ordinary men and women of Lume only resumed their own movements and conversation when the squad was well clear.

Some did not resume normal activity at all, but instead hurried away, presumably to the safety of their own homes. No one seemed inclined to discuss what they had seen.

That universal reaction of silent watchfulness meant that the deputies paid no particular attention to Anrel and Perynis, since they were doing nothing that stood out as in any way unusual. That allowed Anrel to safely stay close enough to catch a glimpse of the prisoner's face. He could not identify the man exactly, but Anrel was reasonably sure he had seen him before—and that he was a sorcerer.

If that was indeed the case, then the true names from the Great List had apparently worked. A dozen ordinary citizens armed with clubs could not have captured a sorcerer without some magical assistance.

Anrel wondered what had become of Lord Allutar; had he been at the Baths that morning? Anrel had not seen him, but his own stay had been very brief indeed.

"What's going on?" Perynis asked, when the warden's party was safely past. "Who are those men with the warden? Who was that they were carrying?"

"I assume those were deputies," Anrel said. "And that was one of the people the Grand Council has ordered arrested."

Her face went pale. "Oh," she said. She glanced in the direction the deputies had gone. "Anrel?"

"Yes?"

"I definitely want to go to Quand."

"I understand."

A few minutes later the pair arrived at the rear entrance to the wine merchant's house, where Perynis knocked loudly. She and Anrel stood on the rear stoop for a moment, waiting, and then the door swung open. Perynis turned to the opening, starting to say something.

Then she froze.

Anrel saw the man standing in the doorway, and recognized him instantly. He was thinner, his hair and beard longer and far more unkempt than when Anrel had last seen him, he stank of sour wine, and his clothes were much the worse for wear, but his identity was unmistakable.

Garras Lir.

"Father," Perynis said faintly.

32

In Which Anrel Visits His Uncle

"Daughter," Garras said. "And Master Murau. I didn't expect to see *you* here!"

"Where's Mother?" Perynis demanded.

"Inside," Garras said. "I haven't touched her."

"We came to speak with her," Anrel said. "If we might enter, please?"

"What did you want with her?"

"With all due respect, Master Lir, our business is with her, not with you."

"She is my wife," Garras replied angrily. "Anything you might say to her is my business!"

"Nonetheless, we are here to speak to *her*," Anrel said. "Please step aside."

"Don't you give me orders, you sorcerer's bastard!" Garras snapped.

"I am assured that my parents were married to each other," Anrel answered calmly. "Can you say the same?"

"Two sorcerers producing a commoner?" Garras sneered. "I know better than that—and I suspect your mother's husband did, as well. That's probably why he killed her."

Anrel dropped his pack to the ground and stepped forward, and without consciously planning it he felt magical power surge up into him from the earth beneath the stoop. He reached to grab Garras, but the other man stepped back into the house.

He was not able to close the door, though, before Anrel thrust his foot inside.

They froze like that for a moment, Anrel squeezed into the opening, trying to force the door open, while the larger, heavier Garras stood behind it, trying to push it closed. Their faces were scant inches apart, and they glared at each other; Anrel could smell alcohol on the other man's breath. Magic tingled in Anrel's gut and in his hands, but he did not know how to use it, what he might productively do with it.

"You should have died in Beynos," Garras growled.

"You did your best to arrange it," Anrel replied.

"You raised our hopes, with that speech of yours, and then Reva died anyway."

"I did what I could," Anrel said. "No one regrets more than I do that it wasn't enough."

"It's your fault my wife left me, with your lies and false hopes!"

"I wish I could take credit for her decision, but she came to her senses without my help." Anrel raised his hand, reaching for Garras's face, thinking that perhaps he could stupefy Garras momentarily and push his way into the house.

Garras saw the motion, and pulled his head back. "What are you . . ."

He did not complete the question; instead there was a loud thump, and Garras crumpled backward, falling flat on his back on the mudroom floor. The door suddenly gave under the pressure of Anrel's shoulder, and he had to step forward, over Garras's outstretched legs, to keep from falling.

He found himself staring directly at Nivain Lir, who stood in the mudroom clutching a cast-iron skillet. Her hair was unbound and in wild disarray; her left cheek was covered by a large fresh bruise just beginning to go purple. Her husband's assurance that he hadn't touched her appeared to have been a lie.

"I don't . . . he was . . ." she said.

"Mistress Lir," Anrel said. He glanced down at Garras, who was blinking at the ceiling; he was obviously still alive, and apparently conscious, though stunned. "I think it might be advisable to come with us."

"Yes," Nivain said. She stepped forward, hesitated, flung the skillet aside, then stepped across her husband.

His hand rose, groping for her ankle, and with a soft gasp she tumbled into Anrel's arms. He quickly pulled her out the door and set her on her feet, where Perynis could take her hand and steady her.

After allowing mother and daughter a moment for a quick embrace and a few words of comfort, Anrel urged them away from the door. "I hear him moving," he said. That was the simple truth; the door had not closed fully, and Anrel could clearly hear Garras muttering to himself and trying to push himself up.

Nivain immediately started away, choosing her direction at random until Perynis caught her elbow and said, "This way."

A few seconds later the three of them were hurrying up the alley in the direction that would eventually bring them to Wizard's Hill Court. Garras staggered out the door and bellowed, "Come back here!"

Nivain hastened her pace, and the others hurried to catch up.

"He's drunk," Nivain said.

"So it would appear," Anrel agreed, as they emerged from the alley.

Nivain started to turn left, and the others caught her, one on either side, and guided her to the right. She looked up at Anrel, startled. "Where are we going?" she asked. "I thought . . . either the tenement or . . ."

"We are bound for my uncle's house in Wizard's Hill Court," Anrel replied. "I will explain why as we walk." He glanced back over his shoulder; Garras was following them, stumbling along the alley with one hand to his head, but losing ground.

"Are you all right, Mother?" Perynis asked. "Did he hurt you?" She studied her mother's face, apparently trying to judge the extent and severity of the bruising. "He said he hadn't touched you," she added accusingly.

Nivain shook her head. "I will be fine," she said.

"How did he *find* you?"

"I don't know," Nivain said. She smiled bitterly. "He complained about how long it took, but he never said how he accomplished it."

"He probably simply asked everyone he met if they had seen you," Anrel said. "You don't seem to have made a point of secrecy, after all; you have been using your own names."

"I never thought he would come here looking for us!" Nivain cried.

Anrel held his tongue.

Nivain looked at him, then at Perynis. "Where is Tazia?" she asked.

"She is to meet us in Wizard's Hill Court," Anrel said, speaking firmly. Nivain did not yet seem fully in command of herself, which was entirely understandable under the circumstances, and he wanted to keep her focused on essentials—most importantly, their destination.

Nivain looked at Perynis, who nodded. "That's right, Mother. She's meeting us there, along with a Quandish sorcerer."

"A what?"

"A friend of mine," Anrel said. "Lord Blackfield."

Nivain turned to Anrel. "You said you would explain?"

"As long as we keep walking, yes," Anrel said. He glanced around. There were relatively few people on the street, and none of them seemed to be paying any particular attention to Anrel and his companions. Anrel thought he could hear shouting somewhere in the distance, but it was far enough away that he felt they could safely ignore it.

"It seems that some members of the Grand Council have finally tired of their pointless hairsplitting arguments, and have chosen to act," he said. "At their orders the city gates have reportedly been closed, Lume is to be sealed off, and wardens and watchmen are gathering up everyone the council considers enemies of the empire. That includes a few dozen sorcerers, perhaps certain troublesome foreigners, and assorted rabble-rousers—including myself. We are to be dragged before tribunals and questioned, and although no one has yet said so openly, I suspect most of us will be hanged as traitors."

Nivain stared at him. "Hanged?"

He snorted. "That's hardly new, is it? I was under sentence of death when you first met me."

"But aren't you a delegate to the Grand Council?"

"I was until this morning, yes. I believe I have now effectively resigned my seat."

"But they . . . how can they *do* that? Did the sorcerers take over the council?"

"Oh, they most assuredly did not," Anrel told her. "No, the radicals on either side have joined forces, each side sacrificing some of its own to accomplish this alliance. Lord Allutar is on their list of enemies, and his name surely comes before my own. They think to appease the mob and make peace." He peered along the largely deserted street. "It may even work, but I am not inclined to donate my life to the experiment."

"So you are going into hiding? But what does that have to do with your uncle, or this Quandish lord?" She glanced at Perynis. "Or us?"

"Lord Blackfield has offered me transport to Quand," Anrel said. "He has been promised safe passage out of Lume until sunset; after that, he is given to understand that he will be unwelcome here, and perhaps anywhere in the empire. At some risk to himself, he has agreed to bring me out of the city in the guise of one of his servants, and I am, I assure you, very grateful for this generosity, but I will not go without Tazia. Leaving her behind in Beynos was the worst mistake of my life, and I have no intention of repeating it. I am offering her the chance to accompany me, and for her sake and yours, I am offering *you* the same opportunity. While I realize Quand is a foreign land that can never be your home in the way Walasia is, witchcraft is legal in Quand, and to the best of my knowledge there are no mobs shouting in the streets of Ondine, nor club-wielding wardens dragging people to unknown fates. I think an extended stay there might be a good idea for us all."

Nivain nodded, chewing her lip thoughtfully. Then she asked, "And your uncle?"

Anrel sighed. "I fear that he and my cousin Saria may be on the list of alleged traitors," he explained. "She is Lord Allutar's betrothed, and my uncle attempted to defend Allutar's home from the mob. I am hoping that they, too, might accompany us to Quand."

"How many people can this Quandishman *take*?" Nivain asked. "How will he transport us all? Does he have a ship?"

"A coach," Anrel said. "And whether there will be room for us all is an open question."

"Are there any others, then?"

"No," Anrel replied. "That's all."

"It seems more than enough. All of us in a single coach, all the way to Quand? It may be a very crowded ride," Perynis remarked.

Neither Anrel nor Nivain bothered to answer that.

Perhaps a quarter of an hour later the trio arrived in Wizard's Hill Court. Anrel was relieved that no warden had attempted to stop them; he guessed that the one he had met before was busy elsewhere, arresting some enemy of the people at the council's behest.

The court was empty. There was no Quandish carriage, nor any sign of Tazia, and for a moment Anrel feared that something dreadful might have befallen her, and cursed himself for sending her alone.

But then, if he had come, there was no chance that Lord Dorias would have admitted them. If all had gone as planned Tazia was inside the house even now, talking to his uncle. Anrel marched up the granite steps and swung the knocker for three deliberate blows.

The wait seemed interminable. Anrel looked back at the entry to the court, at the watchmen's arch; there was no watchman in sight on the walkways, no warden on the streets, but Anrel knew that one might happen along at any moment.

Then at last the door opened, and Ollith stood there.

"Master Murau," he said.

"Good day, Ollith," Anrel said. "Is my uncle in?"

"I have been given specific instructions, sir. You are not permitted in the house, nor is anyone accompanying you, but if you wish to speak to Lord Dorias, and would be so kind as to wait for a moment, he will come out."

That was not a complete acceptance, but it was certainly better than Anrel had feared. "Thank you, Ollith, I will be happy to wait." He glanced at the others. "I believe Mistress Lir is here?"

"She is."

"You might mention that her mother and sister are with me."

"I will do so, sir." He bowed, then stepped back inside and closed the door.

"I don't understand," Nivain said. "Why must we wait out here?" She glanced up at the sun, which was uncomfortably bright and already well past its zenith. None of them had eaten since breakfast, nor had anything to drink in hours.

Anrel admitted, "I am afraid that my uncle and I are not on the best of terms."

301

"But aren't you coming to save him from the mob?"

"I believe that is why he is willing to speak with us at all. I asked Tazia to plead my case, and it would appear she has done so." He glanced at the arch over the court entry, uncomfortably aware that a watchman might appear without warning—though it occurred to him that he had not, in fact, seen a member of the Emperor's Watch all day. The arches and walkways were still there, of course, but he had not seen anyone on any of them, nor had he seen any watchmen at the baths that morning.

He blinked, trying to decide just how unusual that actually was. The watchmen were such a common part of the city's background he no longer consciously noticed them, but an entire day on the streets without seeing one seemed a little peculiar.

He had certainly seen wardens and their deputies, though. He peered under the arch, dreading the prospect of a man in a black coat, or a crowd in red armbands.

He thought he glimpsed a figure in the shadows, but could not be sure. He debated going for a closer look, but decided against it; his uncle might appear at any second, and if Anrel were not immediately ready to talk to him he would most probably take it as a deliberate affront.

Then the black door of the town house opened, and Lord Dorias stepped out.

He was wearing his best wine-colored coat over a cloth-of-gold vest. His graying hair was pulled back in a braid, and crowned with a black hat with a feathered cockade. His badge of office as burgrave of Alzur hung on his chest, supported by a heavy gold chain around his neck. This was not the attire he would wear to speak to his errant nephew; this was the formal garb of an official of the Walasian Empire.

He stopped on the uppermost of the three granite steps and looked down at his visitors.

"My lord," Anrel said with a bow. He made a hasty gesture at his waist to the Lirs, who both reacted by bowing as well, a little belatedly.

"Master Murau," Lord Dorias said.

"I trust Mistress Tazia Lir has explained the situation to you?"

"She has told me that you have some mad scheme to spirit us all off to Quand, abandoning the empire to the mob."

Anrel's heart sank. "My lord," he said, "dear uncle, we do indeed have an opportunity to escape the capital in the company of Lord Blackfield."

"And why should we want to *escape?*" Dorias demanded. "What is there to escape *from?* I am a nobleman of the empire, a sorcerer, and the burgrave of Alzur. Why would I want to flee the very *capital* of the empire?"

"Because, my lord, the capital has fallen into the hands of a group of conspirators within the Grand Council who have used the discontented populace to seize power. They have the support of the burgrave of Lume, and have obtained access to the Great List. They have your *true name,* my lord."

Lord Dorias frowned at him.

"Why would they have *my* true name?" he demanded. "I have done nothing to displease the mob, or to cause the emperor to reveal my name."

"Let us hope you are right, my lord, that you have done nothing to displease the people of Lume, but I fear you misjudge their temper. They are in no mood to extend the benefit of any doubt, and you are known to be a friend of Lord Allutar, who many deem responsible in large part for the worst ravages of the famine that has left the children of the city crying for bread. Indeed, your daughter, my cousin, is betrothed to the landgrave of Aulix. I am also told you tried to prevent the people of Alzur from burning Lord Allutar's house. I believe it likely that these will be seen as sufficient crimes to see you dragged before a tribunal."

"We have done nothing that would cause us to fear a tribunal," Lord Dorias insisted. "And in any case, the emperor would scarcely consider such charges sufficient cause to open the Great List to my name!"

"Alas, the emperor has allowed the Committee for the Regulation of Sorcery free access to the entirety of the Great List. Indeed, I myself was brought to the palace to assist in copying names from it. I distorted those I could, but your name, Uncle, was given to another to record, and I could not prevent its accurate transcription."

"What?"

"It is as I have said. The Committee for the Regulation of Sorcery has recorded the true names of almost every sorcerer in the empire."

Shaken for the first time, Lord Dorias asked plaintively, "Why would the emperor allow that?"

"Because he has been promised the confiscated estates of anyone the tribunals might convict of treason, and assured that these estates can be used to pay his debts." Anrel was tempted to add that the emperor had made a stupendously foolish bargain, but resisted. This was not the time and place to argue the wisdom of His Imperial Majesty's actions.

For a moment, Lord Dorias stared silently at Anrel. Then he said, "What evidence do you have for this fantastic tale? How am I to know this is not all some elaborate lie you have concocted to lure me from my home? If this conspiracy you describe does in fact exist, how am I to know that you are not a *part* of it, hoping to lead me into a trap? Or it could be something far less than that—it might be you are in league with ordinary thieves, who will loot my house once I leave it unguarded. You have certainly demonstrated repeatedly in the course of this past year that you are a criminal and not to be trusted. For that matter, if it *is* true, why would you be here, attempting to aid me? You have scarcely shown any concern for my welfare of late!"

"You are my uncle, my lord. You are the man who took me in when my parents died, and who raised me to manhood. You paid for my education, and saw to it that I wanted for nothing. Whatever strife there may be between us, we are bound by blood, and I owe you a great debt that I cannot ignore. Were I to not do my best to see you to safety, I could not live with myself."

Lord Dorias drew himself up to his full height. "Do not claim to be bound by any sense of honor, Anrel Murau," he declaimed, "for I know you have none!"

Anrel winced. "I am profoundly sorry that you believe that, my lord."

Dorias glared at him, then finally turned his attention to the two women. "Who are these people?" he asked. "What happened to her face?"

Anrel glanced at Nivain. "This is Mistress Nivain Lir, my lord; she is the mother of my beloved Tazia. And this is Nivain's youngest daughter, Perynis."

"Step forward, woman," Lord Dorias said to Nivain, beckoning.

With a glance at Anrel, Nivain took a step forward.

"Do *you* know whether there is a word of truth in my nephew's story?" Lord Dorias demanded.

"I . . ." She threw a quick look at Perynis, then at Anrel, then turned back to the sorcerer. "I do not know, my lord," she said. "I have known Master Murau for some time, and I have thought him to be a good man, but I know nothing of councils or lists."

"Then why are you here with him?"

Nivain touched the bruise on her cheek. "My husband did this to me, my lord," she said. "Master Murau has offered me a way to escape from him, to go to a place where he cannot go. I am not concerned with politics or tribunals, but I would like to start a new life in Quand."

"A fair enough answer," Dorias said. He turned to Perynis. "And you? Are you simply doing as your mother bids you?"

"No, my lord," Perynis said. "I have my own reasons for wanting to go to Quand—and they are mine, and not your concern."

Lord Dorias frowned. "And you know nothing of plots and politics, I suppose?"

"I know that we saw a warden and his deputies dragging a sorcerer through the streets today, on their way to only the Father knows where. That was before my mother joined us."

Dorias blinked. "Did you, indeed?"

"Yes, my lord."

For a moment the sorcerer stared at her; then he turned his attention back to Anrel. "It would seem that there may be some kernel of truth in your tale," he admitted. "Or perhaps this young woman is an accomplice?" He shook his head. "Even if there *is* some truth in it, though, why is it so very urgent that you have come here, have sent that young woman to coerce me into seeing you? What need is there to hurry? Perhaps Saria and I would be well advised to leave Lume, but I see no reason to rush off with that confounded Quandishman."

"My lord," Anrel said, "the gates have been closed, and no Walasian is to be permitted to leave the city. Foreigners are being sent away, and have been ordered to be outside the walls by sunset. Concealing ourselves in Lord Blackfield's coach may be our only chance to get out."

Lord Dorias grimaced, then looked from Anrel to Nivain to Perynis. Then he said, "I don't believe you."

"My lord . . . !"

"I don't believe you," Dorias repeated. "The gates closed? On whose orders? No, this is some trick of yours, Anrel. You seek to kidnap me, perhaps—have you gambling debts that you need my ransom to pay?"

"Uncle Dorias, I swear on my soul—"

"Do not profane yourself any further, Anrel. I will not listen." He turned his back on his nephew. "I will send your wench out, and the lot of you can go to Quand, or to the Mystery Lands, or to perdition, for all I care."

And with that, he vanished into the house and slammed the door.

33

In Which the Players Gather

Anrel stared at the closed door, struggling to control himself as rage and despair seethed in his breast.

"You tried," Perynis said.

Anrel bit his lip, holding back an angry outburst. His mouth twisted. "At least the coach will not be as crowded," he said sourly. Then he shook his head. "But no, I cannot give up. I must *make* him listen to reason—if not for his own sake, then for Saria's."

"You have done what you could," Nivain said. "You cannot save those who refuse to be saved."

Anrel's head snapped around, and he stared at her. "I could not save Reva, to my everlasting shame," he said, "but I intend to do better this time."

"What will you do then, kidnap him, as he believes you meant to do?" Perynis demanded. "He has made his choice, Anrel."

For a moment Anrel did not answer; he *had* no answer, no glib solution. "Perhaps Lord Blackfield may have a suggestion," he said at last. "After all, he is a sorcerer—he may have some spell that can persuade my uncle."

"But Lord Dorias is a sorcerer, as well," Nivain pointed out. "He undoubtedly has wards guarding him against such spells."

Anrel looked at her thoughtfully. "Yes, he is a sorcerer," he acknowledged, "and *you*, Mistress Lir, are a witch. So are your daughters. Is there nothing you can do to convince my uncle to listen?"

"As you so recently reminded me," Nivain said coldly, "I have already lost one daughter trying to enchant a sorcerer. I have no intention of risking another in such an enterprise. I owe you a great debt, Master Murau, for your kindnesses to my daughters and myself, for your aid against my husband, and for your offer of transportation to Quand, but it is not so great a debt as *that*."

"No, of course not," Anrel agreed, abashed.

The latch rattled, and the black door swung wide; Anrel turned to see Tazia standing in the opening, with Ollith behind her, his hand on the door handle, and in the shadows of the passage beyond Anrel thought he saw his cousin, Lady Saria.

"Anrel," Tazia said. She sounded worried.

"My dearest Tazia," Anrel replied.

"I have been asked to leave," she said.

"I know," Anrel said. "My uncle thinks me a liar, and believes my entire tale to be a scheme to somehow extort money."

Tazia had no answer for that; she descended the granite steps, looking shaken.

Behind her the footman started to swing the door shut, but as Anrel put an arm around Tazia he called out. "Hold a moment, if you please, Ollith."

The door stopped.

"Ollith—Master Tuir—please, I ask you, as a personal favor, speak to Lord Dorias. He will not believe me, but in time he will see that he is in grave danger. When that realization comes, for the love of the Mother, do whatever you can to get him out of the city to safety. Lord Blackfield and I will be gone, but there may be some other opportunity, one that my presence will not taint. If you have any loyalty to the House of Adirane, Master Tuir, do whatever you can to encourage my uncle to seize that opportunity."

Anrel thought he saw Ollith's face appear in the opening, then glance back along the passage. Then the door opened a few inches wider, and Ollith stepped out.

"Master Murau," he said, "I hear what you say, and I will take it under advisement. Let me ask you, though—when you were proposing to smuggle Lord Dorias and Lady Saria out of the city, did you give any thought to *me,* or the other members of the staff? Were we to simply be abandoned here, with the house and its other furnishings?"

Anrel's mouth opened, then closed again. Then he said, "I'm sorry. I could make excuses about how you are in no danger from the conspirators, how you are beneath their notice, but I know better. Who knows what they might do? And in any case, we would be leaving you unemployed, among people who are distrustful of anything associated with sorcerers. That would be poor repayment for your years of faithful service, and I profoundly regret my thoughtlessness, Master Tuir."

"I will consider your apology, Master Murau, and will further consider whether I put any more faith in your claims than does my employer. Good day, sir."

With that, he stepped back inside and slammed the door.

"Lord Blackfield couldn't fit the entire household, could he?" Tazia asked. "Not with all of us."

"Probably not," Anrel admitted.

"How long until Lord Blackfield gets here?" Perynis asked.

"I'm not sure," Anrel said, looking at the angle of the sun. "Less than an hour, I should judge."

"I, for one, am eager to be on my way," Perynis said. "I've had quite enough of cleaning other people's floors, and I look forward to working as a witch again."

"You'll need to learn Quandish first," Nivain reminded her.

"Then learn it I will," Perynis said. She turned to Tazia. "We can practice together."

"I'm not certain I'm going," Tazia said.

Perynis's jaw dropped. *"What?"*

"I am in no great danger here," she said. "Not really. The conspirators will undoubtedly be too busy with sorcerers to trouble themselves about witches. Let me leave one more space in the coach for someone who needs it more—that footman, perhaps."

"If you stay, then so do I," Anrel said.

"But they *are* hunting *you*," Tazia exclaimed.

"I have eluded capture before," Anrel said. "I can do it again. I won't leave you."

Before Tazia could reply Nivain let out a shriek; astonished, the others turned to find her staring at the watchmen's arch. Anrel whirled. The shadowy figure he had seen there had emerged.

It was Garras Lir, and he held a chunk of wood in one upraised hand, as if to club someone.

Anrel stepped forward to confront him, uncomfortably aware that he was unarmed—but his feet were on the ground, and he could sense the earth's magic beneath him, ready to be drawn upon and used.

"Get away from my wife," Garras growled.

Nivain and Perynis quickly stepped behind Anrel; Tazia remained at his side.

"Sir, I suggest you leave," Anrel said coldly.

"And *I* suggest you mind your own damned business," Garras replied. "I've heard some of what you've been talking about—the wardens are looking for you, aren't they? If you don't get away from my family, I'll let them know where you are."

"You tried something like that before, in Beynos," Anrel said. "It did not work out well for you there, and it will do no better here. These women want no part of you."

"These women are *mine*," Garras roared. "I paid good money for that one, and sired the others on her, and that makes them mine!"

"Paid?" Anrel directed his question to the Lir women, rather than to Garras.

"We were married by bridal auction," Nivain said. "But that made me his wife, not his property!"

Anrel had heard of bridal auctions, but never seen one; Lord Dorias had not permitted them in Alzur, and in modern times they were a rural custom, not practiced in Lume for a century or more. Still, he understood how they worked, and Nivain was right. The bride had the right to refuse bids from any man she deemed unsuitable, as a bondwoman or slave would not. Nivain had made a poor choice, but it was not irrevocable. "She is a free woman," Anrel said. "You lost any claim to her when you drove her away."

"I'm still her husband," Garras said. "And their father. You step away."

"I don't think I will do that," Anrel said. He began drawing magic up into his chest, around his heart, and tried to remember how to work a warding that would stop a blow.

Garras raised his makeshift club. "I'm warning you, Murau, I will not hesitate to strike you down, or to call for the wardens."

"Go away!" Nivain shouted. "Leave us alone!"

"I *paid* for you!" Garras shouted back. "You owe me!"

"Twenty years of my earnings repaid you a dozen times over!" Nivain retorted.

"Let us be, Father," Perynis said. "We are going to Quand, and you will never see us again."

"You are not going to Quand without *me*," Garras said.

"I think they are," Anrel said.

Garras had no more words; he swung his club two-handed at Anrel's head.

Anrel's hand came up, and the improvised warding thickened the air, slowing the blow so that Anrel was able to catch the wooden bar before it struck his ear. He quickly grabbed it with his other hand as well, and tried to wrench it from the other man's grip.

Garras did not relinquish his hold, and the two men stood face-to-face, each trying to pull the chunk of wood free of the other's hands.

Tazia reached up, trying to grab it as well to help Anrel. Nivain stepped back and looked for some other weapon, while Perynis dashed up the steps to pound on the door of Adirane House.

And then a new figure entered the scene. A tall man stumbled from beneath the watchmen's arch into Wizard's Hill Court. This new arrival wore a fine silk coat but no hat; his hair was in disarray, and blood smeared one side of his head. His right hand held a sword, and both hand and blade were also bloodied.

Anrel was too busy with his struggle with Garras to notice the swordsman at first, but then he saw Tazia step back, and heard Nivain draw her breath in sharply. Without releasing his grasp on the club, he shot a glance toward the arch.

He recognized the man instantly, and froze.

The swordsman stopped for a moment to take in the scene before him, where two men were grappling with a two-foot piece of wood while three women watched; then he saw the face of the younger, lighter man.

"Father and Mother," he said. "You!"

Garras, who had been too intent on the struggle to notice the new arrival, started at the sound of a voice behind him, and tried to twist his head to see who spoke. Anrel released the club and stepped back. "Landgrave," he said.

"What are *you* doing here, Murau?" Lord Allutar demanded.

"I could ask you the same, my lord," Anrel replied.

"I have come to speak to my fiancée, of course."

"And I came to speak to my uncle."

"And who is this?" Allutar pointed his sword at Garras.

"An unpleasant fellow named Garras Lir," Anrel replied. "He and I have been discussing whether or not he has the right to abuse his wife and daughters."

"Ah. Then I suppose that bruise is his handiwork?" Allutar gestured with the sword, indicating Nivain's face. His powers of observation had clearly not been impaired by whatever misfortune had befallen him.

Nivain put a hand to her cheek and nodded.

"Indeed," Anrel said. "But I am at a loss, my lord, to identify the source of your own injuries." He gestured at Allutar's bloodied head.

"That would be the watchman whose sword I bear," Allutar replied.

"And is that his blood upon the blade?"

"It is."

"Then I take it he is not in pursuit?"

"His comrades were," Allutar said. "I hope I have eluded them."

Garras had turned during this conversation and now stood, club raised, facing Lord Allutar. "Who are *you?*" he demanded.

"Dear me, where are my manners?" Anrel said. "Master Garras Lir, allow me to present Lord Allutar Hezir, landgrave of Aulix." He frowned. "You know, I thought you had met, this past winter in Beynos."

"Did we?" Allutar asked, turning his attention to Garras's face.

"Yes," Garras growled, tightening his grip on the length of wood. "I didn't recognize you at first, but I should have, you murdering bastard."

"Oh?" Allutar's grip on the sword, which had been quite casual, suddenly tightened, and the point swiveled toward Garras's throat.

"You hanged his daughter," Anrel said.

Allutar's eyes widened slightly, but remained fixed on Garras. "The witch?"

"Yes," Anrel said.

"How unfortunate. Then these others are her mother and sisters?"

"Yes," Tazia said, glaring at Allutar.

It was at that moment that the front door of Adirane House swung open, startling Perynis so badly she nearly fell down the steps. Lord Dorias looked out at the half-dozen people in the court, and asked, "What is going *on* here?"

"Lord Dorias," Allutar called. "I have come to speak to you and your daughter regarding a matter of some urgency, but perhaps I chose a bad time."

"Allutar? What *happened* to you?"

"It would appear that I have been declared an outlaw," Allutar replied.

"As I told you, Uncle," Anrel said.

"You, an outlaw?" Dorias exclaimed. "That's absurd!"

"Nonetheless, it is true," Allutar said, keeping his attention on Garras and his raised club.

"But you're a landgrave! A sorcerer!"

Lord Allutar grimaced. "At present, my lord, I am a sorcerer in name only. My true name has been invoked, and magic has been forbidden me."

"They have *your* true name?"

"As I told you, Uncle," Anrel repeated.

"It would seem there *is* some truth to your nephew's story," Tazia said triumphantly.

"Indeed," Lord Dorias said, his tone making his surprise and confusion plain. "Who are these others, Mistress Lir?"

"This is my father, my mother, and my sister, Lord Dorias," Tazia explained.

"Your father? He was not here earlier."

"I would prefer he was not here now, my lord."

"I have a right to be here!" Garras proclaimed, taking one hand from the club to point at Nivain. "She's my wife!"

"No more!" Nivain retorted. "You have given up the right to call me that!"

Anrel heard Lady Saria call a question from somewhere behind her father, but he could not make out the words.

"Just a moment, my dear," Lord Dorias replied.

Lady Saria spoke again, and Lord Dorias threw up his hands. "By the Father!" he said. "This is madness, and utter confusion!" Then he stepped back and beckoned. "All of you, pray come inside, so that we might sort this out in peace."

Perynis quickly accepted the invitation, dashing past Dorias. Nivain was close behind.

Lord Allutar hesitated. "I can spare little time . . ."

"Then don't waste any of it arguing," Dorias said. "Come in, please!"

Allutar opened his mouth, then closed it again and shrugged. "As you please, my lord."

"Thank you, Uncle," Anrel said. He turned to Lord Allutar. "Would you care to precede me, my lord?"

Allutar glanced at Garras, then said, "If it is all the same to you, Master Murau, I would prefer to bring up the rear."

Anrel glanced at Garras and nodded. "Of course," he said.

Accordingly, Garras was next to enter, then Tazia, then Anrel, until finally Lord Allutar, bloody sword still in his hand, crossed the threshold, and Lord Dorias, after a final look around at the now-deserted Wizard's Hill Court, slammed the door shut.

34

In Which Important Matters Are Discussed

Ollith took Garras's club, handling it as if it were a guest's walking stick, and a moment later provided Lord Allutar with a cloth for cleaning his blade. He also brought a bowl of clean water and a towel, and while Allutar cleaned his sword, Ollith attended to the landgrave's head wound. While that was happening the others sorted themselves out, occupying every one of the half-dozen seats in the parlor. Lady Saria, not waiting for the servants to act, brought two additional chairs from the salon for herself and her uncle.

The scene seemed oddly homey and peaceful, Anrel thought, despite the wound on Lord Allutar's head, the bruise on Nivain's cheek, and the expressions on many of the faces. The afternoon sun pouring through the lace curtains painted ornate shadows on the Ermetian carpet and the velvet-upholstered furniture, and a fine china teacup stood forgotten on an end table. A scent of lavender lingered in the air, though Anrel was unsure whether it came from some part of the room's furnishings, or from Lady Saria.

Nivain and Perynis were on the settee by the front window, with Tazia at one side and Anrel at the other; an attempt by Garras to take one of the neighboring chairs had been foiled by Anrel. Lord Allutar had the armchair nearest the door to the salon, which relegated Garras to the matching armchair by the hearth, which he turned to face the others. Lord Dorias and Lady Saria placed their own chairs to Allutar's left, facing Nivain and her daughters.

"Now, Lord Allutar," Lord Dorias said when everyone was seated, "would you please explain what brings you hither, and how you came to be injured?"

"I came to warn you and your daughter, Dorias, and to make my farewells."

"Warn us of what?"

Allutar glanced at Anrel, then turned back to his host. "This morning," he said, "I went to the Aldian Baths to take part in the deliberations of the Grand Council, as usual, but instead I found that a coalition of certain elements had taken control of the council and of the city's government. The Committee for the Regulation of Sorcery and the Committee for the Restoration of Order, created from opposing factions and intended to balance each other, have instead formed an unholy alliance, which they call the Joint Committee. With the assistance of the burgrave of Lume and parties within the imperial court, they have seized control of the City Watch and the neighborhood wardens. They have declared a state of emergency, and issued orders for the arrest and interrogation of, by their announced count, perhaps a hundred individuals they deem most responsible for the unrest and misfortunes of the past year, and whom they intend to try for treason." He looked at Anrel again. "About a dozen of those listed had been members of the council, but were expelled this morning. Of that dozen, I believe all but Master Murau were present at the time. I take it, Master Murau, that your friends on the Committee for the Regulation of Sorcery warned you?"

"Yes, my lord," Anrel admitted. "I was a member of that committee, and this morning, when I arrived at the baths, one of my fellows notified me of the planned arrests. I left immediately."

"My compatriots of the Cloakroom were not so generous," Allutar said. "When I realized where the speech was going I knew my name would be included, and I prepared to act. I did not wait to hear every name spoken; indeed, I did not wait for *any* of them, though I did hear a few. When one of Lord Koril's watchmen came up behind me, intending to arrest me the instant my name was spoken, I took his sword away from him, plunged it through his belly, and ran. Most of the crowd scattered before me at the sight of the bloodied blade, but a few did not, and one managed to strike me above the ear, giving me the wound your man, Lord Dorias, has been good enough to clean and bandage, before I could make my way free."

"Horrible!" Lord Dorias exclaimed, clasping and unclasping his hands. "Horrible! How could you have been included on such a list?"

Allutar managed a bitter laugh. "My dear Dorias, my name was *first* on the list! Have you paid no attention at all to the stories circulating here?"

Lord Dorias drew himself up. "I do not listen to lies and slander, my lord."

"You should," Allutar retorted. "Otherwise you will have no idea what others might believe, or what beliefs they might act upon."

"But how could they be a threat to *you,* my lord?" Lady Saria asked. "You're a powerful sorcerer!"

Lord Allutar grimaced. "Oh, at least half the alleged traitors on their list are sorcerers," he said. "And in each case, when they read off a sorcerer's name, they read his *true* name as well. That is a most disturbing experience, my lady, to hear your true name spoken; I hope you never share it. And after my true name was announced, someone—I cannot say who—worked a binding upon it. I cannot use any magic whatsoever, my dear; I have been bound by my true name not to."

"But . . . how did they know your true name?" Lady Saria asked.

Allutar did not reply, but turned to Anrel.

Anrel did not pretend ignorance or outrage. "The Committee for the Regulation of Sorcery," he said. "They made an arrangement with the emperor, promising to pay his debts in exchange for one night's access to the Great List. My dear cousin, I greatly fear they have *your* true name, as well. That was what brought me here."

"And it brought me to you as well, beloved," Allutar said. "I came to warn you that as my betrothed you may be implicated, and therefore endangered." He looked at Anrel again. "It would seem that we are on the same side in this, Master Murau—my name was the first to be read out, but yours, as I heard most distinctly while pulling the sword from its unfortunate former owner, was the second. Rather than appending a true name, as they did for sorcerers, they called you Anrel Murau, also known as Alvos, the orator of Naith."

"Then his story is all true?" Lord Dorias exclaimed.

Lord Allutar looked at him. "I scarcely know what story Master Murau told you, but it was in all probability true, yes. I have never known him to tell a deliberate lie."

This compliment so startled Anrel that he did not speak for a moment; instead it was Lady Saria who said, "But what are we to *do?*"

"I cannot say," Lord Allutar said. "I expect to be apprehended fairly soon, and to either die fighting my would-be captors, or if I cannot manage that, to be executed by them. I sought to warn you so that you might have some time to flee, or go into hiding, before my pursuers find me."

"But *you* can hide, surely?" Lord Dorias said.

Allutar glared at him—apparently the burgrave's foolishness had finally worn down the landgrave's reserves of politeness. "They have my *true name,* my lord," he snapped. "They read it aloud before an audience of hundreds. They can find me whenever they please, or they can simply compel me to return and surrender myself."

"But they have *our* true names, as well!" Lady Saria wailed.

"Are you certain of that, Master Murau?" Allutar asked, turning to Anrel. "I had not known how they obtained the names, nor how many they had."

"They have almost the entirety of the list of sorcerers now living," Anrel said. "They may be missing some of the eldest, and I was able to alter their records of many of the youngest and a handful of others, but only a handful. Virtually every adult sorcerer or sorceress is on their list, and almost all the true names they have are accurate."

"Abominable!" Lord Dorias muttered, shaking his head. "Simply abominable!"

"*You* need not fear their magic, Master Murau," Allutar said to Anrel. "You failed the trials."

"I did," Anrel agreed. "My true name is unrecorded, and I can go into hiding once again with some expectation of remaining undetected."

"But we're going to Quand!" Perynis burst out. "You don't need to hide!"

Lord Allutar shook his head. "The city gates are sealed, and the river is heavily patrolled," he said. "No one is going to Quand."

Anrel hesitated, but decided there was no reason to conceal the truth; for the moment he and Lord Allutar were allies, and the secret would certainly come out when Lord Blackfield arrived, if not sooner.

"Some of us may indeed be going to Ondine," Anrel said. "Your friend Lord Blackfield has been ordered to leave the city by sundown, and has been granted safe passage through the gate. Despite the obvious risk to himself he has volunteered to take a few of us with him, disguised as his servants."

The change in Lord Allutar's expression was startling. Until Anrel spoke he had looked weary but proud, but when he heard of a possible escape, for the merest instant his face was alight with hope—and then he regained control of himself, and settled his face into a calm half smile. "A few of us, you say?"

"Yes," Anrel said.

"There are eight of us in this room," Lord Allutar said. "Can he manage as many as that?"

"There are *nine* of us," Anrel corrected him, pointing to Ollith. "And I doubt Lord Blackfield can fit so many. Certainly, so large a group would arouse suspicion."

Ollith cleared his throat.

"Yes, Ollith?" Anrel asked.

"There are two others on the household staff, sir."

"Only two?" Anrel asked, startled. In Alzur the burgrave had maintained a staff of six.

"Our housekeeper and maid," Lord Dorias said. "The others did not accompany us to Lume."

Something in his uncle's voice told him that there was more to the story than that, and that the circumstances had not been to Lord Dorias's liking. Perhaps there was some unhappy history that would explain why Ollith, a mere footman, appeared to be the head servant, and why Ziral, the family butler, was nowhere to be seen.

But that was not immediately relevant. "Housekeeper and maid . . ." Anrel said, trying to recall exactly who that would be. Then he remembered.

"My wife and daughter," Ollith said, confirming Anrel's memory.

There could be no question of leaving them behind if Ollith came. "Eleven of us," Anrel said. "Lord Blackfield cannot possibly accommodate so many."

"But why would he take these women?" Lady Saria asked. "And who is this man?"

"I'm her husband," Garras growled, pointing at Nivain. "They're my daughters."

"He *was* my husband," Nivain said.

"But what do they have to do with Lord Blackfield?" Saria persisted.

"They're witches," Anrel said. "A third sister was hanged in Beynos this past winter, at Lord Allutar's order."

"Ah," Allutar said, more to himself than anyone else. "*All* witches, then?"

No one answered him. "Witchcraft is legal in Quand," Perynis said. "Mother and I want to go."

"And *I* say you go nowhere without me," Garras replied. He turned to Lord Dorias. "Tell them, my lord—a man is the master of his wife and children, is he not?"

Before the startled Lord Dorias could respond, Nivain leapt to her feet and pointed angrily to the bruise on her face. "Is someone who does *this* truly a man at all? This *person* has taken all the money I have earned for the past twenty years while doing no work himself, has taken the money our children earned, and *this* is what he gives us in return!" Both her finger and her chin trembled. "When our Reva was hanged his first thought was not for her, not for a decent burial or prayers for her soul, but to demand that I give *him* her dowry! All he loves is money—he cares nothing for me nor for our children, save as a source of income, and I will have no more of it! Let *him* go to Quand if he will, for if he does, we will stay here and take our chances with the wardens."

Garras rose as well, fists clenched, but before he could speak he found the blade of Lord Allutar's sword at his throat. The sorcerer had moved so swiftly that no one else had time to react; they all sat or stood frozen as they were.

"Master Lir," the landgrave said without rising from his chair. "Your daughter tried to enchant me in Beynos."

Garras swallowed, staring down at the blade. His hands opened. "Yes, my lord."

"Was that *your* idea?"

"No, my lord!" He drew his head back; the blade followed. "I swear it was not!"

"Was it perhaps *yours,* mistress?" Allutar asked Nivain without taking his eyes from Garras.

"No, my lord," Nivain replied. "Reva accepted the commission against my wishes."

"And she paid the price for her folly."

No one replied to that; Anrel bit back a retort.

"That bruise on your wife's cheek," Allutar demanded. "Is that your doing?"

"I don't—" Garras began.

The sword twitched upward.

"Yes, my lord," Garras said miserably.

"What she says about your daughter's dowry—is that true?"

"It . . . I . . ." His eyes widened, and his hands twitched. "I was drunk, my lord. *Very* drunk. I had tried to drown my grief over the loss of my child, and I was out of my senses with sorrow and wine."

"But you demanded the money."

Garras glanced at Anrel, and saw no sympathy there. "Yes, my lord," he said.

"Are *you* a witch?"

"No, my lord!"

"What is your occupation, then?"

"I . . . I am a traveler, my lord."

"I have not heard that one can earn a living as a traveler."

Garras's eyes darted toward Lord Dorias, but he did not dare turn his head. "I . . . I get by on whatever odd jobs I may find, my lord."

"You live on what your wife and daughters earn as witches, you mean."

Garras's eyes moved from one face to another and found no sympathy anywhere. "Yes, my lord," he confessed.

"And you want them back not out of love, but because your funds have run out."

"Not only that, my lord! She is my wife, and I . . . I . . ."

"You want a woman to share your bed."

"Of course, my lord! And I—" He stopped.

The tip of the sword drew a drop of red from just below Garras's chin, and contempt dripped from Lord Allutar's words. "And even with a sword at your throat, you cannot bring yourself to say you love her."

"She's my wife!"

"She denies it."

"I bought her at auction!"

"Have you a receipt?"

Garras blinked in surprise. "A . . . a receipt, my lord?"

"An indenture, perhaps? Some document that says she has been consigned to your ownership, and is no longer a free woman of the Empire?"

"No, of course not, my lord! But she . . . I . . ."

"I think, Master Lir, that you would be well advised to say your farewells and depart. I do not believe you are welcome here."

Garras stared down the blade at the landgrave. "But you—"

Lord Allutar interrupted him. "My apologies, sir; you are quite right. I am a guest here, just as you are, and it is not my place to say. Lord Dorias, do you want this person in your home?"

Lord Dorias blinked as if suddenly awakened. "No," he said. "No, I do not."

"There you go, then, Master Lir." Allutar snatched the sword away and settled back in his chair, retrieving the bloody cloth to once again clean the the tip of his blade but keeping his gaze fixed on Garras.

Garras stared at Lord Allutar, then cast about the room for some sign of sympathy, but found none.

"Good *day*, Master Lir," Lord Dorias said. "Ollith will show you to the door."

Ollith took his cue. "This way, sir."

Garras glared at the others, clearly trying to compose a parting speech, but finally simply strode across the room. "You'll regret this," he said as he left.

"I doubt that," Lord Allutar said. "Ollith, be sure he has his stick—we wouldn't want him to accuse us of theft."

When Garras and Ollith had left the room Anrel said to Allutar, "I suppose he'll go straight to the wardens—but all the same, that was well done, my lord."

The landgrave looked at him, startled, then smiled. "Thank you, Master Murau. Coming from you, I take that as a great compliment."

Anrel nodded an acknowledgment.

"As for the wardens, his threats aside, I wonder whether such a scoundrel dares to approach any sort of authority," Allutar said. "And if he does, one might hope they would hesitate to believe such an individual. In any case, even should he go to them, with any luck at least some of us will be on our way to Quand before he can fetch them here."

"Let us hope so," Anrel agreed as Lord Dorias muttered something.

"With Master Lir removed, we are ten," Lord Allutar said. "Still too many, I do not doubt. Who, then, is to accept Lord Blackfield's kind offer of transportation to Quand?"

"Nivain and Perynis Lir," Anrel said. "If only to ensure that Garras Lir will not be able to trouble them further."

"Agreed," Lord Allutar said. "Though I wonder that you do not include the other daughter."

Anrel glanced at Tazia. "She and I . . . have matters to discuss," he said.

"Ah. I will leave that between you, then. Let us consider the rest of us."

"I am not yet convinced *any* of us need go," Lord Dorias said. "We are Walasians, and have no business in Quand. Oh, perhaps *you*, Allutar . . ."

"My lord Uncle, you are not safe here!" Anrel insisted.

"So you say, but I—" Lord Dorias abruptly stopped in midsentence, eyes going wide. His voice caught in his throat, and he leaned forward as if gagging.

"Father? What is it? What's wrong?" Lady Saria jumped from her chair and threw her arm around her father's shoulders, trying to support him. Anrel, too, arose.

"Someone . . . someone said my true name," Dorias replied, his voice husky and weak.

"Are you sure? How can—" Lady Saria began; then she jerked upright. "Oh!" she said.

Lord Allutar's smile twisted. "An alarming sensation, isn't it? I think we may consider it settled, then, that you both *are* in danger."

"I feared as much," Anrel said. "Are you . . . have you been ensorceled?"

"I am bound, yes," Dorias whispered. He looked up at Saria and Anrel with terror in his eyes. "Magic . . . magic is forbidden me. I am a sorcerer no more."

35

In Which Help Arrives

"My uncle must go," Anrel said.

"Of course," Lord Allutar replied. "And Lady Saria."

"That's four," Tazia said. She had gotten to her feet, as well. "Lord Blackfield can take four?"

"I think so," Anrel said.

At that moment Ollith reappeared in the doorway and saw his employer slumped in his chair, obviously stricken. "My lord?" he said.

"I am no longer a sorcerer, Ollith," Dorias said.

Ollith looked puzzled and uncertain; he glanced around the room for guidance, but found none.

"What of your uncle's staff?" Tazia asked, gesturing toward Ollith.

Anrel shook his head unhappily. "They are in no real danger here," he said, "and the three of them would crowd the carriage."

"But their master is fleeing the country," Tazia said. "What will they do if they stay?"

"No one will hold them to account for their employer's misdeeds," Anrel said. "They can find another position."

"I don't think many sorcerers will be hiring."

"I know," Anrel said. "But what are we to do? They would make seven, and would fill the coach to overflowing. There would be no room for *you*."

"For *us*," Tazia said. "I will not be parted from you again."

Anrel looked at the footman. "Ollith," he said, "do you *want* to go to Quand?"

Ollith hesitated, and glanced at Lord Dorias. "I would prefer to remain in my present position, sir."

"You can't," Lord Dorias said, his voice hollow. "I am no longer a sorcerer. This is the end of the House of Adirane. I must flee the country, and I have no holdings in Quand, nor in the Cousins. I will be a pauper, a penniless refugee. I cannot pay your wages."

"In that case, my lord," Ollith said, "I would prefer to remain in Walasia. I speak no Quandish."

"Lord Dorias," Tazia said, "what will become of your property here?"

"I don't know," Dorias answered, bewildered. "I have no idea."

"If he is captured and executed," Anrel said, addressing the entire company, "then his lands and possessions will go toward paying the emperor's debts. That was the bargain the Committee for the Regulation of Sorcery made."

"And if he is not captured?" Lord Allutar asked.

Anrel shrugged. "They may be forfeit to the crown all the same; I don't know."

"Lord Dorias," Tazia said, "could you perhaps sign your property over to Master Tuir? As you say, you cannot take any of it to Quand with you."

"If you like," Dorias said, sunk in despair. "It doesn't matter. I am finished."

"Ollith," Lady Saria said, "fetch my father's writing desk, and ink, and paper."

Ollith blinked, and for an instant a smile flickered across his face. It vanished, and he bowed. "Yes, my lady," he said. He turned on his heel and left the room.

"A clever notion," Lord Allutar remarked as he watched Ollith depart. "Let us hope the empire's new overlords will honor this bequest."

"And would you like to make provision for any of *your* staff, my lord?" Anrel asked. "Your man Hollem, perhaps?"

"Oh, they won't honor anything *I* might write," Allutar said, smiling wryly. "I am the monster who poisoned the Raish Valley with the blood of innocents; had you forgotten? No, even if by some miracle I survive, my property will go to the emperor's moneylenders and mercenaries; that conclusion is foregone. I regret to say that poor Hollem must fend for himself in this valiant new empire you and your friends are building."

Anrel could think of no useful way to respond to this—Allutar was obviously correct about what would become of his possessions, and arguing about Anrel's role in events would go nowhere useful.

"You *are* coming with us, aren't you?" Lady Saria asked.

Lord Allutar looked at Anrel, then back at Saria. "That may not be up to me to decide, my dear."

"But you're my fiancé!"

"I am also the man who condemned their daughter and sister to the gallows," Allutar said with a gesture toward the three Lirs. "That would make for an uncomfortable ride, don't you think? And there are certain issues lingering between your cousin and myself, as well."

"But we're to be *married!*" Saria wailed.

"My dear, I think you would be most unwise to wed me at this point," the landgrave replied.

"But . . . but . . ." Saria looked desperately around the room.

Nivain looked from one to the other, then said, "For your sake, Lady Saria, we would tolerate this man's presence."

"Speak for yourself, Mother!" Perynis snapped.

Lord Allutar held up a hand. "Peace," he said. "Let us wait and see what Lord Blackfield says before we commit ourselves. It may be he can accommodate no more than the four we have agreed upon."

"Yes," Anrel said. He might have said more, but just then Ollith returned with Lord Dorias's writing desk, interrupting the conversation.

A moment later, while Lord Dorias was carefully composing a document transferring his worldly goods to Master Ollith Tuir, Perynis suddenly said, "I hear horses."

Anrel had been whispering with Tazia in the corner, discussing irrelevancies and carefully avoiding the subject of their possible escape; now he turned and bent to peer out the window, and saw the familiar blue and black carriage rolling into Wizard's Hill Court.

"It's Lord Blackfield," he said. "He's here."

"Then by all means, let us greet him," Lord Allutar said, rising. The sword was still in his hand.

Lord Dorias looked up from his lap desk. He hastily scribbled a few more words, then signed his name with a flourish. "Everything in this house is now yours, Ollith," he said. "I would give you the house itself if a commoner could own land, but I have granted you a lease in it, insofar as I may."

Ollith bowed, and accepted the desk and document. "Thank you, my lord," he said.

A moment later the party poured out the big front door—Anrel and Tazia, Nivain and Perynis, Lady Saria and Lord Dorias, and finally Lord Allutar—to find Harban holding the door of the coach, and Lord Blackfield stepping out.

"Ah, I see you *are* here," the Quandishman said as his feet landed on the cobbles. "Excellent! And Lord Allutar! This *is* a surprise."

"Barzal," Allutar said, with a nod. "A pleasure to see you again."

Lord Blackfield grimaced. "While I am pleased to see you as well, my lord, I regret to say that I cannot spare even a moment for casual conversation. I passed a large party comprised of watchmen, wardens, and deputies on the way here, and I believe their destination to be this very court. They cannot be more than five minutes behind me. I think it would be wise for all of you to board the coach immediately."

Glances were exchanged, and Nivain and Perynis were herded aboard, followed by Lord Dorias. Lady Saria, though, paused with her foot on the step.

"Allutar," she said, "you *are* coming?"

Lord Allutar looked at Lord Blackfield.

"I will need to ask that you put away that sword," the Quandishman said.

Lord Allutar shook his head. "No, my lord," he said. "I am not coming."

"What?" Lady Saria stared at him. "But there's room!" She gestured at the coach's interior. "We can all fit!"

"We can all squeeze into the carriage, yes," Allutar said, "but then what? I am deemed a traitor to the empire, my dear—indeed, my name was first on their list. They will not rest until I am found, and I *will* be found, whether here in Lume today, or in Ondine a season hence. They have my true name, Saria; they can find me whenever they please. With the aid of any competent magician, be he sorcerer or merely a witch, they can compel me to obedience, and send me to the scaffold of my own volition—as I did to this woman's sister, and to Master Murau's friend Amanir tel-Kabanim. I cannot possibly escape, not for long. Better to die here and now, with a sword in my hand, than in a noose a few days from now."

"But . . . but, Allutar!" Saria cried.

"Go, my dear," Allutar said gently. "I free you from your betrothal."

"I don't *want* to be freed of it!"

"You will be free of it soon enough in any case, as death frees us all. Now, get aboard that carriage, lest you *all* perish."

"But they know *our* true names, as well! If you can't escape, how can we?"

"Your crimes are trivial in comparison to my own, my dear," Allutar said. He smiled wryly. "Ask Master Murau, and he will be glad to recount to you the full extent of my wickedness. I doubt these revolutionaries will trouble themselves to hunt you down. Were Lord Blackfield to take *me* back to Quand, though, that might well provoke yet another war between our nations."

Saria turned hopefully to Lord Blackfield, but before she could speak, he shook his head.

"I can shield you against your true names to some degree, but only somewhat," the big Quandishman said. "I fear that Lord Allutar is correct about his own dire reputation, not merely here, but in Quand, as well. While we care nothing about his politics, he is a black magician, by his own admission, and that is not something my people tolerate."

Allutar gestured theatrically. "There, you see? I have wrought my own destruction."

"I won't leave you!" Lady Saria wailed.

"Your father needs you," Lord Allutar replied quietly. "Go with him, see him safe."

"Get in, my lady," Lord Blackfield said, giving Lady Saria a gentle push. Then he turned to Anrel. "And you, sir?"

Anrel looked at Tazia. "I will do as my beloved chooses," he said. "If she stays, I will stay. If she goes, I will go."

Tazia looked at the coach. "There is room for both of us?"

"I believe there is, yes."

"Anrel? Shall we go?"

And now, at the final moment, Anrel hesitated. He glanced at Lord Allutar, with his bandaged head and bare blade. "I wish I could do more," he said. "I wish there were some way to put everything back as it was."

Lord Allutar laughed bitterly. "You are scarcely alone in *that*," he said. "Everything I have done, I have done to maintain the old order and my place in it, and at every turn I have failed, and done more to harm my cause than to advance it. I sacrificed that baker's son to feed my people, and starved them instead. I murdered your friend, Lord Valin—yes, my lady, I confess, your cousin was right, I deliberately murdered your father's fosterling, and I did it so that his pernicious beliefs would not spread, and they spread all the more swiftly and effectively as a result. I hanged a witch in Beynos to maintain the dignity of my position, and instead you, Master Murau, convinced a thousand commoners that I was a coward and a bully. Had I truly believed completely in the rightness of my cause, had I been as utterly convinced of its inevitability as I claimed, I might not have striven so hard to defend it, and might not have damaged it so severely. The Father has seen fit to cast me down for my pride, and while I very much wish it were not so, I do not close my eyes to the truth. You, Anrel Murau, have been the implement the Mother and Father wielded to destroy me, and you have finished the task they set you. Go on to Quand, then, and see what new task they may set for you there!"

Anrel met the landgrave's gaze. "I pray, my lord," he replied, "that if I have indeed been the tool of the divine pair, that they are now done with me entirely, and will cast me aside. I have had enough of unrest and anger." He turned to his beloved. "Come, Tazia—let us both go to Quand."

With that, the two clambered aboard, Lord Blackfield close behind, while Harban hurried to the front of the coach and mounted the driver's seat. A moment later the harness jingled, hooves clattered, and the carriage jerked into motion, turning tightly around the narrow confines of Wizard's Hill Court and proceeding out under the watchmen's arch onto the avenues of Old Heart.

They had scarcely made the turn when Anrel heard Harban shout a warning; then the horses broke into a trot, and the coach rattled forward at an alarming speed, bouncing wildly across the cobbles.

Anrel lowered a window and leaned out, peering through the dust and looking back the way they had come.

A mob was marching up the avenue toward Wizard's Hill Court, but not a mob of mere citizens. Anrel saw a dozen men in the red and gold livery of the City Watch, and half as many more in the black coats and hats of wardens. Others wore ordinary clothes, but sported red armbands. Several of them were shouting, though Anrel could not make out over the rattle of the carriage what they were saying.

At the head of this forbidding company marched Garras Lir, brandishing his wooden club.

Then out from the shadows of the watchmen's arch strode Lord Allutar, sword gleaming in the afternoon sun. He stopped in the center of the avenue and turned to face the advancing crowd.

The mob stopped, deterred for the moment by this one man, and again Anrel heard unintelligible shouts.

Then the carriage swung around a corner, and the entire scene was lost behind the stone facade of a candle-maker's shop.

Anrel hoped that Lord Allutar would receive the clean and glorious death he had wanted, and in a moment of spite he also hoped that Allutar would take Garras Lir down with him.

Whatever was to happen, though, Anrel would not see it. He might never know how the confrontation ended.

There could be no doubt, though, that he had seen the last of Lord Allutar Hezir, landgrave of Aulix.

36

In Which Anrel Murau Departs the Capital

There was little conversation in the brief ride to the Morvanile Gate; Lord Blackfield was too occupied with preparing a seeming that would get the entire company safely past the guards, and the others were too stunned by the course of events.

The gates had indeed been closed, and the city sealed off; soldiers in red and gold stopped the coach and demanded Lord Blackfield identify himself before allowing Harban to approach the tunnel. No one inside dared say a word as the Quandishman presented his papers to the officers of the City Watch and attested to the entirely fictional identities of his passengers. Anrel was presented as a footman by the name of Lurdon Zuai, and names were likewise invented for the three housemaids, the cook, and the butler who had been Tazia, Perynis, Saria, Nivain, and Dorias. Lord Dorias stirred from his gloom briefly and seemed on the verge of protesting when Lord Blackfield called him a butler, but a glare from Anrel and a tug at his sleeve from Lady Saria silenced him.

Harban, of course, was presented in his true identity, though his duties were given as simply "driver," with no mention of the various other services he had provided.

One of the guards seemed suspicious at the size of the household, particularly the number of females, but another told him, "I've heard of the Blackfields—they're great lords in Quand, very wealthy. Powerful sorcerers, as well. They can afford to travel with all the servants they want."

"But three housemaids for a few rented rooms?"

The guard shrugged. "Sorcerers have uses for women, even more than other men. Haven't you heard about Lord Koril's harem? If this Blackfield wants to call all his women housemaids, it's no business of *ours.*"

Lady Saria flushed red at that, but said nothing.

In the end, the Quandishman's papers and words and sorcery were sufficient, and the coach was allowed to pass. The company remained silent as they rolled through the tunnel and emerged into the late-afternoon sun beyond. Indeed, even when they had successfully passed through the city wall and were on the road west, no one felt any need to speak for some time.

It was Perynis who first broke the silence. "I hadn't known—" she began. Then she stopped and cleared her throat.

"Known what?" Saria asked.

"That sorcerers—that they used . . ." Her voice trailed off.

"Sorcerers can draw power from sources other than earth and sky," Lord Blackfield said. "Lord Allutar drew on blood and death, as you know—my people call that black magic. There are other sources, as well, and some magicians do indeed keep women available for that purpose."

"Some witches use that," Perynis said. "I didn't know sorcerers did."

That led to a discussion of the technicalities of magic. Until then, it had not entirely registered with Anrel that everyone in the coach was a magician of some sort, but of the seven, three were witches, three were sorcerers, and he himself was . . . whatever he was.

They slept that night at an inn in the village of Varth, scarcely out of sight of the capital's towers, but made better time on subsequent days. Rumors of chaos and horror in the capital followed them, and sometimes ran ahead of them, so that whenever they were not traveling they spent much of their time professing to curious locals their honest ignorance of what had actually happened in Lume.

It seemed that the initial round of arrests had missed several of its intended targets—rumor had it that about half a dozen of those named in the Grand Council had not been apprehended. Orders to watch for fleeing traitors reached the watchmen of every town along their route. Only Lord Blackfield's sorcery and Anrel's quick tongue saw them safely through four encounters with sentries and authorities of various sorts.

By the time the coach reached Kallai the empire was ablaze with open rebellion; the Joint Committee had assumed full control of the entire country. The margrave of Kallai had closed his city's gates, accepting no authority but his own until matters were more settled, but Lord Blackfield was able to talk his way past the walls by asserting his status as a Quandish Gatherman, and, Anrel suspected, by the judicious use of both sorcerous persuasion and mundane bribery.

The homunculus-driven coaches that normally carried passengers across the Dragonlands from Kallai to Quand were not available, at the Margrave's direction, but that was of no matter; Harban knew the route, and Lord Blackfield's sorcery was able to keep the dragons at a safe distance. Guarding the coach against the great beasts required Lord Blackfield to ride atop the vehicle and left him exhausted, but another day saw them safely across the wasteland in Redcliff, on the Quandish border.

Lord Dorias and Lady Saria seemed utterly miserable to be outside the empire, but the rest of the party studied the foreign landscape with interest. For the most part, Anrel found it disappointingly similar to the terrain in Walasia; there was no sign of the infamous Quandish mists.

On the other hand, for the first time in his life he heard ordinary people speaking Quandish outside a classroom. He and Lord Blackfield began tutoring the others in the basics of the language, even while Anrel learned to correct his own pronunciation to match the tongue as it was actually spoken.

Two more days from Redcliff brought them to Ondine, the Quandish capital, and to Lord Blackfield's town house there.

It was there that Anrel found himself introduced to assorted Quandish dignitaries, all of them eager for news of the Walasian capital. He was also startled to also encounter other Walasian refugees; apparently his own adventures had not been as unique as he thought.

"What will you do now?" one young Quandish noblewoman asked him. "Now that you're safe."

The question caught Anrel off guard; he had not given the matter much thought. Since receiving Delegate Gluth's warning in the Aldian Baths he had been too busy at first with simply staying alive, and then he had been caught up in the miniature society of the crowded coach, discussing the different varieties of magic and the intricacies of the Quandish language. That had left him no time or energy to make long-term plans.

He started to say he did not know what he intended; then he stopped. He looked across the room at Tazia, who was similarly beset, yet remained calm, polite, and to Anrel's eyes, radiantly beautiful.

"I am going to marry the woman I love," he said. He smiled. "And after that, we shall see."